Green Ray

Book Two of The Race Is On Series

OC Heaton

Rookwood Publishing

Join The Race is On Readers' Club

In return, you'll receive a free novella plus loads more gifts, occasional e-mails from me about my life in rainy Leeds and first notice of when a new book will be out.

If you want to unsubscribe at any time, it's simple to do and I promise never to share your details with anyone. To join the club just scan the QR code below or enter this link into your browser: https://ocheaton.com/mad-offer-greenray/

Contents

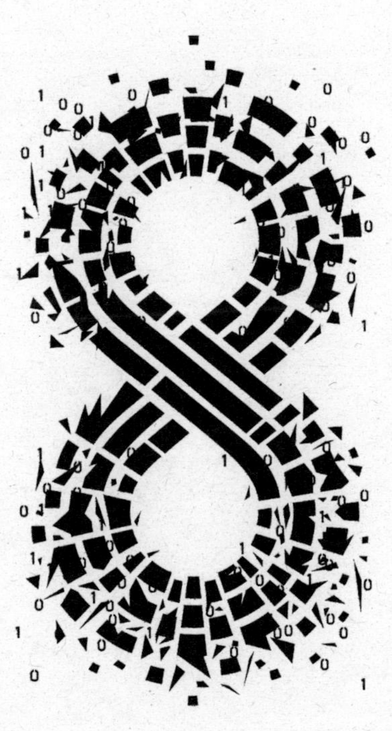

Ghawar Oil Field, Saudi Arabia

2 November 2009, 21:05 hours

The fireball ballooned out into the cool night air, enveloping a nearby stack of oil drums. Within seconds one of the containers exploded, quickly followed by others as the entire stack succumbed to the intense heat, shooting burning blobs of crude oil high into the night sky. They crashed back to earth, enveloping cars, buildings and equipment in fiery explosions that raged across the refinery, each searching out yet more fuel to gorge on. Without warning, a huge explosion tore through the complex as the main collection reservoir for Site 41 detonated.

Ali Jum'ah felt the aftershocks along with his work colleagues in the central control room that served the entire Ghawar Oil Field. It felt bigger than he had intended but the response wasn't—a klaxon sounded and men to his left and right began leaving their workstations and filing towards the two exits either side of the huge screens which dominated the control room. It seemed very orderly but an excited chatter was audible beneath the high-pitched whine, except for Ali who was silent, busy calculating how long he had before the all clear sounded and his team would return to their desks. As the large group of men ambled towards the meeting points outside the main administration building, Ali gradually fell further and further behind until the last man disappeared from his view. He felt nervous and rightly so; the giant field was the jewel in the crown of Saudi Aramco, the state-owned oil company of Saudi Arabia and, depending upon who you believed, produced close to five million barrels of oil a day. That equated to five percent of the entire planet's output. Short of a nuclear attack, there was simply too much pressure to stop production, even for one hour. The diversionary explosions had been timed to bring him thirty minutes at which point Aramco staff would be dispatched back into the control room to continue production. That would be more than enough time to complete the download.

Ali made his way back to the control room and locked the door before returning to his terminal. To one side of the main control screen were four smaller monitors relaying images from CCTV cameras outside. He watched as Aramco staff from all the surrounding buildings waited beside the meeting point, their backs turned to the camera as they looked towards the pyrotechnics show off screen. Every few seconds the image burned to white as another explosion ripped through the complex.

Ali frowned. He had only intended for it to be a small explosion. He didn't want to create an international incident. At this rate every news station across the planet would be picking up the 'terrorist' attack. That would not please his handlers but it was too late to reverse that blunder. He had work to do.

The mainframe of Saudi Aramco's Research and Development Center in Dhahran was his target. Access was easy. As the lead software architect, Ali had helped build it and knew exactly what he was after. However, it still took time to bypass all the security he had written over the last five years. He kept glancing at the quadrant of CCTV images; the group at the meeting point were well into the roll call. They had moved faster than he thought. Too damn efficient.

Bingo. He had found the files. Upload time.

Men were turning now. Pointing back towards the facility they had left less than five minutes earlier.

He could only assume they had discovered he was missing.

Ali flicked open his mobile. Dial in was instant. The satellite link had been set up for precisely this moment, providing him with an upload speed of nearly 15 MBPS. That was fast. Faster than the quickest upload speeds on the market. His online time would be measured in seconds.

A huge aftershock rocked the control centre. Dust and debris rained down on Ali's station. He glanced down at the connection indicator on his phone. It had stopped. His eyes flicked to the screen. It was blank and the first stirrings of panic began to penetrate his calm exterior.

The bottom left CCTV screen showed four Royal Saudi Land Force guards making their way back to the centre. They were not running. Thankfully. Why should they? For all they knew, he had been delayed. He was trusted. He had been working in the facility for over ten years, waiting, watching, searching for the information that the secretive Aramco organisation refused to release to the world. For good reason, Ali suspected. He had stumbled across it only last week. A routine file clearance request had given him the opportunity to snoop and there it was.

His handlers had demanded an immediate upload. They didn't care that his cover would be compromised. This was the sole reason for his presence. His raison d'être for the last decade. Send the information and disappear, had been the order. The explosives had been their idea. Create a diversion.

Without warning, the screens around him flickered back into life. Ali breathed a little more easily as his connection was re-established.

The four guards were inside the facility now, checking rooms on their way back to the control centre. Restaurant. Restrooms. Relaxation suite. Mosque. The search was methodical. Unhurried. Just like everything the Saudis did. Always calm. Never rushed. It had unnerved him to begin with. He couldn't get used to the pace.

The upload began again. Fifty percent. Seventy percent.

The guards were actually in the corridor outside.

'Come on, damn it,' he muttered to himself.

Ninety percent.

The door handle depressed. Relaxed again as the lock caught. Ali could see one of the guards hammering on the door.

Done. The upload was complete.

A huge shudder rippled through the entire building, causing him to stagger against the console. When he looked down, the screen had gone blank again.

Ali ran to the door and unlocked the latch before swinging it open. Two of the guards stumbled in.

'Thank Allah, you came back.'

'The door was locked. Why did you lock the door?' the lead guard shouted, trying to make himself heard above the blare of the klaxon. Ali glanced at the man's shoulder. Two arrows. A corporal. He relaxed.

'I didn't.' Ali held his penetrating gaze. 'It was jammed. The blasts must have warped the door somehow. I have been trying to get out since the alarm sounded.'

'Why didn't you leave with the main party?'

'I was shutting down my system. I couldn't leave. If it had crashed, we would have lost one day's production for the entire southern area down at Haradh. You wouldn't—' The alarm suddenly stopped mid-sentence, leaving him shouting into the guard's face. '—want that. Would you?'

Ali's voice softened but it was too late. The man bristled with indignation.

'Abdullah. Fahd. Escort this man back to the rendezvous point,' the corporal ordered. 'I will search the room with Salman.'

Ali breathed a sigh of relief just as a shrill tone cut through the silence. It was coming from the control room. Even as he turned, Ali realised his mistake.

His phone. He had left his damn phone on the desk. Still connected.

Ali turned to re-enter but the corporal was ahead of him, marching over to the desk where his blue-silver phone lay.

'I take it this is yours?' he announced triumphantly, turning back towards the door, the slim device dangling from the thin wire. Ali panicked. He shoved one of the guards aside and started running down the corridor towards the exit doors. But he didn't get far. Up ahead, three guards blocked his path but it didn't stop him trying to barrel through them, sending all four sprawling to the ground. Minutes later, a triumphant corporal led the now cuffed and sobbing engineer past his bemused colleagues and out into the burning complex.

The Grove Palms Hotel, LA

4 November 2009, 12:03 hours

The two men were standing at the back of the marquee near the exit and despite the scores of industry journalists, local officials, energy analysts and enviros waiting expectantly for the presentation to begin, she had picked them out immediately. In this heat and with this crowd they looked totally out of place. Dark glasses. Black suits. White shirts. Ties. That and their demeanour. They constantly scanned the room as if searching for something. Or someone. It didn't feel right and their reappearance had made her nervous. From the moment she had laid eyes on them last night in the hotel foyer and again this morning in the restaurant, she had experienced a long-buried flicker of apprehension. Of being followed. Kept under surveillance. Of being on the run. She couldn't explain why. It was pure instinct but that was enough for her. She trusted her instinct. It had served her well over the years and she wasn't about to start ignoring it now. She was so preoccupied with them, she almost missed her cue.

'I don't need to introduce the first speaker this afternoon. Our main benefactor and probably the most famous environmentalist in the world. Ladies and gentlemen, may I present, Dr Uma Jakobsdóttir.'

Pockets of applause broke out across the huge tent which felt hot despite the multiple blow tubes pumping chilled air into the car park of The Grove Palms Hotel.

Uma didn't react. She was no longer in California but revisiting scenes usually held at bay until night-time. Dark memories pushed aside her rehearsed launch speech. The axe head buried deep inside Baldursson. Eva's lifeless face. Ethan's broken body at the trauma unit in Manhattan. The images were so clear. As if they had happened yesterday, and the ease with which they invaded the marquee was deeply unsettling.

Jake Burns, CEO of Electro Motors, looked back expectantly but Uma's face was blank. He smiled questioningly at her and, without missing a beat, tried again.

'Busy as always, I see. Ladies and gentlemen, I would like you to join me once again in welcoming Uma Jakobsdóttir, the CEO of our largest benefactor and shareholder, on stage to give you some background about our exciting new venture.'

This time he clapped enthusiastically and was joined by many others in the large gathering. It seemed to snap Uma out of her reverie and she stepped forward hurriedly, grabbing the proffered hand mic from Jake.

Come on, Uma. Pull yourself together, she silently screamed to herself.

'Thank you, Jake. Thank you, everyone. I was miles away. Absolutely miles. Saving the world is hard work.'

There was a smattering of laughter. It bought her some time.

She quickly scanned the crowd but both men had disappeared. *Had she imagined them?* It was too late now. The sea of expectant faces was still there and they gave her the impetus to begin.

'Wow, what a turnout we have today!' Uma said. 'After several years of development we are finally able to unveil the cornerstone of our plans to significantly cut greenhouse gases, initially in the States but eventually across the globe. As most of you already know, cars and trucks account for one third of CO_2 emissions in the States and today's launch will significantly cut into that. However, that is not the only announcement we would like to make. I will also be talking about Green Ray's plans for tackling CO_2 emissions across a whole host of areas. But first, auto emissions.'

Out of the corner of her eye she picked up one of the black suits. Its owner was leaning against the door frame of the middle entrance into the marquee. He had taken his shades off and was staring at Uma intently. He looked mean.

Uma took a deep breath, trying to control her heart rate. Not today, she thought. The day she was announcing the biggest leap forward in environmental planning for the last twenty years.

She forced herself to concentrate.

'Electric cars have always been an attractive alternative to the petrol engine since they are so cheap to run. Even at today's prices, it's the equivalent of twenty-five cents per litre of petrol. However, for many consumers there have always been two issues that have vastly outweighed the cost benefit. Firstly, such vehicles have traditionally had a poor range. Many can only manage 100 to 150 miles on one charge and, secondly, the recharge time is far too long. Eight hours is the average, which vastly reduces the market for this mode of transport. Well, I am delighted to announce that Jake and his team have spent the last two years addressing these issues and have now solved them. Ladies and gentlemen, I am pleased to present, the Electro!'

On cue, a curtain dropped behind her to reveal a medium-sized black car. It looked nondescript. Intentionally so. Like a hundred other nondescript mid-range family hatchbacks clogging the roads of America. Through loudspeakers, U2's *Magnificent* boomed out at the gathered crowd. In perfect synchronisation, all four doors opened and four people emerged, one from each door. An older man and woman from the front and a teenage boy and girl from the back. They were all tall. Big white smiles. Blond hair. Tanned. Dressed casually in jeans and T-shirts, they looked exactly as Jake Burns had intended. The all-American family complete with Labrador Retriever which bounded from the rear boot that had also opened automatically. Uma half turned to glance back as the four models sauntered off stage, leaving the star of the show revolving slowly, gleaming in the bright spotlights pouring down on it. There was an immediate buzz amongst the gathered crowd as journalists jostled to get a better look. Jake Burns stepped forward onto the small stage beside Uma and continued the presentation.

'We were very conscious that 'green' didn't necessarily have to mean un-cool or require design and specification compromises. That is why our model is so much better than what has come before. The Electro has a top speed of 100 mph and can hit 0–60 mph in under five seconds. It has a range of over 500 miles and will retail for less than $20,000. Importantly, it can be charged in five minutes. That's the exciting bit because it offers quick refills whilst on the move. We have been able to achieve this incredibly fast turnaround thanks to a new technology that allows for both a super speedy charge and discharge of the electrical current. It can now be done in a matter of seconds. Now, before we show you the car in more detail, does anyone have any questions?'

The response was thunderous with questions being fired at both Uma and Jake from all directions of the marquee. It took several seconds for the roar to die down and the CEO's voice to be heard above the din.

'Now, ladies and gentlemen, please be patient. One at a time. You,' he pointed at a portly gentleman who was mopping his brow with a handkerchief. "What is your question?'

'Hello. Jed Gartner from *Science Weekly*. Sorry to get technical on you but the bit about the battery doesn't make sense. Unless I'm mistaken there are only two ways of storing electricity. Either in standard batteries or through supercapacitors. The first is great at storing lots of energy but is hard to get at. The latter is quick to discharge and charge but can't hold much. How have you been able to defeat the laws of chemistry to achieve both?'

Jake handed the microphone to Uma. He was a salesman. Technical questions weren't for him.

Uma spotted the second suit. He was at the back of the marquee, standing in the entrance-way, hands clasped in front. His dark glasses looked menacing. She wished she could see his eyes. They looked like security but weren't theirs. They always used Nat Sec. Low key. Casual. Approachable. No heavy-handed stuff. *Maybe they belonged to the hotel?* It was a big event. More than five hundred journalists and news reporters. Perhaps they had felt the need to police it themselves. Uma knew that couldn't be right. What sort of security dressed that way these days?

The faint stirrings of another panic attack began to form. They always began slowly. Usually at night. First, the cold shiver of hot sweat. A quickening of her pulse. That would in turn trigger long-buried memories that slowly materialised, unstoppable in their inevitability. She would always fight. Tooth and nail. But it was pointless. Eventually she would succumb to the maelstrom as it burst upon her, leaving her sobbing like a helpless child after a night terror.

It was hardly surprising. Long days. Late evenings. Longer nights laid awake. And when sleep finally called in the early hours, the nightmares arrived soon after. Ones that left her bed soaked and skull booming. She had tried to escape in her mission to save the planet, one ton of CO_2 at a time. It mostly worked. An exhausting schedule of meetings with government officials, investors, businesspeople, bankers, reporters, lawyers, accountants. A succession of indistinguishable hotel rooms, conference rooms and restaurants. But those were just the days. At some point she would have to rest and the dreams were always waiting. Patiently. Ready to reap their horrors until the next day when she could return to her race against time. One that had delivered today's launch event which in turn kick-started a two-month tour across North America. No wonder her neurosis was working overtime.

Uma dragged herself back to the question.

'Jeff—'

Jake beamed at the room and whispered in her ear.

"Jed, I'm sorry. Don't worry, I'm very good at cheating the basic laws of science. In this instance we have come up with a system that can do both. We have effectively melded one material that is good at storing ions with another that is great at conducting them.'

'Can I ask what they are?'

'Sure. It's no secret, and importantly for us, it's also fully patented. The storage material is lithium iron phosphate which, as you are aware, is the material used in standard batteries. The other is made of a glassy form of lithium phosphate which is good at conducting lithium ions though it cannot actually store many. It therefore acts as a supercapacitor. The really clever bit is how the spheres inside the batteries are made. Jake's team at Elector Motors have perfected a technique that melds the two materials together which ensures there is lithium iron phosphate at the centre but just lithium phosphate on the surface which is glassy rather than crystalline. The result is a battery that charges and discharges in a few seconds.'

Several hands shot up as Uma finished her explanation. She pointed at a tall man, sitting on the front row. As she did, Uma quickly scanned the marquee again. The two suits hadn't moved. Uma tried to ignore them but it was no good. She could feel herself beginning to sweat.

'Yes. Hello. Chuck Fenton. *US Auto*. Let me get this straight. In your introduction you said the car would retail,' he nodded at the slowly revolving vehicle behind Uma, 'for $20,000. How can you afford to do that?'

Jake stepped forward this time, a permanent smile etched onto his chubby face.

'I'll take this one, Uma, if that's OK?" He palmed the microphone and beamed at the audience. "Thanks, Chuck. A very astute observation. You are correct. It is well below the cost of manufacture. Well below by some $18,000. If you were to buy that car at retail price you would pay $40,000.'

There were several whistles in the crowd. Chuck continued.

'OK,' he started doubtfully. 'How are you going stay in business? My maths is bad but surely that is unsustainable.'

'That's where our benefactor comes in,' he replied, nodding at Uma. 'The whole idea is not to make money. It's to save the planet. If we retailed this model at list price, we wouldn't sell any, especially in this market. Our plan is to offer the first 100,000 models at $20,000 on an interest-free payment plan over five years.'

The seasoned journalist whistled incredulously.

'With respect, but that's impossible. It's one reason why our three biggest car makers are facing imminent bankruptcy. That would cost billions. No one can afford that.'

'Two billion actually,' Uma cut in, taking the microphone from Jake. 'It'll cost us two billion dollars to fund.'

For a split second all she could hear was the low whoosh of cool air and then it was drowned out as several hundred voices shouted out questions simultaneously. Uma nodded at another journalist next to Chuck.

'Dave Moretti. *New York Daily*. Dr Jakobsdóttir, how can you afford that amount of money? I know you have a large fund at your disposal but is that a sustainable approach?'

'Of course, it's sustainable,' she shot back. Jake glanced over, frowning. 'As of yesterday, the Green Ray Fund stood at approximately eighty-five billion US dollars. We are currently in talks with several sovereign wealth funds that could comfortably double that amount by this time next year.'

'But surely they have a profit motive? You can't just give their money away.'

'True. But the source of the initial funding to the tune of some thirty billion dollars didn't have a profit motive hook attached. It is effectively subsidising the rest of the fund which will make money from all sorts of different sources. Licensing is a key revenue generator. We have a whole raft of green technical innovations such as the new battery design that have all been patented and will generate substantial returns for our investors.'

'And that business with Rae? Is it—,' another journalist cut in.

'You know the rules, Brin,' Jake cut in. 'No questions on Rae. That business was resolved—'

'—years ago.' Brin Runcy finished his sentence and glanced down at his notepad, searching for his next but he was too late.

'Doesn't that make you the largest foundation in the world?' another reporter shouted out from the back of the tent.

But Uma wasn't listening again. The mention of Ethan had thrown her. She was no match for that name. In an instant Uma was sat in a Jeep next to Ethan or whoever the hell he had been that day. Watching the firestorm that had engulfed the cars across the highway on the road from Reykjavík to the Blue Lagoon. Screaming men. Burning bodies. And yet more explosions until a vortex of fire consumed everything. As she watched in horror, the fire turned hungrily in their direction as thick black smoke spewed into the cabin. Uma could feel the searing heat through the windscreen. If she stayed here much longer, they would be trapped. She had to get out.

Christ she was going to faint.

Uma stood there swaying slightly, breathing heavily. She had never suffered a day occurrence like that. Why now? She couldn't afford to mess this up. Too much was at stake. She took a deep breath and forced herself back into the marquee.

Something about the foundation. Ethan's foundation. Or so he had claimed. Anger washed over Uma, dissolving the fiery vision. That was better. She used the energy to refocus. The impact was instant. The cramp in her chest faded away and the acrid smoke dissipated.

'By some distance,' she croaked, disguising it with a coughing fit that forced her to gulp down what remained of her water. 'To keep our charitable status on the initial infusion of capital we need to donate approximately two billion dollars annually. This phase of the programme is pretty much covered by one year's donations so we are well within our parameters.'

'Dr Jakobsdóttir,' the reporter continued, 'if the whole thrust of your approach is to reduce carbon emissions, why go with electricity? It's a heavy pollutant in its own right. Aren't you cutting off your nose to spite your face?'

Uma felt better. Her pulse was steady. The dizziness had passed. Her eyesight was clear. However, she knew that the fatigue would follow. A bone crushing tiredness that would sap her energy and leave her unable to complete even the most basic functions. She had thirty minutes at best.

'A good question and yes you are right. Electricity is a huge polluter. In fact, it is the second largest producer of carbon emissions in the US. That is what makes it so attractive to us. Our approach allows us to tackle two thirds of the US' carbon emissions in one go.'

'And how do you propose to do that?'

'Well, electricity is the second cornerstone of Green Ray's strategy. The big issue about electricity is that half of it comes from coal-fired stations. There are over 600 in this country alone. We intend to reverse this. Over the last five years we have lobbied hard to prevent new coal-fired power stations being constructed. In fact, through our direct action, we have defeated plans for eighty alone. In addition, we are pursuing two initiatives that will significantly impact how electricity will be produced in the future. Firstly, we are well on the way to announcing just under 150 new wind farms, twenty each in the five largest current producers of wind power in the States; Texas, Iowa, California, Minnesota and Washington State, and eight in Oregon. That will effectively quadruple output from this source from just under 17,000 megawatts up to 64,000 megawatts. We are working in partnership with Gulf Wind Power, the largest operator of wind farms in the US and our investment in this company will be in the region of four billion dollars per year for the next ten years for a total approaching forty billion dollars. In return for that investment, we will have a ninety-five percent holding in Gulf Wind Power. Again, a further return for our growing number of investors.'

'Excuse me, ma'am.' A gruff Texan stood up near the front, his huge gut testing the buttons of his shirt. 'I admire your efforts but isn't this all a drop in the proverbial ocean? The US currently requires just under one million megawatts per year to meet its electricity demands. Coal produces,' he stared down at a notepad, '330,000 megawatts. Even with your planned increases that is barely twenty percent of coal's contribution. Just over five percent of the US' entire requirements.'

'Ah, Jacob, I wondered when you would pop up. How are your masters at Texas Oil and Gas?'

Laughter rippled around the tent whilst Jacob Greengrass, paid lobbyist for the oil and gas industry, took an exaggerated bow and smiled broadly to the assembled room.

'It's small at the moment but it will grow. Firstly, our wind efforts alone will generate over 100,000 jobs during the next five years clustered in these six States where we will be building up unrivalled expertise. With these levels of investment, the costs of production will tumble which will benefit everyone. That's just a starting point. It's a well-proven fact that investment on this scale will attract a similar amount from other sources. We therefore have the likelihood of a further forty billion dollars of inward investment being poured into renewable energy. That is not to mention the activity that is already happening independently of us. Other manufacturers are pouring billions into electric cars. Other companies are doing the same with wind production and other sources of renewable energy. Given our own conservative projection, I have no doubt that in five years' time we could, collectively, be producing twenty, twenty-five percent of the United States' entire electricity production.

'However, I would agree with you, this is nowhere near fast enough. Our other focus over the next five years is smart meters. We will be working closely with the Federal Government and power companies to install smart meters in every home in the US, all 115 million of them. That will allow consumers to monitor their consumption in a way that makes sense to them. Not kilowatt-hours but actually dollars and cents. They will actually be able to see how much it costs to leave lights on and other household appliances. Our research has shown that this could reduce demand from between 5% and 15% percent. Even at the low end of the estimate this will be equivalent to removing nearly eight million cars from the roads.'

'John Lucas. *Green Weekly*. Ms Jakobsdóttir, the benefits of smart meters are well known but it is not a cheap option. Where they have been installed, consumers have ended up footing the bill. In the current climate that is the last thing consumers need. Most are interested in more earthly matters. Such as saving their jobs or earning enough money to put food on the table for their families.'

'John, I entirely agree. But all these initiatives are designed to save money and cost as little as possible. Insofar as the smart meter installation is concerned, we plan to pay for them at an estimated cost of thirty billion dollars.'

There were more whistles in the audience.

'We have already acquired the main manufacturer of smart meters in the US and we plan to begin rolling out pilot projects next week in thirty medium-sized cities. However, it will cost neither the power companies nor the consumers a single cent and could save upwards of fifty to one hundred fifty dollars a year depending on their electricity consumption. Our Electro car will save them thousands more in petrol alone.'

Uma paused for a second to take a sip of water. Her mouth felt parched. The drop was coming. It always started with dehydration. She drained the small glass, motioning to one of the hotel stewards for a refill. It was going well though. She could tell. The audience were listening carefully now. Scribbling down notes. Hopefully by tomorrow every household in the country would be reading about their plans. She had even forgotten about her unwelcome guests. She pressed on, fighting the urge to yawn.

'I think you also underestimate the fiscal stimulus of this level of investment entering the US economy not only in terms of jobs. All of this activity we have spoken about will be US based. Everything will be manufactured here. We will be building up expertise in areas that the rest of the world will be very interested in adopting. By our own estimates, directly created jobs on both the Electro and wind front will be 200,000 not to mention the indirect benefits of that level of investment.'

Had she just repeated herself? She wasn't sure. No one seemed to notice.

'At this rate you will be all spent up by 2012. What's the point of that?'

She turned towards the voice. It was John Lucas again.

'That's the idea. We are in a race against time to reverse global warming. What is the point of hoarding all this money for tomorrow, when at the rate we are travelling there may not actually be a tomorrow?'

'Why America, Ms Jakobsdóttir? Why such a focus in the States. There are plenty of other countries in the world that would also benefit from this approach. Some much closer to home for you.'

'It's business really. Pure and simple. The US comprises just five percent of the world's population but consumes twenty-five percent of its energy. We need to address that now. And as you know it will only get worse as other economies mature and their consumption begins to increase in line with the States. We wanted to hit the source. Hit it hard. Establish the clusters quickly. We realised that in this climate it also had to be really attractive to everyday Americans. The only way to do that is to save them money, not force 'green' down their throats.' Uma suddenly felt tired. Like a marathon runner, she summoned hidden reserves of energy and ploughed on, her voice hoarse with the effort. 'Come on, ladies and gentlemen,' she croaked. 'You know the score. Long gone are the days when we hoped to change the energy habits of human beings by guilting them into going green. If anything, I think the green movement has suffered a bit of a backlash. People are fed up with it. It is yesterday's cause for the majority and the only way to get it back on the agenda is to help them where it currently matters. In their pockets.'

Uma patted her jacket pocket, realising that she was finished. Even if there had been more to say, she doubted she could summon the energy to say it. Rather abruptly, she addressed the assembled crowd one last time. 'If no one has any further questions, I would like to hand you back to Jake.'

She passed the microphone to her CEO and smiled tiredly.

'Jake, I'm sorry for hijacking your presentation. I have developed an unfortunate habit of doing that these days.'

'Not a problem. Not a problem, Uma,' he said, beaming at the room. 'There are thirty billion very good reasons why you get to interrupt me anytime you want. Please everyone, would you join me in thanking Dr Jakobsdóttir for her time this afternoon.'

Uma located the two men. They hadn't moved, their arms still, whilst everyone applauded. Uma slowly made her way off the small stage and headed towards one of the exits. As she reached it, the two men reacted. One started walking down the outside aisle towards her whilst the second disappeared out of the marquee. Uma quickened her pace as she stumbled into the stifling heat of the afternoon sun. There was a covered walkway connecting the marquee to the hotel foyer and she hurried along the weather-faded red carpet. As Uma reached the hotel one of the men emerged from the same entrance she had exited seconds earlier. He was in no hurry and walked slowly towards her. He looked menacing. His hand went to his ear. He appeared to be talking to himself. As Uma entered the cool interior of the Grove Palms Hotel, the other man came through the revolving doors of the main entrance.

Uma raced through the deserted foyer towards the bank of elevators. As she approached, the doors slid open obligingly and an elderly couple emerged. She hurried past them and summoned her floor. As she waited, the other man entered the foyer through the door she had just used. His partner nodded in her direction and both of them bore down on the small opening. Uma felt trapped, suddenly unsure of her decision.

'Come on. Come on,' she muttered as the doors stubbornly refused to close. She punched the > < button several times but nothing happened. The two men were less than five feet away. Neither smiled. Neither hurried. They looked in complete control.

'Close, god damn you,' she cried out in desperation as the doors slid shut. It was tantalisingly close. For a split second Uma thought she had made it but one of the men thrust his arm through the closing gap. The doors jerked back open.

No one spoke. No one moved. Uma could feel her heart beating wildly. And loudly. Booming beats they must have heard. There was no way past these two. Both were pushing six feet and, shoulder to shoulder, completely blocked the doorway. One of them started to say something but he never finished his sentence. There was a whoosh and he collapsed to the floor of the elevator, his whole body jerking spasmodically. His partner stared at the black object in Uma's hand and smiled knowingly. Tasers had one charge.

He touched his ear and spoke calmly. 'Man down. I repeat, man down. In the lobby elevator of the Palms Grove Hotel.' He held out his hand towards Uma. 'Now there is no need for—'

But that's as far as he got. Summoning every last ounce of energy, Uma ducked down to her left in a feint to slip past the man. As he put out his right arm to block her escape, she dropped to one knee, turning to present her back to him, whilst at the same time smoothly taking his wrist in both hands. A split second later the giant suddenly found himself upside down, slammed against the rear of the elevator. Uma stumbled over his partner and staggered towards the main entrance. Through her dazed vision she caught sight of more men running into the lobby, all dressed exactly as the two behind her. They were all holding guns and whispering silently into invisible earpieces.

The one to her right yelled an instruction.

'Dr Jakobsdóttir. Stand down immediately. I repeat, stand down.'

Uma stopped. It was no good. She was thirty feet from the entrance and already more suits were pouring through both exits, weapons drawn.

Not today, she thought. It had been over five years since the government had finally left her alone after the Steven F. Udvar-Hazy Center disaster in Virginia. At first, there had been long interrogations, some lasting days but she had kept her counsel. Maintained her story both about her involvement with Reynolds Air and the disappearance of its crooked CEO. Her initial instinct had been right though. They had nothing on her. Absolutely nothing. Eventually they had stopped calling her as had the hordes of journalists researching the collapse of Reynolds Air.

A voice behind her made Uma turn. He was examining the unconscious men in the elevator.

'Well, I have to say, Doctor. That is no way to treat this country's finest. Have you any idea what trouble you could be in for attacking CIA agents.'

Uma hadn't expected that.

'What the hell does the CIA want with me? I've done nothing wrong.'

'Doctor Jakobsdóttir, we are not here to arrest you. My boss wants to speak to you.'

It was too much for Uma. Without warning, the floor came up to meet her and the last thing she remembered was the look of surprise on the black suit's face as he rushed forward to catch her fall.

Ras Tanura Port, Persian Gulf

4 November 2009, 23:36 hours

The odour was rather pleasant. Slightly sweet, it reminded him of something vaguely familiar but try as he might, he couldn't place it. Ali Jum'ah struggled into a sitting position and surveyed his ... cell. It certainly looked that way. Barely ten-feet square, the small space was practically dark and the little light there was, came from above. The entire ceiling was bathed in a soft blue glow. He guessed it was some form of ultraviolet light. That was possible. The walls were made of ... glass or was it plastic. Ali couldn't be certain because the light reflected off the smooth surface like a mirror. There wasn't really much else to see. Across the other side of the room was a low cabinet. Inside were glowing lumps of what looked like luminous ... rock. He couldn't tell. There were hundreds of them glowing brightly in the fluorescent light that bathed his prison.

And then Ali Jum'ah remembered. The explosions at the oil field. The evacuation. The upload. His discovery. Attempted escape. Then questions. So many questions until one of his interrogators had introduced him to the butt of his handgun. And then nothing. Until now.

Light sweet crude oil. That was it. That was what he could smell.

The Ghawar oil field produced it by the barrel full. Its smell permeated everything and was the best grade oil available. A high quality, low sulphur crude oil that contained large concentrations of the chemicals required to process gasoline, kerosene, and diesel and was, consequently, in great demand by every country in the world.

Was he still at the oil field?

If so, they were holding him in a place he had never seen before and why was he naked? He sensed a movement to his left and looked over. Part of the wall had moved outwards. On closer inspection he now realised it was a door, like the ones found on long-haul flights, its rubber seal making a soft whooshing sound as it was pulled open by an unseen force. He wondered how they were getting air into the room. A light was approaching the opening, its soft glow growing in size until it filled the small cell. Ali assumed it was a lantern but nothing could have prepared him for what entered.

A glowing apparition appeared and hovered in the opening before floating over to Ali where it stopped, towering over the naked man. It filled the small space with an ethereal glow that almost blinded the software programmer's light-starved eyes. He rubbed them in disbelief. Ali wasn't a religious man but the shimmering being seemed almost Godlike in appearance. Covered from head to foot in iridescent white, except for a dark halo around his head. A tight band of finite black, in stark contrast to the infinite white light surrounding it. Ali found himself drawn to the darkness, the narrow sliver growing in size as he stared, until it filled the entire cell, blotting out the warm glow like an eclipse. Ali was transfixed and remained still, unsure what to do as his logical mind sought to explain the heavenly body before him, whilst his soul soaked up the divine vision.

The spell was broken by powerful lights that suddenly cracked into life high above the room. Ali blinked in surprise. Where, moments before a supreme being had stood, fully ten feet in height, an old man had appeared, slightly stooped and of medium height. He had a neat but greying beard and was dressed in traditional Arab clothes; a long flowing white thawb, its high collar buttoned tight. His ghutra was also white and came down well past his hands which were clasped together.

Ali suddenly realised with a slight feeling of dismay how the effect had been created. It was the phosphors in the detergents used to wash the man's clothes. They had converted the UV light into white light which, in the dark cell, had made the white gown and headdress look 'whiter than white'. And the black halo he had seen was in fact an elaborate black and gold agal. The material holding the man's headpiece in place now flashed yellow as bright light reflected off precious metal. Ali had only seen ones like this at festivals and Eids. It looked very formal but also befitted the rank of the man who stood before him.

Abdullah Al Rahman, Head of the Re'asat Al Istikhbarat Al A'amah, Saudi Arabia's intelligence agency, glared down at the former Aramco senior programmer, his hawk nose and hard eyes giving the familiar face a cruel but unmistakable profile in the bright light. Ali knew of him well. He was the de facto head of the unit Ali had worked in for the last ten years. It was a tenuous but obvious link. The agency was responsible for the security of all state information in Saudi Arabia and the computer systems operating the colossal Ghawar Oil Field were obvious points of weakness. Ali had never met the great man personally but his presence in the same room sent a chill down his spine. If he had suspected a problem before, he was now under no illusions as to the seriousness of his predicament. Nevertheless, he tried to go on the offensive.

'What the hell are you holding me for? I have done nothing wrong.'

The Arab ignored him and glided over to the long bench. That hadn't been an illusion. He did, in fact, seem to glide. As he sat down, Ali suddenly realised that the walls were in fact transparent. He had been so distracted by his visitor that he hadn't noticed their loss of reflectiveness as the bright lights had come on. They seemed to be underground in some sort of giant chamber. The lights above him must have been seventy, perhaps eighty feet above the room and illuminated a metal floor that travelled away into the gloom for hundreds of feet all around them. But Ali's gaze was drawn to the rocks in the cabinet on which his captor was now sitting. They had stopped glowing. More importantly, they weren't rocks, he realised. They were scorpions. Black ones. Hundreds of them, three or four deep. He shuddered. They looked especially menacing in the bright lights, although at least they were quite small. Not even three inches across.

His host saw him staring at the black insects and smiled.

'Did you know they glowed in the dark?'

'What?'

'The scorpions. Did you know they fluoresce under ultraviolet light? No one knows why but it makes them very easy to find at night when they come out. To feed.'

His voice was hushed. So much so that Ali had to strain to hear him despite the quietness of the cell. However, it oozed authority and something else. Cruelty, he decided. It was a cruel voice, devoid of all emotion.

'It's called Androctonus Crassicauda. I prefer its more common title. The fat-tailed man-killer.'

Ali didn't like the sound of that.

'We call him Fat-Tail for short and it can be found all over Saudi Arabia. Isn't he beautiful?'

That wasn't quite the description Ali would have used. His captor continued.

'Scorpions are consummate survivors and also quite unique. Some live on saltwater beaches, whilst others are entirely comfortable a mile and a half up in the coldest mountain ranges. They have also been found in rainforests and of course the driest deserts. However, their basic structure doesn't vary. A hard exoskeleton, eight legs, two pincers like a lobster, and a curling tail capped with a needle-like stinger. Looks menacing, doesn't it?'

Now that was a better description. He stared at Ali who felt compelled to nod.

'It's the smaller ones you need to watch. The bigger ones just sting like a bee.'

He laughed. Apologetically, Ali thought.

'Their venom is a cocktail of powerful neurotoxins which are pretty potent. Once stung you will be dead within the hour. That's quite fast, wouldn't you say?'

Ali nodded dumbly again, a sense of despair laced with panic washing over him. He suddenly needed to empty his bladder.

'Don't be fooled. It's a long hour I've been told. First, nothing much happens. Not even the sting hurts. That's not a good sign because it means the poison is working hard elsewhere on your system. Then suddenly, all that background work starts to produce results. Blurred vision. Involuntary muscle twitches. Excessive sweating. Then the fun really starts. Your throat becomes tight. You have trouble swallowing which is a pity because your tongue begins to secrete excess saliva. Lots of it.'

Ali found himself swallowing hard or trying to. His throat felt tense. He wiped a bead of sweat from his eye.

Had he been stung already?

The pain in his bladder was excruciating.

'You become restless. The twitches become violent jerks. Excruciatingly painful muscle contractions. Fluid will be ejected out of every orifice. Violently.'

The last word was delivered with a cruel smile.

'Eventually your respiratory system shuts down. That is usually the cause of death but even if you were able to hang on, it would be irrelevant because all your major organs would be slowly dying. It would just be a question of time.'

The man stood up and walked over to where Ali was slumped, placing a well-manicured hand on his forearm. It was a surprisingly intimate gesture but made his skin crawl. He shrunk further against the glass.

'You seem to have a preoccupation with our oil reserves, Mr. Jum'ah. I don't know why. There's plenty of oil down there and most of it is headed to your great country. Take this vessel, for instance.' His arm swept expansively around.

'It's one of mine,' he said, surveying the vast hold. 'It's called the Scorpion Queen and is the pride of my fleet, measuring one quarter mile in length and the width of a football pitch. Most importantly, it holds up to 500,000 tons of light sweet crude oil and will sail at exactly midday tomorrow morning.'

Ali's new-found imagination shifted from the Fat-Tail to this latest danger.

'In twenty minutes time, at exactly midnight, they will start loading the oil. It takes twelve hours to fill each of the storage chambers, including this one. That's a lot of oil. And it's all going to your great country, Mr. Jum'ah. That should please your masters.'

'I don't know what you are talking about.'

'There is enough oil in this tanker to satisfy the energy needs of Buffalo for an entire year. That's where you were born, wasn't it? Where you grew up before you attended the George Washington University to study advanced computer programming. From there you joined Oracle in their oil division where you worked for five years on the Aramco account before moving across as senior software programmer. At some point you were recruited by the CIA. I am not sure when. It doesn't really matter.'

'You'll never get away with it. There will be an international outcry.'

'They already think you are dead. Killed in the explosion at Ghawar.'

'They won't stop there you know. They will want to investigate further.'

Abdullah Al Rahman, Head of the Re'asat Al Istikhbarat Al A'amah, stood up. Ali couldn't help but notice the ring on the middle figure of his right hand. It was in the shape of a large black scorpion with diamonds for eyes. They flashed menacingly in the bright light.

'Do you know scorpions are loners? They will hate being this close to each other. Leave them long enough in that cage and they will start eating their companions. You see, they don't need anyone else. They are totally self-sufficient in that impermeable armour of theirs. They don't eat much food. Need that much moisture. Or oxygen for that matter. They are able to slow their metabolic rate down to a few beats per minute which will be very useful during the next forty days. Thirty if you are lucky. That is how long it will take to make the crossing to the States. I don't imagine there will be much air in this chamber. Can you slow your heartbeat down, Mr. Jum'ah?'

He stood up and unhinged the top of the cabinet, holding the plastic in one hand whilst he pulled the vertical section upwards. The insects spilled out into the cell.

A small pool of yellow liquid spread out from under Ali's legs as he started to cry. Great racking sobs filled the small room but they made no impact on the elaborately dressed Arab. He walked towards the entrance but just before he stepped outside, he paused and turned one last time.

'By the way. None of these Fat-Tails have been fed for nine months so even by their minimalist standards they may be slightly hungry. Don't worry though, I am not an unreasonable man.'

He felt within the folds of his cloak and withdrew a small device which he threw towards Ali. It landed in the urine.

And then he was gone, his departure preceded by a slight whoosh as the chamber was sealed tight by the closing door. The sound galvanised Ali, who suddenly leapt to his feet and hurled himself at the glass. It was a futile attempt and his efforts didn't even register on the closed door or the departing Arab. Ali watched the white devil glide over to a small platform which started to rise up towards the lights the moment he stepped onto it. Within seconds he was lost to the bright glare and Ali found himself alone.

With the loners.

Room 761, The Grove Palms Hotel, LA

4 November 2009, 14:36 hours

Uma woke suddenly, sitting up in the bed with a gasp. The room was in almost total darkness and for a moment she was completely disoriented but as her eyes adjusted to the gloom, she recognised the layout. It was her suite at The Grove Palms.

She glanced at the TV clock: 2:37. It had been less than an hour since her blackout in the lobby. The recollection triggered a flood of flashbacks that petered out into unanswered questions.

The two suits in the marquee. Another panic attack—one of her worst to date. And on one of the most important days of her life. The suits following her. The fight in the lift. That man had said they were with the CIA. What did they want with her? They hadn't contacted her in years. Why now all of a sudden? And why was she lying in her hotel bedroom in just her bra and panties?

Uma sat up gingerly, bracing herself for the head busters that always followed an episode. Right on cue they dutifully obliged, causing her to groan out loud. It felt as if her entire head was locked in a circular vice that was being tightened ever so slowly, almost imperceptibly, but with each turn of the screw, the pressure became sharper, more unbearable. Uma knew that it was mainly dehydration and the best cure was lots of water and aspirin. She crawled out of bed and made her way unsteadily to the bathroom. The light flickered into life as she opened the tap fully in the vain hope of cooling the tepid water. As Uma waited, she stared at her reflection in the oversized bathroom mirror.

The cumulative effects of the last three months were beginning to show. What little makeup she had bothered with for the launch had run, accentuating the dark rings around her eyes. Her normally thick hair looked limp and in the harsh light of the bathroom, flecks of grey were clearly visible. Her face looked drawn, the skin pulled too tight, the once healthy glow now a pale pallor. She had lost weight. Lots of it. Uma looked down at the large bruise on her right leg. It was already beginning to colour over, although her hip, which hurt like hell, had no visible marks. Must have happened when she fainted in the foyer. She popped out two aspirins from the foil card and washed them down noisily with the tap water.

She carefully removed the worst of the dried mascara and, after tying her hair back, made her way more confidently back into the bedroom carrying a fresh glass of water.

'Dr Jac—'

Uma's scream cut through the darkness as the tumbler fell to the floor.

For a split second she froze, desperately scanning the large suite for signs of where the voice had come from. A light flickered on by the curtains and out of the shadows a figure materialised. He was sitting in an armchair that was pushed into the darkest corner of the room. He made no effort to move but instead sat absolutely still, staring at Uma who shuddered as the intruder's eyes slithered over her body.

'Dr Jakobsdóttir, forgive me. I di—'

'What are you doing in my room?' Uma screamed.

There was a knock behind her.

Uma half-turned towards the door, keeping the stranger in her peripheral vision but he didn't move.

'Is everything OK in there?'

'No!' Uma screamed again. 'There's someone in my room.'

The handle suddenly depressed and as Uma rushed towards the door, it opened slightly before catching on the security chain. The intruder had locked them in. Panicking, she tried to unhook the metal links but the pressure from the other side made it impossible to release. She glanced back towards the window and let out a whimper of fear. The man had got up and was now halfway across the bedroom. He was much taller than she had realised and his long legs unhurriedly swallowed up the short distance.

'Don't you come any closer,' she yelled.

'Ma'am, are you OK?' The voice on the other side of the door sounded puzzled.

'No. There's a man in my room.'

'Ma'am. I know.' There was a pause from behind the door.

'That's my boss.'

The chain suddenly went limp and Uma clumsily unhooked it before flinging the door open. Two black suits stood there, guns drawn, a look of bewilderment on their faces. Uma recognised one of them. He had spoken to her in the lobby, just before she fainted. Their short conversation sliced through the head vice.

What did the CIA want with her?

'That's OK, boys. I can deal with it from here.'

The two men visibly relaxed and reholstered their weapons, whilst continuing to stare at Uma. She pushed past the tall man and grabbed a sheet from the bed before turning on them.

'What the hell are you doing in my room?'

The tall man said something to the two agents who both laughed knowingly. Thanking them both, he gently shut the door before ambling towards Uma, a wry smile etched across his narrow lips.

'Well, Dr Jakobsdóttir, that didn't exactly go to plan, did it? Maybe we should start again?' He extended a long hand towards her. 'Good afternoon. Joseph Ingram at your service.'

Uma brushed the hand aside and shuffled back towards the bed where she sat down, before hurriedly getting to her feet again.

'You don't know who I am, do you?'

'Another goon.'

'Actually, I'm the head goon.'

Uma's face was blank.

'The Director of the CIA.'

Uma hadn't been expecting that.

'I have to say, Doctor. Your reputation precedes you. That was quite a job you did on my two men downstairs.'

'What do you want?' Uma said. 'And what the hell are you doing in my room in the middle of the afternoon?'

The director walked over to the curtains and drew them back. Bright sunlight flooded into the bedroom.

Uma groaned. *That was doing nothing for her headache.*

'I've been asked to broker a meeting.'

'I presume they're important. Otherwise, why would the head of the largest intelligence agency in the world be acting as an errand boy?'

The director tried to smile, but much to Uma's satisfaction, his thin lips petered out into a frozen scowl.

'He is.'

'Are you going to tell me or is that classified information?'

'It is actually but I'll make an exception. He's my boss. The President of the United States of America.'

Uma's heart skipped a beat.

'Why all the cloak and dagger stuff?'

'All that nonsense downstairs,' he said. 'That was for my benefit. An unavoidable consequence of the job, I'm afraid. My men have been watching the building for two days in preparation for this meeting.'

'Does your boss normally extend personal invitations to his guests by half scaring them out of their wits?'

'Yes. I have to apologise for that but your reaction didn't help. The doctor who checked you out thought you'd had some sort of panic attack. Blacked out. You were saying some pretty interesting things earlier.'

Uma began to colour and unsuccessfully fought to contain the red blush that crept up her neck. She pulled the sheet tight to her chin.

'Don't worry,' he said. 'Most of it was unintelligible. Except two names: Reynolds and Rae. You mentioned them repeatedly.'

The names hung in the air between them. The director studied Uma intently, clearly waiting for a reaction but Uma kept her eyes down, desperately trying to avoid a response. It was a losing battle. The silence continued and when she risked a glance, he nodded encouragingly.

'Don't play games with me,' she said. 'I'm sure you know more about me than I do.'

'Sounds like your past might be catching up with you?'

'What on earth does the President want with me? And why now? We've been trying to meet with him for the best part of two years.'

'So many questions. None of which I can answer.'

'You need to do better than that,' she said. 'I'm currently in the middle of announcing the most important step forward in environmental planning this country has ever seen. It's the culmination of over six years of work, not just by me but hundreds of others and you want to pull me off my schedule to have a meeting with a man who has refused to take my calls!'

'I understand your reluctance but I'm not at liberty to disclose that information. If I could, you would be the first to know.'

'Not good enough,' Uma snapped back. The shock of discovering a man in her room had faded along with her headache. Anger was replacing fear. 'I'm due to leave for San Francisco in less than one hour for tomorrow's road show. Before that, I have a slot on Good Morning America where I have an audience with the people of this country to tell them more about Green Ray's plans for the future. If you don't give me a good reason to break that appointment, I'm going to call my lawyers with a story about your goons' ham-fisted efforts to kidnap me in the lobby. Plus, news of this little stunt you've just pulled in my room. By the time you've finished fighting that PR disaster you'll struggle to get a job pulling security down at the local Walmart.'

The director stared at Uma who held his gaze. It felt like a full minute passed and still no one spoke and Uma was damned if she was going to back down. She took a deep breath and waited, even as it occurred to her that he was thinking, deliberating, whether to tell her more.

'He wants to offer you a job in his new administration.'

'I've got a job,' she said, her mind whirling.

The director shifted in his seat, crossing one long leg over another. He reminded Uma of a praying mantis, his large head, perched atop long limbs, completely still.

'This one's better.'

'Mr Ingram, I head up the largest charitable fund in the world. What could the President possibly offer me?'

'He doesn't want you to give it up. He wants you to combine the role with an appointment of his own—Energy Secretary.'

It was Uma's turn to fall silent. That didn't make any sense. But it fitted that day which was rapidly descending into the surreal. Ingram looked unconcerned, as if breaking into other people's rooms was the most normal pastime in the world.

'Why?'

'Ask him yourself, Doctor.' The director's voice had suddenly become business like. He stood up, drawing himself to his full height. 'A private plane leaves for DC in the next sixty minutes. I suggest you get dressed and join me on it.'

Uma couldn't see any downside. The exposure would be invaluable and keep green at the top of the news networks for days. It was well worth the disruption to her schedule.

'If I cancel San Fran, can I mention my meeting?'

'I suggest your team calls The White House Press Office. They can agree a joint statement.'

That was it. The conversation had ended but the director made no effort to leave. An uncomfortable silence descended which Uma felt obliged to fill. She stood up expectantly.

'OK, you've got yourself a deal, Mr Ingram. I need to make a few phone calls but I will be on that plane.'

Still he didn't move. Uma remembered how she had found herself almost naked beneath the covers and shuddered, imagining the man's bony hands on her body.'

'What are you waiting for, director? Or do you want to watch me get dressed?'

She let the sheet fall to the carpet and flung the doors of the wardrobe open.

The director remained for a few seconds, watching her, and then without a word, made his way towards the door.

Then he was gone, leaving Uma alone, pondering her presidential summons. Already the hammers were beating away inside her but this time it was with excitement.

Ras Tanura Port, Persian Gulf

5 November 2009, 01:56 hours

Ali opened his eyes. For a split second he thought he was back in his bed at the Ghawar compound. Alone and safe. Then he remembered the scorpions. He reacted quickly, jumping to his feet as if he'd been stung but when he looked down, they were still by the dismantled cabinet, immobile, silent, and seemingly asleep. The cell was still bathed in the bright lights from above, but the view had changed. Whereas before he had been able to see all around him, now he couldn't. The walls were no longer transparent. They were black. A bottomless darkness with no depth to it. It was also below him. Puzzled, he placed his hand over the blackness. It felt cool. And then he remembered.

The oil!

They had started filling the tanker. He rushed over to a wall and, standing on tiptoes, peered out over the dark swell. Everywhere he looked, as far as his eyes allowed him, was an ocean of black tar. It was as dark as the apparition's halo and behaved in a similar fashion, sucking up the overhead lights hungrily. It was also moving, like a small sea, with its own swell which rose and fell, gently breaking against the wall of his chamber. He realised he didn't have much longer. A few minutes at most before the blackness swallowed the light for good and then he would be left alone with hundreds of hungry scorpions. His skin crawled at the thought but he remained transfixed by the rising tide, determined to absorb the last atoms of light from above before his liquid tomb was sealed.

Imperceptibly, the thick swell rose up the wall. Only a couple of inches to go. He glanced down and saw the device the Arab had thrown him. It looked like a torch. He knelt down and picked it up, turning it on. Nothing. Had it broken on impact? A cruel joke perhaps. Ali glanced up. The jet black liquid was on the roof of his cage, advancing menacingly like a virus, up the roof which was slanted to a conical apex. The oil rose faster now, perhaps sensing the end was near, reducing the circle of light evenly until there was just a small pinprick left, shining down onto Ali's face like a torch and then it too was gone and he was plunged into darkness.

Instinctively, he clicked the button on his device which flickered into life. However, the bulb wasn't white as he was expecting but ultraviolet blue. He glanced down and gasped in surprise. All around his death chamber, hundreds of shimmering jewels were slowly moving towards him. Ali dropped the light and collapsed to the floor of his cell, unable to comprehend the black hell the white devil had abandoned him to.

Charlie-Echo-3, Camp X-Ray, Guantanamo Bay, Cuba

6 November 2009, 02:26

The corrugated roof was rusting. Badly. He could see the reddish brown corrosion clearly despite the late hour. The harsh halogen lights saw to that. There were six of them shining down into the maze of metal cages and he had long ago learnt to nap through their intrusive glare. However, tonight he welcomed their presence and stared at the hundreds of moths fluttering around one of the huge lamps directly above his bed. They were all shapes and sizes and the chaotic scene was oddly reassuring. It seemed so energetic compared to the lethargy of his daily routine. One he had experienced for over four years now.

Or was it five?

He couldn't be sure and no longer cared.

He was going home today!

That is what his handler had told him. A new President. A new policy. They were shutting the camp down and everybody was being sent home. Those were his exact words and he wondered what could be happening on the outside to make them shut this hell hole down. Things must be going badly to cause such a shift in policy. He hardly dared believe. They had tricked him many times before with offers of treats, visits from family, a Human Rights lawyer, but none had ever materialised.

To his right a small tarantula scuttled into view. He glanced lazily over and stared dully at the black spider. There were hundreds in the cells, especially at night, and because the Charlie block was along the outer perimeter, he seemed to get more than his fair share. At first, he had been scared of the furry insects but had quickly learnt that they were harmless, as were many of the other species that crawled, slithered and sometimes flew into his cell. Sometimes hummingbirds, their beautiful and delicate features at complete odds with the ugliness of the prison camp. He looked forward to their comings and goings. They were his contact with the outside. His reminder that beyond the barbed wire fencing lay another world. He envied their freedom. Their ability to come and go as they pleased, when they liked. But soon he would be joining them.

Unless, of course, this was another of their deceptions. It had better not be.

He wasn't sure how many more he could survive. It was all a question of balance, he kept reminding himself. Don't get too low and don't let expectations become too high. He had learnt the hard way by succumbing to their false promises, repeatedly. Each time it had taken longer to recover from the disappointment, so much so that on occasions he had almost given up hoping. He had to believe. If that stopped, he was finished. If they removed that right then life would not be worth living. Cautious optimism, he had learnt to call it.

He would soon see his family.

His mother.

His father.

Two brothers. Sister.

His cousins, perhaps. Maybe not them. He hadn't seen them for so long now. Almost since the day they had both been picked up with him on the camping trip in—

Where was it?

The name was elusive, drifting on the periphery of his tired memory. The Americans had come at dawn. Out of nowhere. A foot patrol. All three of them were still in their tents, fast asleep, exhausted from the previous days hiking out of—

It was no good. He couldn't remember.

However, he had a vivid memory of being pulled from his tent by his hair, his unprotected heels scraping painfully across the sharp shingle of the mountain. They were lined up and shackled. Forced to walk for two days without food or water. In their underwear. Finally, they had arrived at their destination. A camp high up in the foothills of the Safid mountain range. Hot, dehydrated. Feet bleeding. They were chained so tightly they could barely move and then herded like cattle onto a transport plane. That was the last time he had seen his cousins.

Peshawar. That was it.

The capital of the North West Frontier Province of Pakistan. It was where his father's family were from and he had gone to visit them for five months just after graduating with a first in Chemical Engineering. The backpacking trip had been his idea. They were supposed to hike up to the Khyber Pass. They had all the right documentation. The correct gear. They were in the right area but the Americans didn't care. They had decided he was a terrorist on a training camp and that was it. Tried, convicted and sentenced without any judicial process.

The cell door swung open. He looked up slowly and blinked in the bright light. Two men had entered, their heavy protection immediately identifying them as members of the IRF. The Immediate Reaction Force. Even in his reduced state he knew this was strange. They normally moved in groups of five to eight. In fact, it was very unusual to see only two. It was also unheard of to see them at this time of night. The IRF were enforcers. If you broke a rule, they would enter your cage and beat you. It could be for anything. Talking. Humming. Even standing up. You were meant to sit during the day. If you didn't, you were beaten. He stared at them dully. He hadn't even heard them coming.

The taller of the two moved towards him. He couldn't see his eyes. They were obscured by the thick plastic visor covering his face.

'Hey, man. You're going home today. We need to get you ready.'

His voice was soft. Kind almost. That was also very strange. They were never nice to the prisoners but, nevertheless, his heart jumped. He was going home today. He struggled to his feet and staggered forward with the effort of staying upright. The soldier caught him, dropping his plastic shield in the process.

'Steady there, buddy. You need to take it easy. Come. I'll help you.'

He guided the man over to the bed and sat him down, before kneeling beside him and taking his right hand. Then, ever so gently, he began clipping the man's nails. They were long. They hadn't been cut in years or cared for. When they had got too long, he had simply chewed them down.

The man felt like crying. It reminded him of when his mother used to cut them when he was a young boy. Except, back then, he could barely sit still. When the soldier had finished with his hands, he did the same to his toes before carefully collecting the clippings and placing them in a plastic bag, which he pocketed.

The man frowned at the bag.

Behind the mask, he felt the soldier grin.

'Got to be tidy. Come on, you need to get something to eat and have a shower.'

He helped the man up and guided him towards the cell door where his partner stood. Slowly, the three of them made their way quietly down the corridor. As he turned the corner, Mohammed Hussain paused and looked back towards his home for the last time. He stood silently, a welter of emotions washing over him.

'I'm going home,' he mumbled. The long-forgotten sound of his voice was strange to his ears.

'I'm going home,' he repeated.

Satisfied, he smiled at his captor and shuffled off down the corridor.

Foxtrot-Charlie-6, Camp X-Ray, Guantanamo Bay, Cuba

6 November 2009, 02:56 hours

He could smell the sweat. The odours of too many people bunched together in cramped surroundings. All around him people stood glumly staring into space, lost in their morning thoughts, everybody avoiding each other's gaze with the practised experience of city dwellers. The carriage swung left and the tightly packed crowd swayed with it like saplings in a summer breeze. He felt hot. His thick coat made it so. He wondered how his brothers were getting on. He tried to glance at his watch but the overcrowded carriage made it impossible to look down at his wrist buried deep in his coat pocket. No matter. What he had to do wasn't time critical. Just destination specific. His face was almost touching the long hair of the woman just in front of him. It was silky long. He couldn't remember ever being this close to a female except his mother and sisters. He pressed forward, so that some of the golden threads tickled his nose, and breathed in. It smelt wonderful. The scents of morning mixed with western femininity. Hairspray. Perfume. Shampoo. Suddenly everyone jerked forward and he instinctively braced himself on the overhead hand pull, almost nose-butting her head. The train had begun its shuddering braking routine, the shrieking sound of metal on metal making him wince in the confined space. He didn't need to look up to know where they were.

London Bridge.

The penultimate stop. He could feel his heart begin to beat rapidly. The load in his pack felt heavy. The doors inched open but no one got off. If anything, it became even more crowded. The doors shut with a jerk and the carriage began to pick up speed again.

He felt pleased. He had done his homework well.

Today was the day.

Allahu Akbar.

Within minutes, the cramped train began another screeching stop as it approached its final destination.

Bank Station.

The eighth busiest station on the London Underground. Discharging over eighty-two thousand passengers daily into the heart of London. A lot of them finance types, all heading for the Bank of England or other financial services firms nearby on Threadneedle Street and King William Street. A perfect target.

He took a deep breath. There were only seconds now. The carriage had almost stopped. He needed to time it to perfection. The doors jerked open and for a second nobody moved. There were too many people. That was his moment. His hand went to the button in his coat pocket. It was still there, waiting for him, and just before he pressed it, he screamed out:

'God is Great. Allahu Akbar.'

Then the bomb exploded. It wasn't much. Liquid Acetone Peroxide mixed with chapatti flour powder to bind the mixture. And detonated by a booster charge. But that was sufficient to produce an entropy burst where the half-kilo of TATP produced thousands of litres of gas in a millisecond. In such a confined space the result was devastating, made more so by the 250 ball bearings packed tightly around the crude bomb. Instantly, each metal sphere accelerated to speeds in excess of 4,000 feet per second as the gases sought to escape.

Within twelve inches of the blast, every single person was decapitated. He saw the beautiful woman crumple, her golden hair vaporising from the small explosion that ballooned out from his rucksack. He could see her face. She didn't have time to react. No one did. Not even him. The explosion was too fast to register on their minds let alone transmit to their facial muscles. However, he saw the neat cut that separated the top half of her torso from her legs.

Two feet out, the balls began to separate from a solid blade of metal into discernible silver orbs. They were indiscriminate, penetrating soft flesh with the killing precision of trained snipers.

One metre, and the metal bullets ripped through the carriage walls, burying themselves into the concrete wall on the tunnel side of the train. On the platform side, the pressure blast from the explosion fanned out its deadly metal harvest, tearing through everything in its path before ricocheting off the tiled walls behind unsuspecting early morning commuters.

How could he follow this explosion so closely? It was physically impossible. It should have happened too quickly but everything was revealed in super fine detail at a speed that his mind could absorb. Something was wrong. He should be dead. At the very least he should feel pain and also the heat of the blast. He was at the epicentre of the explosion. Yes, he could feel the heat. It was very hot. He was fading. He was dying. At long last, he was dying. He had won.

Martin Belman woke up with a start, his body bathed in sweat. He lay still for a full minute, luxuriating in the clarity of the dream, his overloaded senses reeling from the blast. The sound. The sight. The smell. The heat of the explosion. It was heavenly. Just as he imagined it would be. Except it hadn't happened. He hadn't won. He had failed that day where his brothers had succeeded. And now he was forced to relive the moment every day in this humid hell hole where all he could do was think about his failure over and over again, with no prospect of righting the wrong so that he could join his victorious brothers in heaven.

A sound to his right brought him out of his half-sleep.

He looked over. Three men were entering his cage. Two heavily suited soldiers and a third. A prisoner, just like himself, his orange boiler suit far too big for his scrawny body. He seemed confused. Martin recognised the symptoms of sleep deprivation well. One of the soldiers motioned for him to get up. He did so silently. There was no point in resisting. He had been there too many times. It was too painful. The soldier placed his plastic shield by the door and stripped the thin top sheet off his bed. He held one end whilst his colleague grabbed the other and they began to rotate the sheet so within seconds it had wound itself into a tight rope.

Martin knew better than to question what was happening. That would result in a beating. He looked over at the other cells. They were all empty. That was no surprise. Prisoners had been disappearing for months. It was rumoured they were being released. He doubted it. He wouldn't be. There was no way the Americans would release him, ever. The British had seen to that.

One of the soldiers picked up the slop bucket and upended it, spilling fresh faeces and urine on the concrete floor. He pushed it with his boot towards the centre of the cell, positioning it carefully. Satisfied, he levered himself up and started working on the chain link fence above his head at the point where it was connected to a bar that bisected the cage. Gradually, he worked one of the links free and then moved on to the next. Within minutes, he had worked four of them loose and was able to thread the tightly wound blanket through the small opening, looping it over the metal support and pulling it back down into the cage so that it was supported by the bar. He knotted it expertly at one end before swinging to the ground. Satisfied, he motioned for the other prisoner to climb onto the bucket, pointing up at the knot. The man looked up compliantly.

'What? You want me up there?'

Martin was surprised. He spoke perfect English but it was heavily accented. Sounded Northern. Yorkshire possibly. Did he know him? It sounded odd. Out of place in these surroundings.

'Hey, a fellow—'

The soldier turned on him with his billy club raised. It was difficult to see his face through the plastic visor but the sign language was clear; a gloved finger to the approximate position where his mouth would be. Martin obeyed once again. It wasn't worth the beating. Four years had taught him that. No point in fighting a fight he could never win.

The soldier pointed again at the bucket and beckoned for the man to climb up.

'Look, buddy. It's time to go home.'

Robotically the man obeyed, climbing onto the upended latrine. He needed some help, given his tightly bound hands but he made it with the support of the guard. He stood swaying in the cold morning air. Martin stared at the two of them in amazement. They looked bizarre. The guard covered from head to foot in thick plastic that was able to withstand a knife thrust from close quarters and the emaciated wretch in an orange jump suit who was so weak he could barely stand.

Without warning the other soldier stepped forward and, with a deft and practised movement, placed the tightly wound blanket round the prisoner's neck. Once, twice he wrapped it before knotting it securely on the taut part of the rope. As he stepped away, the other soldier nonchalantly kicked the bucket away from underneath the man's feet and cut his plastic wrist restraints. His hands immediately went to his neck where he clawed desperately at the thick blanket.

Martin was too stunned to respond. He stood watching the death throes of the orange boiler suit. Initially, they were violent but shortly the jerks became weaker and weaker until they were mere twitches. It seemed to take so long. The soldiers stood there motionless, watching the pathetic dance with their arms folded, waiting patiently for the blanket to complete its deadly work. Finally, the body was still.

Without a word, the two soldiers approached Martin who was half-crouched by the door.

'Come on, buddy. It's your turn. Time to go home.'

Martin looked at the swinging body and back at the advancing men. So that's where everyone was going.

He bolted for the entrance, scrabbling through the metal doorway with no certainty of where he was heading. Except to access the shower block at the end of the corridor on a weekly basis, he had never been this far in years. There was clearly nowhere to run but his survival instinct didn't consider that option. Besides which, he still had a reason to live. He wasn't ready to die. Not just yet at least and certainly not like this. However, he was no match for the two men. Within a few strides they reached him. He could hear them coming but didn't have the strength to do anything about it. He pushed forward and in doing so lost his footing, crashing into a metal post. As he blacked out all he could see was the woman's hair and its wonderful smells.

Central Washington, DC

6 November 2009, 10:55 hours

Uma stared up at the ceiling twenty feet above her head and studied the unmistakable profile of a large bald headed eagle cast in white medallion plaster. In its right talon was what looked like a branch of some sort. In its left, arrows. Circling the bird was some lettering.

'... of the President of the United States,' she mouthed again, squinting with the effort.

It was no good. The white letters were almost invisible against the light cream of the ceiling and, whilst there was an identical design imprinted on the heavy carpet beneath her feet, there were no words. She gave up and concentrated on the rest of the room, trying to ignore the two men stood either side of one of the doors, their hands crossed in front of them like some half-hearted act of prayer. They hadn't spoken since entering and continued their silent vigil as she perched self-consciously on the cream sofa.

To her right was a very familiar dark wooden desk. It looked much smaller than she imagined but everything was, including the famous room itself. Despite its diminutive size, the room radiated power and was hugely intimidating. The circular shape drew you in. There was nowhere to hide. No comforting corners to sit quietly in. When you entered this room, you were immediately the centre of attention and given its status, that attention would probably concern matters of national security or global importance. However, the overwhelming sense of power was completely at odds with the room's décor, which was positively plain. The walls were the lightest cream, almost white, and the carpet, couch and chairs a soft shade of barley. Even the fireplace to her left was white marble and gave the office a much warmer feeling than she had ever imagined possible. In fact, if you removed the famous desk, it could have passed for a large but elegantly decorated drawing room looking out onto a formal garden.

The sentinels suddenly shifted to attention as the door magically opened and three men entered. As the guards exited Uma slowly got to her feet, suddenly aware that she was in the middle of the room.

'Good morning, Dr Jakobsdóttir. I'm so sorry to keep you waiting. As you can appreciate, we have a very busy agenda to maintain. However, Director Ingram has already given me a full briefing so I am up to date.'

Uma stood frozen, like a star-struck fan meeting her rock idol for the very first time, unsure whether to curtsy, bow or both. The man in front of her helped. With an easy assurance born of meeting many strangers, both hands travelled to her right and grasped it, gently but firmly. His relaxed familiarity put Uma immediately at ease.

'Hello, Mr President. I am honoured to meet you,' she said before blurting out, 'Congratulations on your recent inauguration. It looked cold out there.'

Jamal Williams, forty-fourth President of the United States of America, smiled warmly down at her.

'I had it easy. Some of those poor souls were queuing for two days to get a good position.'

He turned to the men accompanying him.

'I understand you already know Director Ingram.'

Uma shook his hand, unsmiling.

'Yes, we've met. And been the butt of his rather heavy-handed tactics.'

'Yes, he told me that you hospitalised two of his best men. That's exactly the qualities we need in our new administration. Wouldn't you say so, Joseph?'

'I would indeed Mr President,' Ingram said, his grey eyes revealing nothing.

'And this is John Forsyth, President and CEO of In-Q-Tel.'

Uma gladly turned from the director to greet his other guest and stood transfixed as he took her hand.

'Hello, Uma. A pleasure. I've heard so much about you.'

It was his eyes. They were a deep aquamarine blue. So inviting and so familiar but not of this earth. They were too bright. Too blue if that was possible. *Where had she seen them before?* They were almost preternatural. Wise beyond a normal lifespan but sparkling like a high-spirited child. Compassionate beyond human capacity but beneath the warmth, an arctic chill that was almost Godlike in its detachment. She couldn't hold his gaze. No one could and he knew it.

'In-Q-Tel?' was all she could think to say.

His eyes twinkled with suppressed merriment.

'The CIA's VC Fund.'

'Why would the CIA need a fund?'

It was the Blue Lagoon. His eyes were the colour of the Blue Lagoon.

'The government are not immune to the costs of developing leading edge technology.' Forsyth smiled warmly, his eyes drawing Uma in, completely at home in the powerful room. 'Spying is a supremely expensive business. That's where the fund comes in. We identify, invest in and nurture smaller and promising companies and once we have our technology, we float. We retain an equity stake to control who the technology goes to and also get a return on our investment. We are effectively self-financing. It's all very straightforward.'

His voice was gravelly. She could have listened to it all day.

But what was he doing here? It didn't make sense. None of this did.

'So, to business. I have precisely thirty minutes.' The most powerful man in the world sat down and gestured for his guests to do the same. They all complied. 'Joseph, perhaps you would be so good as to update Dr Jakobsdóttir on where we are.'

'Before he does,' Uma said, 'could you explain to me what I am doing here?'

The President looked surprised.

'I don't understand. I thought Director Ingram had already briefed you.'

'He has but—' Uma said, suddenly tongue tied again, completely distracted by the blue eyes now boring a hole into the side of her head. 'I meant that I understand you want to offer me the position of Energy Secretary in your new administration. What I don't understand is why. We've been trying to engage with your team for the best part of two years through Green Ray but no one would talk to us. I accept that you had the small matter of the primaries and then an election to win but what we stand for is right up there with your own beliefs on climate change. That, and we have plenty of money. We could have been very useful to your campaign.'

The President sat staring at Uma, hands clasped together, thumbs resting against his mouth.

'I admire your frankness, Dr Jakobsdóttir. Not many people can walk in here and speak that openly. I'll return the compliment. We didn't engage with you for one very good reason.' Uma held his gaze. She was determined not to be overawed by the room or her host for that matter.

'Samuel Reynolds III.'

Uma's heart skipped a beat. She hadn't heard the name in years.

'You were simply too close to the events surrounding his disappearance and what followed.' The President didn't need to spell that out for Uma. Reynolds Air had crashed big time, becoming the largest bankruptcy in American Corporate history. Not only that but they were still litigating over what some regarded as the biggest securities fraud ever and, in the words of the man sat before her, 'the most blatant hoax ever perpetrated on the American public.'

'But I had nothing to do with any of that,' Uma said. 'The Congressional Enquiry completely absolved me of any involvement in Reynolds' schemes.'

'Doctor.' The President smiled warmly at her. It was very disarming. 'I'm a politician. I deal in public perception every day of my life. During an election campaign it becomes even more important. You were guilty by association. At least in the eyes of the public. And quite frankly, that's all that matters.'

Uma made to interrupt but the man in front of her cut in smoothly.

'Every poll we ran supported that view and as the election unfolded it became more entrenched, particularly given the financial crisis that was unfolding before our eyes. For many voters the credit crisis was like history repeating itself, except on a much larger scale. They kept referring to the greed of Reynolds and my predecessor's failure to stamp it out, or at least restrict the opportunity for others to perpetuate what he succeeded in pulling off. There was never a chance that we could engage with you. It would have been political suicide.'

'I understand the game you needed to play Mr President.' If there was one thing the last five years had taught Uma, it was the realisation that she could never win this argument no matter what she said. 'However, given that position, it makes the current offer even more mystifying. What has changed in the last few weeks that means you not only want to talk to me but actually offer me the most powerful environmental job in America?'

'Everything has changed Dr Jakobsdóttir.' The President sighed heavily as if the entire weight of the world was on his shoulders. It suddenly occurred to Uma that it probably was and she felt the power of the office again pressing in on her from all sides. 'In a few short months the entire western banking system has virtually collapsed and the world economy has dropped off a cliff face into the worst recession since the 30s. In that short period, we've pumped billions into the system and it won't stop there. Next Tuesday I will sign into the law the American Recovery and Reinvestment Act which will inject a further $787 billion into the economy.'

'So, you want my money?'

'Partly,' the President acknowledged. 'The Act has set aside thirty-nine billion dollars for the Department of Energy. Add that to its annual budget of twenty-six billion and you will have effectively doubled the funds available to Green Ray. Not to mention the power you can wield to get your programmes up and running. The Electro. Your Wind Programme. The Smart Meter. You will be able to move so much faster.'

'And be subject to the same political straitjacket that has torpedoed your Clean Energy Bill. I am not sure I have the patience for that.'

The President laughed.

'You're right. You probably don't, but we need you.'

'But why?' Uma wasn't going to be charmed so easily. She clearly remembered the wall of silence that had greeted her team whenever they had approached any number of the then Presidential Candidate's handlers. 'I'm still as guilty as I ever was in the eyes of the public. Given what you have just said, you would never get my appointment past the Senate anyway. There must be something else?'

'Joseph. Could you please enlighten our guest on what we're facing?'

Director Ingram stood up and went over to the desk. On it were two pieces of paper. He picked up the first and handed it to Uma.

She barely glanced at it before tossing the sheet onto the table.

'OK. You're going to have to help me here. What does this mean?'

'Those,' the director said, 'are the known reserves for the Ghawar Oil Field in Saudi Arabia.'

'And ...?'

'It's the largest known oil field in the world by some distance. So big in fact that, at first, geologists believed it was five separate fields. They nicknamed them The Magnificent Five. It wasn't until 1953 that they realised all five were part of a single field. During the last sixty years Ghawar has produced over fifty billion barrels of oil which is equivalent to almost sixty percent of Saudi Arabia's total output. We have believed for quite some time that it is running dry. Aramco has consistently denied this, claiming there are still over seventy billion barrels of oil waiting to be extracted.'

'And what are these readouts exactly?'

'Earlier this week we received intel,' Ingram nodded at the sheet, 'that confirmed our suspicions. They suggest that the reserves stand at less than twenty percent of the official figure.'

'And?' Uma was beginning to get angry. They had pulled her off the promo campaign for a geology lesson.

The director shifted ever so slightly in his seat. If Uma hadn't known better, she would have said he looked slightly annoyed.

'The US consumes twenty million barrels per day. We produce eight million barrels per day. I'll let you do the math. The point is that we import the majority of that shortfall from Saudi Arabia. If these figures are correct, and I can assure you they are from a very reliable source, we need to accelerate our move towards self-sufficiency. Quickly.'

'And you want me to spearhead that effort?' Uma said. 'There's no way we could make up the shortfall overnight. You know as well as I do that there simply isn't the will. Political, maybe, but unless you have the public behind you, that will never fly. Why don't you release the information? That would motivate everyone. If they knew that they would be losing their precious lifestyles in a few short years, that would spur them on.'

'We can't afford to do that. Can you imagine the impact this would have on the oil price if this intelligence got out? Our analysts believe it would make the $150 per barrel seen last year look like loose change. Let me assure you, Doctor, the world doesn't need that type of shock given the position its economies are in.'

'OK,' Uma said, feeling rather stupid. She was more used to firing back that type of statistic and being on the offensive when it came to discussions on energy usage. 'Why don't you just buy it from elsewhere?'

The director sighed heavily, this time like a school master berating a dim student.

'In the short term, it's not realistic. As you know, once Saudi is out of the picture most other countries with significant oil production and reserves are hardly friendly towards the US' economic interests. Take UAE and Kuwait off the list and you're left with Russia, Iran,

Venezuela, Iraq, Libya, Nigeria, China and Angola. Even if they wanted to, they could never take up the strain and, as you have been so quick to remind us, weaning people off power is not easy.'

'OK,' she said, 'it sounds like you have all the answers here. I guess that brings me back to my original question, what do you want from me? If you can't produce sufficient alternative energy, source it easily from elsewhere and explain to the American public why they should be using less power, I'm not sure I can help you, even if I was Energy Secretary.'

'Welcome to government, Doctor!' the President said. 'There is another way. One I am sure you have considered in the past. Joseph, if you would be so good.'

The director returned to the table and handed the second piece of paper to Uma.

'Recognise this?'

Uma stared at the single sheet, unmoving. Her neat handwriting was unmistakable and the first few words confirmed her worst fears. She hadn't seen this coming. Should have, but hadn't.

Uma placed the letter on her lap and stared at it unseeing, blinking back hot tears. She suddenly realised why blue eyes was here and her heart sank even further.

The power in the room was overwhelming and she felt its full force zeroing in on the hundred or so words before her. The single sheet felt heavy, as if each individual letter was cut from solid blocks of granite. She remembered writing these words. Knew them intimately. Her first instinct was to tear the paper up and run from the room, even as her eyes travelled reluctantly to her letter.

Dear Mr Reynolds,

The crowd in Virginia will be getting agitated now, as will the millions who tuned in to watch you teleport from Virginia to San Francisco. History will shortly be made but not the sort you had intended. Come Monday morning when the markets open, there will be some interesting fall out from your failure to appear on the West coast. With any luck, the airline your grandfather founded will go bust along with your family's trust fund. Gone. Vanished. Faded away, along with your reputation.

Sure, you'll be famous but for all the wrong reasons. You'll be remembered as the one who took down the family business by illegally boosting his failing airline's stock price with made-up stories about teleportation. The desperate ramblings of a desperate man – not quite the legacy you had in mind!

Yours

Uma Jakobsdóttir

'Where did you find this?' Uma's voice was flat as if the life force had been sucked from her, one word at a time.

'On the deep-frozen body of a certain Samuel J. Reynolds III,' the director said. 'In a deserted building in the centre of Iceland. About sixty miles from civilisation. But you already know that.' There was no accusation. Just a statement of the facts.

Uma remembered writing the letter as if it was yesterday, not six long years ago in a hotel room, the night before Reynolds's ill-fated attempt to launch LEAP at the Steven F. Udvar-Hazy Center in Virginia. She had decided to sabotage the event weeks before, once she realised that Reynolds needed stopping. That his relentless pursuit of LEAP had resulted in so much bloodshed. So many deaths: the journalists, dear Frederik and poor Eva. She had known that her actions would kill Reynolds but more importantly, she also knew with an absolute certainty that she would do it all again given what he had done. The thought steadied her.

'What do you want from me?'

'I thought that was self-evident.'

'You really believe it works?'

'We know it does, Doctor. We suspected it at the time but couldn't prove anything. Now we have Mr Reynolds.'

'He doesn't prove anything.'

'Actually, he does. In the short time since we discovered his body, we've been able to establish a number of irrefutable facts.'

Uma slumped back in her seat and stared up the ceiling.

Seal. That was the word. It said, 'Seal of the President of the United States'. She felt as if her own fate had just been sealed.

From far away she heard the director's voice. Something about an autopsy.

'—showed that Mr Reynolds ate a very specific breakfast on the morning of December 17th, 2003. We know this from the hotel records of where he stayed and they match perfectly with the contents of his stomach. Smoked salmon with scrambled eggs washed down with a Mimosa. Several it would seem. His key card was still in his trouser pocket. It was still programmed to Suite 9000 of the Bethesda Marriott. As was his wallet.'

He looked over.

'John, if you please.'

She tried not to look at him but it was impossible. His stare was magnetic and she felt an overwhelming urge to move closer.

'Thank you, Joseph. We've been tracking your patent filings for some time now. As you would imagine, its part of our strategy to spot early-stage ideas that might be of use to the CIA. Quite frankly they are astounding and don't actually make any scientific sense, at least in terms of achievability given our current knowhow. Take the most recent one. An application for a new wind turbine blade constructed from a—' Forsyth glanced down at a file in front of him, '—a morphing composite, that can actually alter its aerodynamic profile when wind and current conditions change and in turn remove unwanted stresses in the actual blades systems.' The filing maintains that it would increase the efficiency of the blades and extend the working life of the generator systems by up to 100%.' He continued leafing through the sheets before stopping at one marked with a red cross. 'Here is another one filed at the beginning of the year. A composite to be used as an alternative lining in nuclear reactors that can resist radiation damage by exhibiting a sort of healing effect by moving its atoms around to fill in holes caused by exposure to the reactor and restore the crystal structure of the material. Again, in the preamble you talk about the fact that current reactors only can burn one percent of fuel. Using your material will allow them to increase the amount of fuel burnt by a factor of twenty and mean less nuclear waste, not to mention extending the lives of existing reactors.' He closed the file. 'Both these composites require you to have a working knowledge of subatomic particles that my analysts tell me is decades away from even the most advanced labs. Doctor, the evidence is overwhelming.'

The last sentence was delivered with a certainty that brooked no argument. Uma didn't even try.

'I vowed never to release LEAP,' she said. 'It's too destructive. In the short time I tried, some of my closest friends died and I lost my twin sister. I simply won't do it. You can't make me.'

'Actually, we can,' Ingram cut in. 'If you don't agree to make the code available to us, we will charge you with the premeditated murder of Samuel Reynolds III. I don't doubt that he deserved it but the fact is that when you transported him to the Interior you sent him to his death. Even if he had stayed put and survived the winter, there is very little likelihood that he would have made it to civilisation. If you go down, so will your fund and that means you will not achieve any of your environmental objectives. Instead, you'll spend the next thirty years of your life rotting away in a high security penitentiary in Virginia whilst the globe suffocates to death.'

Uma laughed for the first time since she had entered the Oval Office. Was that the best he had?

'I could deliver Reynolds to you tomorrow if I so desired. Other than a four-year memory lapse, he would be in perfect physical health with not a hair on his misguided body disturbed. He would pass every conceivable identification test, from the two-inch appendix scar right down to his shrivelled liver. Now that would be an interesting court case. One dead body and one live one. Isn't that the basis of a murder case. A dead body. Perhaps you would both care to opine on the outcome of that line of enquiry.'

The director's grey eyes absorbed Uma's fierce stare with a calm detachment bordering on nonchalance. It was as if the thought of unravelling centuries of criminal law was indeed an everyday occurrence and one he was quite prepared to experience if it progressed his end goal.

'I would welcome it,' he said. 'Regardless of the outcome, your secret would be out and you wouldn't get a moments rest until the day you died. I'm not sure if imprisonment wouldn't be better. At least if you decided to co-operate with us now, we could avoid some of your mistakes that led to so many people dying in the first place.'

The President cut in smoothly.

'Doctor,' he said, leaning forward in his seat. 'Actually, do you mind if I call you Uma?'

She didn't respond and he continued.

'Uma, I understand your reluctance to release LEAP, I truly do, but I need the boost this technology will provide. Not just me but the whole country. My entire election manifesto was structured around delivering real change to this great nation of ours. Change at all levels of society that will deliver affordable health care for all, high quality education for the many, not just the privileged few, and sustainable energy consumption, not only for us but the whole world.'

His shoulders suddenly slumped and he sat back on the couch. Uma thought he looked world weary. Jaded almost, as if his thirty or so days at the epicentre of the storm had taken their toll.

'When I stood on the steps of the US Capitol Building, I meant what I said. I am truly humbled by the task ahead and truly grateful for the trust bestowed upon me. However, I'm also a realist. My background forces me to be. The credit crisis threatens to derail any chance I have of delivering real change. It will swallow up the money, time and energy of the entire country and there will be nothing left for anything else. My words will remain just that and I will go down in history as the hollow saviour who failed his country and, with it, the hope of an entire generation.'

As he spoke, he suddenly came alive. His whole posture changed, his voice had acquired a deep timbre, naturally slowing down to accentuate each and every word with the gravitas he cleared intended.

'With LEAP, we all stand a chance. We could cut our dependence on foreign fuel imports overnight. Push forward my agenda on other forms of renewable energy, particularly for heat and light. I—' he paused and smiled at Uma, '—we could create an unstoppable momentum of economic activity that would lift everyone out of the current crisis. Make a difference to millions of Americans' lives and allow me to push ahead with my health care and education reforms.'

He finished with both arms open, held out towards Uma as if he was beckoning her to join him.

'Nice words, Mr President,' Uma said. 'You put it so eloquently. I understand the need. Both yours and the nation's. Your desire to deliver results. The impact that LEAP could have. You sound like me five years ago and for that I salute your honesty. Your good intentions. But LEAP is a poisoned chalice. It promises a better tomorrow but what good is that if it destroys the present.'

The man in front of her made to cut in but this time Uma continued.

'I lost my present. Virtually overnight and it changed my future forever. My experience represents a microcosm of what I believe would happen if you released LEAP on a wider scale. We, mankind, the human race, is simply not ready for it.'

'What right have you got to sit here and lecture us about the dangers of LEAP when you are clearly using the technology and have been for some time,' the director said.

'Joseph, please,' the President raised his hand slightly. 'The patents John referred to. You're not going to sit there and claim that your team leapfrogged twenty years into the future and developed nano composites that were radiation proof and altered their shape depending on the direction of the wind.'

'But there is no danger in that,' Uma said. 'No one is harmed or hurt by the use of that. In fact, it will help people by taming our energy dependency.'

'Ah. So, you and I have the same aspiration,' the President said. 'That is good to hear and I understand the rationale. It is like the current credit crisis. Money is not inherently a bad thing. Far from it, in fact. It's people that complicate things, especially if they're left to their own devices and remain unregulated, uncontrolled. Then our baser instincts take over and it's open to abuse, not only by a few greedy and irresponsible men but by our collective failure to make hard choices sooner.'

He sat there seemingly deep in thought.

'You know, I think we are getting slightly ahead of ourselves here,' the President said. 'Uma you'll have to forgive me. I have only known about the existence of LEAP for seventy-two hours and if truth be known, since I was introduced to the concept, I have developed a few reservations, which perhaps you can help me with.'

What was he planning now? Uma thought. She instinctively liked him. He was so charming. She already felt she knew him. All of a sudden, the office felt like a family drawing room again and it was as if she was sat on the sofa of an old friend having tea and sharing stories.

But, she reminded herself, he had an agenda. Everybody did but she couldn't, for the life of her, work out what it was.

She couldn't help noticing the director take a surreptitious look at his watch and smiled inwardly. He could well wait all day as far as she was concerned.

Blue eyes didn't say a word. He just sat there staring at Uma, which she found incredibly distracting. She turned her head slightly. Away from him.

The President continued.

'My main problem is this,' he said, collecting his thoughts. 'LEAP is a truly disruptive technology. Possibly the most disruptive mankind has ever encountered. We studied them for a while at Harvard in my second semester of law school. I recall we were trying to understand the different type of shocks that a country's legal system might be placed under and how it would react. Other than the obvious ones like a civil or actual war, we also considered technological advances. The problem, if I remember correctly, is that there's no way you can anticipate the social, political, military, economic or even environmental consequences of such a technology being introduced into the world. It would just be guesswork.

'I was thinking last night of the damage something like this could do to the economy if it was released overnight. Can you imagine the resultant social upheaval through job losses ... the community breakdown ... the business fallout, especially with industries involved in transportation? The impact would be catastrophic, especially in the current crisis. Except of course, it's not that simple. Take Detroit. It's a proud city with a rich history of manufacturing that quite literally stands on the edge of a precipice. Unless Congress comes up with a rescue package, GM, Ford and Chrysler will collapse and hundreds of thousands of jobs will be lost, not to mention the knock-on effects to the wider economy. So, we are now faced with having to pump tens, perhaps hundreds of billions of dollars into the industry to prop it up. I've no doubt they will get their money but then we are faced with a conundrum. Save the car industry but pay for their continued environmental impact in the longer term. However, we can mitigate that through LEAP but if we do all these people still lose their jobs. So, what's the answer? Either path we tread carries an enormous cost socially, politically, economically. It then becomes a question of weighing up which is worse. The lesser of two evils as it were.'

He looked at all three of them questioningly and carried on.

'The answer is in controlling the speed of the disruption—if it is allowed to hit unchecked then we could really have problems that might make what we are currently going through seem gentle by comparison. However, if we could slow it down then the upheaval would be minimised. In one sense, do what you are currently doing but on a bigger scale.'

Uma looked mystified.

'You phase in the technology,' the President said. 'It's the only way. Just like you are doing at the moment. We could say that it doesn't work on people and foodstuffs. Limit it to the transportation of say, inert or non-biological structures. That would give everyone a chance to acclimatise in every sense of the world. Society. Business. Politicians. That's effectively what you are saying, isn't it? That's in fact what you are doing. Phasing LEAP in at a pace that is comfortable for you.'

He looked questioningly at Uma again.

'I guess,' she said.

The President leapt to his feet and began pacing in front of Uma.

'You know, I think it could work. Drip feed the technology to ensure society didn't get left behind but at the same time provide the sort of impact that the world needs.'

'I agree with what you are saying in principle,' Uma said, suddenly on guard. The man was sweet talking her into agreeing a release of LEAP. 'However, I'm not sure that is quite how it would pan out in practice.'

'It would if we controlled the progression,' the President said. 'It's just a question of determining the speed. Given what you've been through, I'd imagine that is going to be very slowly.'

'How do you control that?' Uma said. 'It's impossible. At some point someone would discover ways in which to use LEAP that no one had anticipated? And I guarantee you they won't be legal.'

'That's just human nature,' the President said. Uma felt herself bristling with indignation. She had a feeling this was going to happen, regardless of what she said today and felt the first stirrings of an attack. *Please, not here,* she thought. 'To innovate. That is good for any nation and is something that this great country of ours was founded on and hopefully will continue to drive forward long into the future. By the time that happens it wouldn't matter.'

'Not unless LEAP was used for the wrong reasons. Just like five years ago. I lost family and friends.'

'This is no longer about you,' the director said. 'With LEAP, we could alleviate the suffering for millions of Americans. What happened to your friends and family was unfortunate but in the context of what it could alleviate, the price is worthwhile.'

Uma flushed with anger.

'How dare—'

'Joseph. Please!' the President shot his director an angry glance. For the first time since he entered the room, Uma saw cracks appearing in his calm exterior.

Ingram continued to stare at Uma. Nothing. It was like looking into a grey mist. Nothing moved. Nothing came out. Nothing was allowed in.

'You're right, Mr President. I apologise.' The eyes of a ghost. 'I didn't mean to cause offence.'

Despite her anger, Uma realised that he wasn't scared or overawed by the man to his right. If anything, he was treating him like her. A pawn in his own game, to be moved at will.

'But I don't agree with—'

There was a soft knock at the door. Everyone looked up. A small man entered and without acknowledging anyone, hurried over to the President and whispered urgently in his ear. He sat motionless for a few seconds before addressing the room, his face grim.

'There's a problem at Guantanamo. One of the inmates has hung himself.'

The words hung in the air.

'I'm sorry, Mr President,' the aide said. 'I'm afraid we have to go. We need to fully debrief you for the press conference. It's scheduled to run in less than thirty minutes.'

'Was it one of the releasees?' Ingram said.

'No,' the President said, deep in thought. 'It was a long-term inmate. Belman. An Englishman. He was the sixth London bomber. No loss really, although it will completely overshadow the release of the ten leaving today. A bit of a PR disaster really.' He looked up and smiled. 'OK, Sam. Let's do it. We have some damage limitation to perform.' He rose and turned to Uma.

'It's been an absolute pleasure. I think we can make this work, you know. You have my word on that.'

She made to object but he put up his hands.

'I know. I know. You need to consider the whole proposal. I understand. It's a huge decision. Regardless of what you decide, I will respect your decision but if you do come down in favour of pressing the green button, please be assured that you will receive my full executive support to ensure that LEAP is rolled out at a speed that you are comfortable with. In addition, you will receive the post of Energy Secretary with carte blanche to direct the Agency in any manner you see fit to advance the objectives of Green Ray. In the meantime, Director Ingram has arranged for you and John Forsyth to begin working on a possible roll-out approach. A limited one, that suits your pace.'

More people swept into the room. A television crew. A makeup artist. More agents. Lots of them. The President was ushered over to the desk where he sat down as three aides bustled around him.

'It looks like we have been dismissed, Doctor.' John Forsyth smiled, slowly getting to his feet. 'Come. We have a lot to discuss if we are going to identify some middle ground that satisfies both you and the President.'

John Paul Jones Hill, Guantanamo Bay, Cuba

6 November 2009, 4 hours earlier

The huge blades cut a ninety foot swathe through the early morning heat and, even though they were 150 feet above his head, Weapons Sergeant, Jos Brody of the 1st Battalion, 7th Special Forces Group, involuntarily ducked each time one swooped majestically by. Up ahead his Company leader, Kurt Lee, swore softly as he tried to jerk open the metal door that would lead them into the guts of the wind turbine that overlooked their base, nestling in the bay far below. He glanced up at the brightening sky. Already the sun was beginning to peep over the eastern horizon, illuminating the tips of the Sierra Maestra Mountains directly to his West. It would soon be light and, like every other day for the last three months, it was going to be a hot and humid one.

The door suddenly cracked open and his partner grunted with satisfaction.

'Come on, buddy. Let's get this over with.' And then Lee was gone, swallowed up inside the tall white tube. Brody took a deep breath and entered, trying to keep his breathing steady. He hated heights and was already beginning to worry about the two-hundred-foot drop once he got to the top.

'Did you see that rag head dance?' Lee called down. His voice sounded echoey in the chamber and Brody struggled to hear it above the disorienting drone that buzzed around his head. It was a weird sensation. Every two seconds the metal chamber vibrated as one of the passing blades compressed the air between itself and the tower. It wasn't loud. Far from it but the intermittent bursts made his bones tingle and head hum. At least it took his mind off the drop.

'Button it,' he hissed, suddenly fearful that someone might hear them. But no one would. That was why they were meeting here. The turbines were fully automatic and required no supervision except for a monthly maintenance visit which was not due for another twenty days. Brody had checked the rota himself before they left the base.

As they climbed, the tower became narrower until their arms and shoulders were brushing against the metal of the service chute.

Add small spaces to his phobia list. He was actually looking forward to getting out into the open air.

Brody could feel himself beginning to pant. He could feel a slight sway in the tower which made his stomach turn somersaults at the thought of how high they must be. Above him, Lee paused as he reached the top of the steps. Brody risked a glance up just as his partner wriggled into a narrow tunnel and quickly disappeared from view. Brody followed and continued on his hands and knees. Judging from the noise, he figured that both the generator and the main rotor shaft were directly above them. This close, the vibrations hurt his ears and shook his body till his bones ached. He crawled faster but was hampered by Lee who shuffled along slowly. At last, the tunnel opened out into a small area with just enough space for both of them to stand up, side by side. Directly above their heads was a hatch. Brody had had enough. He pushed past Lee and clambered up the ladder, pushed open the door and scrambled out into the morning air.

For a few seconds he just stood there admiring the heightened view. In the short time they had been climbing, the sun had almost cleared the horizon which gave him an uninterrupted view of the ragged mountains of Haiti only fifty miles to the east. Ahead, the blades continued their tireless work, quietly and efficiently. This close they were even more impressive. As one disappeared below the line of the platform, a chasing blade had already appeared, exactly one hundred and twenty degrees behind, cutting a wide arc through the sky before dropping out of sight as another came into view in an eternal chase. Brody smiled. It felt as if he was in the cockpit of some colossal plane that was awaiting clearance for take off, its massive propellers ticking over expectantly in anticipation of the moment when a surge of power would hurl them into the atmosphere. Far below them the base was coming to life. There were signs of activity everywhere and he suddenly felt very exposed on the narrow ramp.

'What took you?'

He whirled round, instinctively tensing up but then relaxed as Carl Fortune emerged from behind the door.

'Is it completed?' he said.

Straight to business. Brody had known Carl Fortune for over four years now, right from when the agency had recruited him whilst serving out his basic training at Fort Bragg. He knew no more about him now than he had done when they first met. He even doubted his name. It felt fake.

'Sure is, buddy. That rag head didn't put up no fight,' Lee said. 'Like taking candy from a baby. He's gone home and MB has been handed over to his handler.'

'Any problems?'

'Are there ever?'

'Good. Good. Come,' Fortune nodded towards the slowly turning blades, 'walk with me.' Fortune squeezed past them both and strolled out along the narrow platform. Brody kept his eyes focused on his handler's back, being careful not to look down. Up to this point he hadn't even thought about the altitude but now they were on the move, that's all he could think about. At this height the wind was gusting strongly. Maybe thirty miles per hour, he reckoned, and he could feel the whole structure swaying in the breeze. Was it strong enough to withstand these stresses? In his mind's eye he saw the whole structure folding in on itself and crashing to the ground. He fought the overwhelming urge to run back to the service chute and instead concentrated on Fortune who had reached the far side and was staring up at the slowly rotating slivers of polyester.

'Do you know these babies are computer controlled? They sense the direction of the wind and then turn to meet it. Incredible. Come, look at this.' Fortune pointed towards the centre of the structure. It was at this point that Brody realised he was wearing thin black undergloves. They looked so out of place in the humidity of the early morning.

'It has to support about thirty tons. Add in the stresses of movement caused by wind and the blades themselves, and that can treble. It's an incredible feat of engineering.'

Brody doubted Fortune had ever said as much. Nor had he finished.

'I've heard they've become the suicide tool of choice. Must be the height, no?' He looked back at the two men for confirmation before continuing. 'Can you imagine how desperate someone must be to end his own life?'

The irony wasn't lost on Brody who stared at his handler suspiciously.

Fortune leant out over the guard rail to get a closer look at the nose cone. A huge blade slowly descended towards him. It must have been fifteen feet across and for a split second Brody thought it was going to decapitate him but at the last moment it disappeared past his head just as the next blade swung into view.

Lee joined him on one side but Brody hung back. There was no way he was going anywhere near the guard rail. Fortune glanced back at him.

'What's wrong? Don't you enjoy the view?'

'I don't like heights,' he said, before turning away and retracing his steps back towards the tower. He felt lightheaded and his stomach was doing its damndest to repatriate his light breakfast onto the metal walkway.

A scream made him turn. At first, what he saw didn't register. Fortune was leaning out over the edge of the safety barrier. The blades were caught up in their eternal chase. The sun had notched up a few more centimetres. And then he realised what was wrong. Lee was nowhere to be seen. Forgetting his fear, Brody ran back along the walkway.

'Where's Lee?'

Fortune grunted with effort and nodded down. Brody took a deep breath and looked over the side.

Directly below him was Lee, holding Fortune's hand, his face contorted in terror as one of the huge blades completed its rotation just beside him, the outer ridge passing inches from his head.

'Help me,' Fortune grunted, beads of perspiration bathing his forehead. 'I'm losing him.'

Brody had no time to think. As he reached for Lee, Fortune let go. Brody grasped his wrist just in time.

Below him, Lee looked up and let out a scream.

'No, it— a tr—'

Brody could barely hear him above the roar of the wind, his fear, the turbines, the massive blades.

'N—, i— trap.'

He sensed movement behind him and felt Fortune's hand on his shoulder.

'Sorry. Just following orders.'

Without warning, he felt one hand close around his trouser belt and the other grasp his shirt collar. And then he was suddenly jerked upwards. Brody instinctively made himself heavy and slumped hard against the curved railing. The metal dug deep into his armpits but the tactic worked. Temporarily. He was still on the platform.

Fortune grinned and stepped back. Brody knew immediately what he was doing. He was waiting for him to tire. Already his arms were beginning to ache. There was no way he could support Lee for much longer. And he also had to protect himself. Below him he heard another scream.

'Let go.'

'No' he hissed but Lee started to wriggle backwards and forwards and Brody felt his buddy begin to slip from his sweaty grasp.

'Kill that s—'

And then he was gone. His head struck one of the fibreglass blades a heavy blow and Brody saw him go limp as he spiralled raggedly down towards the waiting tarmac. Brody turned away before he hit the ground but as he did so, Fortune struck. He had timed his move to perfection. As Brody let go, his body relaxed. For a split second he was slightly off balance and Fortune shoved him upwards with all his might. Brody had expected the attack but was powerless to resist. As Brody went over the barricade, his nails raked Fortune's face, drawing a scream from his handler. Then he was falling, grasping at one of the huge propellers as it swung by. But it was built to capture the wind and his hands skidded across the smooth plastic before he disappeared, swallowed up by the early morning mist which hung over John Paul Jones Hill.

CIA Headquarters, Virginia

6 November 2009, 15:10 hours

June Fortis risked a glance at the man in front of her. He had been furiously pacing back and forth across the thick carpet for the last twenty minutes, hands thrust deep into the pockets of a burgundy suit, his normally ruddy face a deep purple. The secretary had little doubt this was solely down to the copious quantities of red wine the Director of National Intelligence was rumoured to drink every night. No, something had clearly happened to get him this agitated and she had a very good idea who might have caused this mood. As their eyes locked for the merest moment, she quickly tried to avoid his angry gaze but it was too late. George C. Brown walked over to her desk and June was forced to look up.

'Director Ingram is still in transit. I am told he will be here imminently,' she began, trying desperately not to stare at the huge pot belly that was now less than eighteen inches from her head. She could clearly see the strain it was placing on the lower buttons of his shirt that were stretched to breaking point.

'What's taking him so long?' he said. 'It's barely ten miles from The White House.'

'As I mentioned earlier, there's been an accident on the George Washington Memorial Parkway.'

'Why doesn't he fly like everyone else?'

'I don't know, sir,' June said.

Actually, she did. Director Ingram insisted on being driven. The short drive caused a security nightmare but he liked the solitude. It gave him time to think. He would not take phone calls in the car unless, of course, it was the President. He would always take his call but no one else got through, including his own boss who had resumed his furious carpet crawl. June watched him out of the corner of her eye. He was becoming increasingly agitated, muttering under his breath, his chubby hands clenched tightly into fists. Every so often he would jab the air with a fat finger as if to make a point. June hoped her boss would hurry up. At this rate the Director of National Intelligence was going to have a heart attack. She abandoned any pretext of trying to work and instead concentrated on the huge flat screen TV that dominated the room. It was permanently switched to CNN and according to her boss, was the best intelligence service in the world. Always first with the story, he would laugh. As she watched, the view switched from the studio to an outside scene. It looked warm, the blue ocean framing a sweaty reporter who wiped his brow with a handkerchief before speaking.

'It's been a busy day here at Guantánamo Bay. On what should have been an occasion of celebration for The White House, the planned release of twenty detainees including the British citizen Mohammed Hussain, has been completely overshadowed by three unexplained deaths on the base. Two weapons sergeants from the 7th Special Forces Group were found dead in the early hours of this morning beneath one of the four wind turbines that power the base. Both appeared to have fallen from the two hundred fifty foot structure and an internal investigation has already begun into their deaths.

'In an entirely separate incident a third death is also being investigated. This one concerns the apparent suicide of Martin Belman, the infamous 'fifth' bomber who failed to detonate his bomb during the 7/7 terrorist attacks on the London Underground in 2005. His detainment in the camp had long been a source of acute embarrassment for the British government who allowed him to be transferred to the US under the controversial Extradition Act of 2003, despite there being sufficient evidence to successfully prosecute him in the UK. While many people will not mourn his passing, it looks like the relatives of the victims from that sad day will no longer have the satisfaction of seeing at least one of the bombers successfully prosecuted for the carnage they wrought. Responsible for the deaths of fifty-six Londoners, it remains the worst act of terrorism in mainland Britain since the 1988 bombing of PAN AM flight 103 over Lockerbie which killed 270 innocent people.

'All in all, the three deaths have completely overshadowed what should have been a good day for the young administration as the President sees good on his campaign promise to begin shutting down the notorious Guantánamo Bay detention centres which w—'

'Good afternoon, George. I trust that June has been taking care of you?'

Both of them looked round in surprise at the tall man standing in the doorway. June hadn't heard him enter but was not in the least shocked by his silent appearance. He had been doing it to her for over twenty-five years, from the very first day that she started with him in the old headquarters building where the design of the office meant that his door was behind her station. She would often glance back and find him stood there, like a sentinel, watching his agents in the huge open-plan office.

'Hell, Ingram,' George C. Brown said. 'Are you trying to give me a heart attack?' How long have you been lurking there anyway?'

Director Joseph Ingram ambled over to June Fortis.

'Any messages?'

'Nothing that can't wait, sir. Director Brown has been waiting for you to return from The White House. Would you like some refreshments?'

'That won't be necessary, thank you,' Ingram said. 'I won't be staying long.'

Joseph Ingram winked down at his PA, before turning to face his red-faced boss who had stopped his manic pacing.

'Now, George. What can I do for you today?'

'How dare you cut me out like this!' he bellowed at them both, his short frame shaking with suppressed anger. June felt herself reddening but Ingram just looked puzzled.

'Out of what?'

'Don't get cute with me,' George C. Brown said. 'May I remind you that since 2004 you have been required to report directly into me. I am now the head of National Intelligence. Not you!'

'How can I forget,' Ingram said. 'You remind me weekly. I hope you haven't come all the way over from Connecticut Avenue just to tell me that?'

A vein bulged in his neck as George C. Brown fought to contain his anger. Several seconds passed before he was able to speak. In the meantime, Ingram strolled calmly across the foyer into his office, leaving the puce coloured man alone.

'Just tell me what was so important that the President cancelled his weekly security briefing with me so he could meet with you in the Oval Office along with your lap dog, Forsyth.'

'Oh that.'

'Yes, that.'

Ingram eased his lanky frame onto a long sofa that ran down the entire wall of his huge office. He motioned for Brown to sit but was declined with an angry wave.

'Oh, George. Relax. You're behaving like a spoilt child.'

'You owe me an explanation.'

'I can't tell you what was said,' Ingram said. 'It's highly classified information that concerns the national security of this country.'

'That's exactly what I mean. You're accountable to me,' Brown smacked his chest, 'not the President. It's my job to co-ordinate your findings with other intelligence sources and brief him myself. That was the purpose of this role.'

Ingram studied his boss for a second, his ruddy face and straining shirt evidence of the dinner led politicking he detested.

'What's your concern here? That you've been denied an audience with our great leader or that I'm not following the letter of the law?'

'You cannot cut me out like this.'

'Oh, but I have, George, and, where the security of this nation requires it, I will continue to do so.'

'But you have no right to. It's in direct contravention of the Intelligence Reform and Terrorism Prevention Act of 2004.'

'That piece of legislation is a bureaucratic bungle designed by politicians with no inkling of what it takes to protect our national interests,' Ingram said. He had argued the point a hundred times and knew what was coming. 'It hasn't improved intelligence gathering. It's just added another layer of bureaucracy to the process that has resulted in both delays and obfuscation of the facts.'

'You brought it on yourself, Joseph,' the Director said. 'If you had shared your own intelligence more freely, then 9/11 might not have happened.'

'Is that so?' Ingram was getting bored. He had heard the argument a hundred times before.

'Ninety-six senators who voted the Act into being seemed to think so; they all agreed there were major failings in the intelligence community that allowed nineteen terrorists to hijack four commercial passenger airliners and fly them into the World Trade Centre and the Pentagon. That is why I am here. At their behest, to ensure that we avoid another 9/11 and I will pursue that brief with all the powers at my disposal to ensure that it doesn't happen on my watch.'

'You know what your problem is, George?' Ingram said. 'You and your masters expect us to achieve the impossible. That, I don't mind. I can cope with that but then you tie one arm behind our back and still expect the same results. Except we cannot do that. If it hasn't escaped your notice, we are at war and have been for the last nine years with an invisible enemy that has no scruples. That will stop at nothing to achieve its ends.'

'That doesn't give you the right to ride roughshod over the democratic process.'

'It does when my agents are at risk,' Ingram said. 'Every day, hundreds of them put themselves on the line to obtain information and intelligence that will hopefully make a difference in this unwinnable war.'

'Come on Joseph. They knew that when they signed up. As you said yourself, we are at war and in war there are casualties.'

'Try telling that to three of my agents who won't be joining their families for Thanksgiving this year. They all lost their lives this week obtaining intelligence that directly impacts the long-term security of this country.'

Brown didn't know it but that was the one area that could get a rise from Ingram. Losing agents was his personal failure. Not 9/11. He knew deep down that no one could have stopped the attacks. He just happened to be in the right job at the wrong moment in history. But his dead agents. That was a different matter.

'And you know the worst bit,' Ingram continued. 'When I add their stars to the ninety already on the Memorial Wall, I will not even be able to acknowledge their sacrifice publicly. No one will ever know that they died serving their country. It has to remain secret because what they were doing is so sensitive.'

The director shrugged his shoulders uncomfortably, suddenly unsure of what to say.

'That's precisely why you will never get to know what was said today,' Ingram said. 'You don't deserve to know. You people have no idea what is happening out there. All the plots, the plans, the crimes, the acts of terrorism that we intercept. That never see the light of day. All you care about is your precious process and public reputations so that when it all goes pear shaped you can point the finger at us, conduct your kangaroo courts, pass the blame and secure your next position.'

'Are you questioning my patriotism? How dare you, when I'm simply trying to do my job.'

'You do that George, and in the meantime, I will do mine.'

Ingram stood up and made his way over to the window which looked out onto the huge foyer of the Old Headquarters. Below him he could see the stone mason silhouetted against the shiny white marble of the Memorial Wall. Above the dusty figure were twenty words inscribed into the stone. He was far too far away to make out what they said but Ingram didn't need to. They were imprinted on his memory.

'In honor of those members of the Central Intelligence Agency who gave their lives in the service of their country.'

To the artisan's right the Book of Honour had been moved. It was covered with a plastic sheet to protect it from the fine cloud of dust that billowed out from around the engraver as he carefully cut three stars into the wall with a stone grinder. Ingram had watched him earlier on his way in, painstakingly etching each one into the wall. Each star measured 2¼ inches tall by 2¼ inches wide, was half an inch deep and spaced six inches apart from the next. That was it. A solitary five pointed star to remember their silent and anonymous sacrifice. At least he knew they had died serving the best interests of the country even if no one else did.

When he turned back Brown was still stood by the sofa, watching him carefully.

'George, if you'll excuse me, I have a security briefing starting in five minutes. I need to prepare.'

'More of your secrets.'

'No. You can have this one.' Ingram noticed with some satisfaction the short man visibly coloured again, the vein in his neck pulsating dangerously. 'We are keeping the ten Guantanamo inmates that have just been released under close surveillance. Contrary to popular belief, they are not all as benign as the press would like you to believe. There are some dangerous men amongst them, especially the Siddiqui brothers.'

'You haven't heard the last of this.'

His boss marched across the carpet, his short legs pumping like pistons. But Ingram wasn't listening. He pressed a button on his phone, George C. Brown already forgotten.

'June, get me a secure line please.'

As he heard the dialling tone, Ingram punched in an extension. One ring later, it was answered.

'John, Samuel here. We're in play. Can you move Operation Green Ray into the next phase? That's right. Today. This very second. Thank you.'

He returned the handset to its cradle and sat for a few moments, thinking of the three new stars in the foyer. Three lives lost. But not in vain. They had died defending their country. Preserving a way of life that tens of millions of Americans took for granted. It always hurt to know he was responsible for their deaths but Ingram had accepted a long time ago that was the price to pay. Sacrificing the few to save the many. An approach that men like Brown couldn't stomach, at least not publicly. But politicians came and went whilst Ingram had served out four administrations with his legions of agents. Quietly protecting the nation against a changing kaleidoscope of threats. Most would never know what he did but that's exactly how he liked it. Visible to no one. Indispensable to everyone.

Ingram redialled.

'June, tell the Guantanamo Bay team I'm ready for them.'

Somewhere over Virginia

6 November 2009, 11:47 hours

The HH-60N eased away from the CIA HQ as it began its ten-mile journey into DC. Inside, George C. Brown stared at the cold grey waters of the Potomac River as the helicopter roared south following its loop into the capital. Who drove these days anyway? The man was an anachronism but also a damn nuisance. Had been since his appointment and seemed to be getting more so, blocking his every request and constantly trying to score points. He'd be damned if he allowed that dinosaur to blindside him on this one. It had happened too many times.

He reached for his mobile.

'John, Brown here. I've got a job for you. This morning Ingram met with the President, that green campaigner, Uma Jacobs—'

'Jakobsdóttir.'

'Yeah, that's her. And his lapdog, Forsyth.'

'And?'

'I need you to find out what's going on.'

There was silence on the end of the line.

'Are you still there?' Brown said.

'Yes, sir. I was thinking.'

'That's my job. You just do.'

'It's not going to be easy.'

'Come now, John,' Brown said. 'You work for the CIA. The world's greatest intelligence agency.'

'How far do you want me to go?'

'Let me repeat myself. I need to find out what was so important that the President cancelled his weekly security briefing with me.'

'When do you need it by?'

'Yesterday.'

'Anything else?'

Christ. The man sounded like he was taking a food order.

'No, that's all for now.'

He cut the connection. Just in time. Already they were sinking to the ground over the familiar domed white rooftops. Within minutes the motor had died and Brown was on terra firma.

Now that's the way to travel, he thought as he made his way across the frozen grass towards the West Wing.

Camp Peary, Virginia, USA

8 November 2009, 12:47 hours

The snowflake settled on the windowsill, a perfect six-sided hexagonal crystal formed in the upper reaches of the atmosphere above Chesapeake Bay. It retained its intricate lattice shape for several seconds before disappearing beneath a flurry of frosty clones that suddenly bombarded the farmhouse in the frigid air of the early morning. Within minutes, the porch was blanketed in white. A family of deer foraging for food in the clearing outside faded from view, their ghostly shapes barely visible through the swirling snow. Above them a lone herring gull wheeled away towards the Bay, its brown feathers suddenly invisible against the soft onslaught. Eventually, all that was visible were the ramrod black tree trunks that encircled the isolated building.

Martin Belman shivered and pulled the thick blanket around his shoulders even more tightly. He turned away from the window and wandered back into the living room towards the fire that roared in the large grate. Despite its warmth, he couldn't get warm. Hadn't been warm since leaving Cuba two days ago on a huge transporter plane that deposited him and his handler at an army air base. God knows where. He figured America. That much was clear. They had landed on a beautifully clear morning after a three-hour flight, coming in above the shimmering ocean which gradually morphed into a maze of small bays, inlets, and coves. Then, suddenly, an iron-grey runway had appeared, onto which the pilot slammed the huge aircraft. It had to be military. There were soldiers everywhere but no one gave him or his handler a second glance despite the brightness of his boiler suit. After alighting, they had transferred to a huge Ford Truck inside the hanger. It had an engine like a mini earthquake and they had driven for miles through a bewildering network of unmade roads and mud tracks. All were deserted. Slowly the trees had become denser until his view of the bright morning was streaked with the bare branches of a hibernating wood. During the entire journey not a word was said. And that had continued when they reached their destination. His handler had dropped him off and driven away without so much as a goodbye, leaving him to explore the building on his own.

There wasn't much. Three rooms downstairs and above, two bedrooms and a bathroom. One had been emptied of furniture and converted into a mini prayer room. There was a sink in the corner with a small basin beneath it to wash his feet in. On the shelves above was a stack of towels to dry himself down after his wudu. The floor had been stripped and on top of the bare wood was a prayer mat. It was placed at a very particular angle. Martin wondered whether it was pointing towards Kabah. As he scanned the room, he noticed a small piece of paper pinned to the wall with the word 'Mecca' scribbled carelessly across it. Crude but effective. Beside the mat was a sheet of paper with prayer times. He presumed they were for this part of the world. For this time of year.

In the other room was a bed and wardrobe filled with an assortment of winter clothes. They were nondescript garments which could have come from any out-of-town retailer. However, they almost fitted him perfectly. Downstairs, a well-stocked fridge contained delights he had long forgotten after the disgusting cuisine of the Camp. Someone had gone to a lot of trouble.

Exhausted from the rollercoaster ride of the last twenty four hours, he had bathed, eaten and slept in that order. On the second day, he had decided to explore but didn't get far. Wherever they were was a wilderness of woodland, interspersed by frozen streams and mud tracks. On his first outing he had got lost on the maze of roads that criss-crossed the woods outside the old farmhouse. He had wandered around for hours trying to trace his way back until, in the fading light, he had spotted the lights on the porch, the only illumination for miles. After that he had stayed close to the building, enjoying the sense of freedom that his new prison afforded him. He didn't know what he was doing here or why. All he knew was that whoever had sprung him from the jail wanted him alive. Not only that but they had gone to a great deal of trouble to do so, beginning with the summary execution of the poor soul in his cell, the flight and now this well-stocked building complete with prayer room in the middle of nowhere.

As he stood staring at the crackling fire, a low rumble cut through the quiet.

The Ford?

Sure enough, the huge truck pulled up outside the farmhouse, its bonnet steaming under a fresh coating of snow which continued to blanket the bleak landscape. He half expected his handler to emerge and was surprised to see another figure step down. He looked big. Maybe six foot and at least two hundred pounds. As he approached the front door, Martin suddenly had a premonition.

Was this all a trick?

A clever, despicable trick by his captors to lull him into a false sense of security? Did they want to break him? Offer him the succour of all this before returning him to the horrors of Camp Delta. Or maybe worse, kill him here. His worst nightmare. Not the dying. That didn't bother him but to die here, alone, with his mission unfulfilled. Delivered into heaven with nothing to show for his self-sacrifice. That thought was unbearable. How could he look his four victorious brothers in the eye? They had succeeded where he had failed. He would bake for eternity in purgatory with the shame and knowledge of his failure, whilst they basked on the glory of their self-sacrifice. A death unfulfilled.

As the man entered, Martin's eyes zeroed in on a clear bulge in his jacket. It looked like a gun. What's more, as the door closed and the man paused, steaming in the warmth of the hallway, he reached for it. He wanted to die. But not like this. Martin turned to flee but as he did so, his foot snagged in the folds of the blanket and he crashed to the wooden floor of the house. Scrambling to his knees, he half turned to fend off the expected attack. But none came. Instead, the large man stood there, grinning down at him, a metal tube held in one hand. It looked like a thermos. Martin sat up feeling rather foolish. He brushed the dust from his arms and made to get up. The man offered him a hand and he cautiously accepted it before being heaved to his feet as if he was small child. The man's size belied his strength. Beneath the fat was muscle.

'Thank you,' mumbled Martin, staring at the man. He was huge. Crew cut hair. Square face with an angry scratch across his right cheek. It looked recent. As he stared, the man smiled and removed his coat.

'No problem, buddy. I trust you have settled into your new home. Must be kind of nice after the Bay.'

His accent was American but that is as far as Martin could place it. They all sounded the same to him. His eyes were drawn to the leather shoulder holster around the man's huge girth. The gun was nested on his right side and for a split second he toyed with making a lunge for it. It was in touching distance. One quick movement and it would be in his hands. But then what? He felt the man's eyes on his. They were challenging him to make an attempt and, in that instant, he knew he would never make it.

'Why am I here?'

'Whoa, slow down there, buddy. First things first. The name's Carl Fortune. My buddies call me CF.' He held out a hand again but Martin ignored it and stood there unsmiling.

'I presume you know my name, Mr Fortune, so let's dispense with the formalities. Where are we?'

'Wrong question, Martin. Your first was more relevant.'

'OK. So, what am I doing in this deserted farmhouse in the middle of nowhere?'

Carl laughed. A deep stomach laugh. Despite having watched countless videos of his prisoner being interviewed in Cuba, the sound of his live voice was still a huge surprise. In the flesh, his prisoner's clipped British accent was even more pronounced and totally at odds with the dark brown colour of his skin.

'Yeah, Johnny said you went walkabout. At one stage, he thought he was going to have to come and get you.'

It was still a prison, complete with guards, albeit invisible.

'You, my friend, are being offered the chance to complete your mission.'

Martin's brow furrowed in puzzlement.

'The one you so spectacularly screwed up back in 2005.' Without waiting for an answer, Fortune unscrewed the cap of the thermos, withdrew a piece of metal and threw it over to Martin who clumsily caught it with both hands.

'Do you know what that is?'

Puzzled, he stared at the small piece of metal. It was cylindrical in shape and reminded him of a spark plug for a car. Martin shrugged his shoulders.

'That my friend is a detonator. A very special one. One that will never let you down regardless of the weather conditions, your own incompetence or the preparedness of your target. Nothing will get in its way and prevent it from delivering its precious cargo of energy in the required amount at the exact moment you need it to.'

'Why should I care?'

'Because, Mr Belman, if you are being given one last shot to redeem yourself, I would expect you don't want your equipment to fail you again.'

Martin was silent.

Stunned.

A chance to complete his mission. His dream. To join his brothers. Victorious. For all eternity.

A jolt of excitement tickled his stomach.

'I'm listening.'

'I thought that might get your attention.' Carl Fortune went over to his jacket and withdrew a slightly soggy newspaper which he handed to Martin. It was *The New York Times* and as he stared at the front cover, Martin suddenly realised that he hadn't had access to any news in the last four years. Not a drop of information about the outside world. It had been one of the hardest parts of his internment. Prior to 7th July 2005, he had read a newspaper every day as far back as he could remember. Martin prided himself on his knowledge of current affairs, particularly in the Middle East and Afghanistan. But now he knew nothing and his captor had just handed him the chance to reacquaint himself with the world. He held the paper carefully, almost reverently.

'Front page. Recognise that man? He's your target.'

Martin didn't recognise him and his face said as much.

'Read the caption.'

He looked up, puzzled.

'Is this a joke?' Martin said.

'Do you think we would have gone to so much trouble to play a joke on you? No this is for real.'

'But he's black. And his first-name, its Arabic. How can this be?'

Carl laughed again. The look on the prisoner's face was a picture.

'It's for real, buddy. Believe me, it's for real.'

'But how did that happen? When did this happen? You want me to kill him? Why? When will this happen? Who are you? You must work for the government. No? How did you get me out?'

'Whoa. Slow down there, buddy. Too many questions. We've got plenty of time to answer them all. But first, I need to know whether you are on board.'

'Do I have a choice?'

'That's a strange question coming from you.'

'I didn't mean it that way.'

'What way did you mean it? We are offering you the opportunity to strike right at the heart of our democracy and you suggest that you have no choice. You made your choice the day your home-made bomb failed to detonate four years ago. And subsequently in every interview you have given down in Cuba, you have repeated your choice. Need I remind you?'

Carl made to pull a folder from his coat but he didn't need reminding. The words were emblazoned on his mind.

'Death to your democracy. Its hypocrisy knows no bounds. In its name you kill, sodomise, rape and maim our people. We will not rest until—'

'—the lawns of your suburbs swim with the blood of your men, women and children,' Martin finished softly.

'So, you do remember. I think it is safe to say what your choice is.'

Martin stared at the newspaper, his mind whirling with unanswered questions and awash with mixed emotions. But above them all, like a guiding star, shone a bright light of joy and excitement that crackled through his veins like electricity. He hadn't felt this alive since July 5th, 2005.

It felt like a gift from Allah.

When he looked up, Fortune was standing by the door, pulling his dripping great coat onto his massive shoulders.

'Where are you going? We have so much to talk about.'

'We've done enough for one day. You're going to be late.'

'For what?'

'You're losing your touch, Martin. It's time for your mid-morning prayer. '

'I'm impressed, Mr Fortune.'

'It's in my interests to know these things.'

'Will I see you again?'

'Sure thing. You will be seeing a lot of me over the coming weeks.'

Martin held up the newspaper.

'Do you mind if I keep this. I haven't read a word in four years.'

'Be my guest.'

And then he was gone, leaving Martin in the foyer staring after the departing figure who was soon swallowed up in the swirling blizzard. He stood there for a few moments, staring after him, his mind a mirror image of the chaotic snowstorm outside and then slowly made his way upstairs, the precious paper grasped tightly in his hands.

As he reached the Ford, Carl Fortune glanced back inside the house but his ward had disappeared, presumably to pray to his God. He was unnerved by the man. He couldn't understand why. The clipped British accent. It seemed so out of place. Suggesting an education. Breeding. Class. Intelligence. Civilisation. History. Yet when he opened his mouth, all he heard were the insane ramblings of a deeply misguided man.

Oh, well. His place was not to ask questions. It was to serve.

He checked his watch. Right on time. He pulled a mobile from his pocket and punched in some numbers. It was answered immediately.

'Did he buy it?'

'He's suspicious. Four years in a high security jail will do that to a man. But I think he'll come round. He needs salvation so badly, he's willing to do anything.'

'Good. Keep me appraised.'

The connection was cut, leaving Carl Fortune shivering in the cold morning. He removed the sim card from the phone and took out his lighter. As the small flame played over the tiny square, the plastic bubbled until it became too hot to hold. He let it fall to the porch before recovering it and making his way carefully to the huge Ford which rumbled into life at the first request.

250 miles north of San Francisco

9 November 2009, 11:20 hours

Despite her thick jumper, Uma shivered uncontrollably. It was not so much the cold. That was manageable. But the thick fog that blanketed the coast at this time of year was a different matter. It enveloped the castle in its clammy tentacles and made her bones ache. She paused at the top of the stairs and blew into her cupped hands but it was no match for the moist Pacific air, deeply chilled by the cold waters of the California Current. She clenched them into fists and started down the steep gradient, being careful not to slip on the wet stone steps. There were 121 in total, which wasn't so bad on arrival but leaving always made her calves burn and, for the hundredth time, she regretted locating the LEAP gate in the tower. At last, they levelled out into a short stone corridor into which narrow slits had been cut every five feet and through which the mist continued to invade the fortification. Without pausing, she hurried to the end and tugged open a heavy oak door, bracing herself for the short walk. Far below she could hear the boom of the ocean as it smashed into the base of the remote peninsula. On most days the view was truly spectacular, a kaleidoscopic outlook over the mighty Pacific Ocean that stretched away for thousands of miles. But this morning a grey veil had been drawn across the spectacle. As she hurried along the stone parapet, Uma had a sudden memory of the night she had gone swimming with Ethan in the Blue Lagoon. The fog had been so thick they had lost each other in its cold embrace and she found herself smiling. At surprising him in the warm waters. His angry reaction. Their fleeting intimacy. The laughter. And then, without warning, an axe shaft appeared. The blood welling up out of Baldursson. The black-eyed demon materialising through the fog.

Dear God!

In a second, she was back in the Lagoon.

The slimy goo sucking at her feet.

Her heart pounding in fear.

The heat of the water.

The hypnotic glare of Baldursson's killer.

She stumbled against the wall and instinctively ground her frozen knuckles into the cold stone. The pain cut through her vision and it faded as suddenly as it had appeared, leaving Uma crumpled on the flagstones. She got to her feet and unsteadily completed the rest of the short walk. It was only thirty or so feet but felt like a mile and as the heavy oak door slammed shut behind her, she slumped to the floor, exhausted with the effort. The nightmare had gone but it had left her with a familiar throbbing headache. Uma stumbled along the corridor, heels echoing off the cold stone. Every few yards an ornate torch-shaped light flickered into life as she approached and faded from view as she passed. It felt quite eerie, as if a wide-beamed spotlight was following her progress whilst at the same time illuminating the way. And, of course, the weapons.

Thousands of them. Antiques of every description from every imaginable era. They seemed to be loosely ordered around technological advancement beginning with pre-history clubs, ancient axes, boomerangs, sling shots and unwieldy thrusting spears. On the next floor were examples from early Egypt, Macedonia, Sparta and the mighty Roman Empire with its short swords, array of spears and curved shields made of wood.

The theme was continued on the next level but now the weaponry was joined by military garments. Sinister suits of armour materialised out of the shadows, their hollow limbs host to memories of long-forgotten campaigns in distant lands. The weaponry became more modern. Guns appeared. At first primitive but increasingly more sophisticated. Muskets were replaced by pistols which morphed into revolvers. Then rifles. And finally, machine guns. Uma passed a Gatling gun, closely followed by a Maxim capable of spitting out 500 rounds per minute. It sat motionless on wagon wheels that dwarfed the small metal death dealer. She finally came to a huge circular landing which continued onto a wide sloping staircase that gradually descended to the ground floor. As it did, she was presented with a grandstand view of its centrepiece, a one-hundred-foot metal tower covered with a great fanfare of weapons. All manner of swords lined the structure from Samurai Katanas and Wakizashis to Norman fighting swords, with their unmistakable cross guard shaped pommels. Huge double-handed long swords sat beside lightweight rapiers. Swords morphed into axes. Hundreds of them. Heavy Viking battle axes dwarfed tiny tomahawks favoured by the Native American Indian. Elegant eight-foot-long poleaxes, short one-handed spears, the longer two-handed Greek Sarissa, the heavier Roman Pilas, and the fifteen-foot two-handed Kontos, a wooden lance favoured by the Iranian cavalry.

Uma had long since learnt to ignore the military paraphernalia. Where once she'd been openly sickened by the previous owner's obsession with the artefacts of war, she now walked quickly by, barely noticing any of it. As the stairs levelled out onto the ground floor, she found herself in a huge hallway over which the domed roof towered, some 150 feet above. This was the centre of the mausoleum and off it, four thirty-foot-wide corridors disappeared towards different points of the compass. She chose the northern one at the end of which lay her final destination, a massive wooden door studded with enormous wrought-iron bolts. Twenty-foot-high windows framed the long corridor, against which the white fog swirled and shimmered, trying to find a way into the castle. On either side, silent cannons pointed menacingly towards the centre of the building. She passed them quickly, pausing at two huge cast-iron brutes that sat either side of the door like mighty sentinels. The barrels could easily have swallowed her whole. Beside the wheels of the wooden carriage that supported one of the big guns was a pyramid of four cannonballs. They must have weighed half a tonne each and she shuddered at the thought of one of these metal monsters smashing into the fortifications of some long-forgotten city.

The door was slightly ajar and Uma paused for a second, listening to the clang of metal on metal. It wasn't constant but delivered in ferocious bursts. Her heart sank but she had come too far to turn back and, steeling herself for what was to come, slipped through the gap and into the great hall. Like all the rooms at ground level, the ceiling must have been thirty feet above her head but she still felt claustrophobic. On every wall, enormous tapestries continued the theme of war. Through a soft haze of smoke, ghostly images jumped out at her. Great war horses shrieking with panic, their flailing hooves inches from faceless infantrymen. A dying knight lay in the arms of a comrade, his body armour pierced by a bloody lance. Terrified boy soldiers screaming in fear, their helpless faces hypnotised by the battle charge of fearsome giants. Everywhere Uma turned, the horror of war stared back. Dead men, dying animals, the earth itself was drenched in death. But it was the scene in the centre of the cavernous room that made her heart skip.

A colossal stone fireplace sat halfway down one of the long walls. It could easily have accommodated twenty men had it not been for the roaring inferno, fuelled by massive cuts of timber. Framed in the blaze were two figures that looked to have stepped right out of the garish tapestries. Two devils from another world, encased from head to foot in brightly coloured armour; one a blaze of burnt orange and red, the other a dull blue. Studded gloves gripped curved, slender, single-edged swords. They looked frightening but it was the head armour that made Uma shiver. Mounted by razor-sharp horns, a rounded helmet extended well past the ears and neck to almost touch the shoulder armour. The face of each fighter was protected by what could only be described as a death mask. Each mouth frozen in a cruel sneer, framed by sharp cheekbones that supported a hawked nose and hollowed-out eye sockets. One set flashed vermillion red in the fiery blaze. The other a sparkling cobalt. Uma shuddered. Coming across such figures in open battle would have tested the bravest warrior.

The men ignored Uma as she hovered just outside the ring of light thrown by the great fire. Even from this distance, the heat was intense and she quickly began to sweat in her winter wear. But it didn't seem to hold the men back as they circled each other warily, swords held in mirrored symmetry. Without warning, the larger of the two leapt forward. The other figure moved backwards, his footwork a perfect reflection of the other's attack. Sparks flew from their swords as the smaller soldier parried each blow. The red warrior retreated and the mirror restored as they circled each other once again, their breath ragged in the smoky air. Once again, the larger man drove forward, but his smaller shadow moved with him, shrieking as he did so, the sound a perfect echo of his foe. They remained that way for several seconds, each straining to force the other down. Both locked together in perfect balance. That is, until the red devil headbutted his opponent. The smaller man grunted with surprise and went down. The larger man dropped his sword and in one fluid move grasped the unconscious man by his knee pads and neck armour. Effortlessly, he hoisted him above his head and stood triumphant before the fire. For one moment Uma thought he was going to hurl him into the flames like a sacrificial offering but a shout to her left made them both turn.

'What the hell are you doing?' Another warrior emerged from the gloom of the great hall. He was similarly clad in a dull black armour but his head was uncovered and he was carrying a wooden staff. The red warrior glared at him through glowing red slits before simply tossing his dead weight at the advancing man. Unable to adjust himself fast enough, the man took the full force on his chest and crashed to the carpet where both lay groaning, a crumple of battered blue and black armour.

Their attacker moved away to a series of stands, festooned with body armour, swords and more fighting staffs. He loosened his own helmet but even before he removed it, Uma knew who he was. That final image of him stood, triumphantly in front of the fireplace with the man above his head. She had seen it before. Almost six years ago in the Department of Geothermal Studies. The night she had been trapped on the top floor of her father's old offices, fighting for her life. She remembered the ease with which he had disarmed her own attacker, before dropping him with a sidekick to his chest. As the man lay, bent double with pain, he had also been held aloft before being nonchalantly tossed over the balcony. Uma could still hear the man's terrified scream as he fell, before falling silent as he was skewered on 'The Age of Man' pyramid. His own body weight had carried him down the cold hard marble, finally stopping after it had nearly severed him in two.

Ethan tossed his mask and helmet onto the carpet, as the sprawling figures untangled themselves. One removed his mask to reveal a bloodied nose and rapidly closing eye. The other was soundlessly gulping for breath like a drowning fish. They helped each up before staggering over to confront Ethan.

'What do you think you're playing at pulling a stunt like that?' the winded one gasped. 'You could've killed me.'

Ethan just shrugged as he continued to remove his armour; first his neck protector, followed by the shoulder pads and arm guards. His Katana sword and gloves were already on the stand. Even after five years Uma was still struck by his physique. At the beginning, when she had first seen him bulked up, it had been a real shock; the old Ethan was slim, almost skinny, but the relentless fitness regime had changed him. For one awful moment she had thought it was Anderson, the bodyguard that her CTO had entangled Ethan with. But it wasn't. Ethan didn't have the bulk of Anderson who had looked like a prize heavyweight fighter. Instead, Ethan had the sculpted, slightly leaner physique of a welterweight. *Except his hands*, she consoled herself. They were still the same. Slender. Long fingers. Delicate almost. The hands of a pianist. Her link to the past.

'It was the right move, given the deadlock,' Ethan said, turning his back on the two men as he struggled out of the cuirass, the main body armour. Uma winced. She had forgotten about his back. It was a chaotic scrawl of disfigured flesh and in the flickering flames she could see how deep the scar tissue ran; some were raised high, others ran deep. Ethan had never told her how he got them. Something to do with the crash that had killed his parents, she presumed. If indeed he had. *Christ.* She berated herself angrily. She was getting as neurotic as Ethan had become.

'It's illegal,' the winded one continued.

'There are no rules in war.'

'We're not at war. We're sparring,' the man shouted, squaring up to Ethan who stared at him impassively. 'Remember, you invited us here.'

'Come on, John,' the one with the bloodied nose, interrupted. 'It's not worth it. He's clearly nuts, holed up in this mausoleum. Let's get out of here.'

He steered his partner away from Ethan towards the armour stands where they sheathed their swords, wooden staffs and grabbed their things, all the time muttering angrily to each other. As they made their way across the hall, the one in black turned and gave the room his finger before disappearing with his partner through the huge doors.

Ethan seemed to notice Uma for the first time.

'What are you doing here?'

Uma didn't dare tell him the real reason. Instead, she threw a document onto the faded carpet where it rested between them.

Ethan ignored it, continuing to remove the rest of his armour before towelling himself down. Uma looked away and studied the huge portrait above the fireplace; it featured an old man in flying gear, standing on the wing of a bi-plane. He was scowling down at her, his bright eyes flashing angrily in the light of the roaring fire.

'Impressive, isn't he?'

Uma wasn't sure she would have described Samuel K. Reynolds I, the founder of Reynolds Air, in those terms. He looked mean and hateful to her.

'He detested people, you know,' Ethan continued.

'That explains why he built this—' Uma looked around the room, struggling to come up with the words, '—this, this mausoleum, miles from anywhere,' she said, remembering what Ethan's sparring partner had called it.

'Don't be like that,' Ethan said. 'After flying, it was his great passion. It took him over thirty years to build this place. A fortress to house his collection and keep everyone out.'

'Well, he certainly got his wish. No one would willingly visit, let alone live here.' The building responded with a gentle shudder that shook the entire room, causing the massive chandelier above her head to sway alarmingly and shower soft dust onto the two combatants' thirty feet below. Uma ignored the tremor and turned to face Ethan. He smiled at her. A grimace really, which weakly flittered across his face. It was more haggard than she remembered; dark circles surrounded dull eyes which, in turn, sat deep inside a gaunt face that had faded white from the lack of light. Uma shivered, despite the heat.

'You should never have bought it.'

Ethan shrugged.

'I couldn't resist,' he said. 'Reynolds was responsible for the mess we got ourselves into. Once you took the airline down, the family was desperate to sell everything and anything to pay for the ensuing shareholder lawsuits.'

'A petty revenge bought on the cheap.' Uma hadn't intended for her tone to be so scathing but she couldn't help herself. *This place would suck the life out of anyone.* It was miles from the nearest town and was shrouded in thick fog for most of the year, courtesy of the warm currents of the Pacific. Nevertheless, she braced herself for his explosion of anger. Much less had set him off over the years.

Surprisingly, Ethan just laughed. Of a fashion. It sounded hollow in the cavernous room.

'Ethan, this place is sucking the life out of you,' Uma said, emboldened by his reaction. 'You need to leave.'

'Not this again.'

'I nearly lost you once,' she ploughed on, even as she realised Ethan was in no mood to talk. 'I can't let it happen again.'

'What do you expect me to do?' Ethan said, holding his arms out. 'I didn't ask for this.'

'But I saved your life.'

'You imprisoned me.'

'You did this to yourself,' Uma said. 'You decided to live in this … this crypt, a hundred miles from civilisation.'

'That's not what I meant,' Ethan whispered but he may as well have screamed the words at Uma. She knew what he was referring to; that he was no longer Ethan but someone else. The result of a decision made by Shane Williams, Chief Security Officer of Green Ray, who had bowed to Ethan's pressure on the day everything had gone wrong. The day that James Reagan and Sally Moltex, the two journalists handpicked by Ethan to preview the launch of LEAP, had been killed. The day that the LEAP system had been taken offline following a sustained cyber-attack. The day that Uma had been attacked in her offices at the Department of Geothermal Studies by men intent on killing her, or so she thought. The day that Ethan had been trying to get over from New York City to Reykjavík to rescue Uma. The irony was that, had the system not been down, Ethan would have teleported over and been killed. Ethan was a financier, not a fighter, brought on board to help her launch LEAP to the world. But because it was partially offline, Shane had improvised. He had merged Ethan's brain with the body of the last person who had been scanned into the system for teleportation to Iceland. One of Uma's security detail, a brute of a man called Anderson. Incredibly, it had worked, not only technically because Shane had succeeded in merging the two men, but also tactically. Anderson or Ethan, or whoever the hell he was, had saved Uma but not before he had carved out a trail of destruction across Iceland. Many men had died that day: the men at the Department of Geothermal Studies, the men on the road to Keflavík airport and, of course, the men at the Blue Lagoon, including her dear Frederik. Frederick Baldursson, Chief Inspector of the Viking Squad and her father's best friend, who had died trying to save her. Of course, she had tried to correct what Shane had done at the first opportunity but it hadn't worked. Separating the bodies had been easy. But the LEAP system wouldn't give up his mind so easily; Ethan's memories and God knows what else had become entangled with Anderson's. Try as they might, it had remained that way. Ethan was entangled with Anderson. Anderson with Ethan. Early on, Uma and Shane had decided not to tell Ethan what had happened. It had been Shane's idea but Uma had readily agreed. It made perfect sense at the time and was done so that Ethan didn't suffer the agony of not knowing who he was. Or wasn't. Except that Ethan had overheard their conversation and had gone—hell, was still going—through the nightmare of questioning his very essence. Uma hadn't discovered that fact until much later after she had finally resurrected him from his coma and that's when the endless arguments had started. Ethan blamed her for everything: his entanglement, the collapse of the launch, for leading him on, bringing him back. Nothing she said placated him.

'I shouldn't be here,' Ethan said, almost to himself.

'Then leave.'

'For what?'

'That's not fair. I saved your life.' Indignation stoked Uma's anger as the familiar exchange unfolded.

'I didn't need saving.' Ethan suddenly turned on her, his voice shaking with emotion. 'This was forced on me.'

'What would you have me do? You were in a vegetative state,' she said quietly. 'I watched over you for six months as you faded away.'

'You didn't do it for me,' he said. 'You admitted as much in Reykjavík that night I—' His voice faded. 'It was to assuage your guilt for dragging everyone into your mess and causing so many deaths.'

'What else could I do?' Uma said.

'Come clean with me.' His tone had dropped dangerously low, almost a growl, his eyes narrowing to slits. They reminded Uma of the death mask. Every muscle in his body tensed as if he were fighting an inner demon. *Anderson*, Uma thought, suddenly fearful that he would attack her. 'About the mix up with Anderson,' Ethan continued. 'Why didn't you come to me first instead of plotting behind my back with Shane. Christ, you misled me right from the start—about LEAP and taking my blood.'

Uma felt herself blushing; it was true she had tricked him but only because she didn't believe he would have believed her pitch about

LEAP or agreed to a demonstration. So, she had taken a sample of Ethan's blood without his knowledge to access his DNA. Armed with that, she had set him up in the LEAP system and then lured him up to her offices in the Department of Geothermal. Once there, when he had passed through the LEAP gate, the teleportation had been instantaneous. And it had worked. Ethan had believed, had become an investor, had helped her launch LEAP until that fateful day when everything had gone wrong. Uma had spent hours explaining what had happened to Ethan but he would not accept it. Or couldn't.

'I didn't imagine that you'd end up here, like this,' Uma said

'What did you think would happen?'

'I thought you'd help me continue our fight.'

'Your fight.'

'It became yours.'

'It was never mine,' Ethan said.

'For a while it was.'

'You left me with nothing, whilst you got everything you ever wanted.'

The accusation stung her.

'That's not true.' Uma cried out. 'I very nearly lost everything.'

'I did.'

'Even after Reynolds had gone. When the investigations had died down. The press had forgotten us. We could have had something. Started afresh.'

'I remember nothing of that.'

'Why won't you believe me,' Uma said, tears streaming down her face. It was true, Ethan had no memory of anything after 03:52 on 15 November, 2003. No memory of being arrested by Homeland Security in NYC; no memory of his incarceration in the Homeland Security detention centre on 633 Third Avenue in Manhattan; no memory of Uma impersonating her dead sister, Eva, on national TV in a bid to defeat Reynolds; no memory of his fight with the assassin, Andreus Grond, in his cell; no memory of his subsequent coma; no memory of the endless investigations into the collapse of Reynolds Air; no memory of Uma watching over him for months in NYC;

no memory of Uma moving him to a private neurological hospital away from the prying eyes of the press; no memory of her trying every medical route to revive him, until in desperation Uma had breached her LEAP laws. For the last time, she told herself. She had resurrected Ethan from the dead by restoring him to his last scan on the LEAP system. The one that had taken them all from Reykjavík to NYC at precisely 03:52 on 15 November 2003. So, he remembered everything prior to that moment but nothing afterwards. Uma had filled him in. Tried to explain. Repeatedly, but Ethan was too far gone.

'I was ready to give you everything,' Ethan said. 'Had given,' he corrected himself. 'You had it all but it was built on lies and deceit.'

'That's not true' she sobbed. 'Why can't you accept that?'

'I was never more than an investor to you.'

'I never wanted your money,' she screamed at him.

'I'm not talking about the money.'

The accusation hung in the air.

'Neither am I, Ethan.' She remembered the fight in her father's house. His half-baked declaration of love. Then she remembered Ethan mauling her in the Blue Lagoon but, too late, reminded herself that it was Anderson, not him. She felt a surge of sorrow. What did he remember of that kiss? The groping or the initial tenderness, his lips soft for a moment as she had always suspected Ethan's might be.

'But you took it readily enough.'

'It was a fair trade,' she said, the familiar anger replacing her tears. 'Besides which, I had no idea that you'd transferred your entire fortune into Green Ray.'

'Who else could I give it to?' he said. 'I had no family. No friends. No shareholders. No investors. No one.' His voice suddenly softened again, until it was barely audible. 'Until I met you.'

Uma wasn't so sure but she had grown sick of challenging him. When she had met Ethan, he had been a fearless businessman, happy to risk his entire fortune on the next big thing. Except that investing in LEAP wasn't exactly risky. It was a sure bet. All this nonsense about leaving it in trust with her as the sole beneficiary seemed too convenient. It was just further evidence of his bleak outlook. Besides which, he hadn't left it to her. He was still an active trustee in Green Ray but like every other aspect of his life, he just didn't participate, choosing instead to rot inside this freezing cold mausoleum, perched on a fault line on the edge of the world.

'But you didn't die,' she reminded him. 'I brought you back.'

Ethan shrugged.

'I died that day.'

Which day? Uma wondered. Her arguments with Ethan were never clear cut; sometimes they were calm and easily followed, but mainly it was like chasing a rain drop in a hurricane. Violent and unpredictable, buffeted about by the chaos of his mind. Was it the day Anderson died? Or the day that she rejected his advances? Or the day he was strangled by Grond? Or the day she resurrected him? Or the day he was entangled with Anderson? She took a stab.

'That's not true. Grond killed you weeks later.'

'You still don't get it.'

'I do,' she protested. 'Things could have been so different. You never gave me a chance.'

'I'm not talking about that.'

Uma was silent.

'What did you do with my body?'

'What do you mean?' she said, not completely surprised by the sudden change in direction of the conversation. It had been a familiar feature of their exchanges over the last eighteen months.

'After you switched off the life support.'

'I …' Uma was lost for words.

'You couldn't have two of me running around,' he said. 'What would your precious LEAP laws have had to say about that?'

'I had no choice.' She felt defensive but wasn't quite sure why.

'Did you give me a proper burial?' Ethan continued, his eyes blazing in the fire.

'Not exactly. Why would I? You weren't dead.'

'Well, someone died. It looked like me. Was the original me. It had my memories. So effectively speaking, I did die.'

'Why are you doing this to yourself?'

'So, what did you do?' Ethan said.

Uma paused, belatedly realising the trap he had set. She had done the only thing she could do given the circumstances and Ethan knew it.

'You know exactly what I did,' she said.

'And that was?'

Still Uma wouldn't answer.

'Tell me,' Ethan roared at her, knocking the stand over and scattering Samurai armour across the carpet. Uma shrank away, preparing to run.

'I put you back through LEAP,' she finally said.

'You recycled me?'

'What else could I do?' Uma glared at him, willing him to stop. 'A ... a body could have caused problems. A cremation was too complicated.'

'So, what does that make me?' he said triumphantly. 'What am I? Who am I?'

'It makes you Ethan.'

'But he died. You just said he did.'

Uma fell silent, the well-trodden cul-de-sacs all too familiar.

'What does that make you?' Ethan suddenly asked. This time the question caught Uma off guard. She wasn't sure either but she could never share that with Ethan. Not whilst he was in this state. That she might also be an exact copy of her sister thanks to her father; her dear, rotten, hypocritical father who preached one thing at her for decades about not misusing LEAP for her own personal gain yet practiced the opposite by creating an exact copy of Uma. Or Eva. It didn't matter. Eva was dead so the conundrum was solved but the act couldn't be forgotten. If only Ethan would listen. He would realise that they had more in common than he could possibly hope to imagine. Her father's betrayal had been the final moment when Uma realised that LEAP couldn't be trusted. Or at least the people who controlled it couldn't be trusted; their humanness would never allow them not to copy each other, resurrect each other, save each other from terrible accidents. So, after resurrecting Ethan from the dead, her final act of hubris,

Uma had abandoned her dream of using the LEAP technology to reverse global warming. Instead, for the last five years, using Ethan's Green Ray fund, she had pursued more traditional routes to saving the environment; one's steeped in electric cells, wind farms and smart meters.

'I'm still the same person,' she said.

'You're God.'

'What?'

'With power over life and death.'

'Stop it, please,' Uma pleaded but he wasn't listening.

'What have you unleashed on the world?' Ethan said.

'I haven't.'

'You get to decide who lives. Who dies. Who gets reborn again.' Ethan turned on her, the fire framing his muscular torso.

'No. That's not what I want.'

'And a new race shall walk the earth.' He was shouting now, his voice booming through the great hall. 'The undead shall rise up. Neither living nor dying.'

Uma shrank away from him. Despite her earlier resolve, she couldn't stand much more of this.

'Soulless creatures feeding off discarded atoms like vampires with no memory of their sins.'

As suddenly as he'd started, Ethan stopped and his whole body went limp. Ripped muscle became flesh, fists relaxed into hands and his mask melted away into Ethan's face, one etched with fatigue from the outburst.

'Uma. What are you doing here?' he asked almost normally.

She couldn't answer for a few seconds. Although it happened repeatedly on all her visits, the abruptness of his outburst and sudden transformation always shocked her into silence. She swallowed hard, unsure of whether to continue. But she had nowhere to turn. *I need your advice*, she wanted to ask but wasn't about to. Instead, she nodded dumbly at the forgotten paper on the carpet, between them.

'Are you suing me again?' Ethan said. 'The last lawsuit failed, remember. The judge said it was the most watertight trust he'd ever read. That it couldn't be defeated.'

'They found Reynolds,' she said.

Ethan didn't move. Uma wasn't sure whether he was even listening.

'Tread very carefully, if I was you,' Ethan eventually replied. 'The prophecy might come true.'

Ethan turned away, the conversation clearly at an end. For a moment he was framed in the roaring flames, his ruined back flickering wildly as the fire consumed his silhouette. Uma shuddered.

'Ethan,' she pleaded, very close to tears again. But it was useless. She had lost him. Again. 'I need your help.' Uma tried one last time.

But he didn't move. If anything, the flames seemed to grow higher, burning with a greater intensity than Uma could physically bear.

'One day you will have to emerge from this ... this crypt,' she screamed at him, her voice cracking with anger as she turned away. 'You can't hide here forever.'

But Ethan wasn't listening.

He was staring at the huge portrait of Samuel K. Reynolds I who continued to glare angrily down into the room.

'Yes, I can,' he whispered. 'Yes, I can.'

Homestead Joint Air Reserve Base, Florida

7 November 2009, 15:20 hours

Naveed Siddiqui closed his eyes, luxuriating in the freedom; to smell, to see, to hear, to speak even. To whom he wanted. When he wanted. To shout or laugh. Or simply be quiet. It had been many years since he had freely exercised any of his senses but he had made up for lost time, greedily absorbing every sight, sound, touch and smell thrown his way. And there had been plenty. So many people. All talking. A cacophony of voices that his ears simply weren't used to processing. Their clothes, so colourful. The iciness of the air conditioning, which turned his skin blue. A food court in the main reception area with long-forgotten aromas that he thought were imagined and left him salivating with desire. So many things taken for granted prior to his internment, that now seemed like luxuries. The thin mattress, a king size divan. The cheap linen felt like silk against his skin. The simple meal, a feast fit for a king. And then the hot shower that first morning. The memory brought a huge grin to his thin face. He could have stayed there forever. That was seven days ago. Each sunrise brought new treats and today promised the best one yet—they were going home.

The final debrief had taken place that morning followed by an interminable press conference; a thousand shouted questions that he had been instructed not to answer. Instead, the four remaining Guantanamo releasees had just stood there grinning inanely, waiting for the signal from their handlers that they could leave. From there, they were split up; Naveed and his brother made the short walk to a waiting minibus that was now making the thirty-mile trip to Miami Airport for the final leg of their journey. A nonstop flight, courtesy of Pakistan Airlines. In first class, no less. And finally, to Islamabad where his parents were waiting for them. It had taken the best part of a week to renew their expired passports. Seemingly, no one wanted them.

He glanced over at his younger sibling who was staring out of the window of the small minibus as they sped along Route 821. He looked different. Not just his reduced physical appearance. No, it was something else; he seemed older. Tired eyes swung towards him and Naveed smiled encouragingly. Nothing. It was his eyes. They were blank. Nothing revealed, everything locked down. He knew the look. Had witnessed it in many of his fellow inmates over the years as they had come and gone from his wing. Some in body bags, laid low, not by the beatings, but the hopelessness of their situation. He wondered whether it was too late for his brother. Maybe he was too far gone and prayed that was not the case.

Naveed flexed his aching wrists, being careful not to pull on the tight metal bracelets that were chained to the floor of the vehicle. He hoped they would be removed prior to the long flight home. What did the Americans think he would do? Make a run for it. Just one final indignity before his real freedom.

A siren sounded to his left and he felt himself tense; it reminded him of the claxon at the camp which would sound whenever a squad entered the cell block. Every inmate dreaded it. Who were they coming for? Those few seconds of fearful anticipation were worse than the beatings. He looked over to see a police car pass them at speed, its blue and red flashing brightly despite the early morning sun. He turned to his brother.

'Don't worry. It's not for us this time.' He smiled reassuringly. The van slowed. Up ahead the police car applied its brake lights, forcing the driver to slow down. Through the thick glass he heard the booming instruction.

'Pull over please.'

Their driver swore softly and obeyed, swinging the van roughly onto the hard shoulder of I-821.

'Please stay in the vehicle,' the voice boomed.

'That's all we need,' muttered the driver's partner. He was heavy set and sweating freely, despite the aircon. 'Shall I call it in?'

'Of course,' the driver replied. 'We should be pre-cleared. See if we can get their command centre to let us through. Don't want any hiccups on their big day.' He smiled, glancing back at the two shackled men.

Up ahead, two troopers alighted from the vehicle and slowly made their way over to the van, dark glasses concealing their faces. His brother stiffened. So did Naveed. That was one sense still working fine. The situation didn't feel right and every nerve ending in his body told him to run. As they approached, the men split up, moving either side of the van. His brother started to mutter something unintelligible under his breath. Naveed moved to comfort him but the heavy chain cut him short. Both men made rotating motions with their hands, signalling downwards and the soldiers silently retracted their windows.

'What can I do for you, buddy?'

'Your taillight's out.' The cop spoke in a southern drawl.

Naveed visibly relaxed. A brake light. He smiled at the mundanity of the situation. He had spent way too long in prison. His brother continued to mutter, the words getting louder as his panic grew.

'Are you sure? This van's just been serviced.'

'Are you calling me a liar?' the cop said. 'Did you hear that, Ray. He thinks I made it up.'

His partner remained motionless.

'Hey, there's no need for that. If you say the light's out, I believe you.'

'That's just typical. You army types come down south and think normal rules don't apply.'

'That's not what I meant,' the driver said. 'We have an important cargo. I've just radioed the base to have your command centre let us through.'

'There you go again. One rule for us and one for you lot. I'm afraid that's not going to wash today. You've earned yourself a booking.'

He took out his notebook and licked his pen.

'Got a problem with that?' he grinned down at the driver.

'Hey, cool it, buddy. I'm not trying to avoid anything.'

'Maybe you need to see for yourself,' the cop said. 'Come on, step out of the vehicle.'

The driver sighed heavily and looked over at his partner.

'Best do what he says, John. No sense in antagonising him further over a busted light.'

He nodded in agreement and slowly got out of the van, following the cop to the rear of the vehicle.

Naveed's brother was moaning loudly now, a look of pure terror on his wan face.

The remaining soldier looked back.

'What's his problem?'

'I don't know, sir,' Naveed said. 'He's nervous. That's all.'

'Well, tell him to button it or I'll give him something to get nervous about.'

The radio crackled into life.

'Unit two. We have checked with Miami Police and they don't have any units on I-821 this afternoon. I repeat, there are no units. Can you get further information, please?'

The soldier reached for the receiver but that's as far as he got. It happened in the blink of an eye. Before either brother could react, the trooper leant in through the open window placing one hand on the soldier's chin, the other on the back of his head and then he wrenched hard right. They both heard the crack. Such a small sound but it heralded death and both men knew they were next. Naveed heard screaming. It was pure terror. He turned to his brother who was pulling at his manacles and moaning pathetically. And then he realised the screams were his. The passenger doors were suddenly wrenched open and the first cop was there with bolt cutters. First his chains, then his brother's, slipped to the floor and seconds later they were being led to the troopers' car. Neither man resisted. Despite the danger, they were conditioned not to. Resistance was futile. Resistance was met with a beating that would leave them crumpled up in their cell for days. Or worse.

As they were bundled into the car, the first trooper appeared at his side. Naveed felt a tiny prick in his arm. Beside him his brother's pleading eyes stared back in pure terror.

Washington DC

9 November 2009, 16:02 hours

The water was scalding hot and plentiful, cascading over Uma with a ferocity befitting her mood. Slowly she warmed up and eventually the lingering odour of smoke was washed away along with the ghastly images of war. But even the hot shower could not lift her spirits. She leant her head against the shower cubicle letting the jet of water wash over her.

Where had it all gone wrong?

The question made her flush with shame, Ethan's accusation still ringing in her ears. *Come clean with me.* That was all he had asked and she had failed him. Not intentionally. Uma hadn't intended to mislead Ethan about what had happened to him in his LEAP out to Reykjavik. Shane had been right to keep the entanglement secret from him and she had readily gone along with the plan. Until they could correct what had happened. But they hadn't succeeded despite their repeated efforts. Somehow, for reasons beyond their current understanding, Ethan had become entangled with a mercenary called Anderson. A murderous brute of a man with an ugly temper and complete disdain for anyone other than himself. Worse still, Ethan had found out they were concealing the truth and nothing Uma could say would mend that festering wound. When she had finally decided to resurrect him from the coma, everything had seemed normal. In fact, for the first few weeks Uma had convinced herself that the old Ethan was back. He looked like the old Ethan. Sounded like the old Ethan. And, it seemed, there was no sign of Anderson. To begin with they had both agreed that Ethan should stay hidden. They couldn't risk him being seen in public. That would definitely have raised questions if a fully fit Ethan had been seen wandering around so soon after he had been declared brain dead. When Ethan had decided to buy the Reynolds' old place at Point Humboldt, Uma had jumped at the idea. It was miles from anywhere and anyone and would give them the time to fashion a credible story about his miraculous recovery. Except things hadn't worked out that way. As the days progressed, Ethan had become withdrawn. Refused to talk to her. And when he did it was to accuse her of deceiving him about LEAP and her real motives. Just like today. The relentless exercising had soon started, closely followed by the fighting. Boxing. Wrestling. Karate. Taekwondo. Judo. And his fixation with weaponry. *Damn that place.* What had Shane said? *'This shit can seriously mess with your head.'* It was as if Ethan was discovering the enormity of what had happened to him. And nothing Uma said or did seemed to help.

Eventually she had stopped visiting him and, instead, concentrated on Green Ray. And then one day the summons had arrived. At first, she thought it was from the US Government and their interminable inquest into what had happened at Reynolds Air. But it was from Ethan. She had been to see him immediately but he wouldn't listen to her. Nothing she said would convince him otherwise and instead they had spent months defending Ethan's doomed attempt to wrestle control of Green Ray from her. The Trust had been created to hold LEAP and the bulk of his fortune from the fire sale he had conducted. As the judge stated repeatedly, it was a fair trade for what was involved. Uma had agonised over whether to let him have it all back but it wasn't that simple. If she wanted to pursue global warming without LEAP, she needed the money and Ethan had created a structure that enabled her to do exactly that. By the time he sued her, it was too late. All the investments had been made. With his knowledge.

She wasn't even sure why she had gone today. She should have realised what was going to happen but couldn't help herself. And now she was left facing the biggest decision of her life—release LEAP in return for an opportunity to dictate energy policy within the US, the largest emitter of CO_2 the world had ever seen. Finally, she was being offered the mandate to really make a change. It seemed such an easy choice.

But at what price?

Uma emerged from the steaming shower and wrapped herself in a large terry cloth bathrobe before making her way into the dining area, completely preoccupied with the enormity of her decision.

'Tell me. How long did you expect to conceal it from us?'

Uma's heart lurched. He was impossible to miss, framed in the large window, his back to her, lanky frame leant casually against the glass, staring down into the tree-lined avenue below.

'This is getting to be a habit, Mr Ingram,' Uma said through tight lips, trying desperately to control her breathing. She'd be damned if she let him see how rattled she was. 'Do you not have nothing better to do than stalk me in various states of undress?' Uma swallowed hard, thinking fast. There was a phone in the bedroom. Should she call the police? To what end? He was the Head of the CIA. What would she tell them? If last time was anything to go by, the whole building was probably crawling with agents. Why would they even listen to her? He had a right to see her. But in her own apartment? Uma started to blush, remembering the reaction of his men in the corridor at their previous encounter. Their knowing glances as she stood there half-naked. She shuddered. Ingram hadn't touched her. He was just a creep. Nevertheless, Uma wrapped the large towel tightly around her.

'Conceal what?' she replied as evenly as possible.

'You really are quite the hypocrite, Doctor.'

'How so?' Uma said, trying to look puzzled.

'When it comes to LEAP you seem to have two rules; one for Uma Jakobsdóttir and one for everyone else. You get to use it but no one else does. Is that how it works?'

Uma stared at him blankly.

'We get to transport goods but you use it anyway as you see fit. As your own mini transporter. To save your boyfriend's life.'

'I don't know what you are talking about.'

'Oh, come now, Doctor,' he replied. 'Ethan Rae was brain dead.' The director picked up a file from the low table in front of him and leafed through it before finding what he was after. 'This is the discharge report from the trauma centre at Bellevue Hospital from January 2004: 'Ethan Rae has suffered a traumatic asphyxia which has effectively caused a catastrophic reduction in the amount of oxygen reaching his brain.' However, within six months he is seen walking about with no visible signs of trauma. Physical or mental. A medical miracle. Tell me, how is Mr Rae?'

'You don't understand.'

'Let me take a guess,' Ingram said. 'Something to do with assuaging your guilt. At the deaths of Baldursson. Eva. James. Sally. And the countless others that got caught up in your little subterfuge. Do you feel better?'

'You eavesdropped on me!' she spluttered, self-righteous anger replacing her guilt. If only he knew the sleepless hours she had spent debating whether to bring Ethan back. In defiance of the prime Law that, if your physical body dies in the natural world, your LEAP programme would have to be terminated. It had been so easy to write but the moment she had to enforce it on Ethan, it had felt barbaric. How could you just let someone die or remain dead if you had the power to save them? That was how she had justified it to herself despite knowing that was precisely why she had introduced the Laws after her father's death. But if it was no longer an absolute law there would be chaos. People could conceivably live for ever. A crowded world with finite resources would not stand a chance, even with lowered CO_2 emissions. And that's when she knew LEAP was even worse than the poisoned chalice she had imagined it to be. Despite that knowledge she had restored Ethan, comforting herself with the knowledge that this would be the last time because from that day forward she had decided to bury LEAP. As the years had passed, Uma felt more vindicated as she watched Ethan descend into a self-induced madness. It was more painful to watch than leaving him in a coma could ever have been.

'That's what we do, Doctor,' Ingram said.

'You can't prove anything.'

'I'm not looking to.'

'What do you mean?'

'Life is going to get very complicated for you in the next forty-eight hours unless you start to co-operate.'

'Are you blackmailing me?'

'That's such an ugly word, Doctor.' He tossed the medical report on the table and returned to the window. 'To begin with, there will be the odd story. Rumours, if you will. About where you got your money from. Some vague suggestion that it has an Arab source. We know all about your boyfriend's connections to Saudi Arabia. It'll stick. Perhaps not in a court of law but the court of public opinion has much more relaxed burdens of proof.'

Uma had no idea what he was talking about.

'The suggestion of links to terrorist organisations. That should just about do it.' The director rubbed his hands in a self-congratulatory manner and smiled at Uma. A warm sunny smile. 'Rumours like these are not good for business,' Ingram continued. 'Good old middle America doesn't want to buy cars, however cheap, however green, from a company with links to the men that are sending their sons home in body bags. Then there will be references to Reynolds' death. It will raise the whole spectre of your involvement in that ugly episode. Not good timing given the current mood.'

'I'm not sure your Commander in Chief will enjoy hearing about this,' was all Uma could think to say.

'You really don't get this, do you?' The director shook his head slowly in mock amazement. Uma felt herself reddening. 'He's a hostage to public opinion. As are the Senate. Once this story breaks, your nomination will never get past them. In fact, it would be safe to say that by next week, you will struggle to get a day pass to the Washington Monument let alone talk time with the leader of the free world.'

The director's smile broadened. One of satisfaction at a job well done. There was a long silence in the room.

'Of course, you can avoid all of this unsavoury business.'

Uma sank slowly into a chair, the alternative left hanging between them.

'It doesn't sound like I have much choice.'

'Oh, we all have a choice, Doctor.'

He walked round the sofa towards Uma and settled down next to where she was slumped. Uma's instinct was to pull away but she resisted. Men like this fed on weakness.

'Your move, Doctor.'

'Assuming I give him what he's after, what then?'

'In about an hour you'll get a call from The White House Press Office to discuss your appointment as Energy Secretary. That story will be with every major paper and network by this evening. It normally takes time to get approved but given what's on offer, I cannot see that being a problem. Within two weeks you will have access to the combined budget and political muscle of the Energy Department. Once that happens you will be expected to co-operate fully with John Forsyth to get the LEAP programme into test phase. I have to say, from where I am stood, it looks like a good choice to me.'

Uma didn't move, her mind desperately searching for a way to wriggle free from the trap Ingram had set. But there was no escape from his long embrace. And he knew it, perched there calmly like a praying mantis.

'A phased release, right?' Uma said.

'That's what the President asked for.'

'Can I have some time to think about it?' she replied, silently cringing at her request. It sounded so weak.

'I need an answer now. This is a one-shot deal.'

For Uma, time seemed to stand still. A series of snapshots slid across her mind: Ethan hunched by the roaring fire, looking back at her, his face expressionless; Baldursson laughing uproariously; Eva staring at her quizzically; her father standing beside one of his precious mud holes, a deep frown on his face, looking so disappointed; Reynolds walking towards her, a smile of quiet satisfaction framed on his lips.

'Don't look so despondent. Within the next few days, you'll become the most famous person in the world. Again. But this time round you will be one of the most powerful.'

The director's words seemed to pull her back to the present and she smiled thinly at their irony.

'You really have covered all the bases here, haven't you?'

'I take it that we have a meeting of minds.' Ingram clapped his long hands together. 'Very good. You've saved everyone a lot of unnecessary heartache.'

For a second, he seemed unsure of himself, as if he was in two minds over whether to shake Uma's hand or, worse still, kiss her! Finally, he stood, all long limbs and calm authority, and without another word, walked past her towards the hallway.

'Tell me, Director Ingram,' Uma called after him, 'how did you know I was going to say no.'

He paused and turned to face her.

'I didn't,' he shrugged. 'Except that the longer you remained silent, the greater the likelihood you would decline the President's suggestion. I just prepared for that outcome by uncovering some bargaining chips. That's what—'

'Yes, I know,' she said. 'That's what you do. And you do it very well.'

'Thank you. I've had a lot of practice.' There was no gloating now. Just a matter-of-fact statement followed by an awkward silence

'Are you going to stand there all day?'

'No,' he said. 'I've seen quite enough for one day.'

And then he was gone, leaving Uma crumpled on the couch. Already, the skull crackers were gathering. It was going to be a long evening.

Reynolds' Castle, Point Humboldt

9 November 2009, 12:10 hours

Ethan felt a soft tremor roll across the floor of the small room but ignored it and continued to stare at the frozen image of Uma. He was safe here; as one of ten quake shelters commissioned during the original construction of the castle, each one sat within a cage of reinforced concrete and steel that was guaranteed to survive a Force 8 tremble, equivalent to the one that had flattened San Francisco in 1906. They had been stocked with enough food and water to last a week and this one had also been fitted with a bank of TV screens linked to a network of cameras dotted around the castle. Reynolds' son had apparently been quite the voyeur. After Uma had stormed off, Ethan had retreated to the one just off the great hall, its entrance hidden behind one of the great tapestries. He found the cell-like space comforting. It provided everything he needed: a small camp bed, privy, fridge and microwave. And his research: shelves bulging with files on, and photos of, Ethan, Anderson and Mark Brown. Three separate lives carefully researched in the hope of finding one whole. Five years of forensic investigation painstakingly assembled in neat folders all containing Ethan's achievements, Anderson's military record and Mark Brown's shame.

Ethan winced as shooting pains leapt up his right leg. Had he injured himself during his sparring or was it the metal pins? They had been inserted years ago, just after the crash that killed his parents and, even though he could have easily replaced them with bone, courtesy of LEAP, he had resisted the temptation. As the memories of his parents had slowly faded, he had sought out ways to help him remember. The pins were one such way, a constant reminder of his negligence that night that pulled at his leg like an untreated toothache. But if he was honest with himself, just like the cell he was sat in, they were also a reference point to who he had once been—neither that brute Anderson, nor Ethan the financier, but Mark Brown, teenage son of Simon Brown and Martha Brown.

He blinked as if seeing Uma for the first time and clicked the play icon on the screen. She was crossing the Hall of Steel and he could tell from her gait that she was angry. No, she was mad as hell, and it drew a thin smile to his lips. As she started up the stairs, the camera angle changed, allowing him to follow her all the way into the LEAP chamber where she disappeared. If only it was that easy. Every time he saw her, his heart leapt and stomach churned. Just like the first time he'd met her in the auditorium after her interrupted talk on teleportation. And, of course, their shared kiss in the Blue Lagoon. He traced his lips, feeling the familiar tingle he'd felt that day. The memory was quickly purged by the familiar rage of her betrayal, burning through his loins like an avenging angel.

The anger propelled him back into the great hall as another tremor flittered across the room, causing the huge fire to roar with approval. High above, decades of dust showered the floor below like volcanic ash. Ethan barely noticed as he resumed his position in front of the hearth. Every so often he would glance up at the portrait of Old Man Reynolds. His angry scowl wasn't much help but he didn't look like a man who suffered fools gladly. Ethan wondered what he would have done. Probably embraced his new-found eternity and bestrode the globe like a modern day vampire, regenerating at will, growing his empire whilst everyone around him was brought low by their mortality.

As he stared into the roaring flames, he sensed a presence off to his right. *Had Uma returned?* Whoever it was hung back, though, forcing Ethan to turn. His heart sank. It was Edward Hunter, the only other occupant at Point Humboldt. Emboldened by Ethan's acknowledgement, he cautiously advanced until he was within earshot of his employer.

'Sir.' He shifted uncomfortably on the spot, eyes to the floor. 'Sir, there's a visitor for you.'

Ethan looked up.

'You know I don't see anyone.'

'Understood, sir. That's what I told him. But ...'

'But what?' Ethan said.

'He had a message for you. It makes no sense to me but he said you would understand.'

Ethan was silent. He had already turned his back, the man dismissed.

'He said that he didn't want to talk to you anyway. He wanted to talk to Mark Brown.'

Ethan whirled round.

'He said what?'

'That he wanted to talk to Mark Brown,' the man stammered, taking a step backwards. He hadn't seen his boss this animated. Ever.

'Did he give his name?'

'No, sir.'

'You'd better show him in then,' Ethan said.

'I can't. He's not here.'

'Where is he then?' Ethan said.

'Out at the airstrip.'

Ethan's brow furrowed.

'He won't come here. Says it's far too cold.'

Then Ethan did something that Edward Hunter hadn't seen in his six long years of service. He smiled. Except it wasn't really a smile. More of a ghostly imitation as if his facial muscles were trying to remember a long-forgotten routine.

'Well, you'd better ready one of the Land Rovers then. We can't keep our guest waiting. Tell him I will be with him in the hour.'

And then he turned away, leaving Hunter to make his way back across the huge room. A strange day had just become a little stranger. They hadn't had two guests in one day since he'd started working for Ethan. And for his boss to even consider leaving the sanctuary of the castle. That was a first. Whoever it was must be mighty important.

Reynolds' Castle, Point Humboldt

9 November 2009, 12:15 hours

Bill Grant eased his cramped limbs inside the small van and blew into his hands. He glanced over at his partner who was similarly crunched and looked at his watch. They were five hours in, which meant another seven to go. He groaned.

'What do we do?' asked the younger man, removing his headphone.

'Our orders have changed, Grant said. 'We keep him under surveillance and understand what he is up to.'

Grant had been here before; almost five years to the day after Rae had bought the Reynolds' place. They had watched him for months but nothing had ever come of it. He never came out of the castle. Spoke to few people except the Jakobsdóttir woman. Eventually, Grant had been instructed to mothball the entire operation until last week when the order had come through from DC to restart the surveillance. Amazingly, all the surveillance equipment was working but as before, nothing had happened—until this morning, with the surprise arrival of the woman who, as per usual, had appeared from nowhere. They had recorded the most incredible exchange he had heard in his twenty-five years in the service. Now, barely, two hours later, their target was on the move.

'I guess we move out, then. We have an hour to get to the airport and set ourselves up.'

Grant eased himself into the driving seat and started the engine.

Reynolds' Estate, Point Humboldt

9 November 2009, 12:35 hours

To the uninitiated, it seemed that the fog was playing tricks with the eye, presenting solid walls of timber that were impossibly wide and toweringly high. Ethan knew better. He had only driven the track twice in five years; once when he had flown in to view the castle after learning that it was up for sale and then when he had arrived to move in, two months later. On both occasions it had been a fine sunny day and the ancient forest had been revealed in all its primeval enormity. The sight had been breath-taking; redwood trees had towered above him on both sides of the narrow trail, some nearly three hundred feet high, their ancient trunks bleached grey by the incessant rains from the mighty Pacific. At one point he had stopped his Jeep and stood beside one of the monsters, marvelling at its grandeur. It must have been twenty feet wide and when he craned his neck to look up it had swallowed his gaze contemptuously. On that day Ethan finally understood Reynolds' fascination with the trees and why he had built his castle alongside these two-thousand-year-old timber goliaths that bestrode the earth, much like Reynolds Air had during its prime.

Today was a different matter. The coastal fog had spread its misty fingers deep inland, forcing Ethan to navigate the narrow road with care. In one place it actually disappeared through one of the colossal trunks, swallowed up in one gulp before being spat out the other side. Ethan gripped the steering wheel tightly. He wasn't used to being outside. The fog helped but it felt unnatural. Everything seemed unfamiliar. The texture of the leather on his pale hands. The new smell of the vehicle. The cold. Even the towering trees above him. He didn't belong here. Shouldn't be here. He had stopped the Jeep at least four times, pondering whether he should return to the safety of the castle with its familiar sights and smells. The comfort of the great room beckoned him but he couldn't ignore Mark Brown or the man who had summoned him. He was responsible for who he had become. Was an indelible part of his past. Or at least Ethan's. And that knowledge alone had drawn him from the castle. It was buried deep for good reason because Mark Brown had killed his parents. But that very certainty was also comforting; an anchor point to which Ethan now clung for all he was worth. It represented a past that he knew with absolute certainty belonged to Ethan Rae not some loose gun for hire or an entangled monster or a resurrected vampire. So, he continued, cautiously, inching through the fog that blocked his way. The airstrip was some ten miles from the castle and had been constructed so far away after intense pressure from environmentalists. One felled tree for a boardroom table could be ignored by the politicians but five acres was a different matter. Even Old Man Reynolds had been unable to ignore the outcry when he had proposed building the private airstrip within spitting distance of his new home.

The gates of the landing strip suddenly loomed up out of the fog and Ethan slowed to a standstill. At eight thousand feet, the runway could comfortably accommodate the largest jets and was serviced by a small arrivals hall that had been left in its original luxurious splendour. In its heyday, the castle had hosted a succession of dignitaries, politicians, celebrities and businessmen from every corner of the earth, all drawn to Reynolds Point by the enormous power and wealth that its namesake wielded.

As the gates clanged open, the fog responded with a surge, forcing Ethan to use his Sat Nav to guide him towards the northern end of the runway. Eventually he stopped, cut the engine and sat staring out at the shifting wall of fog, his earlier determination wilting; maybe they hadn't been able to land and his journey had been for nothing. He silently cursed Hunter for delivering the message. He knew better than to disturb Ethan but had ignored his specific instruction, drawing him out of the castle on a wild goose chase. But Mark Brown couldn't be ignored and with considerable trepidation, Ethan stepped out into the white world. Instantly, icy tendrils enveloped him and he shivered despite his thick ski jacket. Nothing. Not a sound or sight. Just a kaleidoscope of white vapours, undulating softly in the frigid air.

How had a plane even landed in this?

Ethan stepped forward and felt the reassuring roughness of the runway beneath his feet. However, there was no sign of the plane.

'Hello? Is there anyone there?'

His voice sounded flat in the thick fog and he peered into the white soup blindly. It was just like that night at the Blue Lagoon which felt like a lifetime ago. As he stood there, Uma's face appeared but this time she was smiling, her long black hair slicked back, accentuating her sharp cheekbones. He was faintly surprised by the memory; his thoughts of Uma were always consumed with anger. Their fiery confrontation just before he died. Their subsequent encounters. Always volcanic. Full of vitriol and blame. He remembered the moment so clearly, their close proximity in the hot waters of the Blue Lagoon, the tension, his secret desire, their soft embrace, a silky kiss. He felt himself stir at the memory. Was he being too hard on her? But she had kept his entanglement secret, plotting to cut him out of the LEAP project. But without her intervention he would have died. That was a certainty. But the nature of his survival was unnatural. By all the laws of medicine he should have died. Would have died. Instead, he had cheated death and returned in someone else's body. Not his own. The most recent memories of his last life had been the argument with Uma in Reykjavík and her rejection of him. And of course, overhearing Uma and Shane plotting against him, where he had learnt they had entangled him with

Anderson, wiped his programme entirely from the LEAP system. But what hurt most was the fear in Uma's voice as she shared her concerns with Shane. Then the reawakening. He had no recollection of his time in the Homeland Security prison, the demise of Reynolds Air or his subsequent death at the hands of Grond. Nothing other than what Uma had told him in the subsequent months following his rebirth. In those long weeks, most of it had been spent alone. It was Uma's idea. She was concerned that people would grow suspicious if he had suddenly reappeared after his near-death experience. He hadn't had the strength or desire to argue and when it was time to reappear, he had not wanted to. Couldn't. The enforced solitude had helped him think clearly. Understand what he had become. A twentieth-century parasite. A scavenger, feeding on the cast-off atoms of others, able to regenerate at will, regardless of what he exposed his body to. Able to reappear with no memory of his demise but with his memory fully intact. It was against the natural order of things, that much was clear. But did it matter? If his body was simply atoms, what defined him? His memories? But his were suspect at best, a concoction of two people's, one of whom was clearly a monster. A series of encoded chemical reactions storing up information in his brain. Yet, if they defined him and he had lost a chunk of his own, was he the same person he would have been had he survived his death at the hands of Grond? Which brought him back to Mark Brown. A constant in either version of himself.

An icy gust brought him back to the freezing airfield. He shivered and thrust his hands deep into warm pockets. As he stood there, feeling utterly alone, the fog parted to reveal the strangest sight Ethan had seen in years.

Bill Grant slowed to a stop outside the main gates of the runway. On the dashboard, a red dot blinked, indicating the location of Rae's Jeep, fifty yards ahead. He had bugged all the vehicles in the huge castle garage five years ago so it had been a simple matter to track his target. The fog was perfect cover. However, they were now staring up at some of the largest wrought-iron gates he had ever laid eyes on. There was no way through these. Beside him, Boyd James sat listening intently, a microphone set clamped to his ears.

'Anything?' Grant asked.

'Nothing. I think he just got out of the vehicle. Not sure what he's doing.'

'OK. Let's wait then.

'Don't we need to get closer?' the younger man asked.

'No, our orders were clear,' Grant said. 'Just watch and listen. Under no circumstances are we to engage with the target.'

Ethan stood there staring up at the largest plane he had ever seen. He had only just missed driving into one of the huge tyres that supported the white monster towering over him. Reynolds Senior would have been proud to own such a leviathan in his fleet which would have dwarfed Ethan's own Challenger 800. At the end of the huge plane, a mobile passenger stair gantry was nestled against the rear exit. Coming down the steps were two soldiers dressed all in black. As they reached the tarmac, they beckoned to Ethan who followed them back up the steps in silence. As he reached the top, Ethan paused and glanced down; fifty feet below the fog had already swallowed up the runway, giving the impression that the plane was floating on top of a cloud bank, thirty thousand feet up. It felt strange, unnatural even, and he quickly walked through the open door which silently closed behind him.

'I've lost the signal,' James said.

'What do you mean?'

'It's gone. One second it was there and the next, nothing.'

'Do you think he found the bug?' Grant asked.

'Impossible. They're microscopic.'

'What then?'

Boyd James sat there for a few seconds, thinking.

'It's being blocked,' he said finally. 'What do you want me to do?'

His partner didn't respond, causing Boyd James to look over. Bill Grant was staring out of the window and he followed his gaze. The fog had parted on the runway to reveal the midsection of a white plane. There were no visible markings on the bit they could see and then it was gone, swallowed up by the fog.

'Did you see that?' Boyd exclaimed excitedly. 'It's the biggest flybird I've ever seen. It must be blocking the signal. We need to get on board.'

'Whoa, slow down there,' Grant said. 'Those are not our orders. We were told not to engage with the contact. Just listen and survey.'

'I'm not going to make contact,' Boyd said. 'I might be able to boost the signal if I can get closer. I'm going to take a look. Are you coming with me?'

Without waiting for an answer, he grabbed his equipment and disappeared into the thick fog, leaving Grant slamming the dashboard in frustration. As he did so, the fog parted again to reveal the tail fin upon which a huge black scorpion glowered back at him.

Reynolds' Estate, Point Humboldt

9 November 2009, 12:55 hours

'Greetings, my friend. Please sit and take tea with me.'

Abdullah Al Rahman, Head of the Re'asat Al Istikhbarat Al A'amah, Saudi Arabia's intelligence agency, smiled up at Ethan. He was sitting on a large cushion and was surrounded by yet more cushions spread out around him like a sea of silk. In one hand he held a large ornate copper teapot from which he carefully poured a dark brown liquid into a tiny cup which he passed up to Ethan. They were alone in the ... tent, since that's what it was or at least had the appearance of one; a huge one that stretched away either side of them and above, disappearing into shadows of soft materials and flickering lights. Ethan had no doubt they weren't alone. Somewhere behind all those drapes would be ten, maybe twenty bodyguards sworn to protect their master's life, with their own if necessary. He sat down, cross-legged, opposite the older man and cautiously took a sip. It was extremely sweet and for a second, he was back in the dusty prison where Mark Brown had lost ten years of his life alongside the heat, the humidity and the sand. The sand had been his constant companion, in his clothes, in his hair, on his skin, in his mouth. There was no escaping it and the memory made him feel better. Another anchor to a certain past.

'Hello, Abdullah. It's been a long time,' Ethan said.

'The mere twinkle of a star. But yes, it has been many years.' His host smiled back.

'How's Hassan?' Ethan was referring to his host's son whom he'd befriended and protected whilst serving a ten-year jail sentence in Al-Ha'ir Prison, a Saudi Arabian maximum-security prison, for allegedly killing the only son of a local sheikh.

'As impetuous as ever. Some would say foolhardy. My chequebook never rests.' The older Arab smiled mischievously at Ethan. 'He mentions you often, as do I. The House of Al Rahman will always be eternally grateful to you for saving his life in Al-Ha'ir.'

'I think of him, too. He was my only friend in that hell hole. You would have done the same for my son, I am sure.'

'Perhaps.' Al Rahman shifted slightly on the large cushion. 'You look well, my friend. Are you fully recovered?'

'It's complicated ...' Ethan began, but trailed off, unsure of what to say. An awkward silence ensued as both men cupped their drinks and stared into the eddying steam.

'Thank you for coming today. I understand from your man servant that you don't see many visitors.'

'I owe you my life. Or at least my new one—my last one,' Ethan corrected, his eyes darting towards the sheikh who remained fixated on his steaming tea. 'I will always have time for you.'

'And what do you spend your days doing, Ethan?'

'Abdullah, I don't wish to sound rude but what are you doing here?'

The older man raised an eyebrow and laughed gently.

'Ah, you westerners. Always in such a hurry.'

He took a sip of his tea and looked at Ethan, his hard eyes glistening in the flickering flames. Ethan wondered whether the lamps remained lit when the huge plane was airborne. He could imagine they would.

'I was in San Francisco on business and couldn't miss the opportunity to visit an old friend and show him my latest toy.' He swept his hands expansively outwards. 'I thought you would appreciate it.'

'I do. In another lifetime I would have probably owned one.'

'I thought so and would be honoured to give you a tour after we have finished our conversation?'

'That is very kind of you, but I am needed back at the castle.'

If Abdullah Al Rahman was disappointed, he didn't show it. Instead, he nodded his head slightly and continued.

'When are you due back? I will make sure that we are finished in time.'

'I'm not sure,' Ethan said, unsure as to why he felt so anxious. This man reminded him of his dead parents whom he had killed. And for the first time in five years, his back prickled in anticipation. Ethan wasn't sure whether to be delighted at the physicality of the memory or terrified. Either way, he felt overwhelmed. 'Within the hour, I suppose.'

'Then we don't have a moment to lose. Come. Surely you can spare an old friend a moment of your precious time.'

A half-forgotten instinct made Ethan pause. *The Head of Saudi Intelligence didn't just drop in for a chat.*

'You didn't fly halfway round the world to show me your new toy, however impressive it might be.'

'Still the same old Ethan, I see,' the elderly Arab chided the younger man. 'I would like to invest in Green Ray.'

Ethan felt wrongfooted. He hadn't expected that. He hadn't expected any of this.

'It's not mine to invest in,' Ethan said. 'You'll have to speak with others.'

'I heard that was the case. We can discuss who whilst we walk.'

Ethan made to reply but Al Rahman held up a hand.

'I promise to have you back inside your castle within two hours.' The old man got to his feet.

'Mohammed, help Mr Rae, will you.'

A short man appeared and held out a hand towards Ethan who paused for a second, wondering if he should just leave and return to the castle now but something made him reach out; maybe it was Mark Brown's name, the memory of his parents or simply scar tissue re-energising long dormant nerve endings.

Boyd James was stood underneath the mobile gantry busy adjusting the dials on his hand-held booster unit. Still nothing. He grunted in frustration and continued to make changes to the settings, looking for a way in.

Whoever it was didn't want to be heard. They had gone to a lot of trouble to cloak the plane. He had never come across anything like it. Boyd was so engrossed he didn't hear the soldier behind him until it was too late. The noise, when it came, was the crunch of wood on bone as a rifle butt smashed into the side of his face.

The white ball glided silently over the lush green felt before striking its black counterpart a glancing blow. As intended, it dropped obediently into the waiting pocket. The white ball skewed back sharply before spinning away left towards the next set up, a lone red, its fate already decided.

'I was introduced to snooker in my first year at Cambridge and have never looked back. I take a table everywhere I go.'

Ethan didn't respond. They were stood in a huge room modelled in the style of a gentleman's club, with dark oak panels adorning the walls and ceiling, with a darker floor to compliment the heavily ornate mahogany table that his host was crouched over. As with everything on board the A380, it was unlike anything Ethan had ever seen and probably ever would. The upper deck had been modelled on a street scene containing an exact replica of Al Rahman's favourite eateries from around the world, most of which seemed to veer towards satiating a very sweet tooth: a boulangerie from Paris displaying bewildering varieties of breads and pastries; a sorbet parlour from Milan featuring a multitude of bizarre flavours. They passed a sweet store, modelled on an old-fashioned English shop, the candy displayed in large glass jars behind the counter. Finally, a crêperie with more sugary desserts resplendent with chocolate, whipped cream and other syrups. Each restaurant was fully staffed and ready to serve their master. In some, members of Al Rahman's retinue were eating, including women wearing the traditional full-length black abaya complete with headscarf that cloaked their faces. Furtive eyes avoided Ethan's gaze. Yet another sweet, forgotten memory of his mother who had detested the curtailment of her rights whilst living in Saudi Arabia. On the second floor were the living quarters for Al Rahman's retinue. There were about twenty self-contained apartments leading off a main corridor, each one individually finished to an extravagant standard. The lower deck was entirely devoted to Al Rahman and contained his private bedroom which led off to several further rooms including a small Jacuzzi, the largest dressing room Ethan had ever seen, a prayer room and finally an office that was off limits. Just beyond his private apartment was a board room that could comfortably have seated fifty people around its smoked glass table that had been inlaid with the light relief of a scorpion. Finally, they had arrived at the snooker room where they had continued their strange conversation.

'You do realise that I'm not involved in Green Ray. Never have been.'

'I understand your old prodigy, Uma Jakobsdóttir, controls the fund now. She sounds formidable.'

Ethan's heart lurched at the mention of Uma but he couldn't help himself.

'How much are you looking to invest?'

'Fifty billion. Or at least SAMA is,' Al Rahman said.

'That's a big punt for a central bank to make.'

'So was investing ten million in an unknown twenty-five year old with a criminal record.'

'That was different; I recall it was a loan for saving your son, Hassan.'

'A gift.' Al Rahman smiled at Ethan. 'Remember, it was a gift. You treated it as a loan.'

'I treated it as seed capital and the foundation stone for the Rae Group. Without it, I could never have achieved what I did.'

'I doubt that,' Al Rahman said softly. 'And the fact remains that you returned one billion pounds to me. That's quite a return, even by our standards. Your track record is, shall we say, persuasive.'

'Don't expect such a healthy return from Green Ray.' As he said it, Ethan felt a surge of guilt wash over him, one he angrily tried to suppress. *Uma had shown him nothing but contempt.* Anger replaced the sense of betrayal. *That was better.* 'This is renewable energy, remember. It's a lot more speculative.'

'Unlikely my friend,' Al Rahman said. 'I doubt 'speculative' forms part of your vocabulary, particularly since you have invested the entire proceeds of your own fortune in it. Besides which, we have money to burn. The recent oil price hike has resulted in a huge windfall for our Sovereign Wealth Fund. We can afford to be 'speculative'.'

'I have to say, Abdullah,' Ethan continued, warming to his theme, 'it looks very strange for the world's pre-eminent oil-producing nation to be investing in a charitable foundation, especially one focused on weaning consumers off fossil fuel usage.'

'Nothing lasts forever, Ethan,' Al Rahman said. 'You should know that. The SWF is focused on the long term and we are planning for a day when oil no longer provides the kingdom's revenue. But you are right. This one needs to go under the radar. I was going to propose—'

There was a soft knock and the short man, who had helped Ethan earlier, entered. He walked softly over to his host and whispered something in his ear. Al Rahman nodded thoughtfully.

'Ethan, my apologies. Something has come up which requires my immediate attention.' He laid his cue on the table and glided round to Ethan, where he grasped his hand firmly. 'So, can you help us?'

'I would love to but ...' Ethan replied. 'As I said, I'm not really involved anymore.'

'So, the reports are correct.'

Ethan frowned.

'I have followed your progress with interest: your near death, miraculous recovery, the dismantling of your business empire, withdrawal from public life, a ruinous litigation. Now alone in your castle. Never seen. Never heard of. What causes a man to withdraw from life to such a degree?'

'As I said ...'

Ethan tailed off but his host continued to grip his hand, all the while drilling Ethan with his coal-black eyes. Eventually, Ethan had to drop his gaze. He wanted to leave now.

'I know,' Al Rahman said. 'I press too much. It's a bad habit, acquired from a lifetime of intelligence gathering for the king.'

The older man smiled.

'For an old friend.'

Ethan shook his head slowly.

'Can I speak to Uma Jakobsdóttir directly?'

Ethan shrugged. Again, that slight lurch of his stomach at the sound of her name.

'She runs the fund,' Ethan said. 'I can't imagine she would turn away such a large investment.'

He finally released Ethan's hand.

'My friend, it has been a pleasure as ever and I am sorry we won't be working directly together again.' Al Rahman bowed slightly and Ethan returned the gesture. 'Do you need any help getting back to the castle? Or did you bring a driver?'

'That won't be necessary,' Ethan said. 'I came by myself.'

'I thought so,' Al Rahman said thoughtfully. 'Look after yourself, Ethan. The next time we meet I want to see you more like your old self, no?'

With that, he bowed once again, before turning to the shorter man.

'Mohammed, will you show our esteemed guest out please. I hope that our paths meet again soon.'

As Ethan exited the room, he turned one last time but Al Rahman was already crouched over the huge table, measuring up the angles for his next shot.

Bill Grant watched Ethan descend the steps, accompanied by a much shorter man in a light suit and two soldiers dressed all in black. They looked Arabic and utterly out of place in the cold wet, clammy surroundings. As they reached the tarmac, the suited Arab shook Ethan's hand and waited until he had been swallowed up by the mist. Before returning back up the steps, he turned and slowly scanned the plane from tail to tip. Bill Grant shrank behind the huge tyres, trying to make himself small. He needn't have bothered. The rubber composites were over six feet in height and comfortably concealed his lanky frame. He counted slowly to twenty and risked a glance around the side of the tyre. The short man had disappeared, presumably back into the plane.

As he watched, other men came down the steps; they were all dressed in overalls and looked like ground staff. Two of them spun off towards the wheels he was crouched behind as others headed down toward the other wing and front of the aircraft. His heart started to beat faster. This was not his remit. He was a low-level intelligence agent, normally desk bound. Not out in the field. He had no idea what to do. Instead, he willed the giant wheels to swallow him up, helplessly praying for the fog he had so freely cursed for the last hour. Already he could hear the voices of the two men. They would be upon him in seconds and he took the only action he could think of.

'Howdy, guys,' he announced, stepping out from behind the huge tyre. The two men stopped in their tracks in utter amazement at the sight of the bedraggled and cold agent and then started chattering excitedly in a language Grant had never heard.

'I'm lost. Could you help me, please?'

Both men looked at him quizzically, so he shrugged his shoulders, nodded his head amiably by way of thanks and started walking back towards the perimeter fence. He couldn't believe it was working.

It hadn't.

He hadn't taken two steps before a loud shout cut across the deserted airfield.

From behind him came the thud of heavy boots on tarmac and within seconds, two armed guards overtook him, one either side, their snub-nosed machine guns wet with dew. For a second Grant considered making a dash for the perimeter fence. The arrivals hall was clearly visible. Maybe thirty feet away. He could make it but realised it was hopeless. Without the cover of the fog, he would be a sitting target. Instead, he raised his arms above his head in submission, as the two soldiers were joined by the shorter man he had seen wave Rae off. He stared at Grant dispassionately before jerking a thumb back towards the plane. In the foreground, the sun suddenly broke through the fog bank, lighting up the huge plane's tail fin. The black scorpion's eye seemed to glow with an incandescent brilliance, forcing the agent to shield his eyes.

'You Americans seem to have an obsession with my business.'

The question came from behind which caused Grant to jump. The voice had a slight foreign accent but otherwise Grant would have said he was English; very clipped, very proper. He hadn't heard anyone enter the room but the quiet roar of the plane's engines masked all noise so he had no idea how long the person had been there or if indeed they were even in a room. He tried to turn his neck but it was impossible. There was some sort of metal vice holding his head tightly and preventing him from turning sideways, upwards or downwards. All he could do was look straight ahead which at the moment meant he was staring at a dusty brown tarpaulin that couldn't have been more than two or three feet away. It smelt strange. Like something had been burning.

'Who are you?' Grant said.

'Do you know what we used to do with spies in my country, Mr Grant?'

'How do you know my name?'

'Because you very obligingly keep a business card in your jacket announcing your name, rank and employer. I presume you work with Boyd James. He is your partner. No?'

'You have him?'

'Aren't you a little off the beaten track? I thought the Defence Intelligence Agency was focused on military intelligence gathering abroad.'

'You seem to know an awful lot about me.'

'That's my job, Mr Grant. To know a lot about everything and everyone.'

'Do you normally fly around abducting Federal Agents?'

'You were trespassing.'

'You're in a lot of trouble,' Grant said. He tried to sound authoritative, but his voice was weak and the man must have picked up the slight tremor.

'You still haven't answered my question.'

Grant was silent.

'Do you know what we used to do with spies in my country?' the clipped voice repeated. Grant didn't answer, suddenly fearful. The man's voice had acquired a cruel edge to it. Dispassionate almost.

'Let me enlighten you.'

Without warning, the dirty tarpaulin dropped to the floor. For a split second, Grant couldn't comprehend what he was seeing and then realisation struck. A low moan of denial exhaled from his lips before his reflexes cut in and his eyes shut tight. But they may as well have been wide open. He fought the restraint, trying to turn his head away from the image that his mind's eye continued to project but he could not escape it.

A body was sat upright in a chair, just like his. It was unconscious. Wearing clothes. A business suit drenched with what looked like blood. Its head was staring straight at him. It had no choice because it was held fast by some sort of medieval contraption that meant it couldn't turn. Just like his.

It was Boyd. Grant was sure of that. He recognised his wedding ring. A large slab of gold that was impossible to miss. He wouldn't have been able to identify him from his face.

Or at least what was left of it because his eyes, his ears, his mouth had all disappeared.

They were just blackened, burnt, bloody holes that had been scorched to a cinder.

Grant started to vomit, hot bile burning his throat and nostrils. He tried to banish the image from his mind. But it was too late. There was no escaping it. That and the horrifying realisation that he was next. And then the vision was joined by sounds and smells as his other senses flickered back to life: the low roar of the aircraft, his ragged breathing, stale sweat. And the smell from earlier—a sickly odour which could only have been Boyd's burnt flesh and blood. And something else. He could barely make it out but it made Grant open his eyes: a low whimper barely audible above the engines.

Boyd was still alive?

A rasping sound was coming from the singed hole that had been his mouth; bubbles of blood frothed from the blackened gash.

'Boyd. It's Grant. Don't talk. We'll get you out,' he whispered.

'Oh, Mr Grant. He can't hear you. That's the point, you see. And even if he could, he couldn't respond anyway.'

'You murderous savage,' Grant screamed. 'What have you done to him?'

'Ensured he will never spy again because without his eyes, his ears, his tongue, he has no capacity to observe or report what he has seen. An effective punishment, wouldn't you say?'

All Grant could do was whimper in helpless rage as the cruel voice continued in his ear. 'We're now flying above the largest body of water on earth—sixty-five million square miles, covering one third of the planet's surface. Once you have been punished for your crime, you will be dropped in it with your partner. All the search parties in the world will not be able to find you. No one will be able hear you, see you or communicate with you. Goodbye, Mr Grant. Mohammed, if you please.'

For a moment Grant was left with the roar of the plane's engines before he became aware of someone to his right. It was the small man from earlier. He was holding something in both hands; a long poker that must have been six inches in circumference at its base. It spat and steamed ferociously and although it was still two feet away, he could feel its heat. Grant shrunk back into his harness, moaning helplessly, his eyes fixated on the advancing metal. As it moved closer, Grant realised the end was shaped like a large scorpion, its pincers clearly visible through the white heat. As the skin around his lips started to blister and bubble, he screamed. A primordial shriek of pure terror that was suddenly cut off as the flaming arachnid struck, driving deep into his open mouth.

Washington DC

9 November 2009, 20:10 hours

The phone rang continuously, demanding to be answered but it remained ignored. Eventually it cut out but almost immediately started up again like a naughty child. This happened at least five times, and each time there was a momentary pause before the incessant ringing began again. Eventually its persistence paid off.

'I asked not to be disturbed,' a voice snapped into the receiver.

'Uma? It's John Forsyth. Are you OK?'

'Mr Forsyth,' Uma said, her tone softening immediately.

'Please call me John. I'm so sorry for calling at this time but I need to speak to you.'

'OK ... John' The name felt unfamiliar. 'Don't worry, I was resting. The last few days have been a little exhausting, to say the least.'

'I understand completely,' Forsyth said. 'How insensitive of me. I was just ringing to offer my congratulations on your new position, Secretary Jakobsdóttir. It has a nice ring to it, don't you think?' He laughed warmly and despite her booming headache, Uma felt herself responding to its agreeable nature. 'I know you feel tricked and let down but I can assure you the President has your interests at heart. He is a man of his word. He will stick to your agreement.'

'It's not the President I'm worried about.'

'Oh?' Forsyth sounded intrigued.

'Look, it doesn't matter,' Uma said. 'Thank you for calling. I really appreciate it.'

'There is one other thing I wanted to talk to you about.'

Uma controlled the urge to slam the phone down.

'Yes?' she responded as evenly as possible.

'Are you still accepting funds into Green Ray?'

'You want to invest? I'm—'

'No. No. You misunderstand,' Forsyth said. 'An investor has approached me.'

'Well, it's probably best directed at our Funds Director, Alex Yorke. I can give you his details.'

'This investor has specifically asked to meet you.'

The headache redoubled its efforts.

'I'm sorry, John. I'm not sure that I have the time. There is simply too much to do.'

'I understand,' Forsyth said. 'I know it's unusual but I think you would want to make time for this one.'

'How so?'

'Well for a start, if it goes through it could be to the tune of some billions of dollars.'

'That's no small amount in this climate.'

'I thought it would pique your interest,' Forsyth said, laughing. 'Look, can you be in San Francisco the day after tomorrow. I know it's short notice but we can double up and address some of the finer points of the LEAP roll-out schedule.'

'Do I get to know his name?'

'Not over an open line, no,' Forsyth said. 'There is some degree of delicacy required. It will become clear when you meet him.'

Uma stiffened. It sounded like something Joseph Ingram would say.

'That sounds a little cloak and dagger. Do I know this person?'

'I don't believe so. He is better known to your former partner, Ethan Rae.'

Uma sat up. Despite her booming head she was listening very intently now.

'That does sound intriguing.'

'I thought that would get your attention.' Forsyth's tone softened, almost to a whisper. 'Maybe if you have time, I could treat you to dinner afterwards. You have time to eat, don't you? Or are you too busy?'

Uma heard herself laughing for the first time in days. Had she once said something like that to Ethan before ... She let the thought go, remembering his latest outburst.

'Yes. I can make time for that.'

'Good. It's settled then. I'll have April, my PA, co-ordinate times with you.'

The phone line went dead and Uma stared at the receiver for a long time.

He knew Ethan! Yet all she could picture were John Forsyth's bright blue eyes. *An investor? Who had that sort of money in this climate?* His handsome face. Grey hair. She suddenly couldn't wait for the time to pass.

East Coast

10 November 2009, 9:25 hours

The weight pressed down painfully, enveloping Martin Belman's upper torso like chain mail. It stretched his arms, dug into his shoulders and pulled at his back. Even his neck felt the great load and he struggled to raise his head in the dim morning light. It was as if someone was sat on his chest. His lungs burned and sweat poured from every pore of his body. He wasn't sure he could go any further. His breath came out in weak plumes of steam barely visible in the freezing air. Up ahead, the track disappeared over a brow. *Is this the top of the hill?* The thought spurred him on and with a superhuman effort he forced his aching legs to carry him the final muddy steps. For a few seconds he was bent double, waiting for the pain in his chest to subside. When he finally looked up, his elevated status offered no comfort or view for that matter. As far as he could see in the dim light, thin trees stripped of their summer coats glared back, their bare branches drooping miserably against the biting winds of the Atlantic. This morning it was accompanied by a sleeting drizzle. Neither snow nor rain, it stung his eyes, rendering him almost blind. He blew into his frost-bitten hands and prepared to descend. It wasn't steep but the slopes were treacherous as he had discovered to his cost over the last three weeks. Icy traps lay everywhere, waiting in the frozen ruts to turn his ankles at every opportunity.

In the beginning he could barely walk, let alone run. Six years in Guantanamo had seen to that. His legs muscles had wasted away from lack of exercise and bad diet. He had no stamina. The very first day he had puked up his breakfast after about 200 yards and, despite Fortune's screaming encouragement, had been unable to continue. Eventually they had limped back to the farmhouse but not for long; an hour later, Fortune had taken him out again. This time he had gone maybe three hundred yards and the same routine had been repeated every day since, until he was covering maybe a mile, with relative ease. That is until Fortune had presented him with the coat; a thick hooded canvas affair filled with hundreds of small pockets full of lead. They were everywhere. On his chest, abdomen, arms and back. Even the collar. It must have weighed 80 lbs and when Fortune had helped Belman into it, he had nearly fallen over. Belman had soon christened it the Jacket. It seemed to have a life of its own beyond its reluctant wearer and every time he moved, the coat seemed to shift in another direction, pulling at his centre of gravity. On that first day he had barely been able to walk, let alone run, with the dead weight wrapped around him. Today felt no better.

Belman shifted in the cold, trying to relieve the pinching pressure on his shoulders but it was no good. Out of nowhere a large figure emerged, moving effortlessly up the hill. It was Fortune. For such a large man he seemed to run with remarkable ease in spite of the large pack strapped to his back.

'Get a move on,' he bellowed at Martin, who ignored him and began to cautiously descend the hill. Not quick enough for his handler who was now behind him jogging impatiently on the slippery slope. He lifted a booted foot, planted it in the small of Martin's back and gave him a vicious shove. The momentum of the push pitched him forward at which point the weight of the Jacket suddenly kicked in, tipping him over so that he tumbled down the steep slope right to the bottom, fifty feet below.

Martin lay for a second, recovering his breath, checking whether he had broken anything. He had a small routine, learnt from the camp after his many beatings: toes and fingers, ankles and wrists, forearms and shins, knees, elbows and so on, until he was satisfied everything was in working order. Behind him he heard the heavy footfall of his trainer, boot camp master and jailer coming down the slope and he struggled to his feet, fighting the compulsion to stay in the snow for a rest.

'Come on, Belman. On your feet. Just one quarter mile and then you can pray to your God.'

That's all that kept him going, just like in the Camp; that one day he would join his God in eternity. And this training would guarantee his place. For the first time in his life Belman finally felt on the cusp of glorious immortality, on this earth and in the next life. That was what kept him going. Not Fortune's boot.

Fifteen minutes later, Martin stumbled onto the porch of the farmhouse and collapsed. He lay there for several minutes until the burning sensation had subsided in his chest. He tried to get up but it was no good; he was a spent force. But through his throbbing head he heard Fortune behind him, his boots heavy on the icy wood. Martin rolled over and lay there, staring up at him.

'When do I take it off?' he eventually managed.

Fortune snorted in amusement. He was barely panting, his breath coming out in steady plumes of steam, partially obscuring his heavy face. 'You don't. You wear it all the time. When you sleep, eat, pray and piss. All the time.'

'But why?'

'You know why—you need to get used to the weight. Explosives are heavy and with the ball bearings, yours will come in at nearly 60 lbs. When you start your mission, I don't want you to even notice the weight.'

Fortune unstrapped his own backpack and slung it on the porch. As he passed Martin, he paused again.

'The day you take it off is the day it takes off. Boom!' He made an exploding sound with his hands and laughed. 'Come on, you need to get some rest. If you stay out here, you'll catch pneumonia and we can't have that.'

He pulled the frozen man to his feet and bundled him into the farmhouse. Once inside, the two men stripped off their outer garments in silence. Again, it had become part of the routine. Belman was used to routines. So, it seemed, was Fortune. Martin had pegged him as ex-army, hence the routine comfort. When he was changed, Martin usually took the paper that Fortune now brought him daily, read it from cover to cover before taking his lunchtime prayer in time for afternoon training. During this time Fortune would disappear. Martin did not know where. He didn't care. He didn't ask. He didn't follow. Not since he had discovered he was being watched. If he escaped or was presumed to be escaping, he would only be captured and returned, or worse still, shot. That would not do. He was where he wanted to be, working towards a goal he had dreamt about for six years. Why would he want to sabotage that? However, this morning there was no paper, which annoyed Belman; he loved the paper. It was his connection to the outside world. His thread to a life, long lost. It was clear to Martin that Fortune wasn't going to raise it either. He would have to. As Fortune turned to leave, Martin cleared his throat.

'Excuse me. Do you have my paper?'

''Fraid not. Not today, son.'

'OK. Any chance of bringing one tomorrow?' Martin couldn't hide the disappointment in his voice.

'What is it with you and your newspaper? Why do you care what happens in the world? It means nothing.'

Martin shrugged his shoulders, suddenly nervous. 'I don't know. I'm just interested in what is going on out there, especially after my incarceration. It was deeply unsettling to be in an information vacuum. To have no idea what is going on in the world around you.'

'The papers don't really tell you what is going on,' Fortune said. 'They tell you what others want you to hear. The real important stuff, the really interesting news, never makes it into the public domain. Besides which, nothing ever really changes?'

'Everything changes but nothing changes,' Martin replied softly. He had mixed feelings about the papers. Britain and America's continued presence in Iraq and renewed incursions into Afghanistan filled him with anger. However, there was something eminently satisfying about the trouble the West had gotten itself into; how it had brought itself to a financial Armageddon.

'Speak English,' Fortune hissed at him in annoyance.

Martin paused a second, gathering, his thoughts. He needed to choose his words carefully. He had no wish to antagonise Fortune who was a volatile character. Besides which, years in prison had taught him to be acutely sensitive to the mood swings of his jailers.

'Well, in the six years I was in Guantanamo, the West's pursuit of material gain has single-handedly pushed the world to a greater catastrophe than we have ever been able to achieve with our bombs. I find that slightly ironic given my own struggle. In the meantime, you Americans and my government have continued to bomb my people out of existence. And now you are in Afghanistan.'

'And?' Fortune said. He sounded angry. Maybe it was because Martin had broken their self-imposed vow of silence.

'Well, maybe if left alone, America will destroy itself from the inside out.'

'Just like the Roman Empire, hey.' Fortune grinned.

'You make a joke of everything.'

'You don't get it, do you?"

Martin furrowed his brow.

'America. Us,' Fortune continued. 'America is a crazy, chaotic, cruel place where a lot is wrong and a lot is broken but it is also a place of self-determination, where an individual can achieve anything from nothing. Absolutely anything. Even a black man in The White House with a Muslim name. That is what drives this country. And will continue to drive it. Sure, there will be hiccups along the way. Sometimes we get it horribly wrong. But this country is great at reinvention and rediscovery. It's a mirror image of the human condition.'

Martin sat in silence. It was the most his handler had ever said to him.

'So why are you supporting this?' Martin waved his hand at the farmhouse. 'Won't your actions bring it all tumbling down again?'

'I follow orders,' Fortune said.

Martin laughed before quickly stopping, remembering his prisoner's code—any sign of dissent got you a beating. He dreaded to think what would have happened to him if he had laughed at one of the guards in Guantanamo.

'That's what the Nazis said. You must be able to do better than that.'

'Sometimes to move forward you have to take a few steps back,' Fortune said. 'We are at one of those inflection points.'

Fortune stood up. The conversation was over. He heaved the backpack onto his broad shoulders.

'I'll be back at two. Meet me on the porch. We will be running again this afternoon.'

And then he was gone, leaving Martin sat on the floor, fingering the Jacket thoughtfully.

San Francisco

10 November 2009, 15:10 hours

'As you can see, we've made excellent progress during the last six months. The team has succeeded in reducing the droplet size below 500 microns which means each one now contains less than 30,000 cells. It's the optimum size to pass through the 3D printer head and ensure a good bond with the hydrogel scaffold. We've also found that, at this size, the droplets fuse much faster which dramatically improves the manufacturing time. Believe it or not,' Dr David Jones could barely contain his excitement, 'we've got it down from ten days to just under three.'

'Only three!' Forsyth exclaimed. 'Incredible. Absolutely incredible. David, I can't believe the speed with which you and your team have moved.'

The younger scientist grinned like a Cheshire cat. As did his two colleagues, perched either side of him.

'It's not been easy,' Jones said. 'We've been pulling triple shifts since Christmas but now the droplet size has been solved, we should be able to move much faster. As this rate I could definitely see us being able to manufacture a human kidney by the end of the year.'

'It's a miracle.' Forsyth stood up as if to emphasise the point and paced around the large boardroom, bright eyes flashing with excitement. 'That's exactly what it is. A miracle. Who would have thought that we would be able to engineer a man-made biological structure that contains all the features for cleaning waste products from the blood stream?' He sat down suddenly, leaning forward in his seat, his voice suddenly taking on a conspiratorial tone. 'So, how much more do you need?'

The question caught the scientist off guard.

'Well, I don't know.' Jones stumbled over his words, looking to his two colleagues for assistance. 'It's so difficult to say.'

'Don't be shy, David,' Forsyth smiled reassuringly but Jones suddenly felt anything but. 'Never be shy of asking me what you need.'

'It all depends on the headcount. The team are stretched to the limit. Perhaps with more people, we could accelerate the schedule and get it back on track.'

'How many?' Forsyth said.

'Another ten at the very least.' Doctor David Jones licked his lips. 'Plus, the extra twelve months to keep the current team going.'

'Would that get us through the trials?' Forsyth said.

'Probably not.'

Forsyth winced theatrically, grinning conspiratorially at the only woman in the boardroom. She was dressed in a tight-fitting business suit that accentuated her graceful figure. She glared back at him, which he seemed oblivious to.

'You're looking at an extra five million. At least. Probably ten to survive the trials.'

'We thought nearer eleven,' Jones said.

'I knew there was a number in you, David! Just waiting for mine, were you?' Forsyth winked mischievously. 'OK. Shall we go with yours?'

The scientist nodded slowly.

'Another funding round.' Forsyth leant back in his seat, arms folded. 'I have to be honest with all of you. It's poor timing.'

'We understand. But we're so close. With the extra funds we could be close to releasing tens of thousands of transplantees from the need to take immunosuppressive anti-rejection drugs.'

'Not to mention the billions we will save Medicare,' Dr Sean Adams chipped in.

'I know the benefits well enough, gentlemen,' Forsyth said. 'That's why I invested. It's the tip of the iceberg; the skin regenerative capabilities alone will allow many of our richest clients to knock decades off their appearance without the need to go through painful surgery. That's why I'm forty million in.' Forsyth looked at each one of them. 'And counting, it seems.' There was silence in the conference room which stretched out uncomfortably. Jones couldn't help noticing his benefactor had stopped smiling. Eventually Forsyth spoke.

'You've got your money, gentlemen.'

The three men clenched their fists with relief. Sean Adams actually leapt to his feet and warmly shook his colleague's hands. The woman didn't smile.

'What's the catch, John?' she said.

Her clients fell silent, a puzzled look on their faces.

'Well, there is a small but.' Forsyth held up his thumb and forefinger.

'Go on,' she said.

'The full ratchet provisions will have to be enforced.'

All three men glanced over at their attorney.

'What does he mean?' David Jones said.

Rachel Glover silenced him with a slender finger to her lips.

'I knew it,' she said. 'What are you proposing?'

'This is the second time we've had to advance funds at an effective share value below our previous investment. It'll be costly for your boys.'

'How costly?' Dr Sean Aston cut in.

'I'll let your lovely attorney answer that question,' Forsyth said. 'She negotiated the clause.'

'You wouldn't dare,' Rachel Glover said. 'It'll leave my clients with less than one tenth of one percent of the business.'

The mood in the room suddenly changed. Everyone stared at Forsyth who beamed back.

'John,' David Jones said. 'You wouldn't do that to us. Would you?'

'It's not my decision, boys.' Forsyth smiled sympathetically. 'It's the investors. They're nervous in this current climate. Many of them have seen hundreds and hundreds of millions of dollars wiped off their investment portfolios. Sentiment has hardened.'

'But we've been working on this for twenty years,' Dr Sean Aston said. 'It's our life's work.'

'I understand,' Forsyth said. 'Believe me. If it was my decision, you would have the full eleven with no dilution. I believe in you. Have done since the beginning.'

'But that leaves us with virtually nothing,' David Jones said. 'It was my kid's college fund.'

'You won't be penniless,' Forsyth said. 'One tenth of one percent of five billion still buys a lot of education.'

'If they survive another investment round,' Rachel Glover said.

'Why wouldn't they? Are you telling me this thing could go out beyond Xmas? If so, I need to know.'

'The trials might not be successful,' Rachel Glover said.

'If they aren't, we're all out of a job, I'm afraid.'

'It's a nonstarter, John, and you know it. One more round and my clients effectively own nothing in the company they founded.'

'Which is currently worthless,' Forsyth reminded her.

'Or potentially worth one billion dollars based on your figures.'

'I understand that, Rachel, but at the moment their company has no tangible value.'

'But the potential is huge,' David Jones said.

'That doesn't pay the bills,' Forsyth said. 'If we pulled the plug today, our investment would be worthless and you're asking me to sanction an extra eleven million dollars.'

'But we are so close,' David Jones said.

'Yes, to being shut down,' Forsyth said.

'You wouldn't dare,' Rachel Jones said again.

'Not my decision, I'm afraid.'

'But at that level, our ownership has just evaporated,' David Jones said.

'It will anyway if I don't stump up this money,' Forsyth said. 'It's not unreasonable to receive extra shares to compensate for the additional investment.'

The three men sat there, deflated. Sean Adams looked close to tears.

'You don't need to make a decision now,' Forsyth said. 'Take a few days to talk it over. If you need a week, you've got it. But remember that my hands are tied. The provision was inserted to protect our investment, which from my position, is not looking great. We're running one whole year behind schedule and still have the clinical trials to negotiate. We could lose the entire fifty million.'

Forsyth stood up, the meeting seemingly at an end.

'Rachel. Call me with their decision. Better still, come over. It's been a while since we had dinner.'

The woman scowled at him and avoided his handshake. Her clients were more accommodating.

After they had left, Forsyth pressed the speed dial on his phone.

'It's done. We'll have control by next week, I can guarantee it. They're trapped.'

He cut the connection and summoned his PA from the other room.

'Alicia, do you have the Jakobsdóttir info yet?'

'Yes, sir. It came in this morning. There's not much, I'm afraid. Simple tastes. Almost monastic. Never goes out. No friends. No family. Just works on the Green Ray foundation. We've found an old interview but it's ten years old. In it, she talks about liking dance.'

'Anything I know?'

'Mainly Latin. Salsa. Rumba.'

'OK. Let's go with Rumba. Can you organise some music, please? And cuisine?'

'Couldn't find anything. I'm sorry, sir.'

'OK.' He paused, thinking. 'Keep it simple. Fish will be fine.'

'Yes, sir. Will that be all?'

'For now, yes.'

The phone on his desk suddenly rang. He hit the speaker button.

'I understand Dr Jakobsdóttir is on her way from the airport.'

'So I understand,' Forsyth said.

'Tread carefully, John.' Joseph Ingram's tone was soft but firm. 'She's at breaking point. We need her on side. Gentle probing please. Nothing too forceful.'

'I'll do my best.'

'Very good. And please behave yourself.'

'I can't promise you that, Joseph.'

Forsyth smiled and cut the connection.

600 Montgomery Street, San Francisco

10 November 2009, 17:10 hours

As the limo pulled up to the kerb, the crowd of reporters, TV crews and other members of the world's media surged forward. Several stumbled into the road and the large car narrowly missed a young reporter. As it rolled to a stop, the police line broke and the throng encircled the vehicle, shouting questions and hammering on the blackened windows. It was some minutes before the SFPD were able to force them back behind hastily erected barriers at which point the back door suddenly swung open and the diminutive form of Uma stepped out. Immediately, the mob pressed forward again but this time the barricades held and Uma made a beeline for the doors up ahead, steadfastly ignoring the questions being hurled at her from either side of the hastily erected cordon.

'Dr Jakobsdóttir, is it true you've invented teleportation?'

'Why didn't you release it back in 2003?'

'Doc, look this way. Please.'

'Uma, do you have a boyfriend? Our readers want to know.'

'What does Ethan think of this?'

'What reaction do you have to the Dow crash?'

Above her, the four-sided pyramid curved gracefully upwards some 850 feet into the blue sky, its black latticework of windows glinting brightly against the crushed white quartz which gave the building its famously clean look. As she neared the revolving doors, a man broke free of the police cordon and rushed forward, his microphone outstretched. But he didn't get far. One of Uma's bodyguards caught the man by his arm and, using his momentum, swung him in a low arc onto the sidewalk. He landed with a grunt, his lungs emptying under the force of the impact. Uma grabbed the Secret Service agent by the shoulder.

'Get off him,' she snapped, kneeling to see how the man was. He lay there, clearly winded, blinking up at her, his forehead reddening where the overzealous agent had shoved it against the concrete.

'Dr Jakobsdóttir,' he gasped, desperately trying to recover his breath. 'Dr Jakobsdóttir,' he tried again, feeling his forehead which had begun to swell up. 'You'll be hearing from my lawyers,' he snarled in the direction of the agent who stared down at him impassively.

Uma placed an arm on his shoulder.

'Are you alright?'

The journalist suddenly seemed to notice Uma for the first time, and with it a dawning realisation that he was now the other side of the cordon. He smiled at her and got to his feet.

'Phil Johnson, *Baltimore Reporter*. I have a question for you.' He seemed fully recovered now. 'Have you traded your technology for the position of Energy Secretary?'

Uma was speechless.

'I haven't got time for this nonsense,' she spluttered, pushing past the journalist who ignored the rebuff and took the opportunity to follow her, his microphone inches from her face. Uma brushed it aside but it came back with renewed force, smacking her in the face and causing her to cry out. One of her agents caught the journalist by the shoulder which further inflamed the crowd. The police barrier buckled under the crush of bodies, forcing Uma to quicken her pace. Her security detail closed around her, fending off microphones, sound boom poles and other recording equipment. Uma stumbled and was caught by one of the agents who did not break his stride. Now they were fighting through the mob, the police cordon absorbed by the crush. Uma felt herself falling but as she struggled to stay upright, the roar of voices suddenly went quiet.

They were in the lobby of the Transamerica Pyramid. It was light and airy. Behind her, the crowd of journalists and TV crews pressed against the thick glass like a mob of zombies, silently howling their inane questions at her. Uma exhaled slowly with relief. This was worse than the media scrum that had erupted after Reynolds' disappearance at the Steven F. Udvar-Hazy Center. Even now it made her nervous around crowds. The agent she had reprimanded came up to her, his face red with anger.

'Doctor. Please. Don't interfere again.' It wasn't a request and Uma responded accordingly.

'But you can't manhandle people like that. It's not fair. I remember how it feels.'

'Everybody knows their place,' he said. 'If they step out of line, they get hit. You can't give them an inch. We have to keep the crowd at bay otherwise we can't protect you.'

'But—'

The agent interrupted.

'Now, I suggest we shift. You don't want to be late for your meeting.'

Without waiting for a reply, he turned his back on Uma and marched towards the elevator.

Uma was still smarting from the reprimand five minutes later as she waited in a large conference room on what must have been one of the uppermost floors of the Pyramid. It was the first time in days that she had been alone, away from the constant presence of her security detail. There was no need for an agent up here.

'So, what is it like being the most famous person in the world?'

Uma would have recognised that deep gravelly voice anywhere and turned rather too quickly. John Forsyth was stood by the entrance to the conference room. He was wearing a black polo jumper which accentuated his tight physique. She had forgotten how handsome he was but not his piercing eyes; they seemed to expose her fragility but she found them immensely comforting.

'I had some experience when Reynolds' business crashed but nothing on this scale.'

John Forsyth laughed. A deep baritone blast that brought a smile to Uma's face.

'I'm afraid you'd better get used to it,' he said. 'I don't think it's going to let up for quite some time.'

'Perhaps. The one thing I did learn about the press is that there is always a bigger, better story just around the corner. They will tire eventually and move on.'

'Spoken like a true pro and in the meantime, life goes on,' Forsyth said. 'We have a huge amount of work to deliver on the President's vision. And yours, of course.' He winked at her mischievously and Uma felt herself beginning to blush.

'Shall we start?' was all she could manage.

'Before we do, I would like you to meet that prospective investor I told you about? He's in my office downstairs.'

Uma followed him into a small elevator and one floor later they entered another space similar to the one they had just vacated; it was more compact but mirrored the fabulous views above.

'Uma I would like to introduce you to one of my biggest investors and a close friend of mine,' Forsyth announced. 'We've worked together for many years, particularly in the development of my business interests overseas.'

A man got up from the couch and turned towards them, a broad smile breaking out over his dark features. He embraced Forsyth warmly before turning towards Uma, bowing slightly but never taking his eyes off her. Uma felt compelled to do the same.

'Abdullah Al Rahman, Head of the Re'asat Al Istikhbarat Al A'amah, at your service.'

For a few seconds there was an awkward silence until John Forsyth spoke.

'Abdullah has championed the use of our clinics in the Middle East both by members of the ruling classes but also by rich Europeans and Asians. We've had a very successful partnership over the years.'

'Tell me, Doctor, how is your new appointment going?' Al Rahman said. 'Your press release was quite a shock. Particularly since I just met your mentor only yesterday and he made no mention of it. It is very unlike Ethan to keep something from me.'

'You met up with Ethan?' Uma said. 'I don't understand. He talks to no one. Including me.'

She caught herself, suddenly aware that she had said too much.

'Interesting,' the security chief murmured, exchanging glances with Forsyth. 'Ethan always has time for me. Our association goes back a long way. Way before you, in fact. I have to say he looks very reduced. What have you been doing to him?'

Director Ingram's words came back to Uma forcibly. What had he said? Something to do with Ethan's longstanding connections with Saudi Arabia. The link to terrorism. How much did he know?

'Nothing,' she said, feeling defensive and annoyed in equal measure. Was this another set up? 'He has not been well since his accident.' Another awkward silence ensued. 'Tell me Mr—'

'Please call me Abdullah.'

'Why were you seeing him?' Uma said.

'Funnily enough I wanted to make an investment in Green Ray, although given yesterday's news I think I would prefer to make it in your new teleporter. However, it looks like Uncle Sam has beaten me to it.' He smiled knowingly at Forsyth. 'Tell me, Doctor, how have you managed to keep such an incredible discovery secret for so long? Men would kill to possess such knowledge.'

'They have,' she heard herself saying. 'Lots of people have died.'

'Have they indeed?' His cruel eyes seemed to glisten at the thought. 'That doesn't surprise me. So,' he suddenly clapped his hands sharply, 'my investment. Ethan suggested I take up my request directly with you.'

'How much are you looking to invest?'

'Fifty billion,' he said.

The figure stood before them. Uma couldn't help herself.

'That's a preposterous amount.'

'I believe you know the state of our oil reserves.' Al Rahman glanced at Forsyth who nodded. 'Add in the LEAP effect and you begin to get a sense of the precarious position we find ourselves in. We must start planning for tomorrow. Energy is all we know. It makes sense to be at the cutting edge of alternative energy production in the most consumptive society the world has ever known. The only condition of our investment is absolute secrecy. I don't think it would be very productive to have the whole world know about our little bet.'

'How on earth do we keep that amount quiet?' Uma blurted out.

'Anonymity will help.'

'We'll never get it past the regulators.'

'That won't be a problem,' Al Rahman said. 'Our lawyers have structured an approach which will satisfy the US Government using offshore accounts; we can structure it as a series of fifty separate investments made over the next ten weeks starting as soon as we have addressed the legalese.'

He offered Uma his hand.

She stared at it, her mind foggy with awkward questions.

'Is that it?'

'I do business the old-fashioned way, Doctor. I've known Ethan for many, many years and that is enough for me.'

'I would need to have the Trust look at this in more detail before accepting such a huge investment.'

Al Rahman shrugged dismissively, his hand still extended

'Of course, Doctor. You need to protect yourself.'

Uma slowly took his hand.

'As they say in America, I think we have ourselves a deal.'

Forsyth clapped his hands.

'I think a celebration's in order,' he said, moving over to a long table and removing three glasses from a counter.

'I would love to, John, but I'm due back in Riyadh tomorrow morning. It's a pity we don't have people-to-people leaps, Doctor. Now that would be interesting.'

He smiled knowingly at Uma who frowned. Did he know about that as well? She wouldn't be surprised. Nothing would surprise her anymore.

'Now. I must be gone,' he was already moving towards the doors. 'John. Good to see you as ever. Please ring me about the new clinic for Dubai. Doctor. Thank you for your time. Our New York lawyers will contact you or should we direct them to Alex Yorke?'

Suddenly Uma was alone with John Forsyth who was already breaking open the foil on a huge magnum of champagne.

Transamerica Pyramid, San Francisco

10 November, 2009 17:36 hours

'Tell me, Mr Forsyth,' Uma said.

'John, please call me John.'

Forsyth returned to the long couch where Uma was sat with two more flutes of champagne. He nestled down beside her and took a long sip. Uma did the same, acutely aware of his closeness.

'OK … John. It's been puzzling me since we met at the Oval Office that day. How on earth does a businessman running a chain of self-improvement clinics end up managing the CIAs VC fund?'

'Joseph and I go back a long way. We first met on the Manhattan Project.'

'Did you know my father?' Uma asked without thinking. As the words came out, she felt a pang of anger. It had been a while since she had even thought of him, let alone mentioned his name in conversation. However, it melted away as quickly as it had appeared and Uma found herself drawn back to Forsyth's reply.

'I knew of him,' Forsyth said. 'We were in totally different departments. Despite my scientific background I was assigned to counter-intelligence where I met Joseph. He was an intelligence officer. Our brief was to understand and confuse the Germans about what we were up to. I was seconded to the department to develop and drip feed credible scientific information into the pipeline. After the war ended, I stayed on and was moved into the War Department, the forerunner to the CIA. Joseph and I worked together for over twenty years, basically doing similar things to what we had done during the war. I was attached to the division that dealt with behavioural science. It was fascinating work and hugely related to what the CIA were doing at the time around anticipating the Russians' next move. The problem was that things moved too slowly so I branched out.'

'Into self-help?' Uma couldn't hide the sarcasm in her voice.

'Don't be like that,' Forsyth said, winking at her. 'It was called personal success back then but, importantly, there was very little thinking at the time, except from people like Napoleon Hill. I picked up where he had left off. Have you read his book, *Think and grow rich*?'

Uma frowned in mock annoyance.

'No. It's a peculiarly American pastime.'

'What?' Forsyth said. 'Growing rich. We don't have a monopoly on that.'

'True but you have to admit you're all obsessed with self-improvement. We Icelandics know our place in the world.'

Forsyth shrugged.

'Spoken like a true European with the self-confidence instilled by millenniums of history to fall back on. Americans don't have that legacy so it's only right that the cult of the individual should pervade our thinking. Hill's genius was creating a formula that puts success in reach of the average person. What gave it credibility was that he based his work on interviewing and understanding how the truly successful people of his day had made their fortunes. Men like Carnegie and Emerson. I did the same thing forty years later, except I focused on the business leaders of my day. I spoke to business leaders like Walt Disney, Sam Walton, Samuel K. Reynolds I.'

Uma shuddered. An image of the old man standing on the wings of his bi-plane rose in her mind, quickly followed by Ethan, his muscled torso silhouetted against the roaring flames.

'Yes, your nemesis' grandfather,' Forsyth said. 'He was a brilliant man. Very driven, if I remember correctly, and would allow nothing to get in his way. Absolutely nothing. I'm glad he wasn't around to see the collapse of Reynolds Air. It would have killed him to see his life's work washed away in that scandal. An ugly business.'

Uma felt herself her blinking rapidly, trying to control her tears. An image of Reynolds' face rose unbidden; he was standing in a room looking quizzically at the floor, a slight frown on his face like a child who had just witnessed the death throes of an ant he had stepped on. Part disgust. Part excitement. But also detached. Except it wasn't an ant; it was her sister lying in a pool of fresh blood, her life ripped apart by a bullet from Uma's hand. *Dear God.* She had killed her sister in the name of LEAP and she had allowed herself to be bullied into releasing it to the world for fear of not seeing through her quest to green the earth. *What had she become?* Reynolds's laughed at her. He was speaking; saying something which she couldn't quite hear. Something about his grandaddy. How he would never have allowed such sentimentality to obscure his path to riches and power. Uma didn't doubt it. She had seen the arsenal where Ethan lived; that was the mark of someone unimpressed by man's humanity. They were simply ants to him, to be herded and controlled and to follow his bidding. Crushed, if they didn't. Uma bit her lip and the pain cut through the vision. She was back in the Pyramid, a handsome grey-haired man was talking to her, framed by the most wonderful view of San Francisco.

'Forgive me,' Forsyth said gently. 'You lost some dear friends as a result of that man's actions.'

His empathy surprised Uma. It was a while since she'd met a man so at ease with his emotions.

'It's OK. Please. Continue,' Uma said, suddenly aware of their close proximity again. His flashing eyes, the soft scent of his cologne and their shoulders almost touching on the deep couch. It felt good.

'Are you sure?' he said, his bright blue eyes boring into her.

Uma nodded self-consciously, quickly draining her glass to break their spell.

'Well, I didn't stop at self-help,' Forsyth started up again. 'I soon realised that once you enabled someone to become successful, they needed help staying there. Initially it was around physical wellbeing: you know, gyms, spas, eating guidance. However, more recently we have expanded into other areas too: plastic surgery, private health care, gene therapy. We now have clinics all over the world that effectively cater for people's wellbeing.'

'But just for those who can afford it.'

'Of course,' Forsyth said, smiling. 'They're an obvious target. The top one percent of Americans earn pretty much one quarter of all income in the States. It's a virtuous self-sustaining circle.'

'I still don't understand how you got involved with Ingram.'

'Simple,' Forsyth said. 'I've spent the last forty years dealing with VCs, first as a borrower but more lately as head of my own fund. Joseph recognised that I could help him run the CIA's.'

'Why would the CIA need a VC fund?'

'As we discussed in The White House, the government are not immune to the costs of developing leading edge technology, particularly in the world of spying. Staying ahead is supremely expensive. That's where the fund comes in; we identify, invest in and nurture smaller and promising companies and once we have our technology, we float. We retain an equity stake to control who the technology goes to and also get a return on our investment. We are effectively self-financing. It's all very straightforward.'

'But don't you lose your edge when that happens?'

Forsyth shrugged. 'We lose either way. If we do it ourselves, we cannot attract the best brains to the task because they are cashing share options in Silicon Valley. Alternatively, we have to buy it which is supremely expensive and we have no control over who it goes to or the direction it takes. With a fund we get the best of both worlds.'

'Why are you in charge of this, then? LEAP is not really CIA territory, is it?'

'My guess is that the President's rewarding Ingram for bringing him LEAP. Plus, he needs to move fast, particularly given the current market and the need to revive his Presidency.'

Uma frowned. 'Revive? He's been in power less than a year.'

'True but in politics that can be a career,' Forsyth said. 'The writing's already on the wall; the deficit has ballooned and will continue to do so, which will hamstring his own agenda. LEAP has the chance to boost his popularity significantly. It ticks all the boxes: job generative, green and energy independence. In short, it can benefit a lot of Americans very quickly. However, he needs to move fast. He knows what will happen if too many people get their hands on this which is why he needs to capitalise now. That's where I come in; I'm used to dealing commercially, in the real world and, importantly, have the knowhow to raise the funds and roll it out quickly.'

Uma recoiled as if she had been stung.

'No one mentioned commercialisation. That wasn't part of the deal.'

Forsyth smiled encouragingly.

'Understood, but it's the only way—'

'No one spoke to me,' she said more forcefully, trying to control her anger. Forsyth said nothing. Instead, he sat there smiling calmly. 'When exactly were you going to tell me? The ink is barely dry and already you've breached my agreement.'

Forsyth seemed unphased.

'I have to confess I don't understand your reluctance. This puts you in a great position.'

'You sound just like Ingram,' she said. 'Why can't the government pay for it?'

'Simple,' Forsyth said. 'Speed.'

'I don't understand?'

'To roll out LEAP effectively on a hub system that mirrors the current distribution one in place, will cost, conservatively, three hundred fifty billion. Maybe more. After what Congress has recently stumped up to rescue the financial system and are likely to pay for the health agenda that the President wants to pursue, he's rightly concerned that it will never get past the Hill. That would be disastrous. You've already seen the impact on the Dow; it's fallen nearly twenty percent since the announcement. We need to stabilise that situation and quickly, otherwise it will only get worse.'

'But nobody told me about this,' Uma said, a great wave of fatigue rolling over her.

'I'm telling you now,' Forsyth said.

'And you question my reluctance. This is precisely why I wanted nothing to do with Ingram.'

'Welcome to politics,' Forsyth said. 'It's a world of compromise. Nobody ever gets everything they want.'

'I don't like to compromise,' Uma said, lying back on the couch, very close to tears. She felt like a boxer receiving one knockout blow after another. Except there was no respite. They kept raining down long after the bell should have sounded. The feeling felt familiar. 'Surely there must be another way?'

'Beats me,' Forsyth shrugged. 'Besides which, the deal Ingram brokered is a good one. You get to advance your green agenda as the head of one of the most powerful departments in the US. LEAP only adds to that.'

Uma didn't respond. There didn't seem to be any point.

'Can I ask a question?' Forsyth said.

'Fire away.'

'If you're so opposed to the release of LEAP, why did you agree to it? It's not as if you're destitute. You still head up the biggest fund in the world, pushing one of the most effective green agendas on record.'

'You were there,' she said. 'I was blackmailed.'

'You could have weathered that,' Forsyth said, with a dismissive wave of his hand. 'There're plenty of PR firms who could have rebuffed Ingram's spoiling tactics.'

Uma looked up sharply. He seemed to know an awful lot.

'So, what's the real reason,' Forsyth said, nodding encouragingly. Uma shrugged. It didn't really matter anymore. Besides which, she found herself suddenly trusting this man. Why, she couldn't explain, particularly given his connection to Ingram. Maybe it was the champagne, but she suddenly felt less inhibited about opening up to him.

'Partly fear, I guess,' Uma said. 'Of losing Green Ray after six years hard work. It was something I threw myself into after LEAP.' The words seemed to come unbidden; Uma couldn't stop them. 'I also thought it was a way to redeem myself, from … from having caused the deaths of so many people. I owe them that at the very least.'

Had she just said that? She stared at the empty flute. She wanted to tell him so much more but all her senses warned her not to. Forsyth nodded sympathetically.

'I told you things get complicated up here.' Forsyth leant towards her conspiratorially. 'So, where does that leave us? I have a feeling this thing is bigger than you or me. Or the President for that matter. You're welcome to fight it, but my experience has proven that the best thing to do is roll with it. Do you have any suggestions?'

Uma stared at him in confusion. She felt uneasy but wasn't sure why. Maybe it was the mysterious Arab.

'Feeling a little trapped, are we?' Forsyth said. 'I remember the feeling well; the day I floated my first company I lost control of my baby. Suddenly, people were telling me what to do. I had to totally change my mindset or get out.'

'I couldn't in 2003,' Uma said. 'I don't see how I can now.' *Worse still*, she thought to herself, *I'm all alone this time round*. Although the man beside her seemed so genuine, sat there so attentively, his bright eyes gleaming with energy and intelligence.

'Nonsense,' Forsyth said. 'There are many ways you can still contribute and with my guidance I will protect you from the worst of it. What I would like to do over the next few days is to present my thinking on the hub-and-spoke system and how existing companies with distribution can access the technology through licences. It's a well-trodden path so the markets will react favourably to the approach and, more importantly, will be able to place a value on it. We can use the money to build the infrastructure, charge them an up-front fee for licensing it and take royalties on what is transported. Probably value based. It will be a self-sustaining system.'

Uma felt her mind drifting. There seemed so much to do: The Electro, the new Energy Plan, relating it to her own efforts with Green Ray. She was due to meet some oil lobbyists next week pushing for guidance on offshore drilling. There was a draft tax rebate scheme for energy efficiency to approve. The budget for next year was due shortly. The list was endless. It seemed overwhelming. And now LEAP was being rolled out. Without her input. She had so much power but no control. Forsyth was talking animatedly. He looked totally in control.

'We need to return some calm to the markets. Can I suggest tomorrow morning? Your office has agreed to move your schedule and I've already arranged a press conference where we can make a joint statement about our ideas. That should work for now.'

'I guess,' was all she could say.

'Enough about work,' Forsyth suddenly announced, jumping to his feet. 'Are you hungry?'

Uma nodded dumbly, her mind still struggling to process Forsyth's news. Everything was moving so quickly. Too quickly. She felt like a bystander.

'Excellent. I've had my chef prepare some delicacies that you might be familiar with.'

Uma got unsteadily to her feet and followed him into another room where a small table was laid for two. A waiter appeared and seated them both. Another followed with wine. After they'd left, Forsyth leant forward towards her.

'So, what's the story with you and the great Ethan Rae?'

The question caught Uma off guard and for a moment all she could see was Ethan's gaunt face, his features contorted in religious fervour, the fire raging all around him. She felt herself bristling slightly, suddenly annoyed by the tone Forsyth was using. The loaded nature of his question. Was it professional or personal? She couldn't tell anymore. Nor did she know how to respond. She stared at the handsome face opposite, his lightly tanned skin, slightly wrinkled. His kind mouth and, of course, his eyes, twinkling with suppressed merriment and energy. And something else she hadn't seen before; a wisdom borne of experience and knowledge. She wanted so badly to trust him. To let him into her confidence.

'Do you do this often?' Another stupid question. Her mind was all over the place. A whirl of fleeting thoughts. Forsyth didn't seem to notice though.

'What?'

'All this,' Uma nodded her head at the table. 'The soft lights. The romantic dinner setting. It all looks very, planned.'

'Occasionally,' he replied with a grin. 'I have needs just like the next man. Even one of my advanced years.'

'Does that explain all the ex-Mrs Forsyths?'

'Have you been checking me out?'

'I was curious, that's all. Especially after our meeting in the Oval Office.'

'Me too.'

'I can see. No one has gone to this much trouble in years.'

'I'm pleased you appreciate it,' Forsyth said. 'You're a very private person. I was worried there would be nothing to impress you with.'

'Ah, so you've been spying on me.'

'Guilty as charged.'

Uma flushed, suddenly embarrassed. It was true. She couldn't remember the last time someone had paid her this much attention. She felt detached from it, though, as if it was happening to someone else and she was watching it unfold from afar. Forsyth stared at her intently, smiling. She was forced to drop her gaze. He didn't seem at all perturbed by his efforts.

'Would you like to dance?'

The suddenness of the question caught her off guard.

'What, now?' she said.

'Why not? It's a beautiful evening.'

'Are you trying to seduce me, Mr Forsyth?'

'Now whatever put that thought in your head?' He stood up, offering her his hand. She hesitated, suddenly feeling guilty. About what?

'It's been so long. I hardly remember how.'

'Don't worry, I'll be gentle. I promise.'

She took his hand and rose from the couch effortlessly, as if she was floating. Around her the room filled with soft music; a light jazz tune which sounded familiar. Where had she heard that before? Again, she felt disconnected from what was happening. Had she drunk that much? No, it wasn't the alcohol; it was something far more subtle, as if she was balanced on the edge of sleep, floating in that delicate place of wakefulness and blissful dreams. Her limbs felt heavy yet wonderfully light. Her mouth felt cottony although she wasn't thirsty. Uma felt Forsyth's arms around her, his hands firmly on her hips, his groin pressed hard against hers, his lips inches from her eyes. It felt intimate but not uncomfortable. In fact, she felt completely at ease in his embrace. Secure and in control. It felt good.

'You move well,' Uma said concentrating on her footwork. It must have been years since she had danced, let alone with a man. Especially one like Forsyth who moved like someone half his age, leading her as the music dictated but always in control. Uma was content to surrender to his lead, lost in the moment. They finally sat down and she felt flushed, unsure whether it was her lack of practice or something else.

'Where did you learn to dance like this?' she gasped, collapsing onto the couch.

'I've danced all my life, from when I was a kid. It was all we had at the time. That and music. I now dance to keep fit. I have no choice.'

Uma looked questioningly at him.

'Occupational hazard I'm afraid.'

'What, keeping fit?'

'This is what people are buying into.' He patted his flat stomach. 'The promise of something better. Something out of most people's grasp.'

'Sounds a little superficial to me,' she blurted out, almost unaware she had said the words before he was answering her.

'It is, but we live in an age of skin deep, especially in the States. All this has to be right before you can reach any deeper. It would make it a lot harder to spread my message if I looked like—'

'Hell!'

Forsyth laughed.

'Not quite but if I was bald and fat with a bad back, I can assure you that my clients would not be so keen to own a piece of what I promise.'

'And I'm sure you make a lot of money from their desire to join your exclusive little club.'

'Of course. That's why it's so rewarding,' Forsyth said smiling. 'I don't run a charity. I run a for-profit business.'

'For yourself,' Uma said.

'Guilty as charged.' Forsyth held up his arms in mock surrender. 'And my shareholders, of course.'

Uma was silent. He seemed so certain of everything. Unlike her. She admired him for that, if not his ideology. As if reading her thoughts, he continued.

'We're not so different, you and I.'

Uma felt herself bristle. But again, it was more to do with the impact on her state of complete relaxation than with the words themselves. Or were the two connected? She couldn't be sure.

'How so?' she said. 'Green Ray is for the good of everyone and I don't profit from the fund personally. Its entire existence is geared to reversing global warming. I can't think of a more selfless pursuit.'

'You miss my point. It's a noble cause, I'll grant you that, but if I was running Green Ray, LEAP would be at the heart of the charity. With the capital at your disposal, you could have released it to the world without any help. And avoided the situation you find yourself in.'

'I tried once,' she heard herself saying, 'but nothing good ever came out of that technology.'

'Joseph has told me of your personal loss. However, you must appreciate the apparent contradiction of your actions. From the outside it looks like the ultimate act of selfishness, especially given what you're looking to achieve through Green Ray.'

In her detached state, Forsyth's words suddenly made sense. There was no judgement in them, just a simple statement of fact. And with them came clarity. Was she wrong to hold back LEAP? To keep it for herself? It seemed a selfish act when he put it like that. But what about everyone who had died? Those considerations were inescapable for her. But also, deeply selfish. She should have risen above them. Put them aside for the greater good of others. Reynolds would not have been troubled by such weak-minded doubt. Nor would men like John Forsyth. So certain of his place in the world. Full of conviction.

'Perhaps you are right. I don't know anymore.'

'Maybe. It's easy for me to sit here and pontificate about what you should and shouldn't do. I haven't lost my sister to it. My friends. Ethan Rae.'

Yes, Ethan. Caught in his existential crisis and unable to move forward. Unwilling to help her or himself. Crippled by self-doubt, just like her. She was nothing like John Forsyth. He was assured; she was weak. He was full of confidence whilst she was fragile and consumed with uncertainty. John Forsyth shifted slightly in his seat, pushing aside his plate. He looked solemn but not for long, as his face lit up.

'There is way too much gravity in this room,' he said. 'We need to clear it out and I know of one sure way to do that.' He leapt to his feet and as he came round the table towards her, the music started up again. This time, a slightly slower tempo and before she knew it, Uma was in his arms again and this time she felt herself surrender completely to the music. And to him and his certainty. She felt herself staring up into his eyes and this time she didn't look away. They swallowed her up in their intensity, stripping away her uncertainty. This time she didn't resist. So that when he kissed her, she felt herself melting into his lips and responding to his soft hands and gentle caresses. She moaned slightly as his lips brushed her neck.

'God that feels good.'

Had she just said that?

She felt his fingers unbuttoning her blouse, caressing her breasts. She gasped as his tongue softly traced alternate circles around both nipples. As they hardened, she pushed herself towards him, enjoying his low moan as she felt the hard outline of his body against hers. She felt her skirt fall to the floor. Stockings gently rolled away. Until she was standing naked in front of him, never once questioning why he was fully clothed. Totally lost in the exquisite pleasure of his tongue and hands. At some point she felt herself being lifted in his strong arms. Of moving upwards. In an elevator perhaps. Light silk sheets caressed her skin and finally his hard body against hers. It felt cool against her own and she abandoned herself completely to him, as she knew she would from the moment she had first set eyes on him.

Washington, DC

11 November 2009, 08:32 hours

The black Cadillac limousine was travelling fast, very fast, sweeping majestically over the Theodore Roosevelt Memorial Bridge in the half light of the early morning. At this time of day, I-66 was deserted, allowing Special Agent Andrew Marks to open up the huge 7.4 litre NorthStar V8 engine, barely slowing as he hit Constitution Avenue. At 18 feet it was the longest vehicle in the fleet and also the heaviest; nearly five tonnes of armour-plated metal, eight inches thick in places, requiring a custom-made heavy-duty truck platform courtesy of GMCs Topkick range. Each door alone weighed as much as the cabin door of a 757. Behind his six-inch-thick bulletproof glass, Marks adjusted his headset as the signal from the two outriders in front of him disappeared for a second. It happened occasionally and he had been reliably informed that it was something to do with interference from nearby National airport. As usual, the link was instantly restored but the momentary loss made him nervous, as he was trained to be in the event of anything out of the ordinary. He quickly checked in with the two black Cadillac Escalades travelling behind him but the reassuring drawl of Agent Coombes and then Agent Alex permitted him a brief smile. He began to relax. Within two minutes they would be inside the security cordon around The White House and his precious cargo would be someone else's problem. It was hot inside the sealed cabin despite the cool morning and Marks cursed under his breath. They had reportedly spent ten million dollars developing this car and hadn't been able to get the air right; it was either too hot or too cold. He pressed a button on the steering wheel and his window retracted just three inches before locking. Moving parts meant security weaknesses and windows were no exception. His was the only one that opened.

To his right, the steps below the Doric columns of the Lincoln Memorial were already dotted with early morning visitors, no doubt looking to beat the crowds that would soon converge on the modern-day temple, before trudging along the Reflecting Pool past the World War II Memorial to marvel at DCs tallest structure, the Washington Monument. Less than 200 feet away he could just see the curve of the Vietnam Memorial wall and, as he did nearly every day, Marks offered a silent prayer to his fallen father, one of nearly sixty thousand names inscribed on the black granite blocks in memory of the men lost or killed in action. For a second, he was fourteen again, perched on his uncle's shoulders, tracing the unfamiliar words with his young fingers. The memory made his fist curl tightly around the steering wheel. He had made a silent vow that day to honour the dead man he had never met through service of his own. Ten years later he had made good on the pledge and twenty-eight years later he still visited the solemn slabs every week as his work detail allowed.

As he neared 17th Street NW, Marks slowed the heavy limo and prepared to turn. Two advanced outriders had already stationed themselves at the lights to block any oncoming traffic but there was no need. The streets were empty, although some early morning cars were already parked at the corner, no doubt sightseers making good their afternoon getaway. Each vehicle would have been scanned and logged as they entered DC, their details triangulated with the Department of Motor Vehicles, local police and the FBI's online database at the National Crime Information Center in Clarksburg, West Virginia. If anything unusual was picked up they would have been impounded or the route altered. Marks completed the manoeuvre, barely moving the gyro level on the dashboard. In fact, if his passenger was even aware of the turn he would have been surprised. That was how it was meant to be. He had no desire to be remembered as the one who upset the early morning coffee. As the limo straightened out, it smoothly picked up speed again and Marks pulled north along 17th St NW towards his final destination. Up ahead he could see more outriders slowing to instruct the Secret Service guards to lower the bollards that would take him onto State Place NW and then The White House. To his left, scaffolding encased the Corcoran Gallery of Art as workmen unloaded a large pick-up filled with yet more iron tubes for the higher floors. There were two large transit vans parked behind them, the front bumper of one almost touching the rear bumper of the second. As he scanned them, a wisp of smoke drifted from the rear. An exhaust? That didn't make sense and he reached for his ear device.

'Central Control. I'm picking up some unusual activity on the west side of 17th St. by the gallery.'

There was a short pause as the agent studied the video feed real time.

'We've got it. Proceed as planned.'

Marks wasn't convinced. The van was blocked in so why leave the engine running? As the Cadillac drew level, he realised the fumes were not from the bottom of the van but halfway up, clearly leaking from the door which was slightly ajar. As the thought formed, the world turned white as the white van suddenly disintegrated. The explosion flipped the steel-plated monster twice as it smashed through the wrought-iron fence onto the grassy area surrounding the 1st Division Memorial. As the car came to rest, the last thing Marks remembered seeing were the gold wings of the angel atop the column of the World War monument. They were slowly fluttering into life, growing in size until they filled his whole vision. Majestically, the giant seraph lifted itself from the stone plinth and swept towards him. As he closed his eyes, Marks realised the angel's face was his father's and he was smiling warmly, his arms reaching out towards him in greeting.

Transamerica Pyramid

11 November 2009, 07:23

The silence felt strange. There was no talking, no noise, no agents, no people demanding her time, forcing her into corners or pushing her down cul-de-sacs of their choosing. But then what had happened last night? It felt like an out of body experience. As if the woman who had succumbed to Forsyth wasn't actually her but a different person who had surrendered to his charm and his clumsy attempts to seduce her. He had even admitted as much and she had allowed it to happen. Had she drunk that much? Her head felt heavy; her body soporific. Uma struggled out of bed and walked over to the window. The room was even more remarkable in the bright sunlight of the morning. It was much smaller than she had remembered from last night. The pyramid shape at the top of the tower simply didn't allow for more than one room and this unusual design, along with its high elevation, meant that Uma was presented with a 360-degree panoramic view of the San Francisco skyline.

To her far right the Bay Bridge curved round past Treasure Island, carrying its daily traffic from Oakland and the huge suburbs of Richmond and Berkeley beyond. Directly ahead she could just glimpse the tiny island of Alcatraz nestling in the misty waters of San Francisco Bay. Beyond, the much larger Angel Island State Park was clearly visible as was the familiar silhouette of Mount Tamalpais, which, along with its cousins, formed part of the California Coast Ranges through which Route 101 pushed north towards Petaluma, Santa Rosa, Ukiah and ... eventually Ethan. She closed her eyes tightly, feeling the faint stirrings of guilt. *For what?* She'd done nothing wrong and angrily pushed the feeling aside as she continued searching the landscape, trying to ignore the silhouette of her former partner framed in the inferno of the fire. Her gaze settled on the familiar orange vermilion towers spanning the Golden Gate. At this time of day, rolling fog banks from the ocean had absorbed the six-lane highway completely so that all she could see were the rusty art deco towers floating on the morning mist like two huge sentinels guarding the Bay from the mighty Pacific beyond.

It was no good, she couldn't rid Ethan from her mind and with him came all the old self-doubt: about LEAP, her sister, her capitulation to the Americans. The list was endless. Where had all the certainty gone from the previous evening? Had it all been a dream? A hallucination spun by a clever trickster, intent on getting her onside and into bed. Or both. But Forsyth's words still made so much sense. Was she asking for too much? She wanted to believe him so badly and just go along with what they wanted; to silently take the deal and advance Green Ray, not to mention American environmental policy. It seemed too good to be true when he had put it to her the previous night but in the cold light of day all the old reservations returned. And they couldn't be ignored. She turned back to the bed. On the side table, her clothes were laid out neatly. They had been cleaned and pressed which she found herself resenting hugely, as if she was a hotel guest or another conquest, passing through his life for one night. She got dressed and sat on the bed, waiting for Forsyth? What was she doing? He didn't own her; she could go when she chose, except she didn't know where to go.

There was a light knock on the door and Uma hurriedly stood up as one of the waiters from the previous evening cracked the door, before coughing politely.

'Mr Forsyth sent me,' the man said. 'He wondered whether you could come down immediately. There's reports coming in from the East coast and it's not good.'

Situation Room, The White House

11 November 2009, 11:45 hours

'At approximately 8:35 this morning, a huge roadside bomb exploded in downtown DC less than one half mile from The White House, where the President was in residence with his young family. It would appear that a government limo was involved in the blast but currently, it's not clear who was in the car. However, The White House Press Office has confirmed that none of the President's Executive Team were involved. Preliminary reports reveal some fatalities, including workmen who were erecting scaffolding on the outside of the Corcoran art gallery and the driver of the limousine. Fortunately, the streets were deserted at this time of the day, otherwise the human toll could have been much greater. As the view from our roving copter shows, the explosion was devastating, causing extensive damage to the adjacent art gallery which has collapsed in on itself. Just in front of the building you can make out the crater which we have measured at nearly thirty feet wide and almost eight feet deep. According to our experts, that would have required a device upwards of five thousand pounds given that the roads in DC are reinforced with over eighteen inches of asphalt and concrete. To put that into context, Timothy McVeigh's bomb, that destroyed the Alfred P. Murrah Federal Building in downtown Oklahoma City on April 19, 1995, was nearly seven thousand pounds in weight. Now we're going to leave the scene for a few minutes to speak with our reporter inside The White House. Sam ...'

Chief of Staff, Mike Jarvis, cut the sound and turned back to face the room. To his right was the President and opposite, George C. Brown. Beside the director of National Intelligence were two men he didn't recognise and to his immediate left the Head of the Secret Service, Jed Groves. Around him, White House staffers were a blur of activity. He had never seen it so busy.

'What's the latest casualty count?'

'Well, Mr President,' he said, taking his seat, 'it's very difficult to determine that. So far, we've recovered six bodies: the driver of the limo, four workmen and one of the outriders, a Sergeant Ronald Giff. In addition, we've twelve wounded—five agents, all of whom were in the two Escalades, but it's mainly breaks and sprains. They were far enough away not to catch the full force of the blast which looks like it was designed to blow outwards onto the street. In addition, we have six more agents all of whom were covering the State Place NW entrance off of 17th Street. Their injuries are rather more severe—first-degree burns, some covering fifty percent of their bodies. Three have lost limbs. Four are in critical condition. In addition, we have twenty confirmed missing, all of them workmen. The blast knocked out a huge chunk of the downstairs floor of the gallery and the floors above collapsed in on themselves. Most of the workmen were inside.'

'Sweet Mother of God,' muttered the President. 'When can I visit the injured?'

'As soon as we've finished here, Mr President.'

'And Joseph?'

Before Mike Jarvis could respond, the doors to the situation room swung open and Joseph Ingram limped in, his right arm heavily bandaged and secured to his chest by a tight sling. The President leapt to his feet, as did the Chief of Staff, rounding on the tall man.

'Joseph. Thank the Lord you're alive,' the President said, as he embraced the Director of the CIA, who winced slightly.

'I'm OK, sir. A few bumps and sprains, that's all.'

'Unbelievable. You must be the luckiest man alive.'

'The car did its job. Almost,' Ingram said, turning to the Head of the Secret Service. 'Jed, I'm so sorry about Agent Marks. May his soul rest in peace. Please accept my heartfelt condolences. He was a good man. I know how it feels to lose agents in the field.'

He bowed his head for a second and stared at the carpet of the Situation Room. He looked for all intents and purposes as if he was praying.

'Joseph, what are you doing here? You should be resting,' the President said, squeezing Ingram's good arm gently.

'I can't, sir. It wouldn't be right. American lives were lost today.'

'I understand, Joseph. We all feel the same way.'

'With respect, sir,' he said grimly, 'I'm not sure you do. My job is to prevent this happening. The CIA is at the heart of intelligence gathering and the fact that this occurred without our knowhow is simply unacceptable. We failed you, the Executive and the people of America today.'

'Come, Joseph, let's not start a post-mortem at this stage. We have more pressing matters to attend to.'

'Understood, sir, but I will not rest until those responsible for this terrible atrocity are behind bars.'

'Well said, Joseph. Well said. Nor will any of us.' The President stood aside and motioned for Ingram to sit down. 'The de-brief has just started. Please, take a seat.'

'If everyone agrees?' The Director of the CIA paused beside the President, who had already sat down. 'I don't want to breach protocol.'

George C. Brown glowered at the thinly veiled slight but said nothing.

'Nonsense, it's during moments like this that everyone needs to set their differences aside and do what is best for the country. Come. Sit.'

It wasn't a request anymore and the lanky director acquiesced, taking his seat beside the Head of the Secret Service.

'OK, Jed. What have you got for me?' the President said.

'At this stage of the investigation, very little more than we have released to the press. There are some—'

'Might I intercede, sir?' George C. Brown said.

The President nodded.

'Given the national security implications of the attack, I think this falls under my jurisdiction. Not only that, but the explosion occurred on 17th St NW, which isn't inside The White House perimeter and is, therefore, not a Secret Service matter.'

Jed Groves shifted in his seat. 'True, but the clear target of the blast was one of my cars. Not only that,' he continued, mimicking the director of National Intelligence, 'you aren't the one scraping your men off the street this morning.'

'Jed, may I remind you that I head up the Intelligence Community of which the Secret Service is but one component.'

'With respect,' Jed Groves said, 'you've no direct line reporting over my division.'

'I'm not trying to pull rank on you, Jed,' Brown said, his face turning a deeper shade of purple in the dimly lit room. 'All I'm interested in is co-ordinating the intelligence follow up, so that I might better advise the President on what sort of threat we are facing here.'

'Quite frankly, I don't care who runs this show,' Mike Jarvis said. 'However, I do care that we need to get some answers fast, given that we've just experienced the most devastating attack on US soil since 9/11, all less than ninety yards from this office. Now then, give me answers. What was the target and who did it? Two very straightforward questions.'

'I might be able to help on that front,' Brown said. 'We've already compiled some very preliminary intelligence on who might be responsible. This is Agent Brad Golder. He's with the Office of Terrorism Analysis and has identified two possible perpetrators.'

The young agent cleared his throat, suddenly aware that he was the focus of all the attention in the dimly lit room. He shifted some papers on the table in front of him and began.

'Well ... er ... I mean ... uhm. The—'

'Look, son,' the President said gently. 'We understand this is short notice. Whatever you have will be useful.'

The younger man took a deep breath and tried again.

'Thank you, Mr President. We're considering two possible groups at the moment: an Al-Qaida cell and a right-wing group. I will cover the latter whilst Agent Maughan,' he acknowledged the man sat next to him, 'will cover the external threat.'

He cleared his throat and began to read.

'Since June 2008 there has been an upsurge in white supremacists and anti-government militia in mainland America. According to the latest stats, the number of cells has more than tripled in just twelve months and now stands at 512, of which 127 possess paramilitary capabilities. The two most active are White Rights and Black Death. Both herald from Montana.'

'I don't wish to interrupt your flow, Agent Golder but if I needed a history lesson I would have Googled 'right wing extremist groups', the Chief of Staff interrupted again. 'Now, get to the point please. Give me something more substantive.'

'Yes, sir. I propose to.' The agent shuffled uneasily in his seat and resumed. 'The relevance of these two groups to this morning's events became an issue after last January's inauguration. Since then, we believe they are responsible for at least eight deaths. All of them ... uhm ... blacks.'

'But why these two, son? I would imagine the vast majority of these groups object to the African American population.'

'Two reasons. They both have a paramilitary arm. White Right's is five strong, Black Death's, a little bigger. The big problem is that, earlier this month, they both disappeared off the radar.'

'How do you just lose two cells?' the Chief of Staff said, 'particularly given the clear security threat you've so eloquently painted.'

'Well, sir, it's not that unusual for these types of groups to vanish, especially the gun-toters. It happened last July when they both disappeared into the Bitter Root Mountains to play their war games. However, what is slightly unusual this time round is the time of year and the length of time. Two weeks is unheard of and that's why we're discussing them.'

'Is this their modus operandi?' The President sounded doubtful.

'Roadside bombs?'

'No, camping in Bitter Root,' Mike Jarvis cut in.

'Not really, sir,' the young agent said, reddening. 'To date, it has been all shootings but our agents in Billings did discover a large cache of ammonium nitrate last month, which might be linked to Black Death.'

'Let me get this right,' Mike Jarvis said. 'We've got two paramilitary groups that have gone to ground, one of which might be running a bomb-making factory and you've lost track of them.'

'Yes, sir. That's about right,' replied the agent quietly.

Mike Jarvis expelled a deep breath, shaking his head in disbelief. 'Is that all you've got?'

'I'm afraid so, sir.'

A heavy burden of silence descended on the group, whilst around them, intelligence personnel, White House staffers and Secret Service agents studiously ignored the heightening tension in the room.

'What about the Al-Qaeda threat?' the President said.

'Well, sir,' the agent said, clearly relieved to be off the hook, 'let me introduce you to Agent—'

'If you please, Brad,' Brown interrupted. 'This is Agent Joe Maughan with the CIA. He has some preliminary intelligence from an Al-Qaeda perspective.'

'Good morning, gentlemen,' Maughan began confidently. 'As you're all aware, roadside bombs have become the preferred method of attack against coalition forces in both Afghanistan and Iraq during the last twelve months, and with good reason. They're extremely effective and, currently, the number one cause of death amongst coalition troops in both—'

'Here we go again. George,' Jed Groves cut in, 'it already sounds like you've got nothing.'

'Actually, sir, we do,' Maughan said. 'I was merely proposing that, given our experiences abroad, an Al-Qaeda cell is more than capable of carrying out this type of attack. Two years ago, I would have said not. Roadside bombs were all power but no punch. That's all changed. The poundage has decreased but they've become vastly more effective; the 17th St. bomb reflects that trend and I'd have to say that if Director Ingram had been travelling in his usual ride, I don't think he would be sat at this table.'

'I have Jed to thank for that,' Ingram muttered. 'He asked me to road test the reserve Presidential limo.'

'Do you think the President was the target?' Mike Jarvis directed his question at the young agent.

'Impossible to say at the moment, sir. We need more information.'

'I might be able to help there,' Jed Groves said. 'Son, do you mind?' He pointedly ignored George C. Brown who looked like he was going to explode.

The young agent nodded, and the Head of the Secret Service conferred with a uniformed sergeant sitting at the head of the table. She typed quickly and the main screen behind her flickered into life.

'Gentlemen, this is some preliminary footage from the offside limo camera, along with selected CCTV cuts of relevant activity in the area, during the two hours prior to detonation.'

As the Head of the Secret Service spoke, a remarkably clear shot of 17th St. West appeared.

'This is the view from inside the limo, just before the explosion,' Jed Groves said. 'We've had it slowed down, so you can pick up the detail. As you can see. the car is just passing the Corcoran art gallery. See the two transit vans; concentrate on the first one.'

Over loudspeakers, the men gathered around the table could hear the exchange between Agent Marks and Central Control. The video suddenly slowed to one quarter speed as the camera drew level with the white van.

'See that smoke,' Jed Groves said.

The fumes were clearly visible.

'It's coming from the rear of the van, through the door which is ajar. Now our preliminary thinking is that the bomb was on a rudimentary charge which was burning out to ignite the explosives inside the van. If so, that would suggest the involvement of the Presidential limousine was purely coincidental.'

Jed Groves nodded again and the video jumped to a new screen.

'Now, this one is taken an hour earlier from a CCTV camera on the corner of E St. NW and 17th.'

The black and white image was much grainier and at first nothing happened, but as they watched, the scaffolding truck came into view followed by a white transit van. Both parked up. A man could clearly be seen getting out of the van. He was tall, of heavy build and wearing a thick jacket with the collar pulled high. In combination with the baseball cap pulled low, it was impossible to see any part of his face. He rounded the front of the vehicle and disappeared into the gallery. Several minutes later the second transit came into view and parked up behind the first. The driver also went into the gallery.

'Gentlemen, a number of things,' Jed Groves said. 'As yet, we don't have a clear ID of either driver. We've checked the plates and they're both registered to Boyd Construction, the contractor on the art gallery. It's an incorporated company operating out of Virginia and all three trucks had security clearance. However, we've just received confirmation from the Virginia State Police that one of their patrol cars was called to a gas station off I-395 to investigate a DB in the men's rest room. They've identified it as the driver of the first transit van. He was en route from the parking garage where the vans are kept overnight.'

'DB?'

'Sorry, Mr President, Dead Body,' Jed Groves said. 'The driver was dead.'

'Joseph,' the President said. 'What's your take on this?'

'Why wasn't I shown these videos?' Brown cut in, before Ingram had a chance to respond.

'No one's seen them, George,' the Head of the Secret Service responded. 'There hasn't been time. We only received them ten minutes ago.'

'Sorry, Jed, I would have to disagree with you,' Ingram said, ignoring the interruption. 'The coincidence of the limo passing at the precise moment the truck exploded is just too great. I don't know what that smoke is, but I would hazard a pretty accurate guess that the van was detonated remotely. Have we checked the radio frequencies around The White House?'

'It's being done right now,' Jed Groves said.

'Agent—' the President spoke.

'Agent Maughan, sir.'

'Right, Agent Maughan. Am I right in saying that there was no unusual overseas activity on the intelligence radar?'

'I'm probably best placed to answer that question, Mr President,' Brown interrupted, before Maughan had a chance to respond.

'As you know, I receive daily briefings from the heads of all seventeen members of the Intelligence Community. As of yesterday, we had no indication of any specific threat in the DC area.'

'This just gets better and better,' the Chief of Staff said, his voice laced with a mixture of sarcasm and anger. 'Let me summarise the sum total of our knowledge so far. A five-thousand-pound road-side bomb was driven in broad daylight to within a half mile of The White House and exploded right under our noses, and we had no indication that it was going to happen and no clue as to who perpetrated it. That's just great.' He stood up and started pacing. 'Just great. The combined might of our intelligence service with an annual budget in excess of fifty billion dollars and this is the best you can do.'

'I resent the insinuation, Mike,' Brown said.

'Really,' Mike Jarvis said. 'The whole point of your appointment back in 2004 was to coordinate inter-agency activity better and prevent another attack. From where I'm sat, that does not appear to be happening.'

'How can it?' Brown exploded, his face plum with rage. 'This has been an accident waiting to happen for six years, as I've repeatedly reminded you and your predecessors.'

'Not good enough, George,' Mike Jarvis said. 'Not good enough. It's beginning to wear a bit thin. You were given control of the National Intelligence Program budget. You can therefore direct the focus of the intelligence activities.'

'It's not enough,' Brown said. 'Never has been and never will be. I don't even have operational control over any of the Intelligence branches. Look at this.' He nodded at Jed Groves, who glared back. 'This is what I have to deal with on a daily basis.'

'That doesn't—'

'Gentlemen. Enough,' the President bellowed, slamming his fist down onto the table. The low hubbub of activity in the room suddenly stopped and everyone turned to face the head of the table who looked totally unphased by his uncharacteristic outburst. 'Good. Now is not the time to start a finger-pointing exercise. Seven American citizens have been murdered in cold blood this morning with the likelihood of many more to follow. Now, unless you have something to say that contributes to the task at hand, I don't want to hear about it.'

There was silence around the table.

'Anyone?'

'Mr President, I think we might be missing one line of enquiry.' Everyone at the table turned to look at Joseph Ingram who sat there, unsmiling, stroking his injured arm. 'Apologies, George. I appreciate that this is your show but I believe we have a possible line of enquiry that you've not as yet touched upon?'

The Director of National Intelligence frowned at Joseph Ingram, who continued.

'What about the two Guantanamo Bay detainees who disappeared outside of Miami?'

'What about them?' George C. Brown said, his mind whirring, trying to spot Ingram's trap.

'Well, according to my security briefing, we considered them to be a clear and substantial threat.'

'And?'

'And nothing,' Ingram said. 'You instructed me to transfer surveillance of all released detainees over to the Department of Homeland Security once they landed on American soil.'

Too late, George C. Brown realised where this was going. 'That's right,' he managed, his cheeks turning into eggplants as he tried to control his response, acutely aware of the President's warning.

'What's happened since? Did you ever locate their whereabouts?'

'Come on, Joseph. You know the drill,' Brown said, glancing over at the President. 'We receive twenty thousand non-specific threats per month through the department.'

'Understood. I receive a similar number a week through my field agents,' Ingram countered. 'I just recall that, in the briefing, we felt that these two presented a real threat given their backgrounds and then they kill their handlers en route from Homestead up to Miami Airport.'

Brown couldn't contain himself any longer. 'It's nothing to do with you,' he thundered at Ingram. 'Your brief ended in Cuba.'

'Two federal officers died at the hands of two suspected terrorists just released from Guantanamo. I have a right—'

Joseph Ingram never finished his sentence. He was drowned out by a distant boom, like thunder, that caused every standing person in the room to stumble as the ground beneath them shook. Part of the suspended ceiling crashed onto the table, enveloping the two agents next to George C. Brown in a cloud of white dust. Two huge video screens behind the President slowly toppled forward off the wall, before crashing onto the carpet in a plume of showering sparks. Before anyone could recover their feet, the room was plunged into total darkness just as the doors burst open and pricks of light suddenly pierced the dusty gloom.

'The President. Protect the President.' Mike Jarvis' shell-shocked voice could be heard screaming above the shouts that surrounded the head of the table.

Shafts of light zipped through the shadows, resting on scared faces for a millisecond before continuing the search for their Commander in Chief.

Brown, his normally ruddy face was a deathly white pall.

Agent Maughan, a ghostly apparition.

Jed Groves, his right eye thick with blood.

Then the President's dazed features suddenly appeared in one beam, then another and yet another, until his face was ablaze with furtive light beams anxiously searching for signs of injury.

'The eagle is secure. I repeat. The eagle is secure.' A disembodied voice cut through the dark.

'What in God's name is happening?'

'We don't know, sir.' The voice was calm and reassuring, as it was trained to be.

'Please, you need to come with us. We have a lockdown.'

'Where are you taking me?'

'The bunker, Mr President. The bunker.'

Within seconds, the beams disappeared. Just as suddenly, the main lights flickered back into life, leaving dazed men and women staring at the empty seat. Through the open doors, the hallway boiled with people all heading towards the northwest entrance.

San Francisco

'Apologies, ladies and gentlemen, for the early morning start but, given the Dow's reaction to last week's announcement, we wanted to follow up with a more detailed statement on how we plan to roll LEAP out. I understand there is a bigger news story playing out on the East coast and consequently we will keep this as short as possible. I don't think my co-presenter needs any introduction,' Forsyth said, nodding at Uma. 'And also—'

'Mr Forsyth, would the Secretary of Energy like—'

'Please, I would ask you not to interrupt,' Forsyth said. 'We understand the media interest in this story and, therefore, I would like to read out a short statement that will hopefully answer some of the questions you have been bombarding us with over the last few days. In addition, you should also be in possession of a detailed press pack that describes our plans in more detail. Following this announcement there will be an opportunity for the more scientifically minded of you to have one-hour sessions with members of the LEAP team so you can understand the technology in more detail. Finally, we have allowed thirty minutes at the end to give everyone an opportunity to question both myself and Secretary Jakobsdóttir.'

Uma looked out into the foyer of the Transamerica Pyramid where a sea of faces was crammed ten deep, as the mob from yesterday continued to jostle for position. Beside her, Forsyth stood confidently, looking assured and fresh. When she had gone downstairs, he had barely acknowledged her, let alone made reference to the previous evening. Instead, he had quickly filled her in on the bomb blast in DC before inviting her into the elevator for what seemed like an infinite journey down into the foyer. He had chatted away amiably about what he was going to say. Uma had stood there in simmering astonishment. Was she his conquest now dispensed with once the chase had ended? Well, two could play at that game. She would not give him the satisfaction of her discomfort and instead returned the pleasantries, matching him smile for smile. Grin for grin. Despite her anger, the logic of his words from the night before continued to gnaw away at her even as they both entered the press conference.

'I'd like to start with some more concrete information on LEAP. Contrary to popular belief swirling around the media we will not be using this technology to transport foodstuffs, livestock or people. Only inanimate objects. That's not to say we couldn't transport food but concerns have already been expressed by certain organisations about the safety of doing so. We are therefore going to conduct full trials over the next twelve months in conjunction with the FDA to reassure ourselves and others about the safety of LEAP. Similarly, the transportation of livestock and, in time, human beings, whilst a close reality, is still not fully finalised. So, for the time being, it is just objects. The second myth I would like to dispel is that the government is not going to monopolise LEAP. We fully intend to commercialise it and will shortly launch a controlling corporation, fifteen percent owned by the government and fifty-one percent by Green Ray. The rest will be available for public ownership and our timetable for that agenda is very aggressive; we are looking at an initial IPO within three months from today's date. In terms of the operating model, it's very straightforward. Our goal is to get this technology out to as many businesses as quickly as possible. To achieve this, LEAP will be licensed out to any US company that passes a few simple tests and, once cleared, they will be allowed to use LEAP to transport their goods. We will own and maintain the assembler and disassembler units and charge a small fee based on the value of the items being transported. At this moment in time that fee has not been determined but it will cover our costs for maintenance. In addition, given the global nature of business, we will allow any US company to station LEAP units abroad. In time we will also start licensing LEAP to other governments.'

Forsyth looked up again. He was finished and the waiting horde wasted no time in bombarding the front dais with questions.

'Secretary Jakobsdóttir, six years ago, following the events down at the Stephen F. Udvar Center in Virginia, you denied any involvement in or knowledge of what Reynolds was up to regarding teleportation, yet here you are presenting your own version of the technology. Can you expand?'

Uma took a deep breath. She wasn't ready for this. Had in fact feared this moment since her confrontation with Ingram, that once the press got hold of the story and its clear inconsistencies, they would hound her relentlessly until they got answers. There was no going back now, though.

'As I said at the time and as I would like to repeat now, my only in- volvement with Reynolds was to promote my environmental agenda. I was merely hijacking his announcement by bringing to people's at- tention what mankind was doing to the planet. What better way than at the centenary celebration of flight. It was and remains one of the most potent symbols of man's systematic and wholesale destruction of the atmosphere.'

'Are you prepared to go on record that you had nothing to do with Reynolds' disappearance or his claims to have discovered teleporta- tion.'

'Look, guys, I know what you are trying to do. There is no smoking gun here. As I have repeatedly said since 17th December 2003, I was not connected to R.A. I thought Reynolds was crazy; a rich kid, pulling some elaborate stunt to promote his failing airline. To be honest, I didn't pay much attention to what was going on. I was pretty focused on my own stunt, as it were. And I might add, it worked. In the immediate aftermath of his disappearance, I received twenty million hits a day on www.theraceison.com'

'How come you have suddenly solved teleportation? The coincidence is simply too great.'

'You can thank Ethan Rae for that; he was developing the technology, not me or Reynolds, for that matter. RA stole LEAP from Rae Enterprises. Well before Mr Rae's accident, he had already liquidated his entire portfolio of companies and transferred the proceeds into Green Ray. That included his work on LEAP. I have merely continued where Ethan left off. It seemed the obvious thing to do and entirely in keeping with my green agenda through Green Ray.'

'But only last week you announced a multibillion dollar investment in a new electric car. Isn't that at odds with LEAP, given its potential for transporting people.

'Not really,' Uma shot back, aware of Forsyth at her side. 'The two are perfectly complementary. Despite Mr Forsyth's optimistic projections, I don't believe people will be leaping anywhere, anytime soon. We will still need clean transportation. That's where Green Ray comes in.

'And how come your version of LEAP works and Reynolds' so patently didn't?'

'Reynolds's stole the technology from Mr Rae and tried to LEAP himself so he could save RA. If ever proof was needed that LEAP doesn't work for humans, he provided it. We're still no closer to solving that part of the equation. Maybe one day but not today.'

'Why did Mr Rae transfer it all to you?'

'I have no idea. You'll have to ask Mr Rae yourself.'

'That's unlikely. He's a virtual recluse. No one's seen him for years.'

'Best of luck then,' Uma said.

'Do you ever see him?'

'Occasionally.'

'How close are you to transporting people?'

'It's difficult to say,' Uma said. 'The base technology is there but as you saw with Reynolds, we've a long way to go. As with all breakthroughs of this nature there is still a lot we don't understand. There are a huge range of tests to perform before we start transporting people here, there and everywhere.'

'So, you are denying that you have already transported a human being.'

'Don't put words in my mouth. I am saying no such thing. Once we are in a position to make an announcement, you will be the first to know.'

'How would you respond to claims that you traded the technology for the position of Energy Secretary?'

'With the derision it deserves. Please remember that the government approached me. They offered me the position. I never asked for it.'

'But neither did you decline it.'

'Why would I?' Uma said, relieved that the questioning had strayed from Reynolds. 'My motivation here has, is and always will be very straightforward. I want to reverse global warming as quickly as possible. Anything that helps move me closer to realising that vision is attractive. The position of Energy Secretary gives me the opportunity to directly influence the energy policy of the largest polluter on the planet.'

'But you understand the concern? Without LEAP you are just a philanthropist, albeit the most powerful one on the globe.'

'As I said, the government approached me. Read into it what you will.'

'We intend to, Doctor, and our take is that the government traded political favours to gain a hold on the greatest advancement in science since the atom was split back in the 40s.'

Uma shrugged and remained silent.

A mobile phone rang towards the back of the foyer.

'Secretary, some would say that you are now too powerful. You run Green Ray. You also dictate US Energy Policy and own LEAP.'

If only they knew the truth, Uma thought.

'I would agree that I'm in a powerful position but that's not my motivation. If it was, I would have kept LEAP to myself. Since day one I have followed the same guiding principles behind Green Ray and that is to create a framework that introduces this technology to the widest number of people and businesses at the lowest possible price. For me, involving the US Government at this stage will further that aim.'

Other phones were beginning to ring and the previously silent foyer was beginning to fill with excited whispers. One or two journalists began to leave, speaking urgently into phones clasped to their ears. As they moved towards the back, they paused to confer with colleagues. Within seconds, the whispers morphed into a low buzz of chatter. Uma looked over at Forsyth who was also staring at his phone. He glanced up, a look of astonishment etched across his handsome face and came towards the podium.

'Ladies and gentlemen, I'm afraid we will have to cut the press conference short. As many of you are clearly beginning to hear, it would appear that there has been another bombing near The White House.'

An excited buzz swept the foyer.

'Initial reports suggest that it was a suicide bomber at the north entrance.'

The Oval Office, Washington DC

12 November 2009, 07:10 hours

Sunlight streamed through the graceful curve of windows that looked out onto frosty gardens and it was hard to believe the nearby horrors that had been visited less than five hundred feet away. The room was peaceful, though unnaturally so after the chaos of the morning. Over the years it had learnt its role well, reflecting and deflecting the mood of its powerful occupant as the occasion demanded. Like a second skin it could draw on over a century's experience as silent witness to decisions that had shaped not only America but the entire world: Theodore Roosevelt's love for the environment; Wilson's pivotal decision to enter World War I; Roosevelt's New Deal; Truman's nuclear holocaust; Kennedy's Bay of Pigs; Johnson's Vietnam; Nixon's Watergate; Reagan's Revolution; Bush's Desert Storm; and, of course, Clinton's indiscretions. And 9/11. Moments in history that showed mankind in all its contradictory complexity: the heights of its achievements; the appetite of its greed; the depths of its cruelty; its jaw-dropping ingenuity; its inhuman savagery; its unparalleled capacity for kindness; and its rank stupidity. However, the room never judged. Never criticised. It just was. Always available, day and night, across the decades, offering solidity and strength in support of one man's lonely job. A quiet oasis at the epicentre of the decisions that had shaped the human race for the previous 100 years.

That man was currently silent. Still. Reading. The room wielded its power effortlessly. No one spoke. It looked like they were waiting for something, although everyone seemed lost in thought. Jed Groves, Head of the Secret Service, was nearest, a small plaster above his eye, the only evidence of his inner pain. His fallen agents. His White House security breached like never before. His only consolation sat before him, a living embodiment of his agency's mission. Beside him, Joseph Ingram's face was unreadable, his lanky frame draped over the cream couch. Opposite, Mike Jarvis silently considered the implications for his boss' ambitious agenda that had promised everyone so much on the campaign trail but was slowly being derailed by one intractable problem after another: a crippling budget deficit, the banking crisis, a shrinking economy and an unwinnable war. LEAP had offered some respite but only until this morning when two explosions had shattered the fragile illusion of progress. He glanced at his Commander in Chief, outwardly calm and exuding quiet confidence. The room was at work.

'I can't say I'm surprised by his decision,' the President said, handing the short press release to Jed Groves who placed George C. Brown's resignation announcement on the table. Everyone stared at it.

'Agreed but the timing couldn't be worse,' Jed Groves said.

'That's George for you,' Ingram said. 'Politics always came first.'

'Sir, his position was untenable. The car bomb was bad enough but to have someone blow himself up in sight of The White House during a lockdown was ...' Mike Jarvis seemed lost for words.

'Unacceptable,' the President said.

'Jed's right, sir,' Ingram said. 'It was unacceptable. He had to go.'

'Talking of which.' Jed Groves cleared his throat and paused momentarily before continuing. 'I would also like to tender my resignation, sir. Whilst intelligence was certainly lacking, there are elements of my security detail that simply didn't work as—'

'Stop right there, Jed,' the President cut him off. 'Director Brown's resignation is enough for one day. You're not going anywhere.'

'I'm sorry, sir. The press will not accept that. Questions are already being asked about security, particularly in the period after the first blast. That's supposed to be the safest time. To have someone walk onto The White House lawn is ... also unacceptable. As Head of the Secret Service, it has placed me in an untenable position. I can't continue,' he said with finality.

'The press is not running the country,' the President said.

'But they shape public opinion and, as has been proved time and again, that's all that matters during a crisis.'

'I won't accept it, Jed,' the President replied, shaking his head. 'Simply won't accept it.'

'Have you seen the front of The White House?' Jed Groves said. 'It looks like a Bagdad mosque. That is the image being beamed on a loop around the world at the moment. That is the message everyone is receiving loud and clear. That the US can't protect its seat of government, not just once but twice. Hardly an endorsement of the Secret Service's credentials.'

'Today is not the day to fall on your sword.'

Groves made to speak but the President quietened him with a small movement of his hand.

'Regardless of whose fault this is, as the Head of the Secret Service you should and will take responsibility. Just not today. If you go so soon after George, what sort of message will that be sending to the world? A nascent administration collapsing in on itself before it has even got out of the blocks. Reconsider your position in three weeks but for the time being I need you here in charge of White House security and cooperating with the other intelligence agencies to understand who did this and why.'

The President stared at the Head of the Secret Service calmly, waiting for a response. The room was silent, waiting too. Jed Groves didn't meet his gaze. Instead, he stared at the carpet for what seemed like an age and eventually shrugged his shoulders in resignation.

'You've got your three weeks, sir.'

'Good. I appreciate your loyalty, Jed.' The President smiled warmly at him before turning to his Chief of Staff.

'Mike. What's next?'

'We need to respond to George's resignation notice with some suggestions as to who is going to co-ordinate the inter-agency response moving forward?'

'Ah, yes, Joseph,' the President said, directing his smile at the Head of the CIA. 'I was hoping you would consider the position.'

Joseph Ingram stirred for the first time. He unwrapped his long legs and turned slowly towards the President, wincing slightly as he did so. Since entering the room, he had barely said a word and Mike Jarvis wondered whether he had suffered more harm during the first attack than he was letting on.

'You know my feelings on this matter, Mr President.'

'I do but now I'm giving you the opportunity to do something about them.'

'That position is a poisoned chalice and you know it.'

'All the more reason to accept it,' the President said. 'If anyone can turn it around, Joseph, you can.'

The Director of the CIA remained quiet for a moment before answering.

'Mr President, I'm honoured by your consideration but I'm going to have to decline on this occasion.'

'And why would that be? I thought you would welcome a return to a role you performed so effectively during the 90s.'

'Actually, sir, not that well, as my critics will be quick to point out were I to accept. I am not sure the Administration needs that level of scrutiny given what has just happened today.'

'We could weather that Joseph and you know it,' the President said. 'Come on, give me your real reasons.'

'May I speak frankly?' Ingram said.

'Do you speak any other way?'

'Mr President, as you well know there is a procedural issue,' Ingram said. 'The Intelligence Reform and Terrorism Prevention Act prohibits the current Head of the CIA acting as the DNI at the same time.'

'My presumption was that you would resign your position first.'

'Why would I want to?' Ingram sounded almost incredulous.

'Well, for a start, you would become my principal adviser on intelligence matters relating to national security, not to mention, overseeing all seventeen intelligence agencies' activities.'

'With respect, Mr President, when I have something to say, I call you direct. As for the other carrot, the position has no credibility amongst any of the agencies, including mine.'

'George had no credibility,' the President said. 'He was a career politician. You are different.'

'As flattering as that sounds, I would have to disagree,' Ingram said. 'George and I had many differences but there was one area that we were in complete agreement on. The DNI was a knee-jerk reaction by the 9/11 Commission and a poorly thought through position with far too many compromises. George knew that and today's attacks are evidence of his weakness to adequately lead or manage the performance of the US Intelligence Community. Why would I want to take that on?'

'To improve the situation. The other heads have enormous respect for you. You understand the intelligence community like no one else I know. Surely that will be a step in the right direction.'

'They knew me before 9/11 and we failed to stop that happening. Why would a second run change anything?'

'What would make you reconsider?' Mike Jarvis posed the question like a threat.

'Give me things that I know I can't have,' Ingram said.

'Like what?' the President said.

'For a start, operational and budgetary control over each agency.'

'Is that all?' Mike Jarvis said.

'Actually, no,' Ingram said. 'For it to work, I would also need control over the National Security Agency, the National Reconnaissance Office and the National Geospatial-Intelligence Agency.'

Mike Jarvis laughed, partly out of exasperation. 'The Defence Department would never allow that and you know it.'

'As I've already said, Mike,' Ingram said. 'But it's the only way to co-ordinate all the activities properly and prevent intelligence leakage.'

The President sat forward, already following the thread of Ingram's suggestion through. 'Joseph, we'd need legislation to make those changes. And you know that we'd would never get it through both houses.'

'In the current climate, I would agree with you,' Ingram said. 'However, until we do, then we risk continued intelligence failings and eventually something will get through.'

'Something has got through.'

'What I mean by that—'

'We know what you mean, Joseph,' the President said wearily. 'Do you think sentiment will have changed after today?'

'I'm not best placed to answer that,' Ingram said, nodding at Mike Jarvis. 'Ask your Chief of Staff.'

'Given our legislative programme, particularly health care, I would have to agree with Joseph,' Mike Jarvis said.

'But Mike, that's no reason for not trying,' the President said. 'We have to deal with what is thrown at us real time.'

'True, but let's pursue achievable aims. We've got another ten months to make an impact. After that, local elections will be upon us and then we are into our re-election schedule. Trying to reorganise the entire intelligence community, even if it is off the back of these attacks, will be well-nigh impossible and require so much horse trading that we'll have nothing left to pursue health, not to mention the environment and education.'

The President sat still for a few moments. The room didn't move and eventually he nodded, seemingly in acquiescence.

'Joseph, I appreciate your candour as always,' the President said. 'Mike, can you have Jim advise the White Press that we'll be putting together a list of candidates to replace Mike. In the meantime, I need a short list of ten suitable candidates.'

'Certainly, sir,' Mike Jarvis said, glancing at Ingram, a hint of relief in his voice.

'OK. Let's move on,' the President said. 'Can someone give me an update on the casualties?'

Mike Jarvis leafed through some papers on his lap.

'Good news and bad, I'm afraid, sir. The death toll from the first blast is rising. We have thirty confirmed missing from the four crews that Boyd Construction had working the Sunday shift in the gallery. All are presumed dead.'

'And the second?'

'We were lucky. Very lucky indeed. No one was actually injured in the second blast. Except the bomber that is.'

'Any idea how he got through?'

'Yes, sir,' Mike Jarvis said. 'From what we can piece together, there were two of them. Both dressed as Secret Service agents. One was injured, or at least pretending to be. Witness accounts suggest that he appeared to be coming in and out of consciousness, which is how he got through the first two perimeter checks—everyone thought he was injured in the first blast. His ID was correct.'

'And the second bomber? If that's what he was?'

'Disappeared off the face of the earth.'

'Any CCTV images?'

'We're working on it.'

'If I may, Mr President.'

'Go ahead, Jed.'

'Given what has just happened, I would like to propose moving you up to Camp David.'

'Absolutely not,' the President said.

'Hear him out, Mr President,' Mike Jarvis said.

'You're supporting this, Mike?' the President said.

'I am. Camp David is one of the most secure facilities in the world. It's remote, heavily guarded and all personnel have undergone a Yankee White security background check. Until we have a better handle on this situation, that's the best place to be. We can control the situation far better from there.'

'Out of the question. I'm not going to hide away like a rat in a drainpipe. That's what they would really like.' The President stood up and marched over to the window where the bright sunlight streamed into the office. He turned back to the seated men. 'No,' he announced with finality. 'I'm not going to do it.'

'Sir, I am not sure that you have much choice,' Mike Jarvis said. 'This is out of your hands now.'

'What do you mean? Of course, I've a choice.'

'White House security has been breached,' Mike Jarvis said. 'Not once but twice in the space of an hour. At the moment we have no idea who or why and more importantly when they will try again. Until we have established that fact, it is my recommendation that at best you retreat to Camp David and, at the very least, cancel all travel and public engagements until we have a better handle on this.'

'No chance,' the President said. 'I'm not going to cancel anything. As far as I am concerned, it's business as usual. If I do what you are suggesting then they, whoever they are, have won. They can claim a victory that they have made the leader of the most powerful nation on earth run and hide like a scared rabbit. What sort of message is that to send out to the world? If there are security implications as a result of that decision, then so be it. If that exposes me to danger, then so be it. I have long ago come to terms with the threat. If I hadn't, then I would never have run for public office in the first place.'

'But, sir,' Jed Groves said, 'you also have a responsibility to protect the office of the President and that means not doing anything irre-sponsible that might put you in harm's way.'

'Jed, I'm well aware of your position in this matter and if you had your way, I would be kept in a secure bunker for the duration of my Presidency. However, we need to balance that against the need to govern effectively. We have talked about this. You know my position.'

Jed Groves tried a different tack. 'Could we at least compromise and have you attend Camp David for the next week whilst we review security at The White House?'

'No,' the President said. 'If anything, I need to be more visible over the next few days.'

'What did you have in mind, Mr President?' Mike Jarvis said, frowning at Jed Groves and motioning with both hands for him to stop the line of questioning. He knew when his boss had made his mind up and there was no sense in arguing. It was time to move onto other things.

'Visit the families of the men lost in the first attack and those of the two officers killed in pursuit of the second.'

Jed Groves couldn't contain himself. 'Mr President, you have a responsibility to—'

'I have a responsibility to the people of this country,' the President said. 'I serve them, not the Presidency. Not the Executive. Not Big Business. Just ordinary Americans who work hard every day of their lives to make a living. I ran on that ticket. I am the people and I will not desert them at the first sniff of danger. If I do, then I have failed. If I have to hide out in a secure compound, then I have failed. I might as well resign the Presidency.'

'But, sir,' Jed Groves tried again even as Mike Jarvis mouthed, 'No' in his direction.

'Mr President, might I make a suggestion?'

'Please, Joseph. Go ahead, so long as it's not more pressure to hide out in a secure bunker.'

'No, sir. It's a compromise,' Ingram said.

'I'm listening.'

'What about LEAP?'

There was silence in the room. The Chief of Staff broke it.

'What about it?'

'We can use it to our advantage,' Ingram said.

'The President's not a product.'

'Joseph, be careful,' the President warned.

'They both have security clearance,' Ingram said. 'Besides which, it makes sense, sir.'

'What's going on here?' Mike Jarvis said, looking questioningly back and forth between the President and the Director of the CIA.

'What Joseph is trying to intimate is that we are slightly more advanced with LEAP than we have let on.'

'How advanced, sir?' Mike Jarvis said.

'Do you recall the discovery of Reynolds?' the President said.

'Yes.'

'Let's say he didn't fly there.'

'I knew it,' the Chief of Staff responded excitedly, jumping to his feet. 'I knew something wasn't right. How long have we known?'

'About three weeks,' the President said.

'How safe is it?' Mike Jarvis said.

'As far as we can tell, person-to-person leaps have been a proven technology for over twenty years now.'

Mike Jarvis and Jed Groves both stared at Joseph Ingram.

'Twenty years!' they both responded in unison.

The President laughed out loud. 'It's not often I get to see that look on your faces. Joseph, will you bring Jed and Mike up to date.'

Ingram nodded and for the next ten minutes the two men sat in silence as the Head of the CIA took them through the discovery of Reynolds' body, Uma's letter, and her subsequent confirmation and acquiescence to the use of LEAP. When he had finally finished, the room was silent, waiting.

Jed Groves spoke first.

'Where would you locate it?'

'Here in The White House, with stations at Camp David and wherever else the President needed to travel,' Ingram said.

'We have mobile units?' the President said.

'Nearly, sir. We have a number of teams working round the clock. It should speed up significantly now we have the access codes.'

'How can we proceed after what we agreed with Secretary Jakobsdóttir?' the President said.

'I'll take care of that,' Ingram said. 'I'm sure she'll understand.'

'And this morning's announcement?' the President said. 'It'll seem very contradictory.'

'We don't make it public,' Ingram said. 'As far as everyone is concerned, it's business as usual. That's what you want, sir, isn't it? You continue to do what you do best.'

'But what does it change?' Mike Jarvis said. 'The President will still be exposed at each venue he visits.'

'Jed, explain to Mike the significance of LEAP for the security detail.'

'Joseph's right, Mike,' Jed Groves said. 'The most dangerous part of the detail is travel which is when we're at our most vulnerable. There are too many variables to consider. Destinations are easier because we know those weeks in advance and can make the necessary arrangements. If we remove the travel element, we can control ninety percent of the risks.'

'What about the security detail?' Mike Jarvis said to Ingram. 'Would they travel with the President?'

'Jed?'

'I don't see why not?'

'What about the press?' Mike Jarvis said. 'How do you keep this quiet?'

'Keep them out of it for now,' Ingram said. 'After today's attacks, security is going to be ramped sky high. We could alter any number of protocols without too much trouble.'

'Any more questions, gentlemen?' Ingram said with a sense of finality.

'Yes.' The President had been quiet during the exchange, but now he spoke, his face grave. 'Joseph, tread carefully with Uma. I gave her my word.'

'All under control, sir. John's been working on her. Besides which, I'm sure, given this morning's events, she'll be more than happy to use LEAP in whatever way is necessary to protect the Presidency.'

'Go easy on her, Joseph. Go easy on her.'

Bethesda, Maryland, USA

14 November 2009, 11:32 hours

The black Chevrolet Suburban moved slowly along the road, its tyres crackling on the frozen gravel. Every so often the vehicle gently rolled to a stop, its blackened windows reflecting menacingly back at the furtive glances from behind dirty drapes, before edging onto the next house. Suddenly, the huge 6.0 litre V8 roared its approval as the SUV performed a U-turn on the narrow street and pulled up outside a nondescript condominium. The vehicle sat silently, a thin snake of exhaust the only sign of life. Five minutes passed. The neighbourhood began to relax back into its squalid torpor just as both doors cracked open and two men emerged. They made a beeline for the scruffy condo, their shiny black brogues stepping cautiously on the slippery path leading up to its front door. Under the faded porch, Special Agent Nick Barnes tried the bell, once, twice and then three times but the interior remained still. He tried the handle, which didn't budge, so he dropped to one knee, inserted something into the lock and turned. He tried again, this time successfully, and they both disappeared inside.

'Oh man, what a stench,' complained Special Agent Chris Moon. 'It smells like something died in here.'

He stopped mid-sentence, silenced by his partner who was already across the hallway come living room.

'Are you sure this is the place?' Chris Moon whispered. 'It's a complete dump.'

Nick Barnes stood surveying the cheap furnishings which were littered with the debris of half-eaten take outs and empty bottles. But what struck him most was the absence of daily clutter that normally provided clues to a person's life, their pastimes, family and friends. Whoever lived here was just passing through. They had just arrived or were about to leave. He peered through a half-open doorway. It was dark inside, courtesy of thick curtains pulled tightly shut but through the gloom he could make out a queen-sized bed against the far wall. Other than a chest of drawers, it was the only visible piece of furniture in the room which was also littered with the turmoil of a chaotic and temporary existence. The stench of stale alcohol mixed with sweat was overwhelming. His partner tapped him on the shoulder and he moved towards the bathroom which was even filthier. The shower curtain was pulled closed and in one corner a pile of dirty white lab coats was piled high. Otherwise, the tiny room was also empty, save for a pair of thick glasses lying on the grimy tiles. As he stooped to recover the cheap spectacles, a low moan came from behind the cover. He slowly drew the thin plastic back.

'Chris, he's in here.'

His partner joined him and they both stood, staring at a short fat man, sound asleep in the small tub which couldn't have measured more than five feet in length. He was fully dressed in a white grey lab coat and cradled a half-empty bottle of Heaven Hill whiskey.

'He's out cold.'

'Well, wake him.'

Nick Barnes reached down and spun the shower tap, pulling back quickly so it wouldn't dampen his black suit but he needn't have worried. A trickle of water squirted weakly onto the sleeping figure's forehead. It had the desired effect, though. Almost immediately, the man started coughing and sputtering as if he had been dunked in a barrel of ice-cold water. Professor Crouch's eyes opened, staring up at the two men above him. He blinked twice and then turned away from them, instinctively shielding the bottle.

'Mine,' he said loudly.

'We're not after your booze, old man. But you do need to come with us.' Without waiting for a response, Nick Barnes bent down and grabbed Crouch's belt, lifting him bodily out of the bath as if a small child, before carrying him into the first bedroom and depositing him onto the bed.

'Do you have anything cleaner to wear? We need you to work.'

Crouch sat up, hugging the bottle like a teddy bear.

'I'm not in school today,' he croaked hoarsely. 'Only Mondays through Wednesdays.' His face suddenly dropped. 'Have I slept in again?'

He sounded fearful.

'Don't worry, old timer,' Barnes said. 'There's no school today. It's Friday.'

Crouch still looked panic stricken.

'You won't lose your job,' Barnes said, marvelling at how the dishevelled figure held down a teaching job. The truth was, he couldn't. Since his humiliation at the Steven F. Udvar-Hazy Center in Virginia, Reynolds' former head of LEAP had stumbled through a succession of temporary positions, each one ending in drink-related dismissals. This was the sixth job in as many years, each one shorter than the last in progressively poorer schools. 'We have some real work for you but first we need to get you sobered up.'

'Real work?' Crouch tried to take a swig from the open bottle but as he tipped it to his lips, Barnes snatched it from his grubby hand.

'You won't be needing any more of that today.'

'Who are you to tell me what to do?' Crouch said, reaching for the bottle which Barnes upturned onto the crud-covered carpet.

'You should treat me with more respect. I used to be famous.'

'I know, old man, and if you play your cards right, you could be again. Come on, we're going to be late. Let's find you some clothes.'

He pulled open the wardrobe. It was empty. As were the chest of drawers.

Crouch cackled inanely.

'I don't need clothes, just my glasses. I'm lost without them.'

'Oh, we know that, Prof. The whole world knows that,' Barnes said, cradling the filthy spectacles as he remembered how the professor had spawned a million YouTube memes that perfectly captured the Reynolds Air collapse. He could still picture the elderly man standing in Samuel Reynolds' San Francisco office, staring uncertainly into the camera, clearly unsure what to do when his boss hadn't appeared. He had eventually made his way over to the empty receiving chamber, a large glass container in the corner of the room. And that's when it had happened. The doorway had been cut out of the glass panel, which meant that there was a four-inch high step-over for Crouch to clear. He had never got close. His right foot had caught the high lip and he had tumbled forward into the transparent room, his glasses spilling from his face and sliding across the shiny white floor. The old man had not hurt himself but was clearly stunned. He had slowly got to his hands and knees and cautiously crawled forward, one arm outstretched, carefully feeling for his glasses, the emblem of RA clearly emblazoned across his back. And that was it, Professor Crouch had become an overnight pariah, further pilloried for his drunken interviews in which he claimed teleportation was real science. Barnes sighed. He almost felt sorry for him.

Barnes wiped the glasses on the dirty sheets and handed then to Crouch. 'We've wasted enough time. It's time to go. Chris, if you would be so kind as to help the esteemed professor, he has some very important work to do for his country.'

Without waiting for a response, they positioned themselves either side of the bed and lifted Crouch up by his arms, before carrying him from the filthy condo to the waiting SUV, which continued to stare menacingly at the fluttering curtains on both sides of the quiet street.

Oil Treatment Centre, Riyadh, Saudi Arabia

14 November 2009, 22:41 hours

The Caspian gull stood stock still, breathing furtively, its once white and pale grey plumage now a sticky black mess. It looked exhausted but was compelled by nature to continue preening, its slender bill searching out feathers to align back into their rightful place and form the bond that would keep out the wind, the water and the cold. Its head bobbed backwards and forwards, dripping black oil as it desperately tried to dislodge the glue-like substance, before continuing its frantic clean-up operation that was effectively accelerating the death sentence granted by the tar. It tried to take a step forward but never finished the motion; great globs of sandy tar hampered its movements, clinging to its feathers and weighing down its limbs. One leg collapsed and it fell to the sand where it struggled to regain its footing. Within seconds, its body was covered in a white frosting which initially glistened under the bright lights of the centre. However, the shine quickly disappeared as the sand soaked up the oil and the bird's feathers resumed their dull black colour. The bird's movements became weaker. It tried to extend its wings but only succeeded in collecting more of the thick treacle which, combined with the fine sand, added yet more weight. Eventually it stopped struggling altogether and lay on its side, trying to blink the sticky stuff out of its eyes.

'Untreated, that bird will be dead in twenty-four hours.'

'I'm not surprised. All that oil will destroy its internal organs.'

'Actually, ingested oil won't kill it.'

'Oh.' Forsyth sounded distracted. 'What will?'

'Its preening instinct. An instinct that overrides all others, including the urge to eat, even evade predators. Can you imagine having that behavioural pattern hardwired into your genes?'

'I could think of a few,' Forsyth said.

Al Rahman ignored him and continued in a soft voice.

'It's trying to sort the position of its feathers out so they overlap to create a tight waterproof and insulated barrier. That's what will protect it from the elements and why they are constantly preening themselves. See there.'

Sure enough, the hapless bird was still trying to arrange its feathers even as it lay on its side, panting with the effort.

'That is why birds spend so much time preening themselves. Unless the feathers are perfectly aligned, it will result in certain death. Unfortunately, the oil makes that impossible. When a bird comes into contact with oil, the feathers separate and expose the skin to extremes in temperature. Its instinct is to preen itself to get the oil off which actually exacerbates the problem. This preening instinct will override everything. Very quickly, they lose weight, become dehydrated and suffer from anaemia. Eventually, if they are not treated, they will die.'

'That's where this centre comes in?' Forsyth said.

'No, not really,' Al Rahman said. 'It's a PR exercise. I would call it a damage limitation centre. Nothing more.' Forsyth looked around the large, windowless warehouse. Across the vast expanse of floor there must have been a hundred other small tables with birds flapping about in various states of contamination.

'I don't understand.'

'Unfortunately, oily birds are very bad for business. There is nothing like a few fluffy penguins drenched in oil to turn the public against us. That's why we have the centre. We are constantly developing ways of cleaning up spills faster and also rehabilitating the local wildlife. Currently it takes two people about one hour and 300 gallons of water to clean one bird. That's not only very time consuming but also very expensive. We are trying to speed that up with new chemicals that disperse the oil off the feathers. Over there, we are trying out a new coating which we spray every bird with before they come into contact with the oil. Once coated, it's supposed to act as a natural repellent.'

'Interesting. How's it going?'

'Not well,' Al Rahman said. 'The birds keep dying. They have very delicate immune systems. I'm not sure it will ever get anywhere but we have to be seen to be trying.'

Forsyth kept abreast of the sheikh as they walked towards the far end of the centre where an area was sectioned off by a glass wall. Inside were fifty or so birds, all clean of oil but, unlike the others, completely motionless, staring, unseeing into the middle distance.

'This is another product we have tried recently,' Al Rahman said. 'It's a bacterium that literally eats the oil from their feathers.'

'It looks effective,' Forsyth said.

'I'm afraid a little too effective.'

'What do you mean?'

'It consumes all the carbon, including what's inside the bird. After hydrogen and water, it's the most plentiful element in all life forms. Without carbon we cannot live. Inside, the bird's body is dead.'

The older man continued walking towards one of the exits.

'The bigger problem is that we don't want to give people any more excuses to look for alternative sources of energy. Oil is dirty; it kills wildlife and is an ugly reminder to the Western world during a spill. Remove the dirty birds and it helps the perception problem.'

Forsyth frowned. All these dying birds made him nervous but what made him more nervous was why his largest investor had summoned him halfway round the world to discuss seagulls. It was obviously to do with LEAP but what he feared most was what Al Rahman would want from him—why couldn't he just ask him outright and dispense with this charade? But he knew from years of experience that

Al Rahman liked to take his time so he had to play along. 'It might be an uncomfortable reminder but so long as you keep the price low, the general public really have no choice,' Forsyth said. 'They're as addicted to oil as everyone else. Anyway, I thought OPEC had the price issue covered?'

'It does,' Al Rahman said. 'We learnt the hard way during the seventies. If we allow the price to rise too high, then past a certain point our customers start to think about alternatives. That's why we keep the price relatively lower than any alternative.'

'Except now your biggest customer has an alternative.'

'So, it seems,' Al Rahman said.

'But it'll take years for LEAP to impact oil usage,' Forsyth said, sensing that the question was coming.

'It's already started,' Al Rahman said. 'There is real consternation in the cartel. I foresee that it will soon collapse as each country attempts to charge what it can.'

'But LEAP only affects the distribution industry,' Forsyth said. 'There're plenty of other uses for oil for many years to come: heating, people transportation, heavy industry. LEAP can't replace anything.'

'Perhaps not, but it will severely disrupt our model. And that props up my country and twenty others. Besides which, I don't buy into this transport thing. Very shortly, LEAP will include people. That will destroy the cartel and we can't afford to let that happen. Can we, Mr Forsyth?' Al Rahman's voice had dropped to a whisper, but the tone was forbidding.

'What do you expect me to do?' Forsyth said, relieved that the reason for his summons was out in the open but also fearful of how his benefactor would react to his response.

'I think you already know the answer to that question.'

'And how am I supposed to help on that front?'

'I thought that was obvious, Mr Forsyth.'

'I don't fancy spending the next twenty years in a federal penitentiary.'

'I'm sure you'll think of a way,' Al Rahman said.

Forsyth shifted uneasily. 'I don't think you understand.'

'No. I don't think you do.' Al Rahman turned on Forsyth, his black eyes glittering with menace. 'We have underwritten your organisation to the tune of two billion dollars over the last decade. Now we are calling the chips in.'

'You can't do that.'

'Yes, we can. This isn't just about business but about the security of the region. One reason our people have remained so, shall we say, compliant is because of oil. Without the long-term security of that then we could face a collapse in the Royal Family's power base and civil unrest.'

'Diversify, like every other Arab country,' Forsyth said.

'As you witnessed the other day, we are doing that, but recent events have overtaken us and I can't afford to miss out on this new opportunity.'

Forsyth made to reply but Al Rahman held up his hand, the conversation at an end.

'You have four weeks and then we pull the plug. You may as well go to jail—by the time your press has finished picking over the carcass of your demise, federal prison will seem like a holiday camp. I trust I've made myself clear.'

Forsyth didn't get a chance to reply. The sheikh was already walking away, leaving him staring at the fifty or so trapped birds.

Virginia

14 November 2009, 11:49 hours

The dark grey metal matched the sky, not just in colour. The clouds were low and looked menacing, as if waiting for the slightest provocation so they could retaliate with everything they could throw at the two men below them. Given the temperature, Martin reckoned that was at least six hours' worth of relentless snow. No, make that sleet, an ugly mixture of ice and water that would sting his eyes and freeze his bones with a never-ending ferocity, courtesy of the heat-sucking wind blowing in off the Atlantic. He had become something of an expert at assessing the weather. All it took was a glance upwards as his senses tested the strength of the wind and temperature. In that moment he would know how difficult his training would be for the day. Two hours ago, he had shuddered at the thought of endless miles through the wretched woods that resembled World War I battlefields in their capacity for generating thick glue-like mud that pulled at his aching boots and set traps for his trembling legs. However, today was different. He had been sat still for the last ninety minutes as Fortune lovingly and repeatedly stripped a dark grey metal gun. As he watched on, trying to keep warm in the bitter wind, his minder drew back the top half of the weapon, which he now knew was a slide, along the continuous metal rail beneath it until he could retract no further.

There was an audible click. Without pausing, Fortune depressed the snap ladder before wrenching the slide in the opposite direction. It slid smoothly off the rail and Fortune placed the main part of the gun on the tarpaulin beside the magazine. He hefted the slide in his hand, testing its weight before turning it over so he could get at its guts. First the recoil spring followed by the guide-spring rod and, finally, the barrel. All were laid reverentially on the tarpaulin.

'That's it. Just six parts,' Fortune said.

Martin was unsure how to respond and remained silent, thinking instead about the last four weeks. The training was going well; he was much stronger now, his wasted muscles built up from relentless exercise, unlimited protein and rest. In fact, he couldn't remember feeling this fit. Ever. Certainly not back in Leeds where his life had been quite sedentary; a mix of rich food, student life and endless hours poring over his keyboard writing software programmes. Back then he had felt lethargic but now energy surged through his body. It felt as if he was surfing the crest of a wave that was slowly gathering momentum, building in speed and power. It was becoming unstoppable and he could barely contain his excitement for the day when it would come crashing down on the beach in a maelstrom of sea, salt and sand. He dragged himself back to Fortune who was still drooling over his gun.

'—it's all down to the German build.'

They both stared at the bits of metal.

'It's great for first-time shooters. Very smooth recoil action because of this continuous rail here.'

He handed part of the gun to Belman who stared at it doubtfully.

'See here,' he huddled closer to Martin, 'it connects all the way through which means that when the shot is made, there is continuous guidance for the barrel.'

'It's heavy,' was all Martin could think to say.

'Best stainless steel on the market,' Fortune said approvingly. 'Again, excellent quality. Look.' Martin was handed another part. 'Even the recoil spring is braided steel. Made from up to three, possibly four strains, which means there is excellent memory retention.'

Fortune started to reassemble the weapon, effortlessly sliding it back into place like a primitive transformer.

'Everyone uses it: Special Forces, FBI, CIA, Secret Service.'

He handed the assembled gun to Belman who hefted it in his hand for the first time. He was surprised at the weight, especially for such a small firearm.

But what did he know? He had never held one before, but it fitted snugly in his hand like an old glove and he instinctively put both hands up to simulate a firing stance.

'Whoa there, buddy,' yelled Fortune, knocking the gun to one side as the barrel swung close to his head. 'Don't point that thing at me.'

'Why?' Belman was genuinely surprised. 'It's not loaded.'

'First rules of weapons training. Never assume a gun is not loaded.' Fortune grabbed it off Belman, pulling the barrel back. As he released, a bullet popped from the chamber on to the tarpaulin.

They both stared at it, thinking the same thing.

'Don't worry, you would have never got the shot off.'

'Why would I want to?' Belman said, shocked at Fortune's insinuation. 'I need you. We need each other.'

'Just in case you were thinking.'

Martin glanced around him. He couldn't see anyone.

'Two snipers. One at twelve o'clock. The other at six.'

Martin didn't answer but silently he offered them both his apologies for having to lie out there in the freezing cold, training their hairpins on his head. He hoped they were warmer than he was.

'Fancy a go?' Fortune jumped to his feet and marched off towards the range without waiting for an answer.

'Sure,' Martin said to himself. He would have preferred a ten-mile hike over spending another second crouched on the exposed hillock overlooking the shooting range. There was no cover for one quarter mile all around them and the wind had taken full advantage, slowly freezing Belman like an open fire spit roasts a joint. He couldn't believe it could get any colder and for the first time since arriving, found himself wistfully thinking about the heat of Guantanamo Bay. Fortune, who was already waiting for him, didn't seem to notice the cold.

'OK, be strong. The kickback is not bad but you need a good stance every time you fire if that's possible.'

Belman complied like an autonoman and fingered the weapon apprehensively.

'Good. Hold steady. Breath. Depress on the outward breath otherwise you'll never hit anything.'

It was too late. The pistol cracked loudly in the clear air and a puff of white powder exploded twenty feet in front of the two men.

'No, not like that. Try again,' Fortune said. But it was no good, Belman could not hit the target. Two, three, four shots rang out. He could sense his jailer getting more and more frustrated. In less than a minute he had emptied the entire magazine and Fortune grabbed the gun off him, checked the safety catch, rammed a new magazine into the handle and rapidly squeezed off three rounds of three in quick succession.

The rapid cracks made Belman jump.

'That's how you do it. Shall we have a look?'

Belman shrugged and blew into his cupped hands. Even the running was preferable to this. At least he had been warm. He looked round the deserted range and shivered. Behind him the black Ford Transporter stood impassively, its entire body coated with a fine white powder. Either side of him was a lonely fence that marked out the perimeter of the range and which he could have stepped over with ease. He looked back. Fortune was already halfway to the targets, three paper-thin soldiers staring grimly ahead, their rifles pointing threateningly in his direction. He trudged over, barely noticing the Jacket which he had quickly grown used to. Fortune was bent over the first target. Belman was impressed. The cutout was peppered with three holes: one in the centre of its forehead and two, spaced neatly either side of where its heart should have been.

He whistled appreciatively.

'You expect me to shoot to that level of accuracy?'

'No. But I expect you to at least hit the target,' Fortune said, moving to the next cut out which sported a neat isosceles triangle of three holes around its chest.

'I thought you wanted me to blow myself up, not shoot people.'

'I do.'

Fortune was now bent over the last target, inspecting the three neat holes, one through each eye and the last one just above its lip.'

'So why the target practice?'

Fortune turned to look at the smaller man, a look of weary resignation etched on his face.

'Preparedness, Martin,' he said, jabbing a finger at his pupil's chest in time with his pronunciation of each syllable. 'Pre—pa—red—ness.'

'I don't understand.'

'You don't need to. Just follow my orders and you will be OK.'

'It would help if I understood a little of what you've got planned for me.'

'You'll find out in good time.' Fortune repeated the same response he had used for the last four weeks whenever the conversation had turned to what Belman was meant to do.

'But why the gun?' Belman said, not even bothering to question Fortune further. 'I don't understand. Are you expecting trouble?'

'What's your concern?'

'I don't want to fail again.'

'You won't.'

'This target practice worries me.'

'It shouldn't,' Fortune said.

'Then tell me why I'm stood here on a shooting range in the middle of nowhere, firing a revolver at paper targets.'

Fortune turned on him. 'It's not a revolver, it's a pistol better known as the Sig Sauer P229. The standard issue weapon for the United States Secret Service.' As Fortune spoke, he cocked the firearm and checked the chamber. 'It's a variation of the P226 but has a significant number of differences, none of which I will bore you with.'

Martin blinked. He was certain Fortune had already done that.

Fortune holstered the pistol before continuing.

'The idea is that you don't get to use it. If the plan works you will access your target without being challenged by a single person, but we need to cover the downside. Work out what could go wrong and arm you to deal with the consequences.'

'What could go wrong?' Martin said.

'You might be challenged by a Secret Service Agent.'

'And.'

'You will have to shoot him before he shoots you.'

'I've never shot anyone before,' Belman said slowly. 'Come to think of it, I've never killed anyone.'

'Not for lack of trying, hey.'

Martin grinned self-consciously.

'You're not really cut out for this are you?' Fortune said.

'I don't understand'

'This.' Fortune waved at the range. 'Guns, bombs, running, pre-paredness. Killing people. It's all completely alien to you. How did you ever manage to get yourself mixed up with those London bombers?'

'I didn't get myself mixed up with them. They were ... are my brothers. We were united by a common cause.'

'A lost cause, if you ask me.'

'No one asked you.'

Fortune ignored him.

'What were you hoping to achieve by blowing yourself up on a subway in London? To stop the war?'

'In time.'

'How? By failing?'

'No,' Martin said, stung by the accusation. 'If we had succeeded, it would have chipped away at the public's view of the war.'

'You think the public care.'

'No, I don't.' Martin said. 'That's the problem. The war is too remote and doesn't impact their lives at all. We need to make it real for them. Have it interrupt their daily lattes. Have them experience what it feels like to have their women and children die indiscriminately. Then they will start to care.'

'It hasn't worked so far,' Fortune said.

'It will. That's the benefit of a democracy. Your governments are too beholden to public opinion. Eventually they have to take notice.'

'Well, it doesn't get much bigger than 9/11—the repercussions of that will be felt for generations.'

Belman shook his head.

'No, it won't. Americans grow tired of this war. So do the British. We're reaching a tipping point. It just needs one act to pass the point of no return.'

Fortune didn't reply. He just sat there fingering the Sig Sauer.

'How else could I make an impact? With words?' Martin said.

'You could've joined your brothers in Afghanistan or Iraq.'

'And waste my life.'

'You're dead either way. What does it matter to you?'

'Hugely,' Martin said. 'The manner of my death is crucial and needs to have the greatest impact possible. Dying on some lonely hillside in Iraq is a waste but creating an international outcry in London is far more effective. As I said, attacking the enemy on home soil is our real weapon. That is what impacts public opinion. Bring the fight to the public. The only way we can do that is to cause death and mayhem on their doorstep. Eventually, if it happens enough, your democratic governments will stop their war against my people.'

'Your people?' Fortune said, shaking his head. 'Have you checked your passport recently?'

'I might be English but I'm first and foremost a Muslim, reacting to the wholesale and indiscriminate slaughter of fellow Muslims on the other side of the world. How do you expect us to react? How would you react if you knew Americans were being slaughtered arbitrarily?'

'That hasn't happened.'

Belman pulled a sheet of newspaper from his pocket. 'It happens every day,' he said, handing the piece of paper to Fortune who stared the headline: 'Iraqi wedding party wiped out by lone US missile.'

'There are dozens more examples. This is just one.'

'It's called collateral damage,' Fortune said. 'That's what happens when you wage war.'

'So was 9/11.'

'No, it wasn't. We didn't go out to intentionally murder those people.' Fortune waved the cutting at Belman. 'This was an accident, a regrettable one, but an accident, nevertheless. The 9/11 bombers, you, your brothers—your intent is the wholesale murder of non-combatants. How can you live with that?'

'We're fighting a war,' Martin shouted at his handler. 'One we didn't start. That is all the justification we need.'

'You'll get your chance soon enough,' Fortune said, but Martin didn't hear. He'd had enough of his handler's righteousness. He was the same as all the others.

'I'm going back to the house,' he screamed back at Fortune as he marched off the frozen hill.

1000 Independence Avenue SW, Washington DC

14 November 2009, 19:44 hours

The man appeared to stumble momentarily but then caught himself and continued walking. Slowly. Very slowly as if he was carrying something heavy. He was wearing a thick coat: standard issue Secret Service winter wear. It looked bulky but gave no indication of what was concealed beneath. He paused for a second, turned slightly, to look back as if someone had called him and then turned again. From this angle you couldn't see his face; the peaked cap was pulled low, covering his features entirely although subsequent reports had indicated he was of Indian origin. The image was frustratingly grainy, a result of the enhancement made by the network, to zoom in on this portion of an aerial shot one of their helicopters had made of The White House. Uma knew what was coming but it still made her jump. Without warning, the image was suddenly returned to its original perspective, sound was restored and seconds later there was a low boom as the man disappeared in a flash of light. At this distance you could see the sound wave ripple away from the blast, as it picked up dust and snow from The White House lawns. Again, the image cut to a different shot entirely, this one taken from just outside the northwest gate on Pennsylvania Avenue. Directly ahead, the entrance veranda into the West Wing had collapsed in on itself, covering a vehicle that was parked outside. All the windows had blown out and the normally white exterior was now a dirty grey. In the background, a shocked reporter was covering the last time The White House had sustained damage of any kind. It had been a fire, cause unknown. You had to go back to 1812 to find any evidence of an attack this devastating. As the reporter finished, the video had already begun the loop again, picking up the grainy images of the man as he made his way slowly across The White House lawn.

Uma dragged her eyes away from the screen. She felt numb. Since yesterday's press conference she'd been immediately recalled to DC for briefing after briefing. Most concerned security which Uma realised was a further intrusion on an already privacy-free existence—a new car, a new driver and round-the-clock bodyguards. It reminded her of Ethan's efforts to protect the development of LEAP but multiplied by a factor of ten. None of it made her feel more secure. If anything, she felt more vulnerable. More cut off from reality and utterly powerless. She had attempted to contact the President, but a wall of silence had descended on The White House through which no one could penetrate. There was really no one else she could speak to—she'd be damned before reaching out to Ingram and after last night, she couldn't even contact Forsyth.

Her eyes drifted back to the grainy image as the bomber looked round slowly. It was hypnotic. The phone suddenly rang, causing her to jump. It was her secretary calling to say that a security detail had arrived to escort her to a dinner on the other side of Washington. Six Secret Service agents accompanied her to the front of the building where more agents lurked, speaking furtively into their palms. *Christ, this was ridiculous*. Two black SUVs bookended her ride and the agents peeled off, three per Cadillac, while Uma slid into the darkened interior of her limo, where she settled back into the soft leather and slowly exhaled.

'Having a tough day, Doctor?'

Uma let out a little yelp of surprise as she turned in the direction of the familiar voice, his lanky frame clearly visible on the opposite seat. She couldn't believe she had missed him.

'Well, Director Ingram, this makes a pleasant change.'

'How so?'

'I'm fully dressed for a start.'

'I must be losing my touch.'

'And I thought this reception was for my benefit.'

'Some of it is. We would hate to lose you, Doctor.'

'And why don't I feel reassured by that.'

Uma could barely make out his face in the dark interior, not that it would have provided her with any clues as to what he was thinking.

'How can I help you, Director? I've got an evening engagement to attend.'

'We're heading over to the Hotel Metropole as we speak. You have plenty of time.'

'I don't know whether to feel honoured or offended that you know where I'm going.' Through the gloom, the director shrugged and Uma was certain a contented smile flittered across his smug face. It angered her that he got a kick out of this but she wasn't going to give him the satisfaction of seeing that. She suddenly had a vision of him talking with Forsyth about last night. Her stomach turned at the thought. 'I know. It's your job,' was all she could manage.

'Have you seen the reports?'

'How can you miss them? It's on a constant loop on every TV channel playing 24/7.'

'You know this changes everything.' It was less of a question, more of a statement.

'How so?' Uma was suddenly nervous but couldn't pinpoint why.

'We need LEAP to protect the President.'

Uma's heart lurched.

'What do you mean?'

'Our security advisors are recommending that he use LEAP to travel for the immediate future.'

'That wasn't the deal. We said no people.'

'No one could've foreseen this.'

'That's not the point.'

'What would you have us do?' Ingram said. 'Expose the President to further attacks when there is a proven mode of transportation that would significantly cut down on his public exposure.'

Uma felt lightheaded. Nauseous. Her anger rising.

Through a thick fog she heard Ingram talking, trying to placate her. 'It won't go public. That's the main thing. Only a few people will know. The President's personal security detail who travel with him at all times. We'll run permanent links out of The White House. Up to Camp David. Others as they fall due.'

'Why did no one consult with me?' Uma said.

'Doctor, have you watched the news recently? We're involved in a very fluid situation. It's changing by the hour.'

Hadn't Forsyth used those words last night? It seemed an excuse to abandon any pretext of the agreement she had struck with the President only days before. She heard herself repeating words used barely hours earlier with Forsyth. She remembered where that had ended and felt her skin crawl at the thought of Ingram dancing with her.

'But we agreed—no teleportation. That we would phase this in at an acceptable pace.'

'What would you have us do, Doctor? Expose the President to an unknown danger simply for the sake of an agreement.'

'I need to speak to the President.'

'I'm afraid that's out of the question. He's up at Camp David, locked away with his Security Council.'

'And he agreed to this?'

'He doesn't have a choice. This is the Presidency we have to protect. That's all that matters.'

'But, Director—'

'Doctor. The decision's been made. I'm here to see you out of courtesy.'

She remembered Forsyth's certainty and his reassurances about the strength of her position—something about a PR company and the control she had. And whether she was being too selfish about LEAP. Before she knew it, LEAP would be everywhere.

'If you go ahead with this, I will resign,' Uma said as firmly as she could manage. 'Make it public.'

'And where would that get you?' He sounded tired of the discussion, which angered Uma even more. 'We've been through this. At the moment, you're inside the circle. If you proceed, you'll be on the outside and there'll be no coming back. LEAP's potential will be out in the open. Everyone will know about it and you will have lost the ability to influence anything. As we've discussed before, I would strongly advise you to reconsider that course of action.'

'But you leave me no choice.'

'As I said before, you have a choice, Doctor. Stick with what you've got.' The director's voice had hardened. 'Co-operate and you can influence the roll out. Help us monitor where the LEAP stations are placed. Ensure they are dismantled. Control who travels. There's a lot you can do to help but there is also a great deal we can achieve without your participation. On the whole, I would prefer you to remain in the loop. It would be so much less complicated for everyone.'

Uma was silent. And what had Ethan said? 'And a new race shall walk the earth. The undead shall rise up. Neither living not dying. Soulless creatures feeding off discarded atoms like vampires with no memory of their sins.' Was this the beginning? It felt wrong and Uma realised that she couldn't let it happen.

'Don't do anything rash, Doctor,' Ingram said. 'Proceed as you're doing and you can still effect the change you need with both LEAP and the green agenda you've set yourself.'

'I'm not sure I want to do this,' she said, trying to sound defiant but it felt pathetic and he knew it. She fought back hot tears. 'The President promised,' she continued. 'He promised.' She was suddenly glad of the dark as the tears finally broke through, streaming down her face.

'Remember why you've come this far. All the work with Green Ray. Six years of your life. You don't want to lose that with a hasty decision.'

There it was again. He seemed to know such a lot about her and what she was thinking. But this was different. The words sounded familiar to Uma. Had he been eavesdropping again? Or had Forsyth told him? She should never have opened up to that man. But it had been so easy to speak, her words flowing out before she had time to think.

'Sleep on it. You'll see things differently in the morning.'

'Not this time, Director. I have compromised enough.'

'Very noble, Doctor. But once you go public, your life will change forever. But if that is the choice you make then I respect your decision.'

The door suddenly opened, the shadow of an agent visible on the street. Uma hadn't realised they'd stopped.

'Have a good evening, Doctor.'

As she turned to get out of the car, the director spoke again.

'Remember. Sleep on it.'

And then he was gone, the huge limo disappearing into the cold DC night, leaving Uma alone on the sidewalk with her security detail.

Washington, DC

15 November 2009, 03:45 hours

The mobile started to ring and should have continued unanswered given the hour but it had barely begun its second chime before being snatched off the bedside table.

'Hello.' The voice sounded out of breath and in pain.

'Uma, is that you? Are you OK? Sorry to ring you so late.'

I wasn't asleep,' she said. In fact, that was an understatement. She'd been racked by night visions since returning from her dinner four hours ago, Ingram's words ringing in her ears. 'What can I do for you, Jake?' she asked irritably.

'We've been raided.' The CEO of Electro Motors sounded shocked but also calm.

'What do you mean?'

'About fifty minutes ago, forty federal agents entered our main facility down in San Mateo. With search warrants. Something to do with their investigations into the DC bombings.'

Uma's blood chilled.

Was this Ingram's idea of a joke?

'It's getting worse by the minute.' He sounded panicked. His usual jovial tone was strained. 'Someone tipped off the press. I've had journalists from both coasts trying to contact me. Almost as the agents arrived. That's actually how I found out. To get a quote for their morning papers. I've got at least seven major news stations outside the office right now. Uma, what's going on?'

'Jake, stay put. I think there's been a massive misunderstanding.'

'Uma, they've threatened to shut us down until the investigation is resolved. This would be catastrophic at a moment like this.'

Uma's phone began to vibrate. It was Yuri Baker, Chief Counsel at Green Ray.

Why would he be calling her? He had nothing to do with Electro, unless he felt it compromised the Fund. A chill flittered down her spine.

'Jake, I've got to go. Yuri on the other line.'

She hung up without waiting for a response from her CEO.

'Yes, Yuri. How can I help you?'

'Have you heard?' He sounded breathless.

'About Electro. Yes, I've just had Jake on the phone?'

'Electro as well! What's happening, Uma?'

'What do you mean, as well?' Uma felt herself lurch outside Ingram's circle even as she asked the question.

'Green Ray has been raided by Federal Agents. About 100 of them across the Manhattan, DC and San Francisco offices. Something to do with irregularities over our funding sources. So far, that is all the detail they will provide me.'

'Yuri, is it legal?'

'You bet your life it is. My desk is stacked high with search warrants all signed off by a Federal Court judge within the last hour.'

'What we can we do?'

'Get them off our backs and quickly. We have a perception problem developing and very quickly. A tainted funds story will kill Green Ray off, particularly in this climate. It will spook our legit investors. It's like a house of cards. Pull one out and the entire stack could come tumbling down.'

'Leave it with me.'

'Uma, your position would also be untenable.'

Her phone had started to vibrate again. It was from an unknown source. That could only mean one thing.

'You bastard. Do you really believe your strong-arm tactics will force my hand?'

'Ah, Doctor. I've been expecting your call.' Ingram's laconic tone filled her ear. 'You're needed tomorrow evening for a meeting with the President. Apparently, there has been some federal activity down at your fund and car company. It's just beginning to hit the wires now. As you can appreciate, this is the last thing the administration needs at the moment. I'm sure it's all a misunderstanding and will be resolved quickly but he would like your personal assurance that nothing is untoward. Will you be able to do that?' Before she could respond, Ingram continued. 'Please don't answer that question now. I'm sure you need to investigate first and reassure yourself that everything is in order. A car will pick you up at 18:30 tomorrow evening. Your meeting will start at 19:00 prompt. Good night, Doctor.'

Fort Bragg, Mendocino County, California

16 November 2009, 9:03 hours

'Let me get this straight. Grant and James went missing last Saturday. Their van was discovered at the old Reynolds' landing strip but there were no signs of any struggle. Just before they disappeared, they called in at 16:00 hours and nothing untoward was reported. They were following Rae, right? Has anyone been to interview him?'

There was silence in the small room. Agent Brody stared at the three men sat in front of him but all of them kept their gazes down, unwilling to take their new boss on.

'Why not?' Brody said.

One of the men cleared his throat, looked like he was going to say something but thought better of it and resumed his microscopic inspection of the table.

'Come on, guys,' Agent Brody snapped. 'It's been a full week.'

Finally, the middle agent looked up. He glanced at his two silent colleagues either side of him and, satisfied that they weren't going to speak, he began.

'Well, Bill Grant was the acting office head. When they went missing, we reported it up the chain of command into Sacramento. That was Monday. We found the van on Tuesday. Up at the old airfield, as you said. We kept the search teams active through the end of last week into the weekend and here we are.'

'Did it occur to anyone to send a team to question Rae at the very least?' Agent Brody said.

Yet more silence. The spokesman had dropped his gaze and was also inspecting his table carefully. This was getting nowhere. Brody thrust his hands deep into his trouser pockets and glared at them. As Brody waited, he glanced out of the window into the street below; an old lady was slowly crossing the intersection. It must have taken her a full thirty seconds to reach the centre line, but she needn't have worried. Nothing troubled her. Turning back to his men, Brody delivered his orders.

'This is what we'll do. Dispatch two more agents up to Reynolds' Castle to interview Ethan Rae. If he won't co-operate bring him in. We can question him here.'

The three men exchanged glances.

'Oh, for God's sake. You two get a car and drive out there now. You.' Brody pointed sharply at the oldest of the three; the sleepy one. 'You stay and maintain radio contact. Any changes, you come get me straight away.'

The men moved. They had their orders. They seemed happy now.

Field Agent Brody shook his head in frustration. This is what happened when you had office geeks doing field work. He had no doubt the two agents were probably wandering, cold and bedraggled somewhere on the Reynolds' Estate. At this time of year there was no chance of them freezing to death. They would be tired and hungry but that was it.

Reynolds' Castle, Point Humboldt

16 November 2009, 12:12 hours

The corridors were colder than Uma had remembered, causing her breath to mist over in great clouds as she made her way towards the great hall, the obedient lights flickering on like a guiding hand. A heavy tremor rumbled across the corridor. She waited for it to pass before continuing reluctantly down the armed corridor. What was she doing here? She must be mad. Ethan had made his feelings very clear the last time she had come. What could she possibly hope to gain this time round? The simple truth was that she had nowhere else to turn; she didn't trust Forsyth, despite the cold logic of his approach to LEAP. Besides, he was too close to Ingram. All she knew was that by the end of today there would be nothing left: no fund, no position in the government and she would be watching LEAP from the sidelines. She had nothing to lose.

Uma looked up at the great doors. Without realising, she had arrived outside the great hall. The huge cannons sat there, unmoved by her personal turmoil. They were waiting silently, obediently, for the order. Ready to hurl their metal payloads skywards as their commander requested. Yet there was no war. No commander. They were historical anomalies, much like the military mausoleum they were housed in. Without pausing, she pushed on the heavy door and it opened quietly, effortlessly drawing her into the great room. It was as she had left it. High overhead, the massive cast-iron candelabra hung heavy; beneath it, the carpets of war cast their grisly images across the great space. The huge fire still burned furiously, long flames licking hungrily in her direction as the brief draught pulled them towards her. Above the fireplace, Reynolds looked almost bemused, a wicked smile threatening to break out across his angry visage.

'Ethan.'

Her voice sounded small in the large space, the high ceiling effortlessly swallowing up her plaintive call.

She tried again, louder.

Still no answer.

By now she was nearly at the great fireplace. She could feel the first prickles of perspiration break out and it made her stop. The room was clearly empty. Uma stood there wondering what to do. On her previous visits she had always come to the great hall where he would be stood staring into the fire or fighting or exercising. She wouldn't even know where to start looking; there must have been over two hundred rooms in the castle. Besides which, if he didn't want to be found, there was no point in even starting.

She checked her watch. *12:26*. Just three hours to go until her meeting at The White House. A sound made her turn back towards the door. A man had entered and for the briefest second, she thought it was Ethan. Her heart sank as the southern drawl of Edward Hunter, Ethan's assistant, echoed across the cold space.

'Doctor. How can I help?'

He didn't seem surprised to see her and Uma suddenly realised she had been watched from the second she had entered the building. She had an image of Ethan sat in a high tower, monitoring her progress through the labyrinth, ready to send in his hired help to get rid of her. He couldn't even bring himself to face her anymore.

'Edward,' she said, her early resolve melting away. 'I was hoping to talk to Ethan.'

'I'm sorry, Doctor. Mr Rae asked not to be disturbed.'

An awkward silence descended on the silent room.

'I understand, Edward, but it's vitally important that I speak to him.'

Her voice sounded desperate. Too much so but it seemed to work. The man's face softened slightly, and he appeared to shrug, clearly caught in a dilemma.

'I'm really sorry, Doctor, but my orders are clear. Mr Rae doesn't want to see anyone.'

'Please, Edward, I beg you. I won't be long. Please.'

The man made a move towards her and Uma peeled away, walking further into the great room. She was shouting now, circling the abandoned armour and weaponry, her arms outstretched. Pleading.

'Ethan. I know you're there. Please. I need your help.'

Only echoes met her desperate cries.

She glanced round. Edward was still there, looking embarrassed.

'Please, Doctor. You need to leave.'

Uma tried again, anger taking over.

'Ethan, damn you. Show yourself. You can't hide forever. Come out. I need you. Isn't that enough?'

Her voice sounded small, swallowed up by the huge room and once again, a wall of silence met her cries. Uma's shoulders drooped. He wasn't coming, and she slowly made her way towards the door, holding back her tears, determined not to embarrass herself even more in front of the older man. Once they were in the corridor, Edward Hunter seemed to relax. He stooped towards her and whispered.

'I'm sorry, ma'am. He won't see anyone, not even me. It's getting worse. I don't know what to do. He isn't eating, barely comes out of his room and when he does, he just stands in front of that fire for hours on end, staring into the flames. This isn't what I signed on for. It's very lonely up here. If it wasn't for the money, I'd be long gone.'

Uma barely heard him. They had reached the Tower of Terror as Uma had nicknamed the armaments display. It bristled above them, all sharp edges and deadly points and Uma shuddered as she looked up. Hunter chuckled.

'It's a sight for sore eyes, isn't it? This whole place is—'

Edward Hunter never finished his sentence.

The stone floor suddenly lurched sideways, throwing them both to the ground toward the tower. Even as she lay there, Uma knew what was happening; she'd experienced enough tremors in Iceland to know the real ones. The ones to fear. The ones that would measure eight or more on the Richter scale. This was one. However, she was helpless to respond. The vibrations continued, scaling at an exponential rate until it seemed the floor itself would split apart, as ancient forces sought to release the tectonic pressure that had built up along the thousand-mile fault line. The tremor faded as quickly as it had hit and Uma's instinct kicked in. Find cover—a table, a doorway. Anything. The tower was her only option and she scrambled towards it as fast as she could.

West Coast

16 November 2009, 13:32 hours

The drive up had been spent in silence. It was partly the weather. At this time of year the rugged coastline was even more desolate than usual, battered into a reluctant solitude by the relentless hammering of the mighty Pacific. Travel-hardened waves arrived with grim determination. Like legions of long-distance runners, they used the sight of the shore to generate one final spurt of energy, some rolling in majestically, holding their shape and formation to perfection whilst others broke far too soon, their arduous journey cruelly wasted, as they arrived spent, barely able to make landfall let alone reduce it. Above them, black clouds scudded low across the horizon, pushed inland by cold winds sweeping in from the west. No traffic braved this wilderness and the absence of humanity was matched by the wildlife. Not even a lone seagull dared the greyness which stretched away as far as the eye could see. The huge seascape was empty. It set the mood and the two agents were happy to comply, still stung by the unjust criticism of their big city cousin from that morning's briefing. Neither voiced their anger, secure in the knowledge that each was thinking the same. What did he know, coming up from Sacramento throwing his weight around and embarrassing them in front of their colleagues? JP would have a field day with this one once he got back. They would be the laughing stock of the department for weeks.

'Ever been to the Rae place?' Special Agent Dan Fellows asked his travel companion.

His voice sounded loud in the quiet truck after the thoughtful silence of the last hour but suddenly both men were happy to be talking.

'Never,' Drew Grange replied. 'You?'

'Once.'

'Did you meet him?'

'Nope. He refused to see us. His butler or man servant or whoever he was, said we would need a search warrant before he would agree to speak to us.'

'And?'

'We left,' Dan Fellows said.

They both sat there, contemplating the reality of what had just been said.

'Do you have a warrant?'

'Nope.'

'That's really going to piss Brody off.'

'Yep.'

And then they started to laugh, a manic laughter that possessed them like a mischievous spirit until tears streamed down their cheeks. It was a welcome release and continued unabated as the coastal road suddenly diverted inland. Within minutes, one natural wonder had been replaced by another as they entered the massive forest of timber surrounding the Reynolds' former family estate. Either side of them the wooden sentinels disappeared high up into the silent sky, the thick canopy blotting out everything. Silence once again descended on the two men.

'We heading inland?' Drew Grange asked.

'We have to,' Dan Fellows said. 'The Reynolds place is built on a promontory that stretches out into the sea. The only way to get to it is to approach from the north, through this redwood forest.'

Drew Grange looked out of the window and whistled appreciative-ly.

'Why did he build it here?'

'You don't know the story?'

'Nope. I'm not from around here, remember.'

Dan Fellows shrugged.

'You've heard of Reynolds, right?'

'Very funny. The whole world's heard of him since that cock and bull story about teleportation.'

'Well, there was another Reynolds before his grandson single-hand-edly destroyed the family name. I'm talking about Old Man Reynolds.'

'Never heard of him.'

'Not many have but he founded the airline which at one time was the biggest company in America and made him the richest man. It allowed him to build his castle.'

'But why here? It's so remote.'

Dan Fellows laughed.

'That was partly the point. Reynolds hated people. Back then this coastline was deserted all the way back to San Francisco and up to Eureka in the north.'

'Sounds like a nut job to me.'

'That's what everyone said but there was also method to his mad-ness.'

His partner's questioning silence invited Dan Fellows to continue.

'San Andreas.'

'What's that supposed to mean?'

'His success haunted him, especially after RA became the biggest airline in America. It drove him like no curse could. He was up at 6 a.m. and working till midnight until the day he died, trying to build a greater company than the one he had the day before. He pushed his staff in the same way, constantly reminding them about the precarious position the business would be in if they relaxed for a minute. As a permanent reminder, he decided to build his place on the fault line.'

'So what?' Drew Grange said. 'I thought everything was on the line in California.'

'But people don't seek it out. Old Man Reynolds did but he took it to the extreme. He wanted something different. A place that had extra resonance. So, he chose north of Point Arena. Do you know why?'

'No, but I'm sure you're going to tell me.' Drew Grange was bored with the story but the older man refused to be rushed.

'It's the very last point on land before the fault enters the Pacific Ocean,' he declared grandly. 'Old Man Reynolds loved the thought that two tectonic plates were slowly crushing themselves together beneath his front door. All eight hundred miles of it stretching away to the south. That's why he built the castle here. Used to fly his entire management team up from San Francisco every week. He wanted to remind them of how unstable their position was, that other competitors were out there waiting to take their position if they relaxed for one second.' The older man chuckled as if he had been there. 'There was a famous story that a particularly ferocious tremor hit the boardroom one afternoon, sending the entire team under the table. Reynolds fired them all on the spot. Said they didn't have the stomach for the sort of business he wanted to run.'

'He was a nut job!' Drew Grange said.

'Maybe,' Dan Fellows agreed, 'but whilst he drew breath, RA was unrivalled. Same story with his son who grew up at Point Arena. However, it all began to fall apart with his grandson. He was a playboy. Moved the family to San Francisco and, as Reynolds predicted, disaster struck.'

'So, is this place still standing?'

'Sure is. That's the genius of the man. Even though he built it during the forties, it was built to last. Apparently, he brought in Japanese engineers to consult on the best building techniques.' As he was speaking, they emerged from the treeline onto a low brow which began to climb steadily back west towards the ocean. 'And as you're just about to see, it has survived intact, despite lying on one of the most active fault lines in the world.'

They crested the incline and sure enough, spread out below them, was Reynolds' Castle. However, the sight that greeted them made Dan Fellows stop the vehicle and they both sat in silence as they surveyed the scene hundreds of feet below. The road continued for another half mile along the top of a barren rocky incline. Either side, the rock face fell away sharply into the boiling ocean below. Drew marvelled at the engineering that must have gone into building the narrow road but that was minor compared to the building itself. As the road neared the end of the small headland, it was swallowed up by a huge structure which looked like it had been chiselled out of the rock itself. Drew couldn't decide whether it was a cathedral or a castle; from their viewpoint it looked like a bottom-heavy cross that followed the natural geology of the outcrop. As a result, the nearest section was long and narrow before branching out along the contours of the promontory in three directions, pointing north, south and finally west into the Pacific. The eastern end boasted a huge tower which was matched by its three cousins or at least Drew figured that would have been the case, except that the west and southern towers were no longer there. They had disappeared into the sea, taking much of the building with them. Drew could see debris littering the surrounding slopes like scree.

'Holy smoke,' he said.

Dan Fellows was silent, staring, his face ashen, absorbing the devastation beneath them.

'What do we do?' Drew Grange said. 'Call it in?'

Still no reply.

'Dan.'

He nudged his partner who blinked in disbelief and slowly looked over.

'What do you want to do?'

'We'd better check it out,' Dan Fellows eventually said. 'See if there are any survivors. Maybe the boys are in there. Maybe we should've come here sooner like Brody suggested.'

'Shouldn't we call it in?'

'Good idea, call the office.'

'What are you waiting for then?'

Dan Fellows gunned the engine and they started the steep descent towards the devastation.

Reynolds' Castle,
Point Humboldt

16 November 2009, one hour earlier

*T*oes. Check.

   Feet. Check.
Ankles. Check.
Shins. OK.
Thighs.

Ethan winced as shooting pains leapt up his right leg. Had he injured himself or was that the pins? Either way it felt good. It meant he was alive. He tensed the muscle once more and this time it didn't feel so bad. He continued his mental checklist, marvelling at how he hadn't suffered more serious injury; the reinforced office had done its job but not much had survived. All the shelving above the desk had collapsed, raining files and photos onto the floor. The rack behind had buckled, almost in two, littering the floor with yet more research. Five years of forensic investigation painstakingly assembled in neat files and now a jumbled mass of paper shaken free by the earthquake which must have lasted a full thirty seconds, growing in strength until Ethan feared the very earth beneath him was going to crack open and swallow him whole. He had instinctively curled up into a foetal position until the shaking had subsided and, finally, stopped.

Ethan struggled to his feet, emerging from the piles of paper like a moth from its pupa. The first thing he saw was the flickering CCTV monitor, somehow still attached to the wall above his head, somehow still transmitting, and its frozen image sucked the air from his lungs. When the quake hit, he had been tracking Uma and Edward across the Hall of Steel. Both were now spreadeagled on the stone floor, Uma face down, hands over her head but his butler hadn't been so lucky—he was flat on his back and protruding from his right thigh was a thick pole. For a moment, Ethan couldn't place it but then realised that the tower must have shaken loose one of the spears that adorned its walls. He felt his stomach churn at the thought of thousands of weapons raining down on Uma. Nobody could survive that downpour of metal. He sank to his knees at the thought he might never see her again, even as the familiar resentment closed over him like a thick crust of magma. He didn't owe her anything. She had lied to him, tricked him, double crossed him, trampled on his heart, entangled him, resurrected him, but none of it was a match for the unfamiliar feelings that bubbled up through a hundred fault lines, each one peppered with memories. The first time he had seen her at the lecture in Reykjavík, her dark green eyes burning a swathe across the audience. The way she had fearlessly confronted the religious nut who had invaded the stage. In New York when she had called his bluff over LEAP, challenging him to walk away from the biggest opportunity of a lifetime. How he had lingered in her arms on his second LEAP, to the Interior, savouring the moment, her body pressed against his, thick curls tickling his face, his hand tightly gripping her shirt, which hours earlier, soaked through by the rain, had revealed more than he had seen in a long time. And later, much later, when Uma had told him that her office in Reykjavík had been destroyed just after Sally and James had died. His reaction had been the same then as now. A primal calling, compelling him to protect her and over which he had no control. It had happened after LEAP had been taken offline, when she'd called, this time barricaded in a back office as someone battered the door down. He could still hear the wood splintering, the surge of adrenalin, his need to get to her even though it was a suicide mission. He wasn't a fighter, not back then at least, he was a financier. But it didn't matter. Nothing mattered. Just like now. Not the fights, not the petty squabbles or his simmering animosity. Ethan stood up suddenly. Christ, what had he done, pushing her away like this? And now it might be too late. He needed to get to the hall as quickly as possible. But first, he needed to escape his new prison.

Ethan tried to open the door into the great hall, but it wouldn't budge. He braced himself against the solid oak and pushed with all his might. It gave slightly, barely a crack, but it was enough to glimpse what was blocking his escape. To provide privacy, one of the huge tapestries had been hung across the entrance but the quake had shaken it free and it was now slumped against the door. Encouraged, Ethan grabbed a long piece of metal that had supported the shelving behind his desk and inserted it into the crack. On his second push, he forced the bar into the narrow gap and was able to punch a six-inch opening into the thick material. As he paused to rest, a wispy cloud of smoke snaked through the gap. *Strange.* That wasn't forest wood from the great fire. It was a smorgasbord of different smells: wood, oil and old carpets. He redoubled his efforts and slowly the gap enlarged to the point where he was able to scramble through into the main hall where all he could do was stand and survey the scene before him.

Opposite, the entire wall containing the picture of Old Man Reynolds had collapsed into the fireplace below, sending huge flames shooting wildly up the outside of the chimney. On one side, a tapestry had become engulfed in the growing inferno, the armoured elephants rearing up on their hind legs as if to escape the advancing flames. Ethan could almost hear the screams of the terrified animals as the heat became too much to bear. Ethan limped into the centre of the hall and surveyed the wreckage. To his left, one end had disappeared completely, buried beneath the ceiling and upstairs floors that had collapsed, concertina-like, into the room. Most of the huge tapestries had shaken loose from their hangings and were now lying heaped on the floor like abandoned carpets, their ghastly images hidden from view. Old Man Reynolds was long gone, erased for all eternity along with most of his castle.

Ethan stumbled as an aftershock rumbled up through the wounded castle like an afterthought. The ceiling seemed to shriek in pain and the huge cast-iron light frame high above him swayed alarmingly. Without warning, two of the supporting chains whipped free from their bolts and the circular structure dropped a foot before the remaining restraints took the weight. Momentarily. Cracking like gunshots, first one chain failed, then a second, a third and finally the fourth tore loose. Ethan barely had time to throw himself backwards as a huge cloud of dust engulfed the centre of the room. Momentarily blinded, he didn't see the great chain, as thick as a man's wrist, strike out like a black sea serpent. The century-old metal, fired in the forges of Detroit, wasn't going to miss him a second time. It clipped his right temple before coiling to the floor. As Ethan lay dazed, he heard a distant scream of agony and puzzled over a searing pain that consumed his left hand from the tips of his fingers all the way to his elbow. And then he passed out.

A primal scream pierced the dark; it was pain filled, part fear, part hurt. The shriek of a helpless animal trapped in the jaws of a snare.

'Is anyone there?' Uma heard herself cry out.

There was no answer. Her voice sounded faint, muffled in the enclosed space. A coughing fit enveloped her as the dust of decades exercised its new-found freedom deep within her lungs.

'Edward? Is that you?' she croaked.

Uma knew it wasn't him. There was no way Hunter could have escaped the collapse of the tower. The cry had come from the great hall. She had been lucky. Her instinct had saved her, otherwise ... she dare not think. What could have happened to Ethan's man servant? Perhaps he had avoided the falling armaments and managed to get away. Maybe he was also under the tower, unconscious or trapped in the twisted metal. But deep down Uma feared the worst. He had been behind her. She was sure he hadn't followed her. Certainly not got ahead of her. Probably wouldn't have known what to do. Years of experience had taught her well. Drop to the ground. Take cover under something. Anything. At home, it had been the kitchen table. It was strengthened with steel bars across the underside but also down the legs to withstand the ceiling collapsing in on them. As children in Iceland, they had practised every day: once before breakfast and once after dinner.

Something clattered high above her. A sword perhaps or axe head broken free from its restraints. It sounded close as it bounced and clanged off the remains of the structure. Uma tried to shift her position, but it was difficult. She was hemmed in by the underside of the tower which was lying at an acute angle. From where she lay, it looked like the concrete base had collapsed, preventing any escape under the tower. Ahead, the small space through which she had scrambled was bristling with weapons shaken free by the quake. She had already tried to shift some of the heavy metal but each piece was stuck fast, wedged against others by its own weight and awkward angles.

Why had she come here? She still wasn't sure. Or didn't dare to admit it. Even now as she lay trapped beneath a collapsed monument to war, miles from civilisation, her thoughts lay with a man who was most certainly incapable of saving her and probably dead. The sudden realisation made her swallow hard. *Is this it?* Was she doomed to die? Alone. In disgrace. Laid low by a ruthless spy chief whose only thought was to keep her in line so he could control LEAP for his idealistic boss.

Without warning, the whole ground shook. Above her, the entire structure groaned in pain and for a moment she thought it was going to collapse. It was Uma's turn to scream.

Ethan felt warm, very warm, or at least his right side did. The left felt strangely cold, except for his forearm. That was burning as if it was being held just above the tongue of the hottest flame. The pain was excruciating and he tried to pull away from the molten fire but his arm wouldn't move. *It doesn't make sense. Why hold it there? Who would do that?* And then suddenly he was awake. And the pain was real now, a physical certainty, gnawing at his nerve endings which made him cry out. He tried to get up but his arm held him back. High above the ceiling seemed to buckle again. Had he dreamt that? It seemed unnatural. The scene from a dreamscape. But as he watched, it went again, rippling away from him like pond water disturbed by a large rock thrown from the shore. This time Ethan followed the wave as it travelled to the far end of the room, to the part that had already collapsed, where it petered out. But as he stared at the ceiling, the wave set off back toward him. Which way was it travelling? He couldn't tell and then, with horror, realised what was happening; the aftershocks had destabilised the entire room. It was too much for the old building and slowly, inevitably, it was pulling the entire ceiling down on top of him. It was as if Mother Earth was gearing up for one last heave to finish the old man's castle off. Galvanised, he tried to sit up again but screamed in agony as his left arm yanked him back, as if attached to some invisible rope. No wonder, his entire forearm up to the elbow was buried beneath chain link, the black metal snaking back to the fallen chandelier, gleaming dully in the flickering flames of huge bonfires that had leapt away from the ruined fireplace. Ethan pulled at the top links with his good hand. They weighed heavily in his palm and he grimaced as the unnatural angle pulled at his shattered arm. One link at a time was lumped from the pile and gradually his forearm came free. Nearby, a huge section of the ceiling crashed to the floor. The blaze raged towards the new heap of rubble as if possessed by Old Man Reynolds' spirit, a spirit that was willing it to consume his now ruined monument to a long-fallen empire. Ethan finally pulled his arm free. It was bent at an odd angle to his wrist and already the skin was blackening.

He staggered to his feet, fighting back waves of nausea, his useless hand cradled across his chest. Another section of ceiling smashed to the floor by the fireplace. Ethan backed away like a caged animal, uncertain of where to run. The building decided for him. With a great roar, the floors above the far end of the Great Hall slowly sank into the room. Ethan turned and sprinted for the doors. He felt the pressure wave propel him forward as a thousand tons of masonry chased him across the long room. He hurled himself under the shattered door as a tsunami of stone, splintered wood and debris spewed him out into the long corridor.

Ethan must have passed out for when he opened his eyes everything was still. He lay there for long moments, performing another mental check. Satisfied, he dragged himself out of the debris, wincing as his crushed arm throbbed with each movement. As he stood, a coughing fit overwhelmed his choked lungs still burning with black dust. He crouched, waiting for it to pass before surveying what was left of the Great Hall. A thirty-foot mountain of rubble greeted him and he realised with a start that his home for most of the last five years had been wiped from the earth, a home where he had trained, often fought, sometimes slept, but mainly sat, just staring at the fire and the menacing portrait of Old Man Reynolds, trying to second guess what he would have done with Ethan's curse. Now it was all gone and he would have to go. There was no saving this place but he could still save himself and, of course, Uma.

The corridor ahead was a wasteland of shattered metal and smashed wood. Several of the massive cannon balls had been flung twenty, maybe thirty feet, by the quake. To his right, the entire glass frontage had collapsed, giving Ethan a bird's eye view of the ugly ocean a hundred feet beneath. It looked dangerous, its iron-grey waters beckoning him down as the frigid winter air pulled at him through the breached windows. Ethan shivered and hurried down the corridor into the central atrium, where he paused to take in the damage. The tower had partly collapsed on two sides, causing it to topple forward before smashing into the top balustrade of the staircase. Most of the weapons had come crashing down but some remained, and he eyed them warily as he stepped into the hall.

'Uma,' he called softly. He throat was dust dry hoarse.

'Uma,' he croaked more loudly.

Nothing. He moved further into the circular hall, stepping carefully over the chaotic arms dump. Nothing could have survived this. Thousands of weapons blocked his way, a minefield of razor-sharp metal and splintered shafts. He stumbled, nearly impaling himself onto an evil-looking spearhead. As he straightened, something caught his eye. It looked like hair.

'Uma,' he screamed, scrambling forward recklessly. Edward Hunter lay still, his mouth a bloody grin, courtesy of a hurlbat axe blade that had split his face from cheek to eye socket. A Mexican macuahuitl sword had severed his body almost entirely from his head, the dull black obsidian fragments set haphazardly into the wooden blade, easily slicing through the fragile bones in his neck. The spear he'd seen on the screen had struck higher than the image suggested, buried deep into his groin, his trousers and shirt soaked crimson red from the severed femoral artery. As hot bile burned his throat, Ethan staggered away through the thicket of weapons like a hapless drunk. As he neared the collapsed tower, he heard a soft cry.

'Ethan, is that you?'

His heart lurched.

'Uma?' She was nowhere to be seen. 'Where are you?'

'Down here.' Her voice was tiny.

He couldn't pinpoint her. There was too much sound: the groaning earth beneath his feet, the shrieking tower above his head. Everything felt fragile as if it was all going to collapse at any moment. The thought made him weak but the desperation in Uma's voice steadied his frayed nerves.

'Where?'

'Over here.' She sounded frantic.

It was clear what had happened. The two front columns supporting the tower had collapsed. As it had fallen forward, the rear supporting legs had shorn clean from their concrete anchors which in turn had caused the base section to break up. Towards the rear it had disintegrated, burying everything in a deep mound of rubble. Nothing should have survived but the front of the tower had held firm. Uma was trapped beneath it, hidden by a thicket of metal and broken wood. He worked quickly but carefully, keeping a wary eye on the remaining weapons that clung like dozing bats to the collapsed tower above him. Every so often one would silently drop. The first he knew was when it clanged onto the ground, sometimes skidding haphazardly off its fallen cousins. Other times it just buried itself deep in the pile, finding the gaps with unerring accuracy. He tried to move faster but his left arm was useless and he fought the waves of pain that washed over him. Many of the larger axes and swords were almost immovable and he wondered how anyone could have lifted them fully fit, let alone wield them in battle. He worked in silence. He wasn't used to talking but every so often he would call her name out and she would respond weakly but calmly. Precious minutes passed. Sweat poured off Ethan. His good hand was bleeding heavily where it had nicked sharp metal. And then suddenly her fingers appeared which became a hand and then a wrist. He could see her, ghost-like beneath the base. But Mother Earth wasn't going to give her up that easily. Without warning, the ground shook and the fallen tower shifted. Another shock could collapse the entire base.

'Please hurry,' she pleaded.

Ethan redoubled his efforts. Choked lungs screamed. Tired muscles protested. A huge sword, at least ten feet long, blocked his way. It was for a giant. Ethan felt the slow rumble before he heard it and knew this was the moment. It gave him the strength and with an explosive roar he pulled the blade free and reached for Uma. His hand, slick with sweat and blood, slipped from hers. He found it again and they both screamed in unison. One in fear, the other from exhaustion. The next thing he knew, Uma was in his arms as the base concertinaed shut and the tiny opening closed off like an ancient tomb.

Ethan lay there, enjoying the moment, her frail body pressed against his, hair feather light on his cheek, heart pumping wildly against his chest. He felt different; there was no anger or resentment, just unfamiliar feelings shaken loose by Mother Nature. He didn't want to let go but as her breathing steadied, she eventually pulled free from their unlikely embrace.

'Thank you,' she said softly. 'You saved my life.'

Ethan shrugged self-consciously, suddenly unsure of what to say.

'You'd have done the same.'

'I did,' she half murmured.

Confusion furrowed his brow. What had he done? Who had done it? Why? He felt like he was standing on the edge of a precipice peering down into the abyss. Behind him, the comforting blackness he inhabited; before him, uncertainty. It made him hesitate. How dare she compare the two? This was different. Familiar resentment flooded his veins. Anger drowned out the flickering feelings.

'It changes nothing,' he said, turning away.

'Where are you going?' she said, her voice incredulous.

'We need to get out of here before this whole place comes down.'

'Why do you care?' Uma said, realisation dawning. 'You're as good as dead.'

He ignored her and started back towards the main entrance, carefully stepping over the glistening minefield. A small aftershock rippled across the floor, making him stagger. Behind him, the familiar metallic clang of metal on metal as more weapons fell to the ground.

'Are you coming?' he growled, half in hope.

Silence.

He continued towards the entrance.

'You can't stay here, Uma,' he called back. 'That tower may come down at any second.'

Still nothing.

He turned round, ready to blast her but she hadn't even moved, just stood there, ramrod straight as if rooted to the spot. It looked slightly unnatural. Around her, huge swords and spears dwarfed her tiny figure. She looked so vulnerable, surrounded by the ugliness of war. Once again, long forgotten feelings. From another life. Another body. Someone else's memories. As he watched, a drop of blood seeped from the corner of Uma's lip and trickled slowly down her chin. The blood so red against her alabaster skin.

'Uma.' He heard himself cry, rushing towards her. But it was too late. She fell forward slowly, the spear buried deep in her back now visible as she collapsed into Ethan's arms.

Virginia

16 November 2009, 18:32 hours

'Let me get this straight.' Crouch paused for a moment, trying to gather his splintered thoughts but it was too much. His body felt unnaturally swollen as if the skin had shrunk overnight, leaving him unable to move for fear of tearing the thin membrane and exposing his aching bones. He remained still or at least tried to but every so often a fit of trembling would overwhelm his limbs, forcing him to hug them tightly but it was to no avail. He gave up and slumped back into the soft couch, watching dully as his defenceless hands surrendered to the manic shaking. The attack passed and he sat straighter, smoothing out his crumpled lab coat. Crouch adjusted his glasses and tried again but it was no good.

'I need a drink' he said.

The men opposite stared back, unmoving, until one nodded, releasing the other to pour a glass of straight bourbon from the once-full bottle by his side. He pushed it across the table towards the old man who grabbed it gratefully in both hands before downing the entire tumbler in one gulp. He smacked his lips and visibly relaxed.

'So, let me get this straight,' Crouch tried again. 'You're offering me a lead role in the LEAP programme.'

'We're offering you so much more than that, Professor. So much more.'

'Like what?'

'For a start, the opportunity to recover your standing in the scientific community as the pre-eminent Quantum Physicist of your generation.'

'I would like that,' Crouch murmured.

'Unless, of course, you're happy to continue teaching high school physics to the students at the Albert Einstein High School in Bethesda.'

Professor Crouch visibly cowered at the threat before a violent fit of trembling wracked his entire body. He glanced longingly at the half-empty bottle on the other side of the table but this time the agents remained still.

'But no more public appearances.'

The agents stared impassively at the broken man in front of them, long grey strands of hair glued sideways over his bulbous head, his pupils grossly magnified by the thick lenses, scraggy wisps of beard matted red with whatever had stained his lab coat.

'I don't think you'll need to worry about that!'

The professor's pudgy lips cracked into a wide grin.

'I'm not good in public.' He stared at the bottle.

'Your reputation was not the only one that Uma Jakobsdóttir destroyed that day.'

The mention of Uma seemed to energise the professor.

'Don't mention her name,' he snapped back, his voice quivering with emotion. 'She ruined me. Made me a laughing stock. I became a pariah. No one would touch me. I couldn't leave my house for months. I never want to see that woman again,' he said. 'Do you hear me? Never.'

'You won't need to. We'll see to that.'

'Good.'

A fresh wave of shivers embraced him like a dark shroud, forcing him to grasp the sides of the couch until the trembling had stopped. He stared at the bottle hungrily, willing it towards him.

'The area we need your help on is at the cutting edge of the programme. In fact, so much so that only a few individuals beneath the President know about it.'

Professor Crouch dragged his eyes from the liquid gold and stared at the man.

'The President?' he croaked.

'Of the United States.'

'Does he have a budget?'

'Unlimited.'

For the first time Crouch's eyes brightened, his burning thirst forgotten for a moment.

'Unlimited?' Crouch repeated.

'There are no restrictions on manpower and funds. It will be the biggest government-funded undertaking since the Manhattan Project during World War II.'

'The Bomb!' Crouch said. 'My father worked on that.'

'Except you'll play a leading role and be provided with anything you ask for.'

'Anything?' Crouch said, staring hypnotically at the half-empty bottle sitting between them.

'Anything you desire.'

Camden Town, London

16 November 2009, 23:50 hours

An anguished whimper escaped the man's tight mouth, his face a study in pain control. Deep crevices creased his dirty grey brow, eyes screwed shut, cheeks sucked in, his thin lips barely visible. The pain washed over him in waves, each one slightly more intense than the last, until, just at the point when he was going to pass out, it would dissipate, radiating out across his battered nerve endings before subsiding slightly, even as the next wave began its patient assault.

'Are you sure you won't take a small sedative?' The doctor sounded concerned.

Ethan managed a weak smile, despite the overwhelming urge to be sick. The agony was a worthwhile sacrifice. It was life affirming, bringing a clarity of purpose he hadn't felt in years. No longer fearful of the future. No longer afraid of the past. No longer avoiding the present.

'I'm sure,' he spat out through clenched teeth. 'Just do your job.'

The elderly man sighed and continued treating the shattered arm, carefully cleaning away small slivers of bone.

'I'm not sure I can do this,' he eventually said, laying the bloody tweezers on the metal tray. 'You should be in hospital. An operating theatre. I can't clean it properly.'

'No hospitals,' Ethan snapped and then more softly, 'I've had my fill of hospitals.'

'The risk of infection is too great. You could lose your arm.'

'Understood, Doctor. No hospitals. OK.'

The response brooked no argument and after a moment's silence, he shrugged and continued his work, admiring the younger man's self-control. Lesser mortals would have broken down long before but not this one. For the next hour Ethan lay there quietly, the only sign of discomfort a stiffening of his body or a slight groan. As the doctor finished up, there was a knock at the door of the study and Georgina Carr entered. Both men smiled at her. She beamed back. The last six years had been kind to Ethan's resident caretaker, chef and housekeeper; a few grey hairs, slightly rounder, the odd laughter line. When he had stumbled into her living room on the ground floor of his old Camden Town property, she had screamed with a mixture of delight and fright. He was punch drunk with pain. More dead than alive but she had recovered quickly, laying him down on the couch, assessing his injuries and calling one of her friends, a retired Harley Street physician who had come over immediately. Never once had she questioned him but behaved as if the last six years had never happened. Ethan marvelled at her stoicism and gave thanks for keeping the property, a decision driven more for her sake than his.

'How's the patient?' she announced brightly, glancing at the thick bandage that now covered Ethan's lower arm. 'That looks better. Thank you, Edward. You've done a fine job.'

'It'll do for now,' he said, turning to Ethan, 'but you need to have this seen to as soon as possible. At the very least an X-ray. Preferably a full examination and proper cleaning. As I said, you could lose the arm.'

'What do I owe you?' Ethan said, cradling his throbbing arm. The doctor exchanged a glance with Ethan's housekeeper.

'Don't worry about that, sir. Edward's due nothing. He's had his fair share of hot dinners over the years, isn't that right, Doctor!'

The elderly man winked back, smiling broadly.

The exchange completely missed Ethan who was concentrating on standing up. The shift in position did not suit his arm. The past two hours of pain seemed to gather up into one concentrated explosion across his shattered arm. He cried out, stumbling back against the table. Georgina Carr stepped forward but Ethan waved her away.

'Well, thank you, nevertheless,' he managed through gritted teeth, shaking the older man's hand with his good arm before turning to his anxious housekeeper. 'Mrs Carr, after you.'

He followed her up onto the second floor as she chatted ten to the dozen about the last six years. The waiting. The knowledge he would return. Ethan, however, wasn't listening. He was thinking of Uma. The moment when she had fallen to the ground, her lifeless body slumped awkwardly. The spear had entered just above her neck and buried itself deep within her body. How far, Ethan couldn't tell but it looked solid. A part of her. He had sat there for maybe twenty minutes cradling her lifeless head in his arms. Even in death, she looked tired. Worn down. Dark rings circled her eyes. Thick black hair now lifeless and dull, matted with dried blood.

His housekeeper stopped outside a bedroom. Ethan put a finger to his lips.

'Right,' she whispered theatrically, a broad grin breaking out across her face, 'I'm going to prepare your favourite meal. I hope you're hungry.'

'Famished,' he silently mouthed.

She shuffled off down the corridor, leaving Ethan alone. He stood outside the door for several minutes, suddenly afraid to enter. Uncertain what he would say. How to even begin. Eventually, he entered and just stood there taking in the large photograph; his parents were still laughing, their merriment captured for all eternity by the black and white print. Ethan smiled back and put two fingertips to his lips, mouthing a kiss. As he did so, the figure in the large bed shifted.

'Ethan!' Uma said his name carefully. He couldn't blame her for that. All the fights, the endless arguments. Ethan was surprised she was even talking to him. 'Can you please tell me what's going on? Who was the old woman watching over me? Where are we? The last thing I remember was jumping from Washington and then ...' Uma paused, desperately trying to remember. '... nothing.'

She lay back on the pillow, her pale face bathed in sweat.

'Annoying, isn't it?' was all he could think to say, his mind casting back to the LEAP when it had all gone wrong. Ethan clearly remembered waking up in Uma's father's house in Reykjavík, the Northern Lights still playing softly in his mind's eye. How long ago was it now? Four ... five years. Probably longer. It had felt hugely disorientating. His last memories peppered his thoughts. The horrific argument with Uma about how to respond to Eva's kidnapping. His tearful confession about killing his parents. Her reaction. His declaration of sorts. Her rejection. The subsequent fight. The ensuing silence. And it had got steadily worse from then on. After their LEAP to New York where they were meant to hand over the LEAP code to some faceless kidnappers in exchange for Uma's sister, Ethan clearly remembered the feeling of betrayal after overhearing Uma and Shane discuss how they had purposely kept his entanglement with Anderson from him. How they had tried to correct it by wiping his LEAP programme but without success and then decided that the monster they had created was too unstable, that he needed to be removed. Even now, he felt suffocated by it. But no longer angry. Seven months of his life had disappeared. His memories wiped. Uma had filled in the vacuum for him: his incarceration at the hands of the Homeland Security; Eva's death; Uma's infiltration of Reynolds' organisation; Ethan's fight with Grond and subsequent coma. Her vigil and the decision to bring him back. And then the last five years, right up to this afternoon. He knew exactly how she felt and would feel.

Ethan winced as he eased himself onto the edge of the bed. Uma seemed to notice his arm for the first time.

'What happened?' she said, concern replacing caution. 'Ethan, what's going on?'

'Do you remember anything?'

'I remember the conversation with Ingram in DC. His threat.'

'Tell me,' he said, stalling for time. 'What did he say?'

She quickly recounted the last twenty-four hours. Ethan was still, preparing his words.

'I had nowhere to turn,' she whispered, turning away from Ethan. The admission hung between them.

'Go on,' Ethan prompted her.

'I remember going to the gate and leaping. Then nothing. Until I just woke up now.' Uma paused and for a moment Ethan thought she'd worked out what had happened. And then she continued. 'Ethan, why are we here? Where is here?'

'You're in London. At my house in Camden Town.'

'But you don't travel anymore,' she said, realisation dawning. 'Unless you're not telling me something. Have you been coming here?'

Her tone wasn't accusatory. If anything, she sounded hopeful.

'No,' Ethan said, 'this is my first visit in over five, six years. I've never left Point Humboldt in all that time.'

'Why now? What's happened?'

He couldn't stall for ever.

'There was an earthquake. A huge one. It completely destroyed the castle.'

A large grin broke across Uma's pale face.

'Well, I can't say I'm disappointed. I hated that place.'

'I know,' he said.

'So, you've moved here?' she tried again.

'Uma, something else happened.' He hesitated, unsure of how to continue. And then he remembered how she had broken the news to him about his coma in her blunt straightforward Icelandic way. He took the plunge.

'You died in the earthquake. In the Hall of Steel. A spear. It was ...' He trailed off, remembering the moment she had fallen forward.

Uma didn't reply, her face revealing nothing. The moment stretched out, compelling Ethan to continue.

'Seeing you there in my arms—so still, so cold—I realised that I couldn't let you go.'

Uma put her fingers to his lips. He fell silent, unable to read her reaction.

'I understand,' Uma said softly. She really did, having already trodden this road once after learning that she was a copy of her sister. Or her sister was of her. In her mind, it was the same thing as this. In both scenarios you were a copy of a copy. Atoms were atoms. With LEAP there was no death. She could rationalise it scientifically. What she had struggled with was why her father had made the copies. He was nothing but a hypocrite with his hollow words and long lectures about the dangers of LEAP. What had he said to her after she had brought him back? 'It will upset the natural order of things. You can't have two of me running around!' Except that it hadn't stopped her father having two copies of her running around. That was precisely why she had created the LEAP Laws, to provide a rule book as to how LEAP should be used. But then she'd promptly breached them at the first hurdle, bringing Ethan back from his coma. What else could she do? And now Ethan had done the same thing for her. She understood exactly why he'd done this. 'Remember. I had to make the same decision. It was the hardest thing I ever had to do.'

'No please. Let me finish. You need to hear this,' he said, realising it was now or never. He swallowed hard, summoning the courage.

'I never told anyone the truth about how my parents died. Who I used to be. You changed all that. Allowed me to believe there was someone I could share my past with. And my future. That night was a big deal for me.'

'I wasn't ready,' Uma said.

'I realised that later, but when you kept Anderson from me,' he said, unable to meet Uma's gaze, 'it felt like the cruellest betrayal.' He fell silent and Uma waited, fearful of the explosion that tended to follow Ethan's brief moments of lucidity. But this time there was none.

'When I awoke from my coma it was the first thing I remembered. And then it took over, like a poison, making me question your motives.' There was no bitterness anymore, just a painful realisation. 'It was like a cancer consuming everything. I couldn't get past it and got stuck on who I had become. What I had become. I couldn't move forward. Until today when you fell to the ground. I sat there for over an hour, regretting what I had allowed myself to become. How I had turned my back on you when you needed me most. How, if I could turn back time, I would do it all differently.'

He glanced back at his parents on the wall opposite, their laughing faces so life affirming.

'I lost you once,' he whispered. 'I couldn't lose you again.'

'Oh, Ethan. I'm so sorry.'

Uma leant forward and hugged him fiercely. He cried out, drawing away from her, cradling his arm. In places, blossoms of red seeped through the white bandage.

'What have you done to your arm?' she exclaimed.

Ethan explained the terrifying collapse in the Great Hall.

'But why didn't you repair it?'

'How?'

'With LEAP of course.'

'I don't want to. It's part of who I am. Just like my pins,' he patted his leg. 'And Anderson,' he said. 'It's changed my present and possibly my future but it won't stop me living. None of this will anymore.' He looked around the room, his gaze settling on Uma.

Uma nodded. There was nothing left to say. He kissed her gently and Uma's lips melted into his. They were soft just like the first time he had kissed her in the Blue Lagoon but this time there was no savage pawing. Just Ethan, gentle Ethan.

Unincorporated Frederick County, Maryland

17 November 2009, 14:34 hours

It looked cold outside despite the bright sunlight streaming in through the wall-to-wall windows which stretched the entire length of the lodge. From his vantage point above the golf course Ingram surveyed the low peaks of the Blue Ridge Mountains in the distance, their slopes thick with denuded oaks, hickories, maple, and tulip poplar. Beneath their bare branches the 5,000 acre Catoctin Mountain Park was asleep, the hundreds of streams frozen over, the campsites empty, its trails deserted. He had hiked many of them over the years, enjoyed the excellent fly fishing on Bug Hunting Creek and holidayed with his grandchildren at Poplar Grove. It still never failed to surprise him that the most powerful man in the world was allowed to share his private retreat with so many others; nearly 700,000 had visited Catoctin last year alone, the vast majority probably completely oblivious that their day trip had brought them within spitting distance of one of the most secure facilities in the country. Only in America.

A uniformed marine came into view and sauntered across the frosted putting green, his M4 carbine pointing menacingly at the ground. Suddenly, others were visible and within thirty seconds Ingram had counted over forty soldiers patrolling the area in front of him. They looked battle hardened and probably were, each man handpicked to join Marine Security Company, an elite unit tasked with protecting Camp David. They would have been put through an intense training schedule to even be considered for this assignment and that was before their Yankee White background check, an all-encompassing investigation into each soldier's life right back to pre-school. He suddenly felt better. It had been the right decision to come. Despite the day trippers this was way more secure than the White House. No one could get at the President here.

A door opened behind him and three men entered; his Commander in Chief flanked by two Secret Service agents.

'Good morning, Joseph,' the President said, making his way to the centre of the room where he slumped down in the deep-seated leather couch and stared at the ceiling of Aspen Lodge. He looked tired. 'You've got me for thirty minutes.'

The two agents exited silently.

'Any breakthroughs?' he finally said.

'We've just had the autopsy reports in on those deaths at Guantanamo.'

'And?'

'The person who hung himself wasn't Belman.'

The President raised an eyebrow.

'Who was it?'

'Mohammed Hussain.'

'One of the releasees?'

''Fraid so.'

The President let out a heavy sigh. He seemed to sink further into the plush couch.

'It gets worse.'

'Go on.'

'The two Weapons Sergeants found on top of John Paul Jones Hill. They were on duty the night Hussain died.'

'Why are we just finding this out now?'

'We knew about the soldiers. Once we discovered the prisoner switch, a full autopsy was ordered. The camp pathologist sent all the bodies over to the mainland for a second opinion. It's standard procedure in a case like this.'

'What did it turn up?'

'Well, this is where it begins to get interesting.'

'There's more?' The President sat up.

'On the right hand of Weapons Sergeant Jos Brody, we found some skin fragments in his nails. We've run DNA tests. They belong to a Carl Fortune.'

'And he is?'

Ingram handed the President a thin folder which he opened and read quickly before tossing it onto the low coffee table.

'We've trained him well,' he said. 'Where is he?'

Ingram sighed.

'We don't know. He dropped off the radar about two years ago.'

'Does he still work for us?'

'Officially, he's never worked for us.'

'Sounds like a dead end to me.'

'Not quite. Jed Grove's people have made some headway on The White House bombings.'

The President looked up sharply.

'That's quick work.'

'They've used CCTV to pick up the movements of the third bomber before he entered the compound. One of his men brought them over this morning. They're all teed up to go.' As he spoke, thick shutters silently dropped from the windows outside. Within seconds night had fallen. Behind the President a flat screen TV flickered into life.

'We've had a team of fifty agents reviewing footage from the 200 or so cameras around The White House. The results are quite revealing.

It's been spliced together at short notice so it won't win any Oscars but you'll get the picture. This first one is taken fifteen minutes after the first blast.'

As he spoke a black and white image appeared. It was surprisingly clear and showed the area just above where the van bomb had exploded at the intersection of Pennsylvania and 17th Street. Three men were walking slowly past the Old Executive Office Building. Around them was a chaos of activity: ambulances, Secret Service cruisers, fire engines, black SUVs, Secret Service agents, SWAT teams, the MPDC. Everyone was there.

'How did you pick them out?' the President said.

'The benefit of hindsight. We've worked backwards from the last blast. We'd never have found them otherwise.'

The men were dressed entirely in black, the tell-tale uniform of the Secret Service Emergency Response Team, their presence entirely in keeping with the aftermath of the van bomb. They were moving slowly, three abreast and it was clear that the middle man, a full six inches taller than his companions, was helping the other two. They appeared to be injured and he half-pulled, half-supported them towards the Northwest Gate. At one point, a uniformed Secret Service agent stopped them. They talked for several seconds and then he pointed towards The White House. The three men continued on their way, even more slowly.

The image faded, replaced by another. It was slightly grainier and must have been taken from the direction of Lafayette Park. There were only two men in frame, the third nowhere to be seen. They had their backs to the camera and were stood by the Northwest Appointment Gate, the sweeping drive down to the West Wing was visible in the background. As they looked into the compound, the taller man fiddled with his companion's hands, squatting down on one knee to fasten something to the fence. As he bent, you got a sense of his size; he was not only tall but broad, his bulk evident beneath the black uniform. It wasn't clear what he was doing though. Whatever it was didn't take long. He swiftly got to his feet and without looking back, made his way across the wide avenue towards the Rochambeau Statue at the southwest corner of Lafayette Park. The man he had left just stood, staring towards the West Wing. Several seconds passed. A uniformed Secret Service agent exited the guard house and walked rapidly towards him. He was speaking urgently into his shoulder mic.

The camera position jumped again, this time urgently zooming in from the direction of the West Wing. As they watched, the agent could be seen talking to the statuesque man who was stood stock still, his face pressed to the bars of The White House perimeter. The guard looked down and suddenly pulled his weapon, turning to shout behind him. Two more guards could be seen running from the guard house, one carrying bolt cutters. The camera jumped again, this time zeroing in on the man. For a second it was an unfocused blur of greys and blacks and then suddenly a pair of hands came sharply into focus. They were clasped together, almost in prayer, either side of a black wrought-iron pole. In the foreground was the unmistakable metal glint of handcuffs. As they watched, the camera pulled away slightly and for a second, they caught a glimpse of his face. He stared blankly back at the camera, his eyes dull, unseeing. Suddenly there was a white flash and the screen went black.

When it returned, again from The White House side, pandemonium reigned. Bodies lay everywhere, some still, many moving slowly, medics, agents, police, huddled in ones and twos around them. In the foreground lay the twisted metal of the fence where the bomber had detonated. Staff hurried across The White House lawn, some with first aid kits, others empty handed, looking panicked, shell shocked. Several uniformed officers were laid on the lawn. As they watched, the larger man suddenly appeared out of the smoke. He was limping slightly, head down. He appeared to be pulling the other man along. It was clearly the last bomber that everyone had seen replaying on endless TV loops around the world for the last three days. The leading man pointed towards the West Wing but the smaller man didn't respond. His companion prompted him forward but still he wouldn't move. Now the larger man grabbed him by the shoulder and pointed again, this time shoving him forcibly towards the West Wing. He stood watching the bomber who stood there, seemingly uncertain. You could clearly see his face despite the peaked cap. He looked dazed. And then he began to walk, slowly but steadily towards the camera. Figures rushed by him all moving towards the Northwest Appointment Gate. No one gave him a second glance. He was ten feet from the main doors when there was another flash. The screen faded to black.

'He never moved his hands.'

'It would appear not,' Ingram said.

'It happened too quickly. Can we get a rewind?'

Almost in anticipation, the image of the last bomber suddenly appeared. He was moving slowly, his hands clearly by his side.

'See, nothing.' The President was on his feet, face inches from the bright screen.

'I agree. No wires. Nothing.'

'Remote control?'

'That's what we're thinking.'

'The big guy? Fortune.'

'Precisely.'

'Why wasn't it jammed?' the President said.

'Not sure. We're looking into it.'

'Got an ID on the bombers?'

'We do.' The image suddenly split into two. On one side was a clear still of the first bomber. Beside him was a mugshot of a prisoner in orange overalls staring dully into the camera.

'We're pretty certain that is one of the Siddiqui brothers.'

The resemblance was uncanny.

'And his partner?'

As the President spoke, the second bomber appeared beside another composite.

'His brother. They both disappeared on their way to Miami after being released from Guantanamo. Their guards were killed. The story wasn't really picked up by the networks because of the LEAP announcement. None of it made sense at the time because they were on their way to the airport to be flown home. Free men. Why kill their escort? But now.' Ingram nodded at the screen.

'And the big guy's Fortune?'

'We think so.'

'How? You didn't get a clear shot.'

'We did actually.'

The screen flicked to another scene, moments before the second bomb went off. A man was crossing Pennsylvania, something clearly grasped in his right hand. He looked back towards The White House and, as he did so, collided with two DC police officers just as the bomb exploded. All three were thrown to the ground in a tangle of black uniforms. As they got to their feet, the larger man adjusted his black beanie which had been knocked almost from his head. The frame froze. It was undoubtedly the man in the slim folder on the table in front of them.

'Do we bury this?' the President said.

'Not sure we can. The networks will probably be doing the same as us, working backwards from the last explosion. They all had choppers which don't offer a great angle but you can follow the flow. We need to release this.'

'What? Tell them about the two brothers.'

'They'll find out anyway.'

'They'll have a field day with this one.'

'We've got no choice. If they uncover this, your Presidency is over.'

'It's not looking too good either way. For God's sake Joseph, we released them from Guantanamo one day as declared innocents. The next day they're blowing themselves up in front of The White House. It's a PR disaster.'

'You're damned if you do—'

'What about Belman?' the President cut in. 'What do you suggest we do there?'

'Keep him quiet for the time being,' Ingram said. 'No one knows. No sense in volunteering that one. In one sense it supports our security lockdown. We can say there's an active suicide cell operating on the mainland. No names. Just the odd detail. Maybe one or two people. ID unknown. You know, create a sense of fear. Get the press on our side. We could start a campaign to find them.'

'And Fortune?'

'Keep that quiet as well. Let's see what our campaign throws up.'

'He had inside help.'

'I know.' Ingram shifted uncomfortably in his seat.

'You need to find out who.' The President sighed deeply. 'What a mess. It's worse than 9/11. If it gets out, we'll look like even bigger fools, especially so soon after that intel disaster.'

Ingram was silent now.

'I know. I know,' the President replied wearily. 'You warned me this might happen.'

'Worse things have happened.'

'Not on my watch.'

'Yours's has only just started. Mine is entering its fifth decade.'

'Shut them down. Whoever is responsible, shut them down. If this ever gets out, I'm finished.'

'You can relax, sir. Be assured that we will throw the combined might of all the available agencies to root out the culprit. We will find them and deal with them.'

The President sighed.

'Anything else?'

'No, sir.'

'The Jakobsdóttir woman?'

'Nothing, I'm afraid. She never contacted me after our meeting.'

The President shrugged.

'Pity. I had high hopes for her.'

Manhattan Island

18 November 2009, 07:10 hours

The lights were hot, unbearably so but this did not seem to deter the many technicians as they scurried around the huge studio moving cameras, furniture, coils of wires, and any other manner of equipment required to make a daily talk show. As they rushed, they chattered constantly into their collars, before listening intently to instructions from the faceless bank of glass where the production team were housed. Despite the chaos, their faces were focused as they scrambled to meet the deadline. By way of reminder, a computer-generated voice suddenly made a booming announcement.

'One minute to live transmission.'

The activity in the room seemed to go up a notch. One poor girl, barely out of her teens, collided with a large fat man carrying a tray of long mics. Both crashed to the floor in a tangle of wires and curses. Nobody stopped to help them. In fact, no one spared them a second glance and it was several seconds before either moved. The girl recovered first and leapt to her feet, leaving the large man sprawled on the floor of the studio.

Uma suppressed a smile, which was quite difficult given all her makeup. She was afraid it would crack and split, leaving her even more exposed than she already felt. A makeup girl fussed over her, applying yet more foundation to the layers already caked on. If it didn't crack, surely it would melt in this heat. Beside her, Ethan was also having the finishing touches applied. He looked better with more colour, although nothing could hide the impact of the last seven years, particularly given the large photo behind them of a much fresher faced Ethan taken in 2002, at the height of his fame. *Just before he met me.*

'Ten seconds to live transmission,' the disembodied voice boomed.

Uma looked over but the fat man had disappeared. The noise reached fever pitch and then, as the countdown petered out, it stopped. The sudden silence felt oppressive as the hundred or so people in the studio moved silently around the five cameras that were now pointed menacingly in her direction. Uma felt like an intruder.

The woman sitting directly opposite Uma and Ethan suddenly came to life, beaming at a camera behind Uma's shoulder before launching into a sunny soliloquy for the benefit of her early morning viewers. Uma disliked her immediately.

'Good morning America. Welcome to the Daily Event. We have two very special guests in the studio today. The former entrepreneur and current billionaire recluse, Ethan Rae, and his protégée, Dr Uma Jakobsdóttir.'

The presenter shifted her gaze onto Uma who felt herself responding to the smile, despite her urge to leave the set. It was magnetic and demanded a reaction. A warm one and she automatically obliged. It felt weird.

'As you know Green Ray is currently the subject of a federal investigation for alleged terrorist links,' Katrina Hoskins said. 'Whilst I must stress the 'alleged' nature of these charges, it doesn't look good, does it Dr Jakobsdóttir? Or may I call you Uma?'

Boy, she didn't mess about. Even as the knife went in smoothly and quietly with the practiced nonchalance of a lifetime conducting broadcast interviews, Uma felt herself responding to the smiling delivery so that she was left grinning like a Cheshire Cat.

She had been set up.

Ethan came to her rescue.

'Nice to see that you haven't lost your edge, Katrina,' he cut in. 'Straight to the point, as always. May I answer that one?' Without waiting for a response, he continued. 'It's very simple really. I've long standing connections with Saudi Arabia that go back twenty years. Maybe the investigation is related to that.'

'Would you care to expand?'

'Sure,' Ethan said. He looked confident and Uma wondered whether he was feeling so relaxed inside. It was a long time since he had been in public let alone subjected himself to an early morning interview in front of an audience of five million viewers. 'What do you need to know?'

'Well, exactly what were your dealings with the Saudis?'

'They bankrolled my very first business venture.'

'I didn't know that.'

'Not many people do.'

'Are you willing to share with our viewers, the nature of their support?'

'Of course.' Ethan paused for a second, looking down at the pink carpet of the raised dais. Then he glanced over at Uma and smiled. In that moment she knew what he was going to do and realised he had planned this all along. It had been his idea to hold an on-air interview with Katrina Hoskins, who anchored one of the most popular morning shows on American TV. He felt it would do their PR good to take their side of the story to the public, but she had assumed an entirely different story, one about LEAP, not this.

'I used to live in Saudi,' Ethan said. 'With my parents. I was only a kid. Maybe fourteen when we moved out there. My dad was an oil man.'

Katrina Hoskins leafed furiously through her notes, simultaneously trying to adjust the mic in her ear, no doubt receiving instructions from her production team.

'I didn't know that,' she repeated again and Uma suppressed a grin.

'Why would you? You won't find it anywhere in your records.'

'We have very good researchers, Mr. Rae.'

'I'm sure, but do they know my name isn't actually Ethan Rae?'

'It isn't?'

'No. It's Mark Brown.'

Half the sheets slipped off her lap.

'It is?' For a short moment, Katrina Hoskins lost her composure, glancing behind Uma again, this time staring blankly at a man with a clipboard who was jumping up and down with excitement. She recovered quickly. Her reporter's instinct kicked in. A scoop was in the air.

'What made you change it?'

'It's a long story.'

'We love long stories on the Daily Event,' she said, settling back into her seat, the notes forgotten. They were irrelevant now. This was all about knowing when to ask the right questions. When to talk. If to talk.

Ethan took a deep breath.

'It's simple really.' His voice dropped to a whisper. Uma held her breath in disbelief at Ethan's newfound openness. 'When I was just a teenager, my family was involved in a terrible road accident.' It was too late. He was committed even if he had wanted to stop, which Uma doubted. Where was he going with this? How could it possibly help her situation? 'We had all been out to celebrate my dad's birthday. I was driving. He had had a drink. So had Mum. Not that it would've mattered. She wasn't allowed to drive out there. As you probably know, the Saudi's have quite strict rules about what women can and can't do.' It was said without any rancour. Matter of fact, almost. 'We were in a head-on collision just outside Riyadh. My parents were killed instantly. The driver of the other vehicle died several days later in hospital. I was very badly injured.' He self-consciously rubbed his thigh. 'Whilst I was in hospital, I was sentenced to fifty lashes and ten years in a Saudi prison for dangerous driving.'

The silence in the studio was joined by a stillness as everyone stopped what they were doing and looked at Ethan.

'Was it your fault?'

'Yes and no. I shouldn't have been driving. I was too young. But the accident itself. I'm not so sure. I stopped at an intersection. It was dark. I went. Another car hit us. It was going too fast. I shouldn't have gone.'

Ethan shrugged, his initial confidence draining away before Uma, who held her breath.

'So why were you prosecuted then?'

Ethan shrugged again, avoiding the reporter's penetrating gaze.

'I hit the wrong person. It was the son of a local sheikh. Very well connected. Looking back, I never stood a chance really.'

'But why change your name?'

'Shame ... Guilt ...' He paused for a few seconds, gathering his thoughts. 'I was only a kid when it happened. When I was released ten years later the memories hadn't dimmed. I didn't want them to but at the same time I was desperate to bury the past. To start over. I wanted a new beginning. I felt ... still feel responsible for my parents' deaths. I would do anything to bring them back ...' he trailed off. For a moment Uma thought he was going to cry as she dabbed at her own tears. So did the reporter opposite although Uma could have sworn there were none. Ethan rubbed his thigh again. 'Somehow I had to get my life back on track. To try and put right what had gone wrong that night. I was a nobody then. A forgotten soul. It didn't seem such a big deal to be honest. But it gave me the new beginning which I craved. Complete anonymity. A reinvention if you will.'

That was how Ethan now referred to his and Uma's reincarnation. 'A reinvention.' Uma didn't care either way. For all she knew, she was a copy of her sister, thanks to her father's meddling. What did it matter if she was now a copy of a copy? Besides which, every LEAP produced a copy. The bit that scared her most were the Laws. It was the reason she had buried the LEAP programme after restoring Ethan from his coma. The first Law had been trampled over once again. This time by Ethan. The first Law, the prime law, was unambiguous. *If your physical body dies in the natural world, your LEAP programme has to be terminated.* What had Ingram said to her in DC? *When it comes to LEAP, you seem to have two rules. One set for Uma Jakobsdóttir and one for everyone else.* He was right but it wasn't meant to be this way. That's why she had come up with the damn Laws in the first place.

But no human could resist prolonging life if they had the means to. Particularly of their loved ones. She had succumbed twice: First with her father and then Ethan. And now, so had Ethan. And the truly frightening realisation was that Uma couldn't deny Ethan what he had done. For purely selfish reasons, she got to finish what she had started and of course to see Ethan seemingly cured. But it left a bigger question which had tormented her for years; if she couldn't resist the temptation to bring people back from the dead, then no one could and now the genie was out of the bottle. At best, all they could do now was be part of the narrative moving forward but Uma still shuddered at the thought of what would shortly be unleashed if Ethan's plan worked.

Uma had been astonished at how quickly he had returned to his normal self, as if someone had flicked a switch, returning Ethan to the man she had first met. They had remained in the townhouse and she suppressed another smile at the memory; feather-light lips, soft skin, moving as one, gently exploring each other. In between their love making they had slept, then eaten delicious meals left outside the door by a giggling Georgina Carr. And talked, for hours on end. At least Uma had. Ethan just listened patiently as she recounted the years following his self-imposed exile. It was only towards the end of the second day that he had grown restless, announcing that they needed to do something if they were going to save Green Ray. Twelve hours later she was sat here listening to his very public confession. Uma dragged herself back to the interview.

'And how is this related to what is currently happening at Green Ray?'

'It's the only connection I have to Saudi Arabia. During my internment I met a young man. A boy really. We were almost the same age. He was slightly older than me. We became good friends. I helped him out. Protected him as best I could. When we were released, his father gave me a gift. For keeping his son alive. That's how I was able to start my first business.'

'What did he give you?'

'Ten million pounds.'

'Ten million!'

Ethan laughed in embarrassment.

'An obscene amount, I know, but back then the Saudis were dripping in oil. It was literally a drop in the proverbial ocean for him and meant as a thank you for what I had done for his son. I didn't want it. In fact, I refused it repeatedly, but he insisted so we compromised and it was structured as an investment in my business. He effectively took a stake.'

'A stake?'

'Yes, a share which has delivered 100-fold since so I guess it wasn't a bad bet.'

'And could this man have connections to terrorism?'

'I doubt it.'

'You seem very certain, Ethan. Or should I call you Mark?'

'Ethan will do thanks,' Ethan said. 'I should be, given who it is.'

'Are you going to enlighten us?'

'Of course. I have nothing to hide any more. It was Abdullah Al Rahman, Head of the Re'asat Al Istikhbarat Al A'amah, Saudi Arabia's intelligence agency.'

Uma's heart lurched.

Green Ray's new investor.

The interviewer rubbed her hands with delight. *You couldn't make this up.*

'Ethan why are you telling us all this?'

'To set the record straight. I care deeply about Green Ray. I don't want to see it collapse in a baseless scandal. It's a charitable institution, for goodness' sake. If anything is worth saving, it's Green Ray. It's a vehicle for good. This has nothing to do with the fund. This is my past. I don't want to see it all unravel and wasted because of that. Besides which, I have nothing to apologise for. Nor do I have anything to hide.'

'Is that it?

'That's the only connection I have ever had with Al Rahman.'

Uma suppressed the urge to cry out. *That isn't true.* She had never mentioned the investment in Green Ray. It hadn't seemed relevant, despite the staggering amount. She had meant to talk to Ethan but with everything else that had happened, it had completely slipped

her mind. And she couldn't say anything now. It would make them both look foolish on prime-time TV. And even if she wanted to, she couldn't. The revelation would trigger a default. The condition of the funding was anonymity. She forced herself to concentrate on what Ethan was saying.

'Well, there could be darker forces at work here. Green Ray is now inextricably linked to LEAP. That technology will change the world and maybe others are looking to discredit Uma and her good work, to force the government to distance itself from her. Perhaps, so other partners can establish themselves.'

'You've never struck me as a conspiracist.'

'Call it what you like but there has to be a good reason for this smear campaign swirling about Green Ray.'

'And who do you believe is behind these allegations?'

'No idea. And quite frankly I don't care. All I want is for them to stop so we can keep up the good work with Green Ray and LEAP. Our partnership with the President is strong and one we are looking to drive forward. Once this misunderstanding has been cleared up,' he added quietly.

'I'm glad you raised LEAP. Why cede so much control to the US Government? Why not launch it yourself?'

'To try and minimise the disruption such a new technology would cause,' Ethan said.

'I don't understand. How could their involvement make any difference?'

'Well, we're all facing a very difficult time at the moment following the banking collapse. I was deeply concerned that LEAP would have the opposite effect and plunge us into a deeper recession as investors took flight from, say, the transport sector. It was too big a risk to go it alone. We needed a strong partner. Who better than the US Government?'

'Many would disagree with you there.'

'Why?' Ethan said. 'We're dealing with a new President. He has given us his word he won't move forward without our say so. Not that he could anyway. We own 51% of the partnership.'

'Are you suggesting that you would pull the plug on LEAP?'

'Not at all. In fact, the reverse is probably true. As you know, Katrina, I move very fast.'

'You used to,' she corrected him. 'You've been out of commission for the best part of five years. A lot has changed during that time.'

Ethan laughed. He sounded genuinely amused. Uma was shocked. She hadn't heard that sound for years.

'I've been recuperating. You have to remember that a maniac tried to strangle me. But I'm fully recovered now.'

As he finished, Ethan smiled at Uma, their eyes meeting for an instant and Uma could have sworn he winked at her before turning back to Katrina Hoskins. It was a deeply private moment in the most public of settings.

'I owe this lady a lot,' Ethan said, nodding towards Uma. 'Not only did she save my life but she helped me convalesce. Literally brought me back to life. And now I'm ready to repay her and help drive LEAP and Green Ray forward as fast as we can.'

The interview was drawing to a natural close.

'From the sounds of it you suffered a very close call the other day at Point Humboldt.'

Ethan held up his left forearm which was encased in a light plastic cast and winced.

'Yes, I was very lucky. We both were.'

'Oh, I didn't realise you were caught up in the earthquake, Doctor.' Katrina Hoskins turned smoothly to Uma.

For the first time, Ethan looked thrown. But he recovered quickly.

'Yes, Uma was with me when the quake struck.' There was an awkward pause. 'If she hadn't been, I wouldn't be here now talking to you. As I keep telling you, I owe this woman everything.'

'And how exactly did you save Ethan?

Uma continued to gawp as if caught in the headlamps of a fast-moving car but Ethan came to her rescue again. He suddenly groaned in pain, cradling his arm protectively. Both women turned to him in concern. Uma suppressed a cry. He looked terrible. A thin sheen of sweat had broken through the thick makeup and now bathed his face.

'Are you OK, Ethan?' the interviewer was forced to ask.

'I'm really sorry. My arm is really causing me trouble.' He winced again. 'The physician warned me this might happen. If it's OK, I would appreciate it if we could wrap up.'

Katrina Hoskins had no choice but to comply and the studio sprang back to life. Almost immediately, Uma's mobile started buzzing, just as Ethan had said it would.

'Well, this is a double first,' Uma said.

'How so?'

'Well, for a start, I'm fully clothed. Secondly, you've used traditional means of communication. Things are looking up.'

'Touché, Doctor.' Joseph Ingram sounded amused, although Uma suspected with a start of pleasure that nothing was probably further from the truth. 'I didn't realise you would bring in the heavy cavalry. The recent earthquake seems to have shaken his cobwebs free.'

'I didn't think you were talking to me.'

'Deadlines are highly overrated.'

'It seems so.'

'The President was quite taken with Mr Rae. Sounds like he has bought you a reprieve.'

The phone went dead, leaving Uma stood there in shock, the funding gaffe temporarily forgotten. Maybe they would get somewhere at long last, just like Ethan had promised.

Virginia

12 December 2009, 10:10 hours

The men stood patiently, their black uniforms in stark contrast to the clinical white of the corridor. Each one effortlessly shouldered a large rucksack, an ugly looking machinegun hanging casually at their sides. No one talked. It was quite eerie, and Crouch shivered involuntarily as he shuffled slowly past them fingering his security clearance. He must have counted over fifty agents. They ignored him completely, eyes forward, almost disdainfully so, perhaps in keeping with the knowledge that they belonged to an elite fighting force. As he neared the end of the line, two guards stepped out into the corridor. Both wore surgical gloves and without speaking, one of them presented a swab to the professor who obediently opened his mouth so the agent could swipe the inside of his cheek. Still no one spoke and, without acknowledging him, both disappeared through a set of metal doors, the sample now tubed and bagged. He knew the drill well. They would submit his saliva for analysis, comparing the DNA strands to the ones held on record. Thanks to the quantum computing power now at their disposal, what would have previously taken several days was now completed in seconds. If they matched, he would be allowed to enter the facility. If not ... Crouch thought of the small army lined up behind him and shuddered again.

This was the third DNA test he had undergone on his journey from the outer perimeter, but that did not surprise him. The world had changed following the attacks on The White House. There was an unsettling neurosis in the air and security was evident everywhere. Who could blame the mood? The DC bombings had brought the raw memories of 9/11 flooding back. In one sense, they were worse. The felling of the Twin Towers was the first strike by a foreign power on American soil since Pearl Harbour. The planes had come seemingly from nowhere on a beautiful sunny day. Without warning. The mere thought was preposterous in its retelling but Ground Zero was a stark reminder of the attacks. The aura of invincibility had been shattered forever. Lessons learnt. Security failings addressed. Borders tightened. Everyone was now ready, under no illusions that a foreign power would dare strike home territory. But it had. Despite billions spent, the monolithic Homeland Security and the endless security reorgs, three small explosions had once again exposed America's vulnerability and struck at the very heart of its democratic process.

A light above his head flashed green and the doors swung open. Crouch entered, an assigned agent followed two steps behind. He would remain his black shadow until he exited the facility, but Crouch ignored him. He was too busy admiring what had been achieved in the weeks since his first visit.

Where previously there had been nothing, a vast empty space the size of many football fields, a small city had sprung up. To his left, a five-storey hotel complex with a gleaming bank of windows over-looked a plaza complete with tinkling fountain and supermarket, several restaurants, even a medical centre. To his right, a semi-circle of offices shone brightly in the artificial light, each thirty feet wide and two storeys high. There were ten in total and each segment was built entirely of glass so Crouch could clearly see into the rooms and beyond. The ground floor areas looked like holding bays and were empty, bisected in half by a glass wall. As he watched, a large SUV slowly reversed into the nearest one. The driver came to stand by the professor whilst a glass wall silently closed so that the truck was com-pletely sectioned off. Above them, technicians in white coats studied their screens intently, peering occasionally down at the vehicle below. Without warning, it suddenly disappeared. One second it was there. The next, nothing. It took him by surprise but not the technicians. He heard loud whoops coming from their vantage point and some high fives were thrown. One of the figures turned in Crouch's direction and waved, beckoning him up. He shrugged his shoulders dismissively and turned away. He had work to do. Much more important work than zapping inanimate objects around the country. Shadowed by his agent he slowly shuffled towards the far side of the glass offices. By the time they arrived, Crouch was sweating freely and gasping for breath. He clenched his fists deep in his lab coat pockets but it was no good. The shake had taken hold and he paused for a few seconds whilst it ran its course. Ahead of him was a nondescript doorway manned by more Military Police. He didn't recognise their insignia but silently submitted to their pat downs before inserting his security clearance into the waiting port.

The door slid open smoothly and Crouch stepped through. Immediately he felt better. This was his territory. More refined. More exclusive. He suppressed a chuckle. Life was good again. He had lots to do today but first things first. At the end of the corridor, he swiped another door open before stumbling through, leaving his shadow outside. It was dark but he didn't pause, walking over to a counter where his hand gratefully closed around a bottle, the other searching out a tumbler. He shakily poured himself a drink and downed it in one. The gold liquid burned his throat but immediately he felt better. The second shot hardly spilt, allowing its calming influence to work its magic across his thirsty body. He picked the bottle up for the third time with a steady hand.

He finished pouring the drink before making his way over to a large desk where he sat down heavily, placing the bottle by his side. He sipped his drink and flicked on the screen which cast a soft white glow across his pudgy features. He cracked his fingers and took a small sip before draining the glass in one go.

'Steady there, Professor. You won't be able to do any work at this rate.'

Crouch didn't react straight away, as if his brain was running slightly behind what his ears heard.

'You've made good progress. Its looks like we made the right decision to bring you on board, despite some reservations.'

The voice came from over by the small kitchenette of the large room. Crouch didn't even look up.

'You needn't worry about this,' he responded, holding up the small tumbler.' It calms me.'

'How is the system handling the frantic pace?'

Crouch laughed contemptuously.

'I would hardly call thirty leaps frantic.'

'And the support team? Doesn't that add complexity?'

'What?' he snorted. 'A forty-agent, eight-hour rotation across a twenty-four-hour period. Even if you factor in all his doctors, nurses, counter snipers, ERT agents, comms engineers, dog handlers, there's barely a hundred people. What I'm building will handle billions of simultaneous jumps.'

'I was thinking more about his LEAP schedule getting ahead of itself?'

Crouch sighed.

'It's hardly rocket science. An empty Air Force One flies to and from each destination. Whilst it's in transit, the President stays at Camp David until the plane arrives at his destination at which point, they teleport him right onto the flight deck. When it returns, he LEAPs straight from the plane back home. It's quite easy out at Camp David because of all the security. Once the plane lands he is free to pursue his normal schedule.' He replenished his glass and took a sip before finally looking up. He couldn't see a thing. 'You didn't come here to discuss the mundanities of the system. What do you want? I have work to do.'

'How's the DNA working?'

'What's that supposed to mean? It's the default security mechanism. It's always been the default, even when ... that woman,' he couldn't bring himself to say her name, 'was running the system for Reynolds. Everyone is swabbed and once on the system, it effectively becomes their biological passport at both ends. Both the ending and receiving gate have to accept the DNA. Without a match, they don't LEAP. It's foolproof.'

'That's what I wanted to talk to you about.'

Crouch was suddenly guarded.

'Go on,' he said.

'We need your help.'

Crouch didn't respond.

'We need to add someone to the system. Without anyone knowing.'

'Impossible.'

'I doubt that, Professor.'

Crouch peered into the gloom but the blackness was impenetrable.

'And why would you want to do that?'

'Your role is not to question. Just to execute.'

'A bad habit I'm afraid. You'll have to give me more than that.'

'How about high school physics,' the voice snapped.

'But I've rebuilt this system for you. Without my input, you would be months behind schedule. With my prior knowledge, you're miles ahead. If I go, it will slow to a crawl.' Despite his bluster, Couch's hand started to shake. 'You wouldn't dare,' he added for good measure as he hurriedly poured himself another drink.

'You don't sound so sure, Professor.'

'But I've done everything you've asked of me,' he whined. 'Why would you do that?'

'We wouldn't. But we need your co-operation. Would it help to know that you could take out the Jakobsdóttir woman?'

The professor licked his lips, a crooked smile breaking out across his pudgy face.

'She ruined me.'

'Now's your chance to even the score.'

'What do you want me to do?'

Something clattered onto the desk, making Crouch jump. He peered at it closely, his nose almost touching the object. It was a plastic test tube containing what looked like a swab similar to the ones used on him earlier.

'Get him onto the system. The President's detail.'

Crouch stared at the tube.

'Who is it?'

'You really don't want to know.'

He drained the tumbler, his mind drifting between images of him stood at a blackboard whilst behind him chaos reigned and of him crawling across a floor, blindly feeling for his glasses, whilst all around him laughter rained down. He started to sweat. His hands were shaking so much he could barely hold the bottle. Neat bourbon splashed onto the table. He gave up and guided the glass mouth to his own, gulping down the fiery liquid until he began to choke. But at least the shaking stopped and the images.

'When?'

'As soon as.'

'Then what?'

'We'll take care of that.'

'But it's impossible. I'm not the only one who checks the security.'

'I'm sure you'll find a way.'

'It'll take time. I need to work out a routine.' His mind was racing. 'How do I contact you?'

'We'll contact you.'

'How?'

There was a soft click as the door opened slightly and the figure exited the room leaving Crouch alone, staring at the small test tube, his bottle temporarily forgotten.

East Coast

13 December 2009, 07:32 hours

He breathed in deeply and savoured the morning. It was heavy with moisture from the unseen Atlantic whose wintery vastness, carried on the strong wind, felt permafrost cold and slightly foreboding. That was evident in the black clouds that broiled angrily above his head. There was something else as well. A lighter, softer undercurrent and he realised with a knowing smile that snow was on the way. Lots of it and it would arrive in the next few hours to blanket the exposed scrubland that had been his home for the last eight weeks. He dropped to his knees, grasping the soft mud in both hands and squeezed hard so that it squelched through his fingers like soft putty. It felt good, life affirming even, to feel the near frozen earth on his skin. His Spartan existence had cleansed him, slowly expunging the poison of the camp with its monastic routine of sleep, prayer and exercise. He no longer missed the papers, a rude reminder of the toxicity that existed beyond the bubble of his regimen. The gluttony. The filth. The wretchedness of mankind. Particularly America with its misplaced nation building trying to impose its childlike will on civilisations that had existed for thousands of years. He spat on the icy earth and jumped nimbly to his feet, continuing to run upwards, cresting the hill fifty yards above him with barely any disruption to his breathing. Despite the Jacket. He hardly noticed it these days, except when he took it off to bathe. Then he would experience that wonderful feeling of weightlessness. For a second, he would be able to imagine the moment when he would sever his mortal coil and float out above the poisoned earth, upwards into the white sky to join his brothers who were waiting patiently for him.

Belman turned and headed back towards the house, settling into a comfortable lope that would return him to his destination in under twenty minutes. He half-glanced round to see if Fortune was keeping up but suddenly remembered—he didn't accompany him anymore. One morning he had turned up as usual but he was anything but. He had cut his hair. Short. Crew cut short and shaved his moustache. It had changed his face shape completely. Knocked years off his look but there was no explanation as to why. He had also been limping. Badly. It hadn't stopped him participating in the daily martial arts tuition and weapons training, but he no longer came on the runs. Instead, he had devised a series of colour-coded courses approximating different distances which he would send Belman out on with threats that if he didn't finish within a certain time, he would deny him his daily prayer. But Belman no longer needed the incentive of punishment to complete his tasks. He felt fit. Pure. Purposeful. Strong in both mind and body. Ready for his mission. He happily ran the distance, never even questioning what would happen if he strayed from his route. There would be no deviation now. He was close. He was ready. He would shortly join his brothers in a glorious death.

Fortune was waiting on the covered porch as Belman took the low steps two at a time. He didn't even look up but pocketed the stopwatch with a grunt and entered the house, leaving his protégé stood there, almost invisible under the steaming cold air that smoked off his warm body. Belman shrugged and followed him inside. The next exercise was already laid out on the floor of the living room.

'What's that?'

'Your failsafe in case everything goes pear shaped. And it will. I've been doing this for twenty years and the only certainty I know is that the best laid plans will go to hell so you always need an alternative. This is it.'

Belman picked up the wristband and examined it carefully. The material was shiny bright and had a metallic feel to it but felt synthetic light. On the inside of the strap were a series of circular pads. He slipped the futuristic device onto his wrist. It fitted him perfectly and felt cool against his hot skin.

'What is it?' he repeated.

'A pulse detonator.'

'What does it do?'

'Guarantees your payload is delivered, even if you are no longer able to do so yourself.'

'How?'

'Your pulse becomes part of the circuit. Break it and,' Fortune scrunched the fingertips of his right hand against those of his left and blew them apart theatrically, 'Boom,' he mouthed silently.

'I'm not sure I understand.'

'It's a trigger point. Once your pulse stops beating, the bomb detonates. That's the mission, right?'

Belman nodded slowly.

'You're ready for your final test. Tomorrow, we're going to run the facility again. I'll collect you at seven. If you're not there, I'll leave without you.'

'Don't worry I'll be there.'

But Fortune had already left, leaving Belman talking to the swinging door.

Washington, DC

13 December 2009, 11:48 hours

He stared at the screen, transfixed. The image rotated slowly, turning gracefully in its suspended electronic animation. The spiral shape looked so incongruous, so primitive, yet it was also elegant and instantly recognisable—the double helix. A simple chemical compound that contained the complete blueprint of what constituted a human being and provided the instructions that enabled the 100,000 or so proteins within each person's cells to endlessly reformat themselves into their shape. No others. Just theirs. Deoxyribonucleic acid. The giver of life but also the keys to LEAP. Everyone who jumped had to be swabbed and once on the system, it effectively became their biological passport. Both the outgoing and receiving gate had to accept the DNA. Without a match, they didn't LEAP. It was a straightforward system to enforce because everyone's DNA was unique which made it completely foolproof. It couldn't be copied. That was its greatest strength but also its greatest weakness. People trusted it implacably and that presented Crouch with the opportunity to meet his master's bidding.

He fingered the thin test tube in his coat pocket and asked himself the same questions that had haunted him since his recent encounter. Who was it? What was their intent? Why the President's security detail? Crouch had no answers. And nor did he wish to fathom out these questions. All he knew was that no good would come of his actions and therefore his approach had to be untraceable. He had two choices: refuse or comply. However, the threat had been clear; if he didn't cooperate, he would be back teaching high school physics. The mere thought was enough to trigger an all-too-familiar reaction which he was helpless to resist. He shut his eyes and waited for it to pass, gripping the silver flask with the strength of ten men. As it subsided, he glanced round the bustling facility but no one was watching him as he hurriedly stole a nip of neat bourbon.

It should have been easy. As Programme Head, he had final say on everything but it was all documented, every keystroke monitored, every call recorded. Every avenue led down a cul-de-sac which meant losing either way: refuse and it was back to school but accept and get it wrong then his reputation would be tarnished forever. And Crouch wasn't going to let that happen a second time. So, he had applied his much-reduced intellect to working out the key. Fuelled by his understanding friend, he had stayed up through the night, during the whole of the next day and long into the subsequent evening, when, overcome by fatigue and alcohol it had come to him. Like all good plans it was shockingly simple and involved others to point the finger at when the dust settled and the inquisitions began.

Crouch glanced up at the line of men on the other side of the screen. Fifty men, fifty swabs, fifty opportunities but he already knew his target. Throughout the long morning, his team of technicians had worked quietly and efficiently, collecting samples, processing them and cross referencing the DNA data back to their military records. Once completed, a soldier's access credentials would effectively go live and he was free to move in the system. Crouch's timing had to be perfect. There was only a ten-second window. If he missed it, he would be finished. The next rotation was not due for another three weeks and that would be too late. Whatever was being planned was due to take place in the next seven days. It was now or never. As he worked, shivery squalls blew across his broken body and by the end of the morning, his flask was empty. He checked his watch for the hundredth time.

The moment approached with an unstoppable certainty. Everything had gone to plan. He started to sweat freely now, the urgency of his plan overriding everything. Three more to go. His unsuspecting target stood patiently, last in line. He watched as one of the many technicians finally swabbed his cheek, bagged it and brought it over. He wiped sweat from his brow, his guilt clear for all to see, except no one was looking.

They misread his shakes, his panicked movements, his nervous glances as the routine of a hopeless alcoholic, struggling to get through the morning, just like every other session he had laboured through since his arrival on the programme. They turned a blind eye to the furtive drinking and ignored the overwhelming stench of neat whiskey. They waited patiently whenever a particularly violent episode threatened to shake him from his seat and wordlessly mouthed condescending obscenities to each other over his shiny pate. Today was no different. Without knowing it, this was Crouch's greatest cover because it concealed the truth.

Oblivious to their mistaken knowledge, Crouch shakily accepted the palm-sized test tube from one of the technicians. He silently counted down.

Ten.

Nine.

Eight.

Seven.

Had he got his timings right? He hoped so. If not, he was finished. The thought brought on a fresh wave of shivers.

Three.

Two.

One.

Nothing happened. The remaining agent stood alone in the corridor, waiting for his first LEAP. The technician by the professor's side ignored the old man's shaking limbs. Crouch's heart was beating so fast he thought it would burst from his chest. He felt sick. Back spots appeared before his eyes. He was going to faint. He needed a drink. There was none left. He closed his eyes, embracing the onrushing darkness. Oblivion beckoned. And then suddenly he heard people's exclamations of surprise. Something crashed to the floor behind him. He opened his eyes and was greeted with a reassuring gloom. The lab was in near darkness. The screens, the overhead lights, the corridor fluorescents, everything had crashed on cue as instructed by his programme introduced ten hours earlier and triggered by a keystroke. His pulse recovered its composure. His plan had worked. The technician by his side wandered off, muttering under his breath. Crouch fingered the tube in his hand. Now was his chance. He flipped the top off the fragile glass, palmed the fiftieth sample, popped it into his mouth and started chewing for all he was worth. He could have used the alcohol now but the flask was bone dry. Crouch slipped the replacement tube into his other palm, placing the lip of one against the other and inverted the two, shaking hard to dislodge the swab.

It was done.

He dropped the empty tube onto the floor, smiling with satisfaction. *Nearly home.* As he ground it into the carpet, the lights suddenly blinked on, closely followed by dormant screens flickering back into life. It had lasted less than thirty seconds, twenty-two to be exact. He sat there blinking with relief as the technician returned to his table.

'Go figure, hey. They spend five billion on the most advanced facilities the world has ever seen but can't keep the lights on.'

The professor nodded, manically trying to swallow the swab. His mouth was dry like sandpaper. He started to retch.

'You OK, Prof? You look like you've seen a ghost.'

Crouch couldn't talk.

'Water,' he croaked.

The technician smiled knowingly.

'Give me two seconds.'

He returned with a small cup which Crouch gulped down noisily. As he wiped his mouth, the technician swore softly.

'The last test tube. You dropped it.'

'No, it's here,' replied Crouch, holding it up. His hand shook nervously but the technician didn't seem to notice 'That's one of the earlier ones.'

The technician shrugged.

'Good, let's do this last one so we can get some lunch.'

'It's not that easy, I'm afraid,' Crouch said, licking his parched lips. He had rehearsed this scene for hours but it still felt forced. 'We can process the sample but he can't LEAP until tomorrow.'

'Why on earth not?'

'Protocol,' Crouch said. 'In the event of a power cut, and I assume that was what we just experienced, all systems have to undergo a full test. It will take ten hours to perform.'

The technician swore again.

'But I'm on leave from tonight.'

'No worries, I can do it.'

'No, I have to see the batch through.'

It was Crouch's turn to shrug.

'It's your vacation,' he snapped back. 'We'd better get this sample processed.'

The technician picked up the test tube, mumbling something about his girlfriend, and removed the small swab, before placing it into the analyser. Within seconds the familiar double helix appeared which he duly linked to the agent's file. He squinted at the screen.

'Another damn hero,' he whistled in appreciation. 'Look at all his medals.'

Crouch squinted at the screen.

'Well, Special Agent McGuire, they won't help you today. You'd better break the news to him that he's got to come back tomorrow afternoon for his first LEAP. Now, if you'll excuse me, I have a system review to organise along with fifty million other things to get this system fully operational.'

Crouch stood up, thought better of it and sat down again, much to the amusement of the technician.

The simple plans had always been the best ones. All that remained was for his new partners to fulfil their end of the bargain.

Camp Peary

14 December 2009, 07:58 hours

The corridor was dark but not blackout dark which meant Belman was able to move with relative ease. Over the past few days, he had trodden this route countless times and could have run it flat out, blindfolded. From his starting point, it was twenty-two steps. Then through a doorway. One level up. Now came sixteen steps that cut left four and brought him onto a small landing. There were four doors off it. Belman chose the third. It led into the current corridor. He was less than forty paces from his target. It was too quiet. There should have been more activity. His heart started to beat heavily and every sense strained to detect movement, any sign of life, any threat that would prevent him from reaching his destination. *Nothing.* He passed a white bust, some long-forgotten leader, his white eyes glowing in the dark, his heavy whiskers carved into a sardonic smile. Nearly there. His hand closed around a heavy handle. As he turned the cold metal, he felt a presence behind but it was too late. As Belman turned, the unmistakable point of a steel tempered blade bit into the back of his neck and a quiet voice whispered in his ear.

'You're dead.'

Belman didn't hesitate. He couldn't. His training didn't allow him to consider the natural reflex—to freeze, to stand still and surrender.

Before the second syllable had reached his eardrums he was dropping to the floor, moving away from the blade. He didn't have long. The blade's owner would be reacting. Quickly. As he fell, he turned, driving the palm of his hand upwards with all the force he could muster. He had timed it perfectly. His hand hit the soft underbelly of the assailant hard and Belman followed through with his other hand to deliver a second savage punch. A satisfying expulsion of breath followed as the figure behind him started falling. He continued his own fall, pushing away with both legs into a rolling recovery to ensure that he wasn't crushed by the heavy weight above him. As he did so, the man behind him sank slowly to his knees, gasping for breath. Already Belman was on his feet, moving swiftly to his side, drawing his own knife, pulling it back for the killing thrust as he positioned himself behind his assailant. At the last moment, he pulled out of the move, instead placing the sharp blade on his assailant's throat. The encounter had lasted seconds.

'I think not.'

Fortune didn't answer. He was still retching for air that wasn't there as his diaphragm continued to expel what was left in his lungs. Several seconds passed. Slowly, his breathing returned to normal and the large man got to his feet. He didn't turn to face Belman but started walking down the corridor away from his student. Belman ran to catch him up and they moved silently through the gloomy facility for several minutes until they reached a door which Fortune pushed open. Bright light streamed in, causing both men to blink.

'You're ready,' Fortune said. 'We move in the next few days.'

LEAP Centre, Virginia

14 December 2009, 19:10 hours

'You did well, my friend.'

Crouch didn't look up, preferring instead to keep his gaze fixed on the screen in front of him. The glare cast a ghoulish half-glow across his drawn features, accentuating his sunken eyes which were almost closed from his afternoon of drinking.

'I assume you haven't come to congratulate me,' he slurred.

'We have one more favour to ask of you. Tomorrow morning you need to complete the upload that you started today.'

'And what about Agent McGuire? What are you going to do with him? We can't have him turn up. And my nosey technician? Too many people involved,' Crouch added in a whisper, almost to himself.

'They're already taken care of. Your assistant will not report into work tomorrow. He has been instructed to continue with his trip. As for McGuire he has been temporarily reassigned. He will be returning to active duty after the weekend. Plenty of time to introduce his replacement into the system.'

'When do you expect me to do that?

'Tomorrow morning.'

'Impossible,' Crouch spluttered. He finally looked up as the latest deadline penetrated his fogged head. 'We're getting ready for the President's LEAP to Copenhagen.'

'A perfect time to introduce the full scan.'

'How so?'

'Plenty of distractions.'

'That's irrelevant. It could be traced back to me.'

'Not our concern,' the shadowy figure said.

Crouch swallowed hard.

'Perhaps not,' Crouch said, trying hard not to scream at the man, 'but it's of passing interest to me. I would like to think I had a future after this little episode is over.'

'Oh, you do, Professor. A very important one.'

'Would you care to elaborate?'

'Not today.'

Silence filled the space between the two men like an evil spirit. The professor looked up again but could see nothing. 'Cover your tracks as you will. Fry the entire system for all we care. It will make no odds after Saturday.'

Crouch pondered these words, not realising until his handler replied, that he had spoken out loud.

'That suggests LEAP will have no relevance.'

'On the contrary, Professor. It will be very relevant. But everything can be rebuilt.'

'Where is the transfer going to take place?

'Camp Peary.'

Crouch desperately tried to remember whether that contained a LEAP gate. His mind drew a blank.

'Never heard of it,' he mumbled. 'What time does the sync need to take place?'

'No later than 21:00 hours.'

'Anything else?'

'No. That's it for now.'

A crack of light spilled into the room as the voice exited. For a moment, the professor caught a glimpse of its owner. He looked awfully familiar, but Crouch couldn't place him. Besides which, he had more important worries. Crouch didn't believe for one moment that he would survive the next few days and the thought terrified him. He reached for the bottle by his side and took a long dark drink, relaxing into the oblivion that it promised.

Transamerica Pyramid, San Francisco

16 December 2009, 16:42 hours

The clouds were low, very low and shrouded the city in an ugly downpour that showed no signs of abating. Everything was hidden by the dirty grey veil of squalling mist: Alcatraz, Angel Island State Park, the Bay Bridge, Treasure Island, Oakland, Richmond, Berkeley. Even the famous towers were gone, their 746 feet of orange steel consumed by the broiling water vapour from above. Every so often the downpour would relent as the Pacific wind adjusted and, for a brief second, she would catch sight of a wet smudge of grey before the clouds closed back in and everything disappeared again. Uma shivered and folded her arms tightly, turning away from the water-cracked glass. It was hard to imagine how different it had all looked on her last visit: a sparkling day; the press crush; Al Rahman; that surreal evening with Forsyth which still felt dreamlike, as did everything leading up to her own resurrection; Ethan's miraculous recovery; and, of course, that afternoon in London. She smiled at the memory. They had talked every day since but didn't see each other nearly enough. Ethan was doing what he did best—organising, dealing, negotiating and driving her Green Ray agenda forward. It felt like the old Ethan, the one she had first met in Reykjavík all those years ago. He was back to his calm and calculating self, beginning with his big reveal on prime-time TV. Afterwards, she had worried that the old Ethan would never have done that but on reflection decided that he would, if he calculated it was the only way to place him in the most favourable position. And it had worked. The federal charges against Green Ray had melted away and communication with The White House had rematerialised, along with her new job.

It was all-consuming, the DEA mandate energy sapping. Among her many priorities was maintaining the safety, security and reliability of the nuclear weapons' stockpile alongside cleaning up the environment from the legacy of the Cold War where fifty years of nuclear defence activities had impacted over two million people. Then there was the small matter of protecting the US' energy security plus overseeing the development of innovations in science and technology. This was the area she enjoyed most, mainly because it gave her the chance to be with Ethan, but more recently, her main focus had been preparing for the United Nations Climate Change Conference in Copenhagen. It had just started and negotiations were not progressing well, with First World nations keen to prevent the Third Worlders emitting up to their levels. They didn't want the poorer nations rejecting the development cap of the wealthy few. It was a familiar fight and there was no easy solution, even with the might of the DEA and Green Ray behind her. She was due to support the President in his closing keynote, two nights from now.

'Everything OK?'

John Forsyth stood in the doorway, his handsome features lit up by a large grin and his preternatural eyes. She hadn't seen him in weeks. Since the morning after that evening, in fact. He walked over and kissed her warmly on both cheeks, European style.

'The weather,' she said, pulling away from him and nodding toward the room-length windows streaked with water. 'All this rain. It's interminable.'

'Shhh,' he mimicked, placing a finger to his lips and looking around conspiratorially. 'You'll put the tourists off. No one realises how much we get at this time of year.'

'It reminds me of Reykjavík.'

'We have so much in common.'

Uma felt herself recoil at the implied intimacy, but Forsyth didn't seem to notice.

'Our jittery geology. The weather. It's home from home for you.'

'I prefer it to DC, if that's what you mean. Too many politicians, if you ask me.'

The older man nodded in acknowledgement, but his smile faded as an awkward silence enveloped the room, the recent past suddenly upon them. Uma had been avoiding him all this time and would have refused his invitation had it not been for Ethan. Immediately after the TV interview, she had told him about the planned Saudi investment in Green Ray. Ethan hadn't been angry about her revelation. It was just another piece of the jigsaw and he had simply got on with ensuring the new venture went through smoothly. Uma had assumed the Arab's interest would melt away after the LEAP announcement but, if anything, the news seemed to have the opposite effect. Facing a complete loss of their oil revenues, the Saudis had pushed for a greater stake in Green Ray and today marked the final payment which would take their total investment to one hundred and twenty billion dollars. As head of the Green Ray Fund, Uma had been invited out to San Francisco by Forsyth to celebrate with Al Rahman. Nothing splashy, just the three of them in a private ceremony. Al Rahman didn't want to advertise that Saudi Arabia had just bet against fossil fuels in their biggest customer's backyard. She had repeatedly declined but at the last minute had relented. Ethan, who knew nothing of Uma's past with Forsyth, felt that not going would start the new partnership off on the wrong foot. So, Uma had reluctantly made the LEAP from her DC apartment to meet up with these disquieting men.

'Where's Al Rahman?' she said. 'I have to get back to DC.'

'But you've only just arrived.'

Uma glanced at her watch. 'You've got me for thirty minutes.'

'Won't you at least have a drink with me, whilst we wait for our guest?'

'I don't think that's a good idea.'

'Just one.'

Uma shrugged in resignation and Forsyth smiled.

'Thank you,' he said, grabbing a heavy bottle from the bar. 'It's a Krug, a Clos du Mesnil 1995. One of the best.'

Was he trying to impress her again, like last time? She wasn't in the mood for this.

'Here we go.' He freed the heavy cork and the sparkling wine began to bubble upwards. 'Whoa!' he shouted, coming towards her with two full glasses.

'To Green Ray.'

'To Green Ray,' she said, sipping the cold liquid.

He grinned at her, raising his glass again in a mock salute, as another awkward silence settled between them. She took another sip. Something about Forsyth's demeanour didn't feel right and then it occurred to her.

'He's not coming. Is he?'

'Who?'

'Rahman.'

'Whatever gave you that idea?'

'This.' She motioned around the empty room which had become noticeably dimmer since she entered.

'He'll be here. Have a little patience, Doctor. Or should I say, Secretary?'

'I don't believe you.' Uma said, beginning to regret making the LEAP without her security detail. She hated their constant presence and would ditch them at every opportunity. Tonight had been easy. Once inside her apartment with two agents stationed outside her door, she had made the LEAP direct to Forsyth's office.

'Top up.' Forsyth nodded at her glass.

Uma looked down. It was empty. *How had that happened?* She didn't remember drinking it. Come to think of it, she didn't remember sitting down either. Forsyth was sat beside her, keeping a respectful distance, although, as he refilled her glass, he drew closer. She could smell his cologne. The scent of a long-forgotten night.

'How did I get here?'

'I presume you leapt.'

'I don't mean that.' Her limbs felt heavy. Her mind slow.

'So, how are those nasty night visions you get?'

How did he know about her night visions? She had never told anyone. She was sure of it. *Had Ingram been watching her sleep?* The thought made her skin crawl.

'Better. Thank you. In fact, come to think of it they've pretty much stopped since Ethan left that place.' She couldn't help herself. Her head screamed stop, but her mouth just ploughed on, pouring out her thoughts before they had finished forming.

'Yes. Quite an escape the two of you pulled off there.'

Did he know about her reincarnation? Uma suddenly wanted to tell him so badly. He was very close to her now, their elbows touching on the deep sofa. She hadn't even noticed him move. When had that happened?

'Do you think he'll rebuild the Reynolds' place?'

'Not if I can help it.'

'That sounds like something my second wife would say.'

Uma giggled.

'We're not married.'

'You won't mind if I do this then.'

Uma tried to push him away as he kissed her, but she couldn't move. His hand moved to her breasts and caressed them roughly through the soft silk of her blouse. Uma felt the panic rising but her limbs didn't obey. It was as if she had no control over her body, unable to resist his advances. She was locked in her head, fully conscious of what was going on but with no way of escaping.

He groaned with desire and was suddenly kneeling over her. The glass tumbled from her hand and she looked up at him helplessly, silently screaming at him to get off, ordering her frozen limbs to move but they ignored her. She could sense his desire as he hurriedly unbuttoned her blouse and pulled her bra up. His stubble felt sandpaper course on her breasts, his hands urgently caressing her thighs. All Uma could do was lie there, silent tears falling from unblinking eyes.

Transamerica Pyramid, San Francisco

16 December 2009, 17:37 hours

The man was standing on a small hilltop, the fading sun directly behind his broad shoulders so that she had to shade her eyes to see him. Even then, it was difficult. But he looked kind enough, was pin-up handsome, with long flowing hair that streamed behind him in the strong breeze. He was saying something—she couldn't tell what—and then he started to chuckle. It wasn't much to begin with, but it took hold and soon engulfed his powerful chest in a deep booming laugh that cut through the silence. There was no hint of menace or danger but was pure of tone and promised a safe haven to all who heard, a place of sanctuary that would protect the listener, that would shield everyone from those with ill intent. So, she walked towards him, trusting in the man. But as she crested the low hillock, the sun snuffed out beneath the horizon and for the first time she could see his face. He was still laughing but his skin began to lose its golden hue and slowly faded to a cold grey. His well-fed flesh took on a hungry look. His lips, previously so vibrant and inviting, thinned out into a cruel sneer. And then, too late, she realised that his laughter was a cloak, a siren, masking the malevolence beneath. It was there to lure the unwary and the innocent into his grasp, where they would be consumed by his insatiable desire for life. Any life. All life. His hair had rapidly thinned to reveal a cavernous skull that towered over a furrowed brow which, in turn, concealed eyes that, until seconds ago, had been light blue. And then they looked down at her and she shrank away in fear because they were now a burning iridescent cobalt that flamed like precious stones in his bony sockets. She turned to run but he did not follow. Instead, he began to fade but not his laugher. That remained, enveloping her in its wickedness, stripping away her dignity, consuming her soul and now she ran as if her very survival depended on it.

Uma awoke, gasping with the exertion of her flight. The image had faded but the laughter had followed and was now behind her. As she lay listening, the hurt returned. A deep burning sensation that ballooned out across her entire body. It felt oppressive and uninvited. Why the pain? Tears welled up to prise open her closed eyes. But she resisted, preferring instead the darkness. However, the laughter remained. It belonged to a man she knew. A deep booming laugh that filled her head and overwhelmed her senses. And then she re-membered. Slowly, feeling followed memory and she became aware of her surroundings. Head bent towards her chest, one arm pinned be-neath her side, knees pulled up tightly into a protective ball. Forsyth's laughter filtered down the corridor into the conference room. Had he drugged her? Is that what had happened last time? The laughter was mocking her as she lay there. Laid low by his trickery. And then the anger surged, burning through her veins like a transfusion. Giving her strength where previously there had been none.

Uma opened her eyes. Night must have fallen, the black glass imper-vious to her suffering, but as she stared, a lightning strike forked diag-onally across the entire window-scape. For a millisecond she glimpsed the storm outside, the massed clouds, the sheeting rain, the raging winds. Barely had it faded when a thunderous rumble shook the building and she felt the foundations groan. Then the laughter again. She arched her neck towards the open door, a corridor beyond. It was softly lit, more like an apartment than an office complex. Then she remembered, this was Forsyth's private quarters. They were eight hundred feet above the streets of San Francisco. Alone. The only way out was in his private elevator. Or the LEAP chamber. Uma uncurled her aching limbs and groaned softly. Her face felt sandpaper rough, both wrists burned sore and her right shoulder pulsed with pain. She gathered herself and stood up. For a second the room swam lazily but she forced herself forward, numbly recovering torn clothes from which she salvaged her skirt and bra. As she left the room Uma grabbed the opened bottle of champagne which she hefted in her right hand. It felt reassuringly heavy.

Forsyth was making no effort to conceal his presence but there was another voice too. It was heavily accented, English, very precise, every syllable unnaturally accentuated. So, Al Rahman had come after all. She thought Forsyth had been lying. Had he seen her? Had he joined in? Uma suppressed the urge to run and hide, forcing herself to listen.

'We're nearly there, my friend,' Al Rahman said.

'It's been a long journey.'

'It's only just begun. The House of Al Rahman will live forever.'

'When will you make the announcement?'

'Soon, my friend. Soon. Once the final payment has been made.'

'Do you think the public will buy it?' Forsyth sounded doubtful, but about what? Uma moved closer to the open doorway through which the two voices filtered into the corridor.

'Perception is reality.'

'I know but—'

'No buts,' Al Rahman said. 'The weight of evidence is too great. All fingers will point to Rae and his fund once we broadcast our ownership. He will find it hard to deny the connection or his motive, especially after such a foolish denial on daytime television.'

'Manna from heaven. I suspect he will regret that interview to his dying day.'

'A rare mistake by the great Ethan.' The voice sounded almost regretful.

'You're not getting sentimental on me?'

'We go back many years,' Al Rahman said. 'He's an honourable man.'

'Nevertheless, nothing gets in the way?' Forsyth shot back. He sounded panicked.

'I'm not doing this for myself, old friend,' Al Rahman said. 'This will secure the future of my country for generations to come.' Uma heard him sigh. He sounded tired. 'Rae's involvement is unfortunate but very necessary. Everyone needs to know that I'm at the heart of this acquisition, both here and abroad. It will consolidate my position with the factions. They only respect strength and no one must be able to deny my purchase of LEAP from Ethan Rae.'

Uma nearly dropped the magnum. *Ethan had sold LEAP.* She inched her head round the door frame. Forsyth lounged at a long mahogany table, his back to her, and for a second she thought Al Rahman was sat opposite. But something was wrong. He seemed slightly reduced and then she realised that Al Rahman wasn't there. He was being broadcast onto a large screen that occupied the entire end wall of the office. The quality of the image was pin perfect. No wonder she had been fooled. Uma hefted the heavy bottle and entered. The elderly Saudi barely moved but his eyes betrayed her presence and Forsyth glanced back.

'Uma. Glad you could join us,' he greeted her cheerfully. 'We're talking about your boyfriend.' He paused for a second. 'You might want to get some clothes on, darling. This is a two-way video conference and Saudi has a slightly stricter dress code than over here.'

Uma launched herself at Forsyth who easily dodged the tired swing.

'I'll call you back,' he continued, turning to face Uma.

'Is everything OK, my friend?' Al Rahman said, watching the confrontation with interest.

'You know what the fairer sex can be like behind closed doors,' Forsyth said, drawing his head back as the heavy magnum narrowly missed his cheek.

Al Rahman laughed gently.

Uma channelled her rage into the next blow but pulled out at the last moment. It worked. Forsyth moved to the right and as he did, half-turned his head to press a small button on the desk behind. The picture cut out. But instead of following through, Uma diverted the bottle sideways. Forsyth caught the correction, but it was too late. He couldn't pull back in time and the heavy glass caught him a crunching blow on the temple. He cried out and fell forward across the desk. Uma dropped the bottle and pummelled his head with both fists. He groaned but didn't move and Uma grabbed his hair, meaning to turn him over. As she did, a great clump came away in her hand. Where previously there had been thick curls, a glistening crown shone brightly.

She shook the hairpiece free, raking her nails across the pale skin of his skull. Forsyth cried out and rolled over, pushing her away before struggling to his feet. He moved unsteadily, the deep cut to his temple dripping blood.

'You'll pay for that,' he roared, grabbing a handful of Uma's hair and flinging her across the office into a glass bookshelf. Hardbacks rained down as the shelves shattered and she sank to the floor, stunned.

'What have you done?' Uma groaned. 'What have you done?'

'Just taking care of my business,' Forsyth said. He looked different beyond the obvious but in her groggy state Uma couldn't pinpoint why.

'Ethan would never sell LEAP to you.'

'Oh, but he has. One hundred and twenty billion dollars has been transferred into Green Ray's bank account. That will take some explaining.'

'But that was an investment by the Saudi Royal Family in Green Ray.'

'Why would they sink all that money into renewables?' Forsyth said. 'It was a payment for the LEAP technology. When Al Rahman announces the acquisition, that payment will back up his claim.'

'How did you get hold of it?' Uma said, remembering Al Rahman's earlier words. Had Ethan double crossed her? The mere suggestion made her nauseous.

Forsyth didn't answer and she suddenly realised what was different. 'Your eyes. They've changed.'

Forsyth grinned but his lips were thin. Like the man in her dream. She realised he was sneering at her, his once bright irises now a pale blue.

'A little parlour trick I learnt twenty years ago for my presentations,' Forsyth said. 'It's amazing how many more people listened after I started using contact lenses.'

'You're a fraud.'

'That's ripe coming from the woman who wants to save the world but keeps LEAP for herself. Regenerates not only her boyfriend but herself. You don't deserve your gift.'

How did he know that Ethan had regenerated her? It had to be Ingram. He was everywhere and sharing it all with Forsyth.

'You don't have the vision to understand what it can do for mankind. In the right hands, we'll live like Gods. Look like Gods. We will be Gods.'

'A few of you will.'

'There you go again with your double standards. At least LEAP will benefit more than two people.'

'You'll go down for this,' Uma said, fighting back tears.

'No, I won't. You will, though, and quite possibly Rae. Think about it. Why would the Saudis invest billions in unproven alternative energy? They've bought LEAP fair and square from two profiteering lovers that kept it for themselves all these years.'

Forsyth's words silenced Uma but she wasn't going to let him know how hard hitting they'd been. 'I meant your little stunt earlier,' she said. 'You drugged me.'

'Oh, that,' he said. 'Something I picked up through the CIA fund. It's powerful stuff. Makes suspects very compliant. They'll tell you anything. Let you do anything. Will do anything for you. All with no memory.'

A veil lifted in Uma's mind.

'You used it before,' she gasped. 'When we first met here.'

'My, my, we are on form tonight.'

'You raped me.' The words sounded remote, as if spoken by someone else.

'Far from it,' Forsyth said. 'I'm afraid you'll struggle on that count as well, given our current romantic entanglement.'

'We're not together.' Uma spat the words out.

'Oh, but we are.' Forsyth turned and pressed a few buttons on his keyboard. The entire wall lit up with a huge PC desktop. He opened a folder marked 'conquests' and a hundred crisp images filled the wall. Uma blinked. They looked like women, all in states of … undress. He double clicked one and the screen flickered into life. Even before the video began, Uma knew what he had done. Two figures writhed on a large table, both naked. The woman on top of the man. Uma flushed with embarrassment as Forsyth caressed one of her breasts in the video and she responded, moaning with abandon, her breathing heavy with desire. As she watched, a tear slipped down her cheek.

'We're an item, you see. Have been for a while and tonight proves it. No one will believe you once they've seen this.'

Uma couldn't drag her eyes from the screen. All she could think of was how Ethan would react if he ever saw these images. And she would make sure he never did.

'You'll never get away with this,' she whispered, almost to herself.

'Your word against mine. And as I've discovered in the past, video evidence can be extremely persuasive.'

He laughed his mocking laugh and moved over to where Uma lay crumpled, his trainers crunching on the shattered glass.

'Now, if you don't mind,' he said, crouching above her, his bald pate glistening in the lights of the room, his rheumy eyes dull with age, 'I have somewhere to go. You know your way out. Oh, and there's some spare clothes in my bedroom. I'm sure you'll find something that fits you.'

Forsyth stood up and made to kick her, causing Uma to shrink back. Satisfied, he disappeared through the open door, leaving Uma staring at the pulsating wall, her humiliation complete.

'Not like this,' she muttered.

Uma struggled to her feet and for a moment, just stood, punch drunk with pain, swaying with the effort of remaining upright. The screen moaned and the sound gave her strength, first to stumble over to the empty magnum, then to pick it up and, finally, with an anguished scream, to hurl it at the screen. The bottle hit with a dull crunch, where it hung like a piece of wall art, flat champagne dribbling from its open neck. For a moment, nothing happened and then the whole image fractured, before the entire wall turned black, just as Forsyth's laptop monitor flickered into life and the scene continued to play. Uma screamed with rage as she grabbed it with both hands and started smashing it down on the table, again and again until the screen detached itself from the casing, closely followed by the keyboard, its innards spilling out onto the table like a gutted fish. Uma grabbed the hard drive and hobbled towards the door in search of Forsyth. It wasn't difficult. He was making absolutely no effort to avoid her. She could hear him whistling and followed the flat tune into another room where he was busy at a terminal. As Uma entered, Forsyth grandly pressed a button on the keyboard and walked through into a second glass-walled anteroom, shutting the door behind him. As it closed, he winked at her and blew a kiss.

And then he disappeared.

It took Uma a few seconds to register what had happened. He'd made a LEAP! But the gate was on the floor below. She hurried over to the console and studied the screen, realising as she did that it wasn't quite the same. The differences were subtle: the layout of the icons, the colours, the naming conventions. No wonder she hadn't known. It was another system. But how? No one had the source code but as the thought materialised, Uma remembered—she'd given up the source code in exchange for her sister's life, the life she'd taken after discovering Eva's treachery. Had Reynolds come back? Had someone got hold of it? The monitor flicked to a new window, displaying details of Forsyth's LEAP. He was going to Dubai? There was something else. She stared at his atomic structure. It looked strange. The compositions were wrong. She ticked them off in her head, running down the list: oxygen, carbon, hydrogen, nitrogen, calcium, phosphorus, potassium, sulphur, sodium, chlorine, and magnesium but ...

'Methyltrichlorosilane,' Uma mouthed silently. 'Methyltrichlorosilane?' She repeated the word in confusion. And then for the first time since she'd arrived in the Transamerica Pyramid, Uma smiled. She had a few seconds before his transfer was complete. If she was going down, so would Forsyth, but not in a way that he could have anticipated.

Washington, DC

17 December 2009, 00:01hours

'But he's made it our problem,' Ethan said. 'It's no one else's.'
He was sat opposite Uma and had come over to her apartment as soon as she had called him about Forsyth's plan with Al Rahman. The last three weeks had been kind to him, softening out his once-hard features, so much so that he looked more like the old Ethan, albeit with a slight greying of his hair. Uma thought of Forsyth's bald pate and shuddered at the memory. After Forsyth had made his LEAP to Riyadh, she had returned to DC and somehow filled a bath, shed her borrowed clothing and then collapsed into the scalding water. Hot tears had followed until her eyes ached. Until there was no more poison to shed. Until she had scrubbed her skin red raw. Until she realised that Forsyth was right—Uma couldn't tell anyone about her ordeal, despite recovering the hard drive from his laptop. A creep like that would have backups, lots of them to keep his 'girlfriends' quiet and she couldn't take the risk that he didn't. Besides which, she'd hopefully got her revenge and even if that hadn't worked, they had enough on their plate with Ingram and Al Rahman. An alleged rape followed by a sordid trial was a step too far. The press would have a field day. It was in that moment she had decided to bury it deep and not tell anyone, especially not Ethan. He would never forgive himself for sending her there in

the first place and she dreaded to think what his reaction would be if he ever found out. The image of Ethan bodily lifting the Samurai above his head and nonchalantly throwing him at his other sparring partner arose unbidden and she stifled a shudder; who knew what he was capable of if pushed? And Uma wasn't going to be that person, especially so soon after she had just got him back. No, it would remain quiet. She looked over at Ethan who caught her glance and held it for a moment, during which she was certain he had read her mind. She suddenly felt like crying again.

'What do you mean?' she said, swallowing hard and turning her head slightly so that thick hair covered her face.

'We accepted the money. I made the denial on television. I have the relationship with Al Rahman. It makes repudiation all but impossible.'

'But we were tricked. That money was invested for Green Ray related matters: the wind turbines, the Electro, smart meters. It's well documented.'

'By the time we established all that, it'd be too late,' Ethan said, stroking the plastic covering over his forearm. 'It's a question of how it all looks and from where I'm standing, it doesn't look too good.'

'Could we make a pre-emptive announcement?'

'I don't think so. The investment was made anonymously.'

'Well, they're hardly playing by the rules.'

'Yes, but we'll spook everyone. The regulators. Other investors in Green Ray. More than likely the fund will collapse, especially after this recent investigation by the government. It will be seen as related.'

'Well, it's going to collapse anyway. We've nothing to lose by going public.'

'I think we do,' Ethan said. 'It'll have a pyramid effect on everything. You'll have to step down from your current position. I'll become a pariah, just like Reynolds. On top of that, I suspect the US Government will also have something to say about it.'

Uma looked questioningly at Ethan, trying to keep up, but all she could think of was Forsyth's hands on her skin. She suppressed the urge to cry out and hardened her resolve; no one would ever find out.

'Meaning litigation by the bucketful,' he said. 'At the moment they have an exclusive. That was the plan. Without that, their investment is worth much less.'

'What are we going to do?'

'There is one way but it won't endear us to the US Government so at the moment it isn't an option.'

Ethan stood up, walked over to the window and stared down into the street below. With a start, Uma realised Ethan was stood in almost the same spot that Ingram had stood when he'd come to blackmail her that day. That was the day she'd realised that Ingram had turned his surveillance apparatus against her. He'd known everything, including her innermost thoughts about the deaths of Baldursson, Eva, James and Sally, and her use of LEAP to bring Ethan back from the dead. At the time, she'd assumed he was simply using it to blackmail her into sharing LEAP with the US Government but now she realised it went much further than that. Somehow, he had, along with Forsyth, discovered the source code for LEAP, the one she'd given up in return for Eva's life. That'd been his real plan all along. The rest had been a diversion and now they didn't need her, LEAP or Ethan.

'It's our only option really. We—'

His mobile buzzed impatiently, rising in volume as it remained unanswered. Ethan grabbed it from the table.

'Shane? What can I do for you at this time of—' Ethan glanced at his watch, 'the morning?'

For what felt like an eternity, Ethan didn't say anything, and just when Uma was going to ask him what was going on, he said, 'We'll be right over. Don't do anything.'

He exited the call and looked up at Uma.

'Our problems mount up. We need to meet him at the LEAP centre. We can jump from here.'

The White House

17 December 2009, 00:04 hours

There was a low knock on the door and for a second the man seemed not to hear but the sound came again, more forcefully this time. He ignored it, or tried to, knowing full well it would continue. That certainty made him look up, glancing sideways at the clock on his desk: 00:04. He stretched with fatigue and slumped back in his chair, staring at the draft speech in front of him. It was covered in his neat handwriting but there were more deletions than text, repeated throughout the draft, the seventh since Monday. Was his Director of Speechwriting losing his touch? It had never taken him this long to capture the essence of what his boss wanted to say. He laid his pen on the jotter.

'Yes. What is it?' he called out, struggling to hide the irritation in his voice.

Margaret Scott, his secretary of fifteen years, swept into the room.

'Director Ingram wondered whether you could spare him ten minutes. He says it's important.'

'Of course,' the President said, glancing down at his draft. 'And after you've shown him in, can you ask Chuck to come through. This needs work. Perhaps you'd like to remind him that my address to the Copenhagen Climate Conference is in less than twenty-four hours.'

'I'm sure he's well aware of that, sir,' she said, removing the thin sheaf of papers from his desk.

'Anything else?'

'No, other than you need to get yourself home. We've got a busy day tomorrow.'

'It'll be no different to the last hundred days—start at six and finish sometime after midnight.'

'Are you counting them, Margaret?'

'Just the overtime you owe me.'

'Ah, it's the money you're after. I knew there had to be some reason why you did this job.'

She smiled and busied herself, fluffing up the cushions of the cream couch in the centre of the room. She had supported him through his unsuccessful bid for a seat in the House of Representatives over fifteen years ago but had stuck with the young politician, because, like many, she saw something in his demeanour that promised great things. Four years later, her foresight had been rewarded as he secured a Senate seat at the first attempt. From then on, she had been a permanent presence in his life, protecting him from the world at large in what she called the 'inner bubble' into which few people were allowed to enter. That had been severely tested since the bombings but she had stuck rigidly to her task and hoped that she'd shielded her boss from the worst of it.

Ingram must have overheard the exchange because he'd already entered the room.

'Thank you, Margaret.' The lanky frame of the director towered over the prim woman.

'Just make sure you don't keep him too long.' She waved the paperwork in Ingram's direction. 'He's got this to sort out.'

Ingram nodded and turned towards the President.

'Good evening, sir. Thank you for seeing me at such short notice,'

'Always happy to see you, Joseph. It's a pleasant distraction from the complexities of solving global warming. What have you got?'

'We've found Fortune.'

The President looked up from pouring two large whiskeys, one of which he handed to Ingram who cradled it between his left palm and right wrist which was lightly bandaged. He seemed to have aged ten years since the blasts. They both did.

'Go on.'

Ingram took a large swallow, savouring the rich flavours.

'We think he's hiding out at the Farm.'

The President looked puzzled.

'It's a term of endearment we use for the training facility up at Camp Peary.'

'Near Williamsburg?'

'The one and same.'

'He's got some nerve.'

'Classic counterintelligence. If you're covert, hide out in the place people least expect you.'

'How?'

'It's big enough. About 10,000 acres, 8,000 of which are scrubland containing about twenty safehouses. It's perfect. A lot of them haven't been used in years.'

'And you're sure he's there?'

Ingram nodded.

'How did you find him?'

'We got lucky. A CCTV camera picked him up on I-64 just outside Richmond at one of the toll booths just after the bombings. We've only just made the match, given the volume of intelligence we've had to sift through. After that, we flooded the area with agents and picked him up again. We've had him under surveillance for the last twenty-four hours.'

'No interception.'

'It's not the way now. We track back. See who he knows. Is involving. Understand if there is a wider support network in place.'

'And?'

'He's hooked up with Belman.'

The President was silent, so Ingram continued.

'He's training him. Physical. Weapons. Bomb making. Self-defence. Given the recent bombings, the other two from Guantanamo ...' Ingram shrugged.

'Sweet Mother of God. You're telling me we have a rogue CIA operative running an Al-Qaida terrorist training camp on our doorstep.'

'It looks that way. We'll know more soon enough.'

'Who's helping him?'

'We don't know that yet. Normally we would watch him for fourteen days, even longer, but it looks like they're winding the camp down. We think that whatever they have planned is going down shortly.'

The President shifted uneasily.

'Don't worry, sir. We're going to take him out this evening. We can't afford to wait and track back. However, I think, on balance, this is not the best place to be.'

'Understood. I have my speech to finish and then I'll leave for Camp David. I have to, anyway. Air Force One leaves in one hour for Copenhagen. I LEAP tomorrow morning at 10. I want hourly updates.'

'I'll be personally supervising the operation from The White House Situation Room. As soon as there's anything to report, you'll be the first to know.'

Ingram drained his glass and stood to leave.

'There's going to be hell to pay once this gets out.'

'You'll get through it.'

The President stood up and moved behind the Resolute desk, between the two flags, staring out into the dark night. Ingram made his exit, leaving the President alone. The room was calm. It had seen worse, much bleaker days than this and knew there were bleaker days ahead.

LEAP Centre, Washington, DC

17 December 2009, 00:06 hours

Uma blinked, shielding her eyes from the overhead lights fifty feet above. After the soft gloom of her apartment the glare was painful, as was the noise. Around her, construction crews mingled with soldiers, military police, technicians, scientists and workmen, their shiny hard hats reflecting yet more light in her direction. It left her feeling even more exposed, but no one was looking at Uma. The forty thousand or so personnel swarming the huge facility were focused on a million different tasks all designed to complete the LEAP centre by the end of December—that had been the deadline delivered by the President and their industry reflected the challenge. As she followed Ethan and Shane across the plaza, they skirted a group of men and women eating fast food by the fountain which cascaded flashing water high into the air. They were all laughing at something and for a moment Uma thought it was directed at her. They'd seen the video and couldn't believe how stupid she'd been to fall under the spell of a common trickster. She felt the urge to run and hide but was struggling to place one foot in front of the other as she trailed behind Ethan and Shane. To her left, the glass offices were seething with white coats, flickering screens and the detritus of long days that started early and never finished. She felt tired and would have happily slept if presented with the means but deep down Uma knew that sleep was impossible. Ahead of her, Ethan and Shane chatted quietly like co-conspirators and Uma quickened her pace, easing herself between them before slipping an arm through Ethan's. He smiled down at her.

'I picked up the LEAP this evening.' Shane was talking, his voice, normally so calm and dispassionate, thick with excitement. 'It got flagged because it wasn't a point to point but began and ended in the same place which is normally associated with DNA confirmations.'

'Where was it coming from?'

'Camp Peary.'

Ethan frowned.

'It's a training camp for the CIA. In Virginia.'

'What's a LEAP gate doing out there?'

'No idea. It's not on any of the authorised lists.'

'I'm not sure that means anything,' Ethan said, glancing over at Uma.

'Have I missed something?'

Uma quickly filled Shane in on her discovery of the new LEAP system in San Francisco and Forsyth's subsequent escape. She didn't mention anything of her ordeal.

'Well, this LEAP gate is definitely one of ours.'

'If that's the case, who set it up?' Ethan said.

'I think it might be something to do with the President's security detail. The LEAP was made by Agent McGuire who's with the Secret Service Emergency Response Team and should have been on the LEAP Protection Team guarding the President. However, he was reassigned shortly after his upload. In fact, the day after.'

'Where to?'

'Afghanistan. Kandahar province.'

'It doesn't make sense,' Ethan said. 'Is he under cover for some reason?'

'I've checked with all the units. No one has authorised this LEAP.'

'Why confirm him now? I thought they were done the same day.'

'It is normally. On the day he was processed, there was a power cut in the LEAP centre which prevented it from happening. It should've been done the next morning, but it never was.'

'Why not?' Uma said.

'Because Agent McGuire had already been transferred,' Shane said, glancing at Ethan. 'To Afghanistan.'

Uma nodded, not registering their exchange.

'Who was in charge of processing that day?' Ethan said.

'Crouch. It's always him.'

'Professor Crouch?' Uma gasped, slowing to a standstill and forcing the two men to stop.

'The one and only.'

She unhooked her arm and faced Shane. 'No one told me this. Where on earth did they drag him up from?'

'Not sure. He runs the CBL Division.'

'CBL?' Uma and Ethan both said together.

'Carbon Based LEAPs: Us. You. Me. Humans. No one knows about it because Uma's agreement with the President prevents human LEAPs, at least publicly. Consequently, they're carried out in a different part of the facility.'

'So, why do you know?' Uma asked as Ethan talked over her with his own question: 'Can someone please tell me who Crouch is?'

'Woah, one at a time please,' Shane glared at Uma. 'Firstly, it's my job to know these things and secondly,' he turned to Ethan, 'Crouch was Reynolds' old CTO. Remember? His career tanked at the Udvar-Hazy Center when Uma sabotaged Reynolds' launch of LEAP.'

Ethan looked blank. He had no idea what Shane was talking about and the mention of Reynolds' name unsettled him. A burning portrait smouldered in his mind's eye, the flames licking hungrily at the canvas, the oil blistering, an old man beginning to fade from view. How long had he spent staring at that picture, wondering who he was and blaming Uma for his predicament? He quickly doused the image. It was all in the past now and he'd be damned if the mere mention of a name was going to derail him.

'The Wright brothers' anniversary,' Shane continued. 'You were ...' he trailed off. 'I'm sorry, Ethan. I forgot.'

But Ethan did remember; he'd been languishing in a Homeland Security Cell for weeks, unsure of who he was, convinced that Uma, and Shane by association, had double crossed him once they'd realised that he was unstable and a threat to the LEAP programme. Familiar feelings of helpless rage reeled through his guts, igniting the dormant scars on his back.

'Don't worry. I remember Uma telling me about him,' he replied, his face a tight mask of boiling recriminations. 'What on earth is he doing here, though?'

'Not sure.' Shane shrugged, his forehead resuming its familiar frown as he felt Ethan's stare rake his face. 'Prior knowledge, I guess. It's been in short supply around here. He's got experience of LEAP—Christ, he built Reynolds a new system with the stolen code. And has clearly reinstated it, given what Uma's just said.'

'Who oversees him?' Ethan ploughed on, redirecting his gaze to Uma. It was like flicking a light switch and the pin pricks subsided as quickly as they had appeared. He took a deep breath and relaxed his clenched fists.

'No idea. CBL's a law unto itself.'

'Can we talk to him? Find out what's going on?'

Shane paused before answering Ethan as a squad of heavily armed soldiers approached them at speed. They were grouped in twos and the lead pair guided the snaking line of sixty or so men in such a way that Uma was separated from her companions and forced to wait as they clattered by. She was suddenly aware of the mass of people around her and felt an overwhelming need for silence so she could rest her crowded mind and battered body. However, the thought of lying still even for a second, catapulted her back to San Francisco and the feeling of helplessness as Forsyth slithered over her. The memory jolted her back and she realised that Ethan and Shane were stood waiting, a quizzical look on Ethan's face.

Christ, he knows.

'Are you OK, Uma?' Ethan walked over to her.

'I'm fine, just tired,' she replied. 'Shane, you were saying, about talking to Crouch. I presume that's why we're here, isn't it?'

'We can try but CBL's off limits. Even to me. Always has been. Why don't we just pass our concerns onto The White House. Let them deal with it.'

'Have you not been listening to what I've just said,' Uma snapped. 'We can't trust anyone. If someone's tampering with the President's security detail, that can only happen with collusion at the highest levels. Ethan's right, we need to sort this out ourselves.'

'So why would Crouch even talk to us if he's involved with that lot?'

Uma fell silent. Shane was right.

'Where's the CBL unit housed?'

Shane pointed Ethan in the direction of the departing soldiers. 'They're the returning security detail from the Copenhagen talks and will have made their LEAP into the CBL unit.'

'OK, can you take me there? It's time we had a chat with Professor Crouch.'

'We don't have access rights to the CBL unit. No one does. And even if we did, Crouch would never agree to see us, let alone talk.'

'Don't worry about that,' Ethan said, winking at Uma. 'I know just the person who can help us get in.'

Ethan set off in the direction the soldiers had come from but, realising Shane and Uma hadn't moved, stopped and gestured for them to join him.

'After you,' he said, standing aside for Shane, who sighed and took the lead, guiding them through the throng of people and deeper into the cavernous building which resembled a huge construction site. They passed a group of workmen gathered round a partially completed glass structure, which Uma realised was a massive LEAP chamber and could have comfortably swallowed up a two-storey building. Ethan paused beside a stack of wooden poles about five feet in length and knelt down to inspect them. He lifted one from the pile and flexed it, before trying another. This was also rejected but he seemed satisfied with the next and ran to catch up with Shane and Uma.

'What do you need that for?'

Ethan ignored Shane and stopped again, this time to try on a number of abandoned hard hats. One seemed to fit, and he nodded for Uma and Shane to do the same as he struggled into a dayglo coat, with 'LEAP CONSTRUCTION' stencilled on the back. It was far too small for him but he didn't seem to notice as he handed out the garish coats to his companions. Shane couldn't restrain himself any longer.

'Are you going to tell us what you've got planned?'

'Nope.'

'You mentioned someone else.'

'The less you know, the better. It'll ruin the element of surprise. Just get us to the CBL unit.'

Shane looked like he was going to argue but thought better of it and marched off, muttering under his breath, which gave Uma her chance to tackle Ethan.

'Do you really think this is a good idea?'

'We've got limited options. If we can get to Crouch, we might be able to stop whatever he's got planned. Unless you've got a better one, then this is what I intend to do.' He twirled the wooden pole around his good hand before trapping it abruptly between his ribcage and inner arm. Ethan winked at Uma again but before she could reply, he was already four paces way from her. She followed, her heart beating rapidly, as she suddenly realised where she had seen sticks like that before—stacked up beside the armour in Reynolds' Castle.

Camp Peary, Virginia

17 December 2009, 00:09 hours

Something was wrong. He couldn't put his finger on it but over the course of thirty years working undercover, Fortune had come to trust his instinct. It had saved his life on numerous occasions. And now it was telling him that something was very wrong. He stared out into the cold night but black mist swallowed up his gaze. It was quiet as hell. Too quiet. He turned and re-entered the large grey building, bolting the door behind him. He checked the lock twice. It was solid. Nothing would come through without his knowledge. Behind him, the soft lights of a plush corridor disappeared into the distance. It had started with a call earlier that day. From his handler. It wasn't scheduled which never happened. All his calls were scheduled. Contact was never made except though a request lodged several days in advance either by him or his handler. Except on this occasion, the call had come in unannounced. Second problem, the hit had been moved from next week to that evening. Hits were never moved. Aborted. Yes. Things happened to prevent something going ahead. But never re-scheduled. And when they were, he had always aborted. It was too risky. But his handler had been specific. It had to be tonight. A precise time. A precise window. He wouldn't take no for an answer. He effectively ordered Fortune to proceed. Hadn't given him a choice, screaming at him down the line to make the play. No questions. No discussions. The whole thing stank. But there was no going back now. If he pulled the hit, what then? There was no second chance. The mission would have failed. If he continued, the mission might fail. That was enough for Fortune. He didn't care if Belman didn't make it. He cared about the mission failing. He had an unblemished record to protect. He could survive a hiccup, even one as high profile as this. Was he being set up? The thought had crossed his mind. The incident in DC had rocked him, particularly seeing his photo in the paper. It was many years since he had taken a hit. It wasn't serious but it had stayed with him, forcing him to relive the job, trying to work out where he had gone wrong. He couldn't lay his finger on it. Maybe it had been dumb luck but that never played a part. Planning reduced the incident of luck. That was his mantra and it had never let him down. Maybe that was it. Was he being manoeuvred to fail? But why and what could he do about it?

Up ahead, he could just make out Belman waiting for him. The man looked nervous. A combination of pure terror and excitement. Anticipation of his impending death tinged with fear of a repeated failure that would sabotage his second attempt at a glorious afterlife.

'Are you ready to rejoin your brothers?'

Belman nodded, his mouth contorted into a fixed grin.

'I've dreamt of this day for six years. I can't believe it's here. Praise be to Allah.'

'It's got nothing to do with him. This one will be courtesy of Uncle Sam himself,' Fortune muttered under his breath. 'Now, remember the procedure when you come out of the gate. You will feel nauseous. That's normal and it won't be as bad as this morning.'

'Are you sure?

Fortune hoped so. Belman had thrown up for a full thirty minutes and taken another fifteen to recover his balance. He had been briefed about the effects of a first LEAP but the severity of his charge's reaction had shocked him.

'Can we do another one? Just to make sure.'

''Fraid not. The risk of detection is too great.'

Belman looked uncertain.

'It's very simple now. Things will go wrong. They always do. That's why you've been training so hard. To stack the odds in your favour. It's going to be up to you and there is one absolute certainty. If you don't make it tonight, you will never join your brothers in heaven. Your entire life will have been a failure. Either way, you will die tonight. Make sure it's under the right circumstance.'

Without warning, Belman suddenly sank to his knees, clasped his hands together and began muttering inaudibly, his eyes tightly shut. It lasted several minutes and when he had finished, he looked up at Fortune.

'I am ready to face my destiny.'

'Good. Let's do this.'

Belman bent his head again as if praying at Fortune's feet.

'But first, I would like to thank you ... for your help. I could never have done this without you. I will forever be in your debt.'

There was no response from his handler and after a few seconds, Belman looked up. Fortune was already marching down the corridor towards the LEAP chamber.

LEAP Centre, Washington, DC

18 December 2009, 00:54 hours

Shane had missed the entrance twice but it was only after they'd doubled back the second time that Uma realised why. There was nothing to indicate that it accessed the CBL unit, no obvious security, no checkpoint, no scanners, not even any guards. It was just a door on the edge of the facility with 'Supplies' painted above but, within seconds of stopping outside it, four men had appeared, all dressed in sneakers, jeans and white T-shirts. Uma knew immediately they were Ingram's men. Despite their casual attire, it was still a uniform of sorts and they oozed CIA like a bad smell. She thought Ethan would spring into action, but he'd been courteous, informing the agents that they were lost and asking for directions back to the entrance, which they'd readily given. One of the agents had walked with them, just to make sure they knew the way, although Uma thought he was suspicious, or maybe it was because her nerves were so frayed. Ethan, on the other hand, seemed to be in his element, chatting and laughing with the agent until he'd left them, almost at the entrance to the LEAP centre. They'd shared a pizza from one of the many restaurants that ringed the plaza, or at least Ethan and Shane had. The thought of food made Uma nauseous, so she'd stood with them, trying to concentrate on the stilted conversation. Finally, they'd retraced their steps, hiding in a deserted storage container about five hundred feet from the CBL entrance. That was ten minutes ago and since then Ethan had been stood, watching the door like a coiled sentinel. Once again, Shane couldn't contain himself.

'What's the plan, Ethan? I thought you wanted to get in?'

'You're the security expert. You tell me.'

Shane was too surprised to reply but Ethan answered for him.

'We know there are four guards, probably more. We have no means of entry. What are you proposing exactly? We knock and they let us in with an escort to Crouch?'

Shane didn't get a chance to reply as Ethan suddenly set off towards the door, which Uma realised, had started to open. Two men emerged, both in white coats, the second carrying a laptop. Like everyone else, they looked exhausted.

'Hey, you,' Ethan called out as he broke into a jog. 'Can you hold that, please?'

It seemed to work. The trailing technician clipped his foot round the door and waited as he continued his conversation. To her left, Uma saw the same agents appear. One of them was talking into his hand and, as another pointed in her direction, all four broke into a run. It reminded Uma of the car launch in LA and that had ended with her lying in a bed, half-naked. An image of Forsyth appeared, his bald pate shining as he laughed uproariously at the memory, his eyes silently undressing her just like Ingram had. She shivered involuntarily and nudged Shane.

'Come on.'

It was a straight race as they all sprinted towards Ethan who had reached the two technicians. Without breaking stride, he jabbed the staff between the frame and the door, whilst punching the closest man in his stomach. As he sank to the ground, gasping like a beached fish, Ethan grabbed the laptop from his startled companion who squared up to Ethan, thought better of it and ran. Ethan pulled the winded technician to his feet and, with his good hand, clamped vice-like on the man's arm, spun round once, twice, like a hammer thrower as he advanced towards the onrushing agents. On the third rotation, he released the man who flew into the lead agent and they both collapsed in a tangle of limbs and curses. Ethan darted back to the door and crunched the laptop into the face of the card reader before switching the crumpled machine for his staff. He pirouetted to one side as the second agent arrived, whipping the staff onto the shoulders of the on-rushing woman who continued into the wall with a sickening crunch as forehead met breeze block and she slumped to the ground, unmoving. The remaining agents slowed to a walk, eying their unconscious partner warily. The delay was decisive. Uma flung herself through the gap, Shane just behind her. She heard the door slam but Ethan hadn't finished.

'Come on,' he yelled, pushing past them, and sprinting down the short corridor towards another door through which a man was emerging, gun drawn. Realising he wasn't going to cover the ground, Ethan used the staff like a polevaulter, planting one end on the floor and launching himself onto the agent's chest, feet first. The impact drove the agent back through the doorway and into his partner. As all three crashed to the floor, Ethan leapt to his feet, smashing the pole down onto the second agent's head before jabbing it into the other's throat. The first's scream morphed into the second's anguished gurgle as Ethan beckoned Shane and Uma through the door, which he slammed shut before marching over to a low metal-framed table. He punched his foot through the glass top and grabbed a leg, before returning to the door and slamming the table down onto the handle which sheared off after the third blow.

'That should hold them for a few minutes,' he said, flinging the frame away and stepping over the two groaning agents. 'Now, Shane, where do we go?'

Shane just stood there, his face slack with amazement.

'What the hell just happened?'

'Anderson happened. Remember, the monster you merged me with. Now, think, where do we go?'

'I haven't got a clue,' Shane said, looking round the room. 'I've never been in here.'

As he spoke, two more white coats appeared through a door on the opposite side of the waiting room. Ethan marched over to them, brandishing his pole.

'Where's Crouch?' Ethan screamed at the startled men, grabbing one by the throat before head butting him. The man's nose exploded in a crimson burst as he crumpled to the floor. 'I said,' he bellowed at the second, 'where's Crouch?' Ethan took the man's right forearm and twisted hard down. The man screamed and fell to his knees, his arm bent at an unnatural angle.

'Last time, and I break each finger. Where's Crouch?'

The man nodded backwards at the door he'd just come through.

'Which room?'

'LEAP4.'

'OK, but just in case you're lying, you can come with me, and if you are ...' Ethan released the man's wrist and grabbed the right hand of his companion, who, sensing more pain, curled it into a tight fist. Ethan prised his middle finger loose and snapped it back. The man's groans turned to screams as his companion stared up at Ethan, his eyes slick with fear.

'I've got a wife,' he moaned. 'And kids.'

'Then let's hope you're telling the truth,' Ethan said, pulling him to his feet and ripping the lanyard from around his neck before sliding it over the card reader. 'Keep up, you two.'

Uma and Shane followed dumbly as he tore the door open, grabbed a fire extinguisher on the other side and decapitated the handle of the closed door with one savage jab of the metal cylinder.

'Two extra minutes to find Crouch,' Ethan said, setting off down the corridor, dragging the helpless man by his coat collar. At one point, he stumbled and Ethan hauled him to his feet before slamming him against the wall.

'Keep up. We don't have time for this.' He pushed the man out in front of him. 'Now find Crouch. And be quick.'

Shane placed a hand on Ethan's arm.

'Steady there, Ethan. He's an innocent in this.'

'Stay out of this, Shane,' he snarled, turning on his CTO. 'You don't know what you're talking about. If you want to help, carry this.' He hurled the fire extinguisher at Shane's feet and stormed off to catch up with the technician.

Uma and Shane exchanged glances.

'Christ, what's happened to him?'

'You made him!' she shot back, before hurrying after Ethan, her mind whirling. She'd seen that look before, in the Department of Geothermal Studies, the night that Ethan had become entangled with Anderson. On that occasion, he'd killed all the men sent to silence her, the last of whom he'd casually thrown over the balcony as if he was a sack of potatoes. She'd seen enough to know that interrupting Ethan was not advisable. The rage scared and excited her in equal measure. She felt safe around it, invincible even, and given what had just happened, that felt good. Given half a chance, she wished she could have fought the agents, smashed their faces with her fists, pummelling them all to a bloody pulp.

Up ahead, Ethan and the unfortunate technician had disappeared through a double set of doors. She pushed through them but they were nowhere to be seen. Uma felt a spiral of panic and began to check each door, her heart pounding. *What had the technician said? LEAP4? Or was it 5?*

She stopped at LEAP4 which was locked and she continued to the next. That was also locked. Hinges squeaked behind her but it was Shane coming through the swing doors. As he did, Ethan's head appeared out of LEAP4.

'Are you two coming?'

He disappeared and they rushed into the room.

'Can you manage the door?' Ethan nodded at the fire extinguisher that Shane was holding. Without waiting for a reply, he turned to the technician and removed his lab coat before forcing him into a chair. He tore the garment into long strips and bound the man's arms and legs to the chair. Behind him, Shane was struggling to break the handle.

'Christ, do I have to do everything?' Ethan wrenched the fire extinguisher from Shane's grasp and smashed it down onto the handle, which clattered to the floor. Ethan dropped the extinguisher and slowly exhaled, eyes shut, hands on hips. As Uma and Shane watched, his shoulders relaxed and the tension seemed to drain from his body. He arched his neck back, rotating it from side to side, grimacing as he did, before breathing in deeply. Finally, his eyes opened.

'What now?' Uma asked cautiously. Ethan nodded past her into the room where an elderly man was slumped in a chair, snoring loudly. It took Uma a few seconds to place him before recognition dawned: Professor Crouch. Time had not been kind to him. His large head was virtually bald, deep under eyes shadowed his face like black clouds, which were in turn framed by beetroot cheeks that had seen too much alcohol.

'You realise that we'll probably get incarcerated for what you just did.' Shane glared at Ethan.

'We had no choice.' Ethan's voice was measured, calm almost, but something in its tone stayed Shane's response. 'We needed to get in here quickly and all we had was the element of surprise. As it is, we've probably got two, maybe three minutes to interrogate Crouch and find out what's going on before those doors give, so I suggest you and Uma do your worst and we can run a post-mortem later.'

'We're not going to get much out of him,' Uma said, nodding at the comatose man.

'You could at least have warned us what you were going to do,' Shane said.

'I didn't know myself,' Ethan said, picking up a half-empty bottle from Crouch's desk. As he did so, a grubby hand snaked out and felt around the table. Finding nothing it paused, resting like a five-limbed arachnid. Slowly, Crouch opened his eyes and stared at Ethan before catching sight of Uma, at which point he broke out into a hollow cackle.

'Oh, you're done for. You really are.'

He stared longingly at the bottle and licked his dry lips.

'He stinks,' Uma said, grabbing the professor's arm and pulling him towards her.

He yelped with feigned pain and laughed again.

'You're too late. The damage has been done.'

He stared at Uma, his bulging eyes rheumy with drink, a manic grin plastered across his veined face, and then, overcome by exhaustion but mainly neat whiskey, his head tilted slowly to one side like a deflating hot air balloon and he resumed his snoring.

Uma pushed his chair to one side and studied the screen on Crouch's desk, before motioning for Shane to join her. 'What do you make of this?'

It took her a few seconds to realise that Shane hadn't moved but was still stood by the bound technician, glowering at Ethan's back.

'Shane, for God's sake. Ethan's right. If he hadn't done what he did we'd still be outside talking about it. We need your help now. This is why you came.'

A hammering behind Shane made them all start. Through the door they could hear raised voices.

'This isn't finished,' he snapped at Ethan, before marching over to Uma and studying the screen. 'He's scheduled another LEAP, tonight, in the next—' he glanced at his watch, '—few minutes. It goes right into the West Wing. To the President's private gate.'

'How's he done that?' Ethan said.

His only response was the rapid clicking of the keyboard.

'I'll be damned.'

'What is it?' Ethan said.

Shane was silent, studying the screen. He whistled in amazement.

'It's been set up to look like it came from your office.'

'How did he do that?'

'Not yours,' he snapped. 'Uma's.'

'What do you mean? My office?'

'He's hacked into the DOE network.'

'Impossible.'

'See for yourself,' Shane said, moving aside to let Uma confirm what he already knew.

'Why would he do that?'

'To make it look like you set this whole thing up. Whatever it is.'

'He's right, Uma,' Ethan said. 'Shane, can you cancel the LEAP?'

Shane's brow had resumed its familiar worry lines and this time he answered Ethan directly.

'It'd take too long.'

'Can we LEAP ahead so we're there to meet whoever's been sent.'

'It's too dangerous,' Shane said. 'Who knows what we'll—'

The door splintered in quick succession as five shots rang round the room. It made everyone jump again and the technician screamed in agony as the right arm on his white coat suddenly blossomed like a red rose.

'You've shot me,' he cried. 'I'm not with them. I work here. In D Lab.'

Whoever was standing on the other side of the door didn't respond but the corridor fell silent as Ethan wheeled the whimpering technician to one side and applied a tourniquet to his arm, with the remains of the shredded lab coat.

'It's just a flesh wound,' he said, turning back to Shane and Uma. 'We need to make a decision. Ideas anyone?'

Beside her, Shane sat frozen at the keyboard, fingers poised, waiting for an answer that would never come. Ethan looked exhausted and Uma realised his entire forearm was cherry red in stark contrast to his wan complexion. She'd forgotten about his shattered radius. How had she missed it? How had he managed the fight? Behind her, Crouch had woken up again and his triumphant cackle crawled across her scalp just like Forsyth's had. She'd be damned if it finished here, trapped in a room like a rat after everything she'd suffered, not just in the last six weeks but since she'd first approached Ethan and people had started dying. The anger surged through her limbs like a tidal wave, sweeping aside her fatigue and leaving her clear headed. The solution followed moments later, in the way lightning strikes a weathervane. Uma couldn't believe she hadn't thought of it earlier. She pushed Shane, who was still crouched over the screen, aside and, ignoring his protests, began to type.

'Well, I'll be dammed,' she heard him murmur. 'Do you think it'll work?'

'It'd better do. Crouch's transfer's just about to go through.' She studied the screen intently. 'Now.'

'What if it doesn't?'

'Get us to The White House, Shane.'

Uma looked up. Ethan was stood there smiling down at her, his face weary with pain. She carefully took his arm in her hands and inspected the casing; it looked intact, but blood was oozing freely through the joins.

'It's too dangerous,' Shane protested. 'Do you remember what happened last time I sent you to Reykjavík?'

'We have to make sure that what Uma's done has worked.'

'We'll find out in time.'

'It'll be too late by then.'

'You could both be killed, and I doubt you'll be allowed to come back this time. If Ingram is behind this, he won't risk it. You ... I ... we ... all know too much.'

The three of them fell silent as Shane's words sunk in.

Ethan recovered first.

'On that basis, we're all as good as dead whether we stay or go, so we've got nothing to lose.'

They looked up as the hammering resumed but this time it sounded solid, and quickly settled into a rhythm that shook dust from the door frame.

'That's not going to hold much longer, Shane.' Uma began to set up the LEAP. 'You just need to shut this console down so when they break in, it'll take them a few minutes to discover where we've gone. In that way, you won't have our blood on your hands like last time.' She glanced up, remembering how she'd berated him for entangling Ethan with Anderson. How she'd blamed him for the ensuing chaos but in reality, it hadn't been his fault. He was simply reacting to an extraordinary situation, making decisions that weren't simply right or wrong but bad or worse. She knew how that felt. 'Can you do that for me?' she whispered to him.

Shane nodded, understanding flittering across his furrowed brow.

Uma stood up and took Ethan's good arm, before intertwining her fingers through his and squeezing tightly. They made their way over to the LEAP gate and just as they stepped across the threshold, Uma heard a crash behind her. As she looked back, her brain registered snapshots of activity, like panels in a comic book: three men framed in the doorway, Shane face down on the floor, Crouch's bulbous head turned towards her, a look of surprise slapped across his face.

And then everything disappeared.

The West Wing

17 December 2009, 01:35 hours

Black dots pinged across his peripheral vision and an uneasy wave of weightlessness washed over him, causing his stomach to somersault in protest. For a second, he thought he was going to vomit again and sank to his knees in anticipation. Nothing. Fortune had been right. As he crouched, the dizziness quickly passed, allowing him to stand and study his surroundings. It looked very similar to where he had come from but he had been warned of this. The practice centre at Camp Peary was an exact reproduction of its famous cousin 110 miles north at 1600 Pennsylvania Avenue NW Washington, DC 20500. Everything was the same. It had to be, otherwise the Secret Service teams couldn't practise in what Fortune referred to as 'live' conditions. He quickly performed his kit check: wrist monitor, Sig Sauer P229, two combat knives, one on his left shoulder, one on his right hip, four extra clips. Everything had come with him. Nothing was dislodged. Beneath the Kevlar assault suit and ballistic vest, the Jacket was satisfyingly heavy, weighed down with heavy metal and high explosive. He felt secure with it on. Almost superhuman, as if the thick covering could protect him from anything—knives, certainly bullets, even explosions. Death itself. Except it would also soon deliver him up to the promised land seven years later than hoped for but at long last he would be reunited with his brothers. He would finally be able to embrace each one of them, victorious, having dealt a mortal blow at the heart of the enemy that would have repercussions far beyond what they had hoped to achieve with their attack on the British Underground system. His name would live forever.

'Don't dawdle,' had been Fortune's other command. 'Time is your enemy once you enter the West Wing. Assume you've been discovered the moment you arrive. Move quickly. The success of your mission depends on it.'

He complied, moving towards the door and slipping into the corridor.

It was dark and seemingly empty. Perfect. Fortune's advice rang in his ears: 'Behave as if you belong there. It won't be unusual to see a member of the ERT patrolling the corridors but if you are engaged, you know what to do.'

Belman knew what to do. The problem was that he had never done it.

As he moved down the heavily carpeted passage towards the stairs leading up from the basement onto the first floor, he checked his watch. Seventy-two seconds. Belman was shocked. In training he had reached this point within thirty seconds of leaving the LEAP chamber. Fortune was right again. The real thing would eat up his time. He needed to move faster. The longer he took, the less likely he would succeed. Fortune had estimated he had precisely 180 seconds from arriving to make his target otherwise he was moving into what he called zero sum time. *You will be probably be dead by then and not in a good way.* At that he would laugh. The prospect filled Bellman with terror. So close yet so far from his target. That would be a repeat of seven years ago except this time he would meet his brothers empty handed, having died a meaningless death. No, he didn't want that to happen and quickened his pace.

As he neared the top of the stairs, whispered tones floated down the stairwell.

Flutters of excitement hiccupped through his belly as Belman reached for the Gerber combat knife on his left shoulder pad. The

TacHide handle clung to his palm which was just as well. He was sweating freely. He paused, straining every nerve as a door opened. The voice faded as it entered the first floor, his floor. Belman moved up a level and entered the corridor. It was dark. Up ahead he could see the outline of a guard. He had his back to Belman and was speaking softly into a phone or radio.

He grasped the Gerber tightly.

The man hadn't moved.

Belman felt so alive, all his senses fine-tuned to perfection

The blade was soundless. There was hardly any resistance. Just a sharp intake of breath followed by a gasp, almost of surprise.

He didn't look back. Fortune had warned him to keep moving and Belman obeyed. Past the Vice-President's office. The Chief of Staff's. He thought he heard voices. More like whispers.

A beam of light swept up ahead.

His heart skipped a beat.

The final corridor.

Either side, advisers' offices.

To his left, the Roosevelt room.

Almost there.

He could see the door up ahead.

He had made it. Fortune said he could detonate from this point onwards. He was entering from the NWW entry point. The room was just short of thirty-six feet in length along its north-south axis. The blast radius was forty feet. It would be enough, but not for Belman. He wanted to see the whites of the Presidents' eyes. Hear him apologise for American foreign policy and then he would detonate. It would be a glorious death.

Belman's hot hand closed around the cool handle of the Oval Office.

The Oval Office, Washington DC

17 December 2009, 01:37 hours

The President looked up sharply. The ringtone was slightly different, probably not noticeable to others but he recognised it and was at the table before the third ring.

'What have you got for me?'

'We're at Camp Peary.'

'And?'

'Five fire teams have entered the West Wing training centre.'

'They were using the training centre! Good Lord, Joseph. How did they get in there?'

'Let's conduct the post-mortem later, sir. In the meantime, we're ready to take him out on your command.'

'Do it,' the President said.

'I'll call you when it's completed, sir.'

'Thank you.'

The line went dead, leaving the younger man staring at the phone.

How had they managed to stay concealed for so long? In a CIA training centre so close to DC? No matter. It was nearly over. Joseph had been right. They could order an inquest later. It would be a rare glimmer of good news to have caught the bombers so quickly. The fact that it was a CIA-supported terror cell on mainland America comprising of escapees and releasees from Guantanamo Bay, was a whole different ball game.

He sat down at the desk and continued working on the Copenhagen draft. Where was Chuck? He should have been here by now.

As the thought formed, the door leading out to the Roosevelt room began to open.

The Oval Office, Washington DC

17 December 2009, 01:37 hours

The bullet caught Belman high up on his back. One second he was upright, half-crouched, savouring the moment of glorious victory as he entered the office of the President of the United States of America, the most powerful man on the planet. In the most powerful room. The next, he was sprawled flat on his face, gasping for breath, fighting a crushing weight that threatened to snap his spine in two. For an awful moment he thought he was going to pass out with the pain, his breath sucked from him by the powerful projectile. His first instinct was to curl up into a tight ball, like a well-trained detainee: defence first. Above him, the door was beginning to disintegrate under the fuselage of fire. Then it all came back to Belman: Fortune, the training, his mission, the Oval Office. How had they found him? Was it a trap? No time for that. His target would be moving. Trying to get out of the room. Agents would be zeroing in on the Oval Office to protect their man. He had to detonate before the President escaped and moved out of range. But the room seemed empty.

He ignored the searing pain in his right shoulder and struggled to his knees, his left arm hanging like the torn limb of a rag doll. Hot metal zipped above his head, making him wince. Where was his target? Behind the desk, cowering like a rat? He stumbled across the room before crashing into the old wood panelling as he lost his footing under a sustained burst of fire from the corridor. He must be there. Had to be there. Suddenly he felt fearful, the possibility of failure too much to bear. Belman crawled on all fours, groaning with the effort. He had to see his eyes. Begging for mercy as so many of his brothers had done. Feel his fear before the detonation ended his life on earth and dammed him in the next, whilst Belman would be delivered, victorious, into the afterlife. Behind him, an explosion rocked the room, showering him with plaster. The force knocked him forward past the desk where he lay crumpled against the far wall, staring at the empty footwell.

West Wing

17 December 2009, 01:40 hours

Fortune broke consciousness, gasping with surprise at the cold ache as his life force slowly pulsed out of the neat puncture wound in his back. It was too high for a clean kill but it was deep, cutting through soft tissue and key arteries that would never heal. He should have known, the last words before he blacked out ringing in his head: 'Get out of there. It's a trap.'

Then he'd fainted. Of course, it'd been a trap. Fortune's instinct never let him down, but it had been too late. After Belman's jump, he had made his way back towards the exit when the call came in. For a moment he had debated whether to answer, but curiosity got the better of him. His handler was breathless with excitement. It sounded like he had been running. He had just heard that a Special Ops hit was to be made on the Camp Peary Training Centre. Tonight. Within the next few minutes. Belman had started asking questions, his anger overriding any number of field protocols. And then, suddenly, it had gone dark, as the knife sliced through his field jacket like scissors through crepe paper.

Up ahead, his assailant was paused outside the Oval Office, hand on handle. He looked familiar, but Fortune's fading senses refused to accept what he saw. And then, as the shooting started, realisation cut through him like the sharpened steel that would shortly end his life. He saw Belman pitch forward into the famous room as if he'd been kicked from behind by a horse. The door disintegrated under a barrage of light ordinance. How had they found him? What had gone wrong? Who had betrayed them? A moment of clarity burst over him. This mission had never been intended to succeed. Or not at least by Fortune's definition. That could be the only answer. He couldn't have made a mistake. Could he? Maybe. His mistakes may have brought five teams to Camp Peary but couldn't have returned Belman to the training centre. Had he even left? It was clear that Belman thought he was in the real Oval Office and was intent on completing his mission. The ease with which Belman had overcome him brought a macabre satisfaction as his life ebbed away. Fortune braced himself for the explosion but it never came which meant Belman must be alive. For now.

Death didn't scare him. He was a soldier and had lived with death all his life, had caused it and had trained others to deal it. And like Belman, Fortune understood the certainty of death except in his version, there was no afterlife. It just ended. For him it would go dark as his life force was snuffed out. His heart would simply cease to beat as his body drew its last breath and then in the next second, nothing. An infinite darkness as decay set in and his cells continued their eternal rotation back to base elemental atoms. He felt no remorse or fear. It was simply the end. Of everything.

The Oval Office, Washington DC

17 December 2009, 01:42 hours

Belman wept softly, staring at the empty space beneath the table. Around him, shrapnel hissed and whined. Was it another trick? A cruel hoax cooked up by the Americans to punish him for all eternity, on this earth and in the next life. A failed soul consigned to wander aimlessly through the eternal passage of time without the succour of success as his companion. He would never meet his brothers on the other side. His name would never go down in history as the man to breach the Americans' aura of invincibility, a calling cry to his brothers across the world to take up arms against their Western oppressors and push them from their territories. Their cruelty knew no bounds.

His helplessness was profound. It froze his limbs and deadened his mind. It bore down on him, crushing his unlikely dream, slowly grinding his glorious victory into dust. Reducing it to nothing, just like his life. A worthless and meaningless existence that would follow him into the afterlife. An abject failure for all eternity, that would remain by his side like a sad spectre, haunting each moment as time stretched away into eternal oblivion.

What could he do?

His only option was to push the button and take down as many as he could.

It would be an inconsequential Pyrrhic victory. A meaningless footnote in the history of his brother's struggles but now his only future. That or surrender meekly and rot in prison until his death, crippled by regret. He couldn't do that. Better an eternity with a courageous death, however underwhelming, than one in the shadow of a cowardly surrender and natural death. He would need to time it to perfection. Would they find the explosives and defuse them? Unlikely. Fortune had thought of everything. They were buried beneath his vest in the Jacket. He wore two bracelets: one on his wrist, the other on his thigh. If either were removed, they would detonate. If he died, they would detonate. He squeezed the cool metal of his hand trigger which he could depress for an immediate explosion or set it to countdown. That was his best option, a countdown. Two minutes should do it, a double click.

He caressed the silver cylinder as a stifling memory of that hot morning on the London Underground surfaced. The crush of bodies, the smell of her hair, its texture so soft and pure. Like the virgins he would unite with in heaven. But he had never made it. On that day the detonator had failed, his malice exposed after his glorious shout, his failure complete as he was tackled to the ground by courageous passengers, his last memory of the woman, a furtive glance back as she fled the carriage. One filled with fear and blind panic.

As he kissed Fortune's detonator for the last time, the entire office exploded in a flash of white light. He instinctively drew both hands to his eyes as the dazzling burst seared his retinas but it made no difference. The phosphoric shower continued to burn across his internal vision like a solar flare as a blast of energy washed over him. He felt rough hands grab his legs and arms, which felt jelly weak. His Sig Sauer P229 went first, then the two combat knives along with his boots. He felt razor sharp restraints pull tight around his wrists. As they lifted him, hot tears burned his blind eyes, but his failure burned brightest, blazing through his heart like an avenging demon from the depths of hell and onwards into his soul.

Washington, DC

17 December 2009, 02:03 hours

Fortune's eyes flickered open. Was he dead? The dull pain in his side suggested otherwise. He felt lightheaded. Short of breath. What was he still doing here? Around him, soldiers were gathered in small groups. Some talked but most stood, silently waiting for their orders. The smell of burning magnesium hung in the air. So, they'd used a stun grenade. Why would they want Belman alive? That didn't make sense. Operations like this always had a no-survivors outcome built in. Belman should be dead. Unless they knew about the Jacket. The pulse detonator. Then he would have to be alive until they could work out how to defuse it or at least get him to a place where he couldn't do any damage. Either way, Fortune couldn't afford that—Belman was a loose end.

Ahead of him, five men exited the Oval Office, walking in his direction. Belman was third, wrists strapped securely behind his back, head slumped down in surrender. Fortune had a chance to finish this. A slim one but he had nothing to lose. He felt the reassuring imprint of the Sig Sauer against his chest. Had the teams assumed he was friendly and left it in his jacket? He had one, maybe two seconds tops, before he was shot. More than enough time to squeeze off five rounds. No body shot. It would have to be the head. A clean kill. Already the group was upon him, all eyes on the prisoner. As the second soldier stepped over him, Fortune slipped the gun from his holster. Belman saw the movement, and their eyes met. It was fleeting but felt like an eternity for both men.

Belman's mouth curled into a smile.

One of the soldiers shouted a warning but it was too late.

Fortune began firing.

Belman screamed, 'God is Great. Allahu Akbar.'

The Jacket burst into life.

The White House, Washington, DC

17 December 2009, 3:39 hours

The metal cut deep into his flesh and he stifled a cry, relaxing his arms, so the pressure abated. There was no way he could wriggle his wrists free, particularly with his damaged forearm. The hastily applied field dressing had long since saturated to a bloody red and every movement pinged bolts of pain deep into his armpit. Ethan tried to sit up but his wrist cuffs were attached to his ankle cuffs by a short length of plastic and it felt like a full body work out to lever himself upright, so that, eventually, his hands were pulled forward towards his feet in a grotesque forward bend. But at least his arm felt more comfortable and he exhaled deeply. One of the agents glanced over. He was young, maybe mid-twenties but boy, he knew how to fight, as did his five companions. They hadn't exactly been waiting for them when Ethan and Uma appeared in the room. In fact, the LEAP chamber had been deserted which in of itself was both puzzling and worrying. Why would the President's personal LEAP gate not be guarded twenty-four hours a day? The implication had propelled them into the corridor outside where the question was answered in brutal fashion. There were six guards: two sat, one either side of the door into the LEAP room, whilst their companions patrolled the corridor. They seemed surprised to meet their unexpected guests. Uma had tried outranking them, reminding them who she was and that they had come to see the President. Not without an appointment, had been the response. But they had an appointment, she insisted, except it wasn't on their schedule, was the counter. Voices rose as positions became more entrenched, so much so that Ethan had assumed others would arrive but no one did. He didn't know the layout of The White House, had never been to The White House but remembered from newspaper articles that it was small so there must have been others close by, within hearing, but no one came. As the argument built like the crest of a breaking wave, Ethan realised it was going nowhere, not that Uma seemed to pick up on that. Her tone became more argumentative and to be fair, the agents didn't react which only seemed to infuriate her even more, as if she was trying to goad them into doing something. Eventually she'd announced she was going to the Oval Office with or without them. Which is when things had turned ugly. One of the agents had placed a restraining hand on her arm and suddenly he was upside down with Uma's scream of 'Don't you goddam touch me' ringing in all their ears. As the second faced her down, she hadn't paused, driving her foot into his groin before unleashing a barrage of punches, first to his chest and then to his face as he sank to the ground from the first kick. Then they'd made their second mistake: one of the agents had grabbed Uma's long hair, tugging her back so forcibly that she'd lost her footing, crying out as she was jerked backwards. Ethan wasn't fully aware of his actions from then on, a bit like when he'd gained entrance to the CBL unit. Just a procession of fleeting images: the wooden pole, freeze framed, crunching down on an unprotected forearm; a fist, his fist, buried in a cheek; a man, spreadeagled on the floor, his arm bent at an unnatural angle. And then shouts, shots fired, agents everywhere, lots of them, too many to fight and finally a sharp pain in his neck followed by an explosion of fireworks. And then he blacked out.

When he came round, he was back in the LEAP room, trussed up like a turkey for Xmas. Uma was lying next to him, still unconscious, a light bandage on her forehead the only clue as to why she didn't respond to his repeated attempts to get a response. Around him were the agents from the corridor, all standing, talking and eyeing him warily whenever he demanded to see the President. Eventually, he'd fallen silent and lay there wondering what had happened. Had the plot worked? Was the President dead? Why were they alive? Surely it meant the President was still alive and that they would soon be free. That, at least, was his logic but Ethan didn't find it reassuring and kept returning to Shane's words just before they made the LEAP—if Ingram was behind this, they'd already be dead but they weren't which meant the President had survived or Ingram wasn't behind it?

He shook his heavy head, trying to dislodge whatever was shooting tiny slivers of pain up into the roof of his skull but it was no good. The slivers morphed into splinters and soon became tree trunks, crashing around his brain like a threshing machine.

Uma groaned softly and her eyes fluttered, before opening fully. Ethan smiled down at her.

'Good of you to join us.'

Recollection cleared her blank face as she struggled into the contorted yoga position.

'Did it work?'

'Not sure. We're alive, so maybe.'

'Hey, you,' Uma called out to the nearest agent. 'If we can't see the President, can we at least see your boss?'

The man scowled down at her, rubbing his shoulder, and turned away.

'What do we do?' she said, shifting her position to face Ethan. She looked exhausted, fatigue draped across her pale face like a mourning shroud. Ethan wished he could reach out, cradle her in his arms, stroke her thick hair and tell her it would be alright. The familiar surge of helplessness washed over him, a lesser version of the tsunami that had engulfed him in the castle when she'd sank to her knees, the spear that had snuffed out her life still piercing his memories. It did so daily but it had also lanced his resentment, purging his body of the poison that had infected so many years of his life. In that moment, as she lay there, he'd vowed to protect her, to never let anyone harm her. Except he couldn't even do that. The fury clawed at his insides, raging to be unleashed, but there was no outlet for that. He needed Ethan, cool, calculated and logical if they were going to get out of this.

'Wait,' he said. 'Whatever you did at the CBL centre must have worked. The President is still alive otherwise this place would be crawling. When they're ready to see us, someone will come and get us.'

The agents suddenly stood to attention as a familiar figure entered the room. He grinned down at Uma and Ethan before motioning to one of his men.

'Davies, you can release these two. The President is ready to see them.'

'Yes, Director.' The younger man, who'd turned his back on Uma, produced a knife from his waist belt and sliced through the plastic tie connecting the cuffs, before motioning to the other agents who hauled Uma and Ethan to their feet. Once they were stood, he unlocked their cuffs.

'You bastard,' Uma launched at Ingram but her cramped limbs had other ideas. She staggered forward into Davies' arms but Uma barely seemed to notice. 'You're responsible for all of this,' she continued, jabbing a finger at the director. 'With your creep, Forsyth, and his Arab paymaster.'

Ingram smiled benignly at her, as a parent might a small child.

'Interesting theory, Doctor, but as usual, you're a country mile off. Thanks to your efforts, we apprehended the assassin two hours ago at Camp Peary. Your CSO, Shane, filled us in at the CBL centre. I have to say, your methods were quite brutal.' He looked over at Ethan. 'Were they entirely necessary? I've got nine men with various breaks, sprains and injuries from your wrecking spree.'

Uma suddenly noticed Davies for the first time and wrenched herself away. Ethan stepped forward as she nearly fell, cushioning her into his chest.

'Uma,' he tried, 'we've no proof of the director's involvement in any of this.'

'Bullshit,' Uma spat back, pulling herself away from Ethan and lunging at Ingram. Several of the agents stepped forward but the director motioned them back, leaving Uma stood in the middle of the room, swaying like a late-night drunk.

'Listen to your boyfriend,' Ingram murmured. His tone was condescending, designed to rile and Uma obliged, swinging a punch in his direction but it was feather light and he evaded it easily, towering over her like a giant insect hovering over its prey. 'Steady there, Doctor. If you don't stop, I'll instruct Davies to cuff you again.' He paused, waiting for some acknowledgement from Uma which was never going to come but she stayed still this time, eyes fixed on his, her fists clenched, waiting for an opening which her tired body could no longer exploit. Satisfied, Ingram continued, 'We've had our doubts about Forsyth for quite some time. His business interests were propped up by Saudi oil funds which Al Rahman leveraged to force him to transfer over the LEAP tech that Reynolds developed with Crouch's help.'

Uma just stood there shaking her head and it was Ethan who stepped forward.

'So, who's behind the plot to assassinate the President? That really doesn't fit well with your explanation.'

'A distraction, perhaps? What better way to mask the theft of LEAP than by assassinating the President of the United States? The ensuing chaos would have kept everybody focused on the fact that LEAP was instrumental to the attack. It would have set the programme back years, allowing Forsyth and Al Rahman to sell their version to other nations unhindered by a rival product. This is all supposition, of course. I have no idea but it's a compelling theory, don't you think?'

'It's bullshit,' Uma whispered but she made no move towards Ingram.

Ethan was impressed. It was a compelling theory.

'So, what happens now?'

Ingram turned to Ethan.

'Not sure. First you get your audience with the President, if you can calm the doctor down, that is. Then we need to try and recover the LEAP tech to protect our new investment.'

'Can you give us some time?' Ethan said, nodding at Uma.

'Of course.' The director motioned towards his men. 'You've got five minutes and then the President leaves for Camp David. He's due in Copenhagen tomorrow, with—' he glanced at Uma. 'Maybe not,' he said with a wry smile.

The room was suddenly quiet as the door clicked shut and Ethan took Uma in his arms as she started to cry.

'Are you going to tell me what's going on?'

'That bastard is getting away with it.'

'So might we if everyone buys into his version of the truth.'

'But he's guilty. He's set this up from the get-go.'

'And how are we meant to prove that? He seems very adept at having others do his dirty work.'

Uma buried her head deeper into Ethan's chest.

'Look, our goal from the outset was to reverse global warming. We need Ingram to ensure that Green Ray remains intact. Besides which, if the President's still alive, it means all your environmental goals are too.'

'How can you remain so calm?' she cried out, lifting her head towards him. Her face was streaked with tears and blood.

'Because I can't win every battle. Only some. And my priority, especially after what happened in California, is to protect you and ensure the LEAP programme is delivered out in some format resembling your original vision. If that means Ingram gets away with what he's planned, so be it. What's your priority?'

Uma didn't reply straight away. The weight of the last twenty-four hours suddenly reasserted itself and she slumped against the wall. She was sure Ingram knew about Forsyth and his little video recordings. Christ he was a spymaster. It was his job to know. But it was more than that. He was a creep; all she could think of was his eyes slithering over her body when they'd first met in LA, and then in DC when he'd entered her apartment uninvited. An image of him watching the video of her and Forsyth on the table in San Francisco arose unbidden and fresh tears burnt her battered face. Maybe he had his own video collection of conquests but none of it mattered. She'd already decided to bury the rape so regardless of how much Ingram knew about it, she could never tell anyone, especially not Ethan. Ingram had outmanoeuvred her again but to what end, she no longer knew.

'It's OK, Uma.' She heard Ethan through the fog of her thoughts and looked up. His kind eyes were creased with worry but also something else—pain. And for the first time since leaving the CBL centre, she noticed his bloody arm.

'I'm OK,' she whispered through her tears. 'We really need to get that seen to.'

The Oval Office, Washington, DC

17 December 2009, 04:06 hours

Uma gently rubbed her sore wrists as she looked round the room. Nothing had changed in five weeks—the eagle above, the silent sentinels behind her guarding invisible doors and to her left, the white marble fireplace. Except, of course, everything had changed. Ethan sat opposite, nursing a fresh dressing but the clean bandages didn't mask the toll of the last five hours. A deep cut framed his right cheek, which in turn sat above an egg-shaped bruise along his jawline which had spattered blood on his shirt already soaked red by his leaking forearm. Ingram paced in front of them, head bent so low she thought he was going to topple over. Behind his desk, the President was surrounded by advisers. All were staring expectantly at a phone that had, so far, refused to ring. That was how Uma and Ethan had found the President when they were ushered into the Oval Office by Ingram less than five minutes ago.

The shrill tone made her jump.

Ingram stopped pacing as the President hit the speaker button.

'Your Royal Highness, thank you for accepting my call at such short notice.'

'Mr President, as always, it's a pleasure to speak with you. I was expecting your call, despite the late hour in DC.'

'I'm sure you were,' the President said, glancing towards Uma. 'Given the background to this, I'll dispense with the pleasantries. We know about the theft of LEAP.'

'I would prefer to call it an acquisition. A rather large one, actually, to the tune of one hundred and twenty billion dollars, paid in kind to Ethan Rae. Or rather his environmental fund fronted by your Energy Secretary.'

'We know about the transfer of funds. Green Ray is co-operating fully with us.'

'I would imagine so. You are their main partner in the LEAP technology and later today, the fund will probably cease to exist once we make our announcement.'

'As you correctly say, we're partners and intend to prosecute your theft with every legal means at our disposal.'

'How very American of you but we have paperwork to prove that a proper and legal transfer took place.'

The President looked over at Ethan and Uma. Both of them frowned, shaking their heads.

'That's not quite how we see it at this end. That money was an investment in Green Ray by a country running out of oil and seeking to diversify its carbon-based revenues with greener ones. It was not an acquisition of LEAP.'

'Are you sure you want to go down this route, Mr President? We have been your staunchest ally in the Gulf for over half a century. We trade hundreds of billions of dollars each year between our two nations. Do you really want to place that relationship under such strain over this technology?'

'Might I respectfully return the question, Your Highness? Why indeed would you want to test over seventy years of co-operation with such aggressive tactics?'

'I thought that would have been obvious. The basis of our relation-ship has been oil. Once that has been removed from the equation there is, shall we say, much less incentive for such a close collaboration.'

'Oil will still continue to play an important role in the world econ-omy despite LEAP. Transportation is not the only use for oil.'

'It has still rocked the markets. The spot price for crude has fallen eighty percent in the weeks since your announcement. You left us no choice once the tie up with Green Ray was announced.'

There was silence.

'And therein lays our difference, Mr President. And you question the aggressiveness of our tactics. Besides which, we don't only just have a demand problem.'

'How so?'

'Come now, Mr President. We've known about Ali Jum'ah for a while.'

One of the men gathered round the President mouthed, 'No'.

'I don't follow.'

'Please, don't patronise me, Mr President. You're not the only ones with a functioning secret service. We've had him under surveillance for a while but the pyrotechnics at Ghawar last month caught us unawares. The data theft forced our hand. We couldn't afford to have that sort of information in the public domains.'

'I don't think the Ghawar oil field's short comings were such a big secret.'

'Tell me, Mr President, if that was the case, why have Ali Jum'ah spying on it for the last ten years?'

'I guess, like you, we were protecting our national interests. We're hugely reliant on your oil imports. We needed to understand how bad the problem was.'

'A typical double standard.'

'How so?'

There was a short pause. For the first time the king sounded irritat-ed.

'It's OK for you to protect your national interests by spying on our national oil company but we are expected to 'toe' the line when the reverse is true.'

'I take it that you will not stand down over LEAP?'

'That's correct.'

'If you were to return the LEAP technology to us, I'm sure we can come to some arrangement over licensing it to you on a favourable basis.'

'It's too late, I'm afraid, Mr President. As we speak, several of our neighbours have already expressed an interest in licensing the technology from us. They also have no choice and we will work closely with them to ensure we can all combat the collapsing oil price using LEAP as the foundation for our new economy.'

The President looked up at his advisors who all stared back at him helplessly.

'Well, Your Highness, I, as ever, appreciate your candour on this topic. We, like you, have our national interests to protect and once we have conferred, I will ensure that you will be the first to hear of our decision.'

'Likewise, Mr President. It has been a pleasure and I only wish it was on a more equitable basis. Good night.'

The line went dead and the President replaced the receiver.

The room was tense. It sensed a moment and was right to pause.

'Suggestions anyone?' the President said.

There was silence as everyone avoided his steady gaze. The room seemed to magnify the moment until Uma felt she was at the heart of a vacuum which sucked the events of the last six weeks into its centre, to a moment of truth that would define their futures for decades to come. And at the apex of that moment, at the moment when she doubted it could extend out anymore, Uma spoke.

'Actually, yes. I have a suggestion. It's not ideal for anyone. Me, Ethan, Green Ray or yourselves, but it will get us all out of this mess Forsyth and Al Rahman have landed us in.'

Riyadh, Saudi Arabia

18 December 2009, 11:32 hours

The old man moved slowly, stopping every so often to catch his breath. He was clearly struggling and as he drew closer to the far end of the room it became clear why. Half his face seemed to be missing. Where his nose had been, a ragged hole bubbled bloody mucus. His lips hung like dry leather across toothless gums so that the lower half carried the pinched look of an ancient man, except around his cheeks and forehead. Here, the skin seemed too big for his skull, giving the impression that his entire visage had slipped two or three inches below where it should have been. He paused and patted his mouth with a blood-soaked handkerchief which required him to readjust both canes which supported his shaking body. Satisfied, he continued, grunting painfully with the effort before finally drawing up beside two chairs framed by a large window. He slowly sat down and looked over at the figure beside him who hadn't moved since he had entered the room over five minutes ago. The man didn't return the glance.

'So, the reports are true.'

'I'm afraid so.' His words came out slurred.

'How did it happen?'

'That Jakobsdóttir woman removed everything.'

'I don't follow.'

'All the silicone, the Botox, my implants. The whole lot. Gone.' He lifted a gnarled hand into the air, mimicking an exploding bomb. 'Phwoof!'

'Why can't you recover it?'

'She scrubbed my DNA profile. Erased it so there was no return reference.'

It was only then that Al Rahman turned to gaze at the pathetic creature, his beaked nose wrinkled with disdain.'

'There's nothing you can do?' he said.

'Seemingly not. The physicians I consulted say that my body is too weak for any major surgery. Plus, my age.'

'It's caught up with you.'

The man turned and for a second, his flaccid brows lifted with annoyance. Beneath, his eyes burned bright blue before snuffing out as the heavy skin folded down like a second eye lid.

'So, you're stuck with ... with that.'

'For the time being.'

'What are you going to do?'

There was a silence in the room as John Forsyth contemplated Al Rahman's question.

KSA2, Riyadh, Saudi Arabia

18 December 2009, 13:36 hours

The makeup girl worked quickly, applying the foundation evenly over his face. Either side of him, the foreign ministers of Abu Dhabi, Oman and Dubai were receiving a similar treatment. Abdullah Al Rahman, Head of the Re'asat Al Istikhbarat Al A'amah, smiled to himself. Today was a great day. The day that his family name would become synonymous with the dawning of a new age of Arab ascendency across the globe, his nation's future secured for generations to come. He studied the group of men in the mirror. They looked tired, especially him, the events of the last few weeks visibly taking a toll on their elderly bodies. However, if there was an elixir of life, they were just about to drink from its fountain. In just ten minutes they would announce to the world their acquisition of LEAP, along with five-hundred-year licensing agreements for his three Arab partners, with twelve more in the pipeline. He had already recovered the payments made to Forsyth and Green Ray tenfold and secured a half percent recurring fee for every LEAP transfer made through the gates for the next half millennia. Today, indeed, was a great day. There was a knock at the door and a face appeared.

'Two minutes to transmission,' the production assistant said. 'If you would be so kind as to follow me.'

All four men stood and were ushered down a narrow corridor, into a large holding room just off the main recording studio at KSA2, the Saudi Government's news channel. At one end of the room was a refreshment table loaded with local delicacies. Above it, a huge flat screen TV, around which were gathered a large group of advisers. Al Rahman made his way over to a couch and sat down with the other foreign ministers. He would never forget the telephone falling silent as the President of the United States of America, the leader of the world's most powerful economy, absorbed the full ramifications of what he had done. It was a priceless moment and would live long in the memories of all who had been present, particularly the king. The old man's eyes had lit up with satisfaction at the position the US Government found themselves in.

'Can we ask you all to come through to the studio please?' a production assistant asked them. 'We need to get you seated and wired up in time for the transmission.'

As Abdullah Al Rahman made his way towards the studio entrance, the large screen caught his eye. Two familiar figures were stood behind a podium. He stopped and watched as the camera panned back to reveal the image of a heron flying across a field of poppies and white flowers. Below it the words, 'United Nations Climate Change Conference.'

What were they doing there?

'Please, everyone,' he said, holding up a hand.

Several people beside him fell quiet, others followed, and within seconds the low hubbub of voices were silent.

The President's lips were moving silently.

'The sound. Turn the sound up,' Al Rahman motioned impatiently.

'—is the world's largest economy and that brings with it a great price in terms of pollution. It's no secret that this great nation of ours was responsible for one quarter of global CO2 emissions last year and we have been justly criticised for not doing enough about it. However, that has paled into insignificance over the global condemnation we've been subject to since our announcement that LEAP is a viable science and can transport non-human life forms. It's rightly rocked the markets the world over and we've worked steadfastly to reassure everyone of our honourable intentions with a technology that can clearly have a significant impact on global warming. Well, we've listened carefully, and I stand before you today to make two announcements. Firstly, that LEAP has progressed in the last four weeks. As you know, we've assembled a team of scientists and engineers unrivalled since the Manhattan Project during World War II. They now number over one hundred thousand and have been working non-stop to commercialise LEAP. Not only that but within the last week our partners in this undertaking, Green Ray, headed by Ethan Rae and Uma Jakobsdóttir ...' The President motioned to his right and the camera swung left to zoom in on a tired looking Uma. '... have confirmed that we have perfected human-based teleportation.' There was an audible gasp around the chamber. The President held up his hand and gradually the huge audience fell silent. 'However, unlike six years ago, when Reynolds Air announced a similar development, this is not, I repeat, this is not smoke and mirrors. In fact, to prove the technology, Dr Jakobsdóttir and I teleported to the conference this morning from The White House. A trip of over four thousand miles, that would normally take eight hours on Air Force One, not only took only a matter of seconds,' the President clicked his fingers, 'but also saved 22,000 gallons of fuel and prevented nearly 200 hundred tonnes of CO2 being spewed into the atmosphere.

'The United States of America has always led the world and we fully intend to do so with LEAP. Therefore, in recognition of the enormous good that LEAP can clearly deliver to the environment and global commerce, we have decided to continue that tradition of leadership, one that will provide the correct climate in which real and long-standing change can be made to global warming and, more importantly, catapult each and every economy out of the recession that has gripped our planet for the last year. Therefore, we have decided to make the technology available to every nation in the world. For free.'

There was uproar in the chamber as delegates leapt to their feet, applauding the President. The cheer rose in volume, sweeping over the two people on stage.

Abdullah Al Rahman didn't move for several seconds. He was aware that all eyes were on him. No one spoke, the only sound, a booming applause in Copenhagen as delegates from every nation celebrated the President of the United States of America. He seemed to be smiling directly at Al Rahman. So was that cursed woman, their reputations preserved for all eternity. Slowly, very slowly, he made his way from the holding room, each step seeming to slightly reduce him, so that by the time he exited, the proud and confident bearing had been replaced by an elderly man, stooped at the waist and burdened by his mortality.

Oil Treatment Centre, Riyadh, Saudi Arabia

21 December 2009, 12:00 hours

The figure was unmoving, holding the same position that only a statue knows how. He was staring into the middle distance, studying something intently but it was not clear what. The vast chamber, normally alive with the chatter of a thousand seagulls, was silent, their tiny silhouettes also unmoving, like a black terracotta army frozen in time. The sand he stood on covered his ankles like soft boots and in places had been stained black by the oil that cloaked his body like a thick shroud from the top of his headdress, down to the soles of his feet. But he did not seem to notice as his eyes continued their vacant inspection of the oil treatment centre.

There was a slight movement in the sand. The powdery silicon collapsed in on itself as if something was tunnelling underneath. A pincer slowly emerged. Then another and within seconds a black scorpion had materialised onto the sand. It scuttled towards the stationary figure, clambering over the dried tar like an all-terrain vehicle. Finally, it stopped and seemed to look up at the man, but he did not look down.

Al Rahman couldn't—there was nothing left to process the images captured by his eyes.

The Rose Garden, White House, Washington, DC

25 March 2010, 12:10 hours

Birds chattered excitedly in the Katherine crabapples, so thick with spring blossom that the white columns of the West Colonnade were almost invisible behind their gnarled limbs. Beneath their cream bounty, the flower beds were a riot of spring colour; red tulips towered over the bowed heads of pink-purple fritillaria and yellow jonquil jostled for position with blue grape hyacinth. It could have been a scene from any country garden, except in this garden the lawns were crawling with Secret Service agents. Overhead, Uma counted four black helicopters hovering menacingly in the sky. It was a fitting show of strength given the several hundred dignitaries waiting patiently in the spring sun for the President to appear. The warmth faded as the sun disappeared behind a bank of clouds moving in off the Chesapeake Bay and Uma suppressed an involuntary shudder. She suddenly felt alone on the dais and glanced towards Ethan for reassurance. He was talking to two men she didn't recognise. One of his companions said something, causing Ethan to laugh. He looked good. A far cry from the battered body that had emerged from The White House three months ago. His face had healed to a healthy tan and his arm was safe in a protective sling. It could have been the old Ethan, except it wasn't. He glanced over and she smiled back at him. It was the eyes—they were different, less remote than before, definitely more relaxed, peaceful but also wiser. He excused himself and made his way over, stooping to kiss her warmly on the lips. She never grew tired of their silky softness.

'Looking forward to the presentation?' Uma said.

'You know I'm not.'

'It's not every day a Brit receives the Presidential Medal of Freedom.'

'I think it's safe to say that I'm riding on your coattails this time round. Your father would have been very proud of you.'

'He would have hated this,' Uma said sharply. She hadn't thought of her father in months and wasn't inclined to. She still hadn't told Ethan that she might be a copy and frankly saw no point. The past was the past and along with what had happened to her in San Francisco, would remain that way. 'His great fear was that LEAP would be misused and, so far he's been proven right.' And there it was, the constant fear that had gnawed away at her insides after she'd made that fateful announcement in the Oval Office.

'Nonsense. You single handedly revived a Presidency, saved Green Ray and nullified the Saudi threat. And let's not forget making you the toast of the green movement the world over. And for achieving your original goal. Albeit seven years later than you intended. It doesn't get much better than this,' Ethan said, craning his neck towards the sun, eyes half-closed. He breathed deeply, a smile played out across his face.

Despite the warmth, Uma shivered again. She knew her father was right, had admitted as much after Eva's death when she'd decided to bury LEAP, but her hand had been forced in the last year. Repeatedly. And here they were stood, LEAP out in the world with all its great potential to slash carbon emissions alongside its potential to distort mankind's position in the world even more, just like every technological innovation had since early humans invented stone tools in the plains of Africa more than two million years ago.

'Ah the great Uma Jakobsdóttir.' Uma stiffened and they both turned towards the familiar voice of Joseph Ingram. He was stood behind them, his long bony hands clasped together as if in prayer. 'All hail the master tactician pulling the strings of power like no one I have witnessed in forty years of service to this great country of ours.'

'I sense this is just a game to you.' Uma couldn't help herself. 'That we're just pieces on a board to be manoeuvred at your bidding.'

Ingram grinned, clearly enjoying Uma's discomfort. 'Not this time. I was merely an observer. Like everyone else.'

'That's not entirely true, is it?' she said, struggling to keep the annoyance out of her voice.

'I don't follow.'

'I hardly call being made de facto head of the US Intelligence Services the actions of a mere bystander.'

'I gain no personal satisfaction from that appointment,' Ingram said, beaming down at Uma.

'Nevertheless, it's quite an achievement, wouldn't you say? No one thought it would ever get through the Senate.'

'They had no choice.'

'That's precisely my point.'

Ingram continued to smile but it appeared frozen and Uma could have sworn his long limbs tensed ever so slightly.

'Enlighten me.'

'Having experienced your techniques firsthand, I wonder whether they were given any choice.'

'Everyone has a choice, Doctor Jakobsdóttir. Isn't that right, Mr. Rae?'

Uma held herself in check even though she wanted to tear the smug smile from his thin lips. What was he getting at? Her decision to stay silent about what Forsyth had done to her? She was sure he knew, probably had the video. Was he threatening her again? To release it to Ethan? But to what end? Christ, his games were endless. She took a deep breath and calmed her racing heart. Not today.

'Not if they're pushed hard enough,' Uma said through clenched teeth.

Ingram shrugged and turned to Ethan.

'The simple truth of the matter is that the DC bombings proved our post 9/11 intelligence service was not fit for purpose. The Senate was faced with a simple choice: maintain the status quo or try a new approach.' Ingram unfolded his hands and drew himself up to his full height. 'Now, if you forgive me, I have more pressing matters to attend to. Doctor, my congratulations once again. Mr Rae, as ever, a pleasure.'

They watched the director amble off the dais and into the Oval Office where the President was just visible, surrounded by several assistants who all seemed to be talking to him.

'Do you think he was behind it?' Uma said.

'Probably.'

'He must have made some sort of mistake along the way. I'm sure we could take him down.'

'Oh no, you don't,' Ethan said, laughing.

'What do you mean?'

'Not another cause, please. I'm still dealing with the last one you got me involved in. And that's barely begun. We have a global teleportation system to roll out quickly and fairly, so we can start reducing your precious CO2 emissions.'

Before Uma could reply, a group of people entered the rose garden from the Oval Office and, as the President of the United States stepped up onto the dais, the large crowd took their seats. He was beaming wildly, and the grin felt infectious. Uma found herself responding. Maybe Ethan was right. She finally had something to show for all her struggles of the last seven years and for those who had died: for Sally Moltex and James Reagan, the two journalists who were meant to break the LEAP story; for dear Fredrik; even for Eva, poor lost Eva, consumed by greed; and for all those nameless men and women who had lost their lives as they became caught up in the race to own LEAP. Nothing would ever replace them but at least their deaths had not been in vain. For the first time in decades the planet had a chance to reverse global warming and she would be at the forefront of it along with Ethan.

At that moment, the sun broke through the clouds, flooding the rose garden with rays of soft light that lit up the candy floss laden trees and flowers beneath. Uma sought out Ethan's hand and squeezed it tightly.

Maybe today was a good day after all.

Epilogue

25 March 2010, 20:54 hours

Toba Kakar Mountain Range, Kandahar Province, Afghanistan

The green figure looked angry, its deeply furrowed over brow towering above slitted eyes, flared nostrils bellowing imaginary steam, open mouth roaring silently into the relentless downpour, comic book muscles bulging through ripped clothing. Staff Sergeant Lee McGuire of the 2nd Battalion 12th Infantry Regiment stared at the miniature Hulk figure on the rock in front of him wondering what Jake was doing. His twelve-year-old son was a Marvel nut, Hulk his favourite character, the figure his most prized possession and he'd pressed it into to his dad's hand just as McGuire was leaving the house for his next rotation in Afghanistan. What had he said? 'He'll keep you safe, Dad. Give you strength.' That was two months ago and so far, Hulk had been a bust but on every call, Jake would ask him if the green man was doing his job and McGuire would roar theatrically at the screen, drawing curious glances from other soldiers in the VC suite.

McGuire fist bumped the small figure and dragged his focus back to the drab settlement fifty feet below. The night goggles gave the buildings a gloom-laden tinge. They looked deserted but he knew this wasn't the case. Surveillance had reported their targets entering the ramshackle buildings thirty minutes ago and their orders were to root and shoot, no survivors. He shifted his position, flexing cramped muscles frozen numb by the sub-zero rain sheeting up the narrow valley. At least this part of the mission was working. Until early evening, when the storm system had scuttered in off the Hindu Kush mountain system, they'd had three straight nights of clear skies blasted white by a billion stars. He wiped the lenses of the NVGs and looked right, then left. Excluding his strike buddy, Boyle, aka Jaw Bone, the remaining squad of six was split into three fire teams. Two pairs were arrayed either side of his position, crouched low amongst the slick boulders, sights trained on the huts. They were all waiting for Max and Gabe to circle east and prevent any escape out of the narrow valley. To avoid more mistakes, everyone was to maintain radio silence. However, they'd know when the third pair had reached their position.

Right on cue, a flare exploded overhead, casting a muted glow through the rain-sodden night, but it did the trick. A shadow appeared in the doorway of the closest building. As McGuire brought him into focus, the figure looked up into the drenched sky, his Pakistani issued G3S assault rifle clutched tightly to his chest. For a brief second his face appeared, lit up by the cigarette hanging from his lips and then jerked back as the bullet from Ground Hog's Barrett M82 exploded his skull.

McGuire tapped his voice mic.

'This is Red Bull. Rock Star and Ground Hog, you take the three far left buildings. Butthead and Turtle, you take the right two. We'll take the middle one, copy over.'

'This is Fire Team One. Copy that, Red Bull. Copy over.'

'This is Fire Team Two. Copy that, Red Bull. Copy over.'

'This is Grid Iron. Don't be greedy. Leave some for us. We're freezing our butts off up here. Copy over.' Lee smiled. He'd worked alongside Max for three years now, all of them in Afghanistan. They'd were on their eighth tour and Max was still the best sniper he'd come across. With his elevated position on the east side of the valley he'd have a clear shot at anyone leaving the buildings.

'This is Red Bull. Eyes sharp, Grid Iron. Let's avoid last week's shit show. Copy over.'

The radio stayed silent and McGuire knew he'd hit a nerve. Intentionally. On their last mission, just four nights ago, they'd lost men and it was his fault. Same settlement. Similar night. But he hadn't deployed his two snipers. Hadn't needed to. There were only three T-Men. But the intel was bad and they'd walked into an ambush: three dead, including him and Max. Which meant this was their chance to get it right and he wasn't going to let it pass. Treat each mission as a training exercise, his CMO had said. With LEAP, you get a second chance and a third and a fourth. Until you get it right. Except he had no memory of that night because his body backup came from the outbound journey into Kandahar, two days before the shitshow had actually happened. All he had was a debrief from the surviving members of his squad. And tonight, he got to do it all again. And get it right.

The sharp clatter of an M4 cut through his thoughts and his heart scuttered with excitement. It was too early for engagement. What the fuck was going on? The three-round burst had come from the left, Rock Star and Ground Hog's patch.

'This is Red Bull. Fire Team One, what is your status? Copy over.'

'This is Rock Star. Enemy engaged. One T-Man down. Possible look out. No other casualties. We will continue to target. I repeat, continue to target. Copy over.'

'This is Red Bull. Confirmed. Copy over.'

He pocketed the plastic figure and squeezed it tightly, before turning to locate Boyle who was crouched behind a boulder the size of a family sedan. McGuire pointed at him with his right arm horizontal, palm facing up and jerked back towards his own face. Satisfied that Boyle was following, he made his way down the steep valley side, being careful to keep his footing on the treacherous rocks, suddenly grateful for the downpour. It had been raining last time, though. A chill sliced across his back, causing him to involuntarily tighten his grip on the M4.

'Keep it together, Mac,' he muttered. The last thing he needed was an involuntary discharge.

As he levelled out onto the valley floor, he held up his hand to halt Boyle who automatically made himself prone, ready to cover

McGuire, who drew a deep breath and sprinted across the open patch of ground. This was where he'd taken a bullet, the hot lead severing his femoral artery, or so the watching Boyle had reported. He would have bled out in minutes and the thought it could happen again adrenalised his run even as the unmistakable flash of automatic fire from the building up ahead cannoned his body into the mud. He heard return fire raking the space where the night had lit up. Then a scream. For a second, he thought it was his own but then realised Boyle had hit the target. Without waiting, he scrabbled forward across the final yards, pitching himself behind an upturned cart. His radio crackled.

'This is Jaw Bone. I've never seen you run so fast. T-man is down. I repeat, down. Cover me. Copy over.'

McGuire peered through a broken slat and rattled a three-round burst into the building, following it with a second for good measure. He heard Boyle approaching before he felt him slide across the wet mud, almost upending him.

'Steady there, buddy,' McGuire admonished the younger man. 'I'll take the front. You take the side. One flash. Then proceed to the rear.'

Boyle nodded and was gone, skirting the side of the building at speed. McGuire saw him remove a flash grenade from his belt which disappeared through a broken window. McGuire instinctively ducked as the low thud of a concussive explosion briefly lit up the building. Before it had faded, he was on his feet and in through the entrance door, rolling hard right to avoid the prone figure slumped in the centre of the room. It was the man Boyle had shot. McGuire relaxed, wondering what had killed him first—the explosion of red across his chest or the ugly puncture in his neck. Either way, both looked fatal.

The room was empty, save for an old couch slumped disconcertedly along one wall and a lit fireplace nursing a bubbling pot. On the hearth were three steaming plates with a fourth upended on the floor, its contents still slithering down an open door leading into another room. McGuire unclipped a stun grenade and tossed it through the opening before crouching low beside the fire, eyes shut, hands clasped to his ears. The concussive blast made him jump. They always did but today felt louder with the resultant smoke cloud ballooning through the doorway like a malevolent weather front. He took a deep breath and scrabbled into the second room on his haunches. It saved his life. A burst of automatic fire decapitated the thin door and he fired blindly, pitching forward behind a bed, using instinct to judge the position of the shooter. The G3S rattled again and McGuire reciprocated with a long burst into the rear, left corner of the room. Outside, the evening erupted into life as automatic fire argued back and forth like recalcitrant teenagers. And then silence.

'This is Jaw Bone. Two T-men down. What is your status, Red Bull? Copy over.'

McGuire pressed his neck.

'This is Red Bull. A OK. There were four T-Men. Repeat. Four T-Men. Copy over.'

'Roger, Red Bull. Eyes open. Copy over.'

McGuire remained hunched behind the bed, assessing his options. It was highly unlikely the last soldier was still in the room. The grenade would have rendered him deaf and blind, possibly unconscious. He must have been waiting outside, at the rear of the building along with the others. He counted to twenty before peering over the bedstead and finally stood up, weapon trained on the door through which they'd sprung the ambush. Nothing. He relaxed but his attention was drawn to the opposite corner where a body lay crumpled, face down. US army fatigues. No weapon. McGuire suppressed a shudder and touched his neck.

'This is Red Bull. Dead body. One of ours. Will report back. Copy over.'

'This is Jaw Bone. Who is it? Copy over.'

'This is Red Bull. Not sure. Copy over.' But he was sure, he just wasn't ready to admit it.

'This is Jaw Bone. Be careful. Copy over.'

McGuire took a deep breath and exhaled slowly as his certainty solidified. Christ, was it him? Or Max or Sanders? None of them had been recovered. He approached the body, noting the rusty brown staining on the soldier's trousers. He'd been shot in the groin but so had Max, according to the team. There was no pooling of blood so it could be either of them. Whoever it was must have been brought here after being captured. Maybe already dead. Poor bastard. Alone in this hovel. With these savages. Seven thousand miles from home. He got down on his hands and knees and checked round the body, gagging as he did. Christ, it stank. McGuire stood up, satisfied there was no wiring, but it could be a pressure IED using the weight of the body to keep the pin in. When it was turned over, the device would trigger, exploding upwards.

'No mistakes tonight,' McGuire muttered to himself, suddenly realising that his dead body could be responsible for his own death! Christ, this was a mind fuck. He'd heard the odd account of this happening in the last six months from some of the other units but never thought it would happen to him. All thanks to LEAP.

He traced the hard outline of Jake's gift through his army fatigues and removed a thin line of rope from his pack, which he tied to the body's webbing, before looping it over a low beam. Satisfied that the rope was secure, he retreated into the front room and heaved backwards, tensing, waiting for the explosion. But the room remained silent. McGuire inched back through the doorway struggling to hold the weight. The main trunk was now suspended two inches above the floor, its arms and legs spread like a decapitated spider. McGuire exhaled heavily, releasing the tension and the body settled back onto the floor. He grabbed the man's webbing, retching as he pulled the dead man towards him. As it turned, something fell from the folds of the man's tunic. Something small. Plastic. Angry. And green.

He staggered back onto the bed, mind whirling, stomach heaving as he stared at the dead body of Staff Sergeant Lee McGuire of the 2nd Battalion 12th Infantry Regiment. He'd died painfully, his bloated face frozen in a morbid scream, bared lips exposing yellowing teeth. He unconsciously licked his own, struggling to contain the bile boiling in his guts. He knew he was dead, had been briefed back in Virginia that he was dead but, until now, the knowledge had felt unreal. Why shouldn't it? After the last mission he'd been restored from the most recent copy, the one saved when he'd made his LEAP into Afghanistan. That was seven days before he died which meant there was a memory gap. All he could remember was saying goodbye to his family in the morning, joking with Max as they waited in line to make their LEAP. Then his next memory was waking up in the same room from which he'd made the LEAP. From there, he'd been led to the debrief to be told he'd died. So what, he thought at the time. I'm alive, sat here, feeling fine. But here he was, sat, looking at himself. Dead. He swallowed hard, grasping for an explanation that would allow him to rationalise what he was seeing.

Nothing except the cold hard logic that the army had applied when announcing the initiative. For them, the benefits far outweighed the moral conundrum. The cost for one; upwards of one million dollars to train a US soldier for combat. Why waste that money and experience by having them killed on a mission, not to mention the human cost of families losing a loved one? It had been run as a beta for three months and now, with the announcement that Rae had perfected human-to-human LEAP, was shortly to be applied to injuries. Another cost saved. No rehabilitation. No expensive medical bills. No ruined lives caused by IUDs ripping limbs from bodies.

He heard a movement to his left but reacted too late. A man was stood in the doorway, head covered in traditional garb, garments soaked through from the rain, his long beard matted to his sodden chest, red with blood. McGuire reached for his gun, but it was lying beside his dead body. Not that it would have made any difference. He reached for his handgun, but the man was way ahead of him, lifting the barrel of his Russian-made Kalashnikov towards McGuire. The first rounds caught him in the leg as they arced across his body, ripping soft tissue on his stomach, shredding ribs and up into his neck.

As his lifeless body fell back onto the mattress, a small green figure slipped from his hand and lay still, staring at its counterpart.

To be continued in ATOM, Inc, Book 3 of The Race is On Series

What Next!

Did you enjoy Green Ray! You can be the difference.

As an Indie Author, reviews are **THE** most powerful tools in my quiver when it comes to getting attention for my books. It's the only way I can compete against the financial might of the big publishers who can command unlimited budgets for advertising and an army of marketeers to promote their writers.

However.

I have my own army.

An army that the big boys would love to get their hands on.

My faithful readers.

An honest review of my book is worth a thousand ads. And ten thousand marketeers! It provides social proof of my writing to other readers and more often than not, persuades them to hit the BUY button.

So, if you enjoyed this story, I would be eternally grateful if you tell others what you thought about Green Ray on the book's Amazon page—it can be as short as you like. Just scan the QR code below or type the following into your browser: https://geni.us/GreenRayReview

Thank you so much.

Fancy some exclusive swag?

Building a relationship with my readers is the very best thing about writing—I'm blessed to call many my friends and a few even help me with my writing; spotting typos, correcting research errors, suggesting plot improvements or simply agreeing to join my infamous ARC teams!

I email a newsletter every three weeks with details of new releases, special offers and signed giveaways. Oh, and the odd snippet about my life in Leeds and that of my writing buddy Max—an aged, often bad tempered, but very lovable brown Labrador.

In return, you'll receive the following gifts, which are all exclusive to my club and can't be obtained anywhere else:

1. A free prequel novella called MAD, introducing The Race is On series—amongst other things, it explains why Uma's father created LEAP and how Uma became a copy of her sister. It's a doozy and one of my favourite stories, although the plot nearly cleaved my mind in two!

2. A short dossier that answers some of the questions that you might have as a reader about Green Ray, including what is made up and what is actually fact. And how I merged the two.

3. My date and time ss which I created to track the timelines in Green Ray—sounds small, but endless hours were poured

into this baby and I want you to see the blood, the sweat and the tears in those 1,080 cells as I worked to create a sense of urgency across Reykjavík, London, Copenhagen, Riyadh, Afghanistan, LA, Virginia, Washington DC, San Francisco and Guantanamo Bay.

If you want to unsubscribe at any time, it's simple to do and I promise never to share your details with anyone. To join the club and receive the novella, dossier and ss, just scan the QR code below, or type the following link into your browser: https://www.ocheaton.com/mad-offer-greenray/

I've dreamt of becoming a writer for years and, like many, believed there was at least one book in me. Having passed that hurdle, I've discovered there're loads and look forward to sharing future stories with you as I create them.

OC

Leeds, England

About OC Heaton

I write what I love to read—big issue tech-nothrillers, with a side of sci-fi, that are super well researched inside a complex plot full of twists and turns.

When I sit down to write a book, I have three non-negotiables:

1. It needs to concern a current or recent real world issue that I can deeply research (I love research!) and weave my fictional story into. Hopefully, so tightly that you struggle to spot where one stops and the other starts.

2. It has to have a complex plot full of twists and turns that'll leave you guessing right until the end.

3. It must contain grey characters, even the good guys. This makes sense to me. First, as a reader I hate stereotypical/one-dimensional characters and second, grey is real life,

right?

When I'm not writing I relax in my hometown of Leeds in the UK with the love of my life and our two daughters.

And Max—my aged, often bad tempered, but lovable Labrador—who features a lot in my newsletters. It rains a lot in Leeds but that works out well for me—loads of time for research and, of course, writing!

Here are some ways that you can talk to me:

Email: oc@ocheaton.com

Web: www.ocheaton.com

Facebook: https://www.facebook.com/ocheatonauthor

Instagram: https://www.instagram.com/ocheaton

The Race is On Series Listing

MAD—Prequel novella to The Race is One Series

1986. Reykjavik, Iceland.

rilliant quantum scientist Jakob Arnasson is on the brink of immortality. After years of fervent anti-nuclear activism, he has finally brokered a nuclear disarmament summit between two of the world's greatest powers: the USA and the USSR.

But on the eve of the talks, Jakob is forced to use his LEAP teleportation device to save his own life — an action that has far-reaching consequences. It resets his memory to the day of his first "leap", in 1954.

Thrust into a future-altering weekend without any recollection of why he should be there, Jakob's responsibilities suddenly multiply when the CIA recruit him for a dangerous covert operation to save the talks.

And just as he looks set to lose everything, a much greater threat appears on the horizon...

FREE to download when you join my Readers Club. Just scan the QR code below, or type the following link into your browser: https://www.ocheaton.com/mad-offer-greenray/

LEAP—Book 1 of The Race is On series

One small step could ruin mankind's greatest leap...

Ethan Rae is known for his billions, but his latest business venture is about to really put him on the map: a quantum teleportation system that would solve global warming for good. Known as LEAP, the system is capable of providing Earth's ultimate second chance...until it falls into the wrong hands.

When playboy CEO Samuel Reynolds III snatches LEAP out from under Ethan's nose, he adds insult to injury by attempting to destroy Ethan's business partner, Uma Jakobsdóttir. But this is no malicious whim. As the daughter of its creator, Uma enforces the LEAP Laws.

Because of its potentially devastating capabilities, LEAP users must not clone people, revive the dead, or merge minds and species. But in the race to recover their precious piece of tech, Ethan and Uma are faced with sacrifices that push their resolve to breaking point.

From the frozen wastelands of Iceland, to the leafy suburbs of London and the mean streets of New York City, LEAP is a technothriller that will keep you questioning what it means to be human.

LEAP is **free for Kindle Unlimited Readers!!** Or BUY IT at your local Amazon store. Either way, just scan the QR code below or type the following link into your browser: https://geni.us/WOFbk9

Green Ray—Book 2 of The Race is On series

No good deed goes unpunished...

Six years after the near-catastrophic hijacking of LEAP, Uma Jakobsdóttir is determined to find a safer path to environmental salvation.

So, with her father's invention back under wraps, Uma turns her attention to the $85 billion-dollar Green Ray fund with the intention of renewing the planet—minus any teleportation.

But when the capabilities of LEAP are discovered by the U.S. government, it sets its sights on using the device to protect the country against economic collapse. When the White House proposes a new set of rules for LEAP—ones which would only allow the teleportation of goods, not people—Uma's objections are steamrolled by powerful forces.

Then the President's life is endangered, and the rules of the game suddenly shift again—leaving Uma in ethical turmoil as she races to stop the full power of LEAP from being unleashed on an unsuspecting world...

ATOM, Inc—Book 3 of The Race Is On series

No one is above the Laws...

Seven years after its conception, LEAP is finally about to spell the end of global warming. For Uma and Ethan, this means personal and professional triumph – but quantum teleportation is an unwieldy beast, held back by those fighting to dominate the new world order.

As LEAP's roll out slows to a trickle, a greater threat emerges when a stealth attack on US troops leaves thousands dead. With the finger of suspicion pointing to a LEAP copycat, Ethan and Uma are forced to condone a breach of the Laws to reverse the massacre.

As LEAP's new rival continues to show their hand, Ethan is dragged back into a nightmare he thought he had escaped. One that may finally claim his sanity, and that pushes Uma to the limits of hers, to defeat an evil that no longer plays by the rules.

ATOM INC hits AMAZON on 29th February 2024 – To pre-order ATOM INC NOW, just scan the QR code below or type the following link into your browser: https://geni.us/6zpC

Dedication

To the one and only love of my life, Lillian. And, of course, our girls.

Acknowledgements

My thanks go to my partner, best friend, adviser and sounding board in this latest adventure, Lillian Ayala. Your love, enthusiasm, patience and wisdom know no bounds.

I am also extremely grateful for the assistance I received from the following individuals whose input helped me shape, write and eventually publish *Green Ray*: Chris Wood and Julie Hoyle.

Copyright